Swifty

Swifty

∞

Roger F. Greaves

Copyright © 2009 by Roger F. Greaves.

Library of Congress Control Number: 2009911445
ISBN: Hardcover   978-1-4415-9416-7
                 Softcover   978-1-4415-9415-0

All rights reserved. No part of this book may be reproduced or transmitted in any form or by any means, electronic or mechanical, including photocopying, recording, or by any information storage and retrieval system, without permission in writing from the copyright owner.

This is a work of fiction. Names, characters, places and incidents either are the product of the author's imagination or are used fictitiously, and any resemblance to any actual persons, living or dead, events, or locales is entirely coincidental.

This book was printed in the United States of America.

To order additional copies of this book, contact:
Xlibris Corporation
1-888-795-4274
www.Xlibris.com
Orders@Xlibris.com
70240

To Erika, who defines me.

Thanks to Connie and Rog Greaves for their edits and advice, and to Jim Fraser for his encouragement.

Special thanks to John Yeager for the cover design and to Isa for being "Isa!"

Contents

PROLOGUE 11

PART ONE

CHAPTER 1	COLIN KOENIG	15
CHAPTER 2	ARTIE	22
CHAPTER 3	JAKE	26
CHAPTER 4	PELTZ	30
CHAPTER 5	KIM	33
CHAPTER 6	THE LAW	37
CHAPTER 7	THE TRUTH?	40
CHAPTER 8	THE FEDS	42
CHAPTER 9	THE MEET	46
CHAPTER 10	REMORSE	50
CHAPTER 11	SCIENCE MEETS THE UNDERWORLD	55
CHAPTER 12	UNFAIR CHOICES	57
CHAPTER 13	MEANWHILE, IN THE SNOW	59

PART TWO

CHAPTER 14	REALITY	65
CHAPTER 15	KIM ALONE	76
CHAPTER 16	THE GENIUS	86
CHAPTER 17	SAFFORD U	89
CHAPTER 18	THE ESCAPE	93
CHAPTER 19	THE QUICK TURNAROUND	100
CHAPTER 20	TIME MARCHES ON	103

PART THREE

CHAPTER 21	THE REBIRTH	109
CHAPTER 22	THE ADJUSTMENT	115
CHAPTER 23	KYLE AND JAKE	120
CHAPTER 24	THE GRAND PLAN	124
CHAPTER 25	THE OTHER GRAND PLAN	133

CHAPTER 26	SWIFTY KING, ADVICE	136
CHAPTER 27	WHEN A PLAN WORKS	143
CHAPTER 28	THE WORKS	150
CHAPTER 29	SWIFTY AND ARTIE	155
CHAPTER 30	THE REAL MR. KING	163

PART FOUR

CHAPTER 31	SUCCESS	165
CHAPTER 32	NO IMMUNITY FROM TRANSFORMATION	168
CHAPTER 33	THE GREAT CHALLENGE	175
CHAPTER 34	EMERGENCY	178
CHAPTER 35	GLADDIE	187
CHAPTER 36	CONNOR GROVE	195
CHAPTER 37	DESERT OASIS	196
CHAPTER 38	THE PARDON	202

PART FIVE

CHAPTER 39	BRECK	207
CHAPTER 40	MATURITY	215
CHAPTER 41	THE FUTURE	219
CHAPTER 42	SPIRIT	221
CHAPTER 43	JUSTICE?	227
CHAPTER 44	IN RETURN	234

EPILOGUE ... 245

The trick is in what one emphasizes. We either make ourselves miserable, or we make ourselves happy. The amount of work is the same.

– Carlos Castaneda

When the first shot downed the figure in front of him, Swifty made a slight head fake right then moved to his left, but too late. He felt the searing heat in his chest, then the pain. He couldn't breathe. The images before him faded. Something struck his left knee, then his right . . . next came his face. It was the hard pavement. He tried to retch but he couldn't make it happen. The street became a sea of burning oil and he was in it. Then . . . nothing but blackness and a humming sound.

PROLOGUE

SWIFTY KING IS a unique character, a contradiction in ethics, and a good man to have on your side when your conscience and your courage get into a wrestling match. When political leaders or corporate CEOs are bound by law from getting down and dirty, sometimes they call Swifty. He is good on the personal front too. That may be why his card reads *Swifty King, Advice.*

I have been his close friend for over four decades and I owe Swifty a great deal. He helped me to gain self-respect, which led to my progressing in business, though not so much in love. I guess I have always been jealous of Swifty's success there, and I have probably always been a little in love with his wife. He knows that. He knows all about me. Swifty is the one guy I share almost all my feelings with. My name is Kyle Kenneth Faust, and I am what you might call a success. Throughout this story I refer to myself in the third person and often leave editorial notes signed *KKF*. So get used to it.

I own businesses and pieces of businesses all over the world. My five children are all college graduates, and two of them are physicians. One of my kids, surprisingly, is a general in the U.S. Air Force. The other two are in business with me. I also have three rather wealthy ex-wives, thanks to generous settlements negotiated by Swifty King and the best lawyers money can buy. My money.

Yesterday, Swifty and I traveled from Bahrain to Frankfurt by private aircraft supplied by the sultan. We then traveled by special unmarked DC-10 to Washington DC, where we boarded one of my corporate airplanes, which transported us to Scottsdale Airpark in Arizona. Swifty had been visiting an influential business associate in the Middle East who had been asked, very discreetly, to intercede in a delicate matter involving the misbehaving girlfriend of a member of the Saudi royal family.

Ali Muhammad Hassan Bellia, better known as Al Bell in New York, is a "fixer" for the Saudis; one of many. Prince Siad Nadir Bandar-Khu, a confidant of the king, likes the ladies. One of his recent "squeezes," Pol Snowrule, a thirty-year-old cocaine-sniffing "go-go" dancer from South London has been terrorizing the prince's number one wife and demanding a seat at the royal table. The prince wants Pol to cool it and the wife wants her to go away. Al Bell was tasked to quiet Pol down, stick her in some remote corner, give her enough "blow" to make her happy, but keep her from going to the press. Al called Swifty for advice.

"My dear friend, Swifty, it is my duty to keep this young woman from embarrassing the prince, and for that matter the royal family, any further. The wives of the prince are of no concern, other than a bother, but they annoy the more senior family members, through their wives, and this cannot be allowed. She must disappear." Al added a slight bow.

"Permanently?" queried Swifty with a wry smile.

"If need be, yes. I have already identified a suitable replacement for this Pol person. Swifty, I beg you, just make her go away."

Swifty did. But he needed help, and there I was again, risking everything to fly a drugged passenger with no passport across the world, bypassing customs. Oh we cleared all right, and so did my son Ken the physician, who supplied the sedatives and the three-member crew. But Pol Snowrule, or "Polly Snowpile," as Dr. Ken called her, snoozed away in a specially designed compartment below the floor and above the cargo hold of the company G-5 after her oxygen-supplied "coffin" – with a hydrating IV feeding her fluids and a continuous stream of a sedating substance – was transferred there from the DC-10 at a remote site at Dulles.

My son Ken, or Kenny Faust, spent seven years with the National Security Agency after med school. For six years now, having completed his residency in anesthesiology, Dr. Kenneth Faust, father of two, has been a partner in the Scottsdale Anesthesiology Group, supporting complex surgeries around the Valley of the Sun. While money, thanks to Dad, is not an issue, he does very well on his own. However, like Dad (me), Dr. Faust has fallen under the spell of Uncle Swifty and cannot possibly say no when "Svengali" asks him to break every rule in the book.

Late last night we deposited the still very drowsy British blonde at the maximum security Southfork Honor Ranch and Hospital, just north of Wickenburg, Arizona. Pol will likely be pissed off for a few hours, then in some pain as she comes down from her drug habit. But, in two or three months, she will be ready to negotiate her safe and very rich return to the British Isles, leaving her Saudi experiences permanently behind.

As I lifted my Cessna 414 off the Wickenburg runway for the short hop back to Scottsdale Airpark, where we had left the G-5 for refueling the previous night, I thought back to the time when Swifty and I first started running together and how my buddy got his rather ignominious start:

CHAPTER 1

COLIN KOENIG

SWIFTY HAS ALWAYS been an ambitious guy, even back in the '50s when he was Colin Koenig. As a kid, he ate his dinner as quick as he could so he could get back to his job sorting beer and soft drink bottles at Johnnie's Market. He'd run there after school, break at six o'clock, and then go back after dinner until nine o'clock. Johnnie would give him $0.10 a case for beer bottles and $0.5 for pop. Johnnie's delivered groceries in the neighborhood for a slight fee and volunteered to clean the old bottles out of your garage, giving you his estimate of the value off on your account. About a third of the bottles were "throwaways," but the rest were pure gold. Johnnie inflated the grocery bill, collected extra for delivery from the two breadwinner families in the area, and gave them a fifty percent haircut on the bottles. Johnnie could afford to have Colin Koenig sort them out for a few dimes.

So, because of his speed in cutting through his evening meal to be taken advantage of by Johnnie's bottle scam, his dad called him "Swifty." Later, he said they should have called him "dummy" for letting Johnnie stiff him so badly.

When he got a little older, Swifty moved from Johnnie's five blocks east to Kraft's Flowers up on Long Beach Boulevard, in Lynwood, California. At Kraft's he delivered, cleaned up, and helped put together some of the arrangements. He had no knack for design, but the kid worked hard. Kraft's liked him.

After high school, Gladdie Ames, his girl, married a football player from USC. Swifty was devastated to find out she was pregnant by this other guy when she dumped him. He headed right for the air force recruiting office. Swifty was a hard worker in the military too, but it wasn't performance that got you promoted there, it was luck. So Swifty didn't make rank, got out at the end of his four years, and headed back to his parents' home in Lynwood.

No longer fearful that people would remember how he was disgraced by Gladdie's choice, Swifty went to visit her parents, half hoping she had left the football guy and come back home. No such luck. Gladdie was the happy mother of two, living in Palo Alto with the football player/stockbroker husband.

Gladys Ames was tall, with long strawberry blonde tresses, the real homecoming-queen type. In fact, she was the homecoming queen as well as the valedictorian of her class. Smart, beautiful, and somewhat progressive for the age, Gladdie would do anything to advance toward her ambitions. She wanted to be rich and famous. There were rumors that she had had an affair with a chemistry teacher before she started going with Swifty. Everybody knew that she was playing Swifty in his senior year. While he was busy trying to please her by making the baseball team, she was cavorting with the USC Letterman whose father was a senior partner at Merrill Lynch, Fenner, and Smith.

So, to Swifty's surprise, it wasn't Gladdie's mom who'd answered the door, it was Kim, Gladdie's by-then very grown-up kid sister. Four years younger than Gladdie, Kim let Swifty know on their first date that she had fallen in love with him the day her sister brought him home from school. Swifty guessed she must have been thirteen then, but now at eighteen she was something! Shorter than the tall, willowy Gladdie, Kim was five foot two with trim blonde hair worn in little ringlets around her forehead that kind of rolled out into small waves on the sides and flipped up in back. She had perfect olive skin, slim hips, a tiny waist, great legs, and a bust that was almost too big for her petite body. Her lips and nose seemed to turn up into a perpetual, coy smile, making her always look like she just got away with something naughty. Later, when she was way over forty, some people thought she had an early facelift, but not so. It was just pure, natural beauty.

Swifty learned that her beauty extended to the inside too. Unlike her sister, Kimmie was true-blue; the soul mate type and a perfect match for Swifty.

Swifty was a good-looking guy, medium height, kind of slim, five-eleven, and one sixty or so. His hair used to be thick, dark brown, and curly. His eyes and skin matched. The long lashes and the hair made him look a little effeminate. Swifty always talked a little gruff to compensate. Later, the hair straightened and thinned, turned a little gray; he added twenty pounds, and a few wrinkles replaced the smooth, olive complexion. Personally, I thought Swifty looked better as he got older. Oh, and he lost the gruff talk over the years too, becoming a smooth-enough talker to play a con man on a daytime soap opera.

Swifty was back working at Kraft's when they got married at the close of the Johnson era. By that time, he had almost three years of college in, one he picked up in the service and the rest when he could stack it in around work. Kimmie helped the bookkeeper at Harvey's Furniture Store, three blocks up Long Beach Boulevard from where Swifty worked. She planned to go to school when Swifty finished. They had lunch together whenever schedules would permit and called each other five times a day on the pay phone. Everybody knew it was true love and that these two would make it all the way. They knew it too. They were going to have their educations, their great jobs, their house, and then their family. Everybody said it: these kids couldn't miss.

Things change. Lynwood, as a later article in the *LA Times* put it, went "downhill on the freeway." About the time Swifty and Kim were getting reacquainted, the much-anticipated Century Freeway cut the little town of four square miles in half. Though the freeway was not complete until thirty years afterward, it devastated the "All-American City" of 1962, and by '70, it was well on its way to urban blight. Harvey's went broke and Kim went to work at Thrifty Drug. Then Kraft sold to a consortium of black businessmen who planned to resurrect the local businesses in a new format.

Mr. Kraft told Swifty, "Kid, Mom and I got our eye on a place in Scottsdale, Arizona . . . out by Phoenix. Lotta hotels and resorts there. Harder to get and keep flowers, but its gettin' to be a convention spot. Money to be made. You and Kimmie want to make the move, you always got a job with me."

They talked. "It'd be an adventure, honey. Oh, it's hot, but you dress for it. They got a school, Arizona State something. We could go there. You been wanting to study real estate and design. They've got that. Kraft'll make me assistant manager," he said.

Kim was dubious. "Gee, hon, what about my folks? And all our friends . . . gosh, I don't want to leave where I grew up. Where'll I find a job?"

Swifty, good salesman that he was, persisted. "But, honey, you can visit your folks, they can visit us. It ain't that far . . . maybe four hundred miles by car or the bus. Hey, the bus is cheap. You can get a job easy, cute as you are."

Kim relented, as she always did back in those days: "Oh, Colin, oh . . . okay, I guess."

So they moved; took a little bungalow thing right near Scottsdale and Third. Kraft set up shop just around the corner on Main, later moving it to Scottsdale and Lincoln. Kim got on at the Furniture Mart their third day in town. She started studying for the real estate exam right away, taking a class offered at an office in the Mart. It seemed to work for them from the start.

The "hippie" stuff was less an issue at Arizona State than it was at, say, Berkeley or the Ivy League. AZ State was a party school, stressing football and fun. Tempe was long hair, short skirts, booze, some drugs, but no serious demonstrations. In fact, if one broke out, it was either disrupted by the football team or interrupted by a spontaneous beer bust. Swifty thought it was kinda fun. Plus, his classes were easier than they had been at Long Beach State and he didn't have to drive that seventeen miles down the freeway. Tempe was just across what passed for a river. Unlike the 1960s, the Salt River has now been dammed and made into the Tempe Town Lake. It looks like the LA River after a heavy rain, but people like seeing water once in a while in this part of the desert.

Soon after moving to Scottsdale, things got more intriguing for Swiftly and Kim. An encounter occurred in the summer of '68 that would change their lives. They met Artie Leonardo, or at least, Swifty met the man who would influence the rest of his life.

One night Swiftly was making late deliveries and trying to keep flowers alive in the heat. His last stop was the Camelback Resort, which was in its heyday.[1] Since then it's had its ups and downs, but then it was way up. It was in the so-called convention center, a separate building from the main lobby containing a series of meeting rooms of various sizes, that Swifty ran into a man of some prominence and heft in the local community and far beyond.

Mr. Arthur Leonardo was in the process of arranging a late-night business meeting with some associates who were expected on the last flight from the East. Unusual as it seemed to Swifty for so late in the evening, Mr. Leonardo wanted a flower arrangement and a few other accoutrements in place when his visitors arrived. The hotel was not too responsive due to the unevenness of the schedule. Mr. Leonardo grumbled a few words to Swifty about his problem.

"This is supposed to be a goddamn service business and these shitheads can't get anything right! No water, no glasses, no pencils, no easels . . . no booze. I'll tell ya, kid, if I owned this place, it would be run like the army and the customer would be the general." Artie Leonardo wore a light summer suit, french cuffs, loafers, and a bright pink tie. Tall, slim, an athlete's build, ruggedly handsome, with piercing gray eyes; Swifty thought he looked like an old movie star.

There was a roughness about his manner, but gentleness in his bearing. Swifty couldn't quite put his finger on it, but it seemed like he could be as tough or as friendly as he needed to be. Swifty wanted him to be friendly.

---

[1] "The Camelback Inn, built in 1936, was the premiere resort in Scottsdale until the '70s. It continues to thrive, but is a far cry from the dusty destination on the dirt road called Lincoln Drive frequented by the rich and famous of the day.

"Sir, most big customers like you usually bring some staff along to help. I mean, like somebody from your office."

"Yeah, yeah, I know that, son. I did just that. But my help ran into a bad salad or something. He had to stay back at shop with a stomachache. College graduate, from right here at State, I figure he thinks this kind of work is not befitting his station. Anyway, I'm here, he isn't, and I can't get things the way I want 'em."

"Now, let's see, you're just a contractor right? You're not a hotel guy?" Artie squinted.

"No, sir, I mean, yes, I'm a contractor for the flowers, which are still fresh at nine o'clock at night, I might add."

Leonardo made a sideward glance, dug into his pocket, and pulled out an uneven stack of bills. He peeled off a ten and waved it in Swifty's direction. "Thanks, young man."

"No, no, sir, I can't accept a tip for doing the job. Anyway, I'm sort of management with the flower shop . . . it wouldn't be right." Swifty had not yet learned to never refuse a buck.

"Okay, but wait. Do you know the 'go to' guys at this place? I mean, do you know who I can talk to to make the things happen I need before my people show up at eleven o'clock?" This guy was about fifty, Swifty guessed, and a cross between Jeff Chandler and Broderick Crawford.[2] He was built like Chandler and had his looks, but Crawford's raw toughness blinked out at you like a strobe light. Those gray eyes made Swifty want to go sit in the corner, face to the wall.

Swifty wrinkled his brow. "Sir, I guess I could give you a hand. I know the guys here pretty well. There have been a lot of changes. It's kind of a new place . . . at least the management is. I can call some people."

"Kid, if you stick around here and watch my back till about one thirty, there's a grand in it . . . that is, if everything goes right. How's that?"

"A thousand dollars? Whose did you say you wanted me to kill? Yes, sir, all I have to do is call my wife to let her know I won't be home and I am all yours."

Swifty accepted the man's handshake and steely gray smile, called Kimmie to explain, and set out to energize the evening staff of the Camelback. Booze with setups, ashtrays, writing pads, easels, pencils, mints, water, sandwiches to be delivered at eleven o'clock – and even ice, which was not a simple trick; it was all in place when the limos dropped off the out-of-towners.

"One last thing, lad."

---

[2] Jeff Chandler (Ira Grossel) was a handsome and virile movie star of the '50s who died prematurely, and Broderick Crawford was the Academy Award–winning movie tough guy who later stared in the TV series *Highway Patrol*.

"Sir?"

"You stand outside that door. When the sandwich waiter leaves, nobody comes in, nobody, no time. Got that?"

Swifty nodded.

"You wait, I'll pay you at the back end."

The men who entered were average looking. Two wore sport coats with open shirts, one wore a stylish long-sleeved shirt with matching slacks, and another wore a wrinkled business suit. They looked like accountants or lawyers off on a golf trip, justifying the expense with an evening drink and talk fest. Only one carried a briefcase. Swifty did notice the man with the disheveled suit had a peculiar bulge on his hip. No phones or pagers back then. No X-ray machines at airports either.

Swifty nodded, smiled, and faded back. He sat to the left of the door for two hours, reading the paper, glancing up at every sound, drinking a couple of Cokes.

That was it. At one o'clock the door opened; the men exited behind a cloud of smoke. There was small talk, and then the men drove off in the limos. Swifty checked the room and called the desk for cleanup.

"What was your name, young man? Did that waiter call you Swifty?"

"Yes, sir."

"Sounds like something out of Damon Runyon . . . there's a hotshot lawyer over on the coast named that. I met him once. Yeah, Swifty Lazar."

"Mine is Swifty Koenig . . . really Colin, Swifty is a nickname from my kid days."

"Why, you a runner?"

"No, just a fast eater, Mr. Leonardo, was it?"

"Yeah, Arthur Leonardo, Swifty, and I don't like to be called Art or Artie. Got that?"

"Yes, sir."

"Okay then, let me be sure all the papers are out of here, Swifty, will you please tear at least five blank sheets off that chart pad until there are no impressions left on the sheet below. Thaaank you." Leonardo folded the blank pages and put them and all nine writing pads left on the table into a large briefcase he had left next to his coat on the table. He picked up both and motioned for Swifty to follow him outside.

"Swifty, I checked my wallet and I have but three hundred eighteen dollars in cash with me. So, you follow me home and I'll give you the rest. How's that?"

"Where would that be, sir?"

"Well, it's over at the Biltmore Hotel, actually. You know where that is?"

"Yes I do." Swifty thought for several seconds. Did he really want to risk going to the Biltmore with this stranger, who may or may not actually give him all this money? He made an unusual decision for a young guy short on cash. "But could I come tomorrow? My wife is probably waiting up and, well, I don't want her to lose too much sleep." Swifty realized immediately how dumb this sounded . . . seven hundred bucks for practically no effort . . . but he had said it.

"Suit yourself, lad. You did real fine tonight. I appreciate your help."

He dug into his breast pocket and produced a business card. "If you can swing by the office after nine o'clock, either I or a senior person will be there with the other seven hundred."

"Yes, sir."

Swifty didn't look at the card until a long gray Lincoln eased out of the winding drive, with Arthur Leonardo resting comfortably in the backseat. "McDowell? Shit!" It was downtown. He'd have to drive all the way to downtown Phoenix to get the money tomorrow. Hey, for seven hundred, he'd go to New York.

Kimmie was so excited when he told her, she just kept giggling

"Do you really think he'll give you the rest, honey? I mean, gee, you already got the three hundred for only a couple a hours. Gee!"

"He'll give it to me. I can tell he's honest. Beside, I have his license number." Cute. Swifty had no idea who Arthur Leonardo was, no idea at all. He might as well have Joe Louis's license number.

CHAPTER 2

ARTIE

ARTIE LEONARDO HAD spent more than a decade of his fifty-three years in various correctional institutions. A self-educated man, having read widely during his nearly eleven years, in three separate stretches in Dannemora, Terminal Island, and Lompoc, Artie had diverted his interests from street hustling, hijacking, and extortion to the more esoteric methods of cash flow. Money laundering was not yet a widely understood practice, nor had the term been formally coined; but Arthur Jacob Leonard had convinced heads of the New York and Chicago mobs they could move cash discounted from gambling, extortion, and other traceable and illegal transactions offshore and bring back "clean" currency in exchange.

Within two years this son of a Jewish father and Italian mother, who added the *o* to his last name to fit in, had expanded his operation to more profitable areas. He devised a scheme to hold and cleanse untaxed income from various business activities in nine banks whose charters he had acquired in the Bahamas and the Caymans. Artie had gotten very rich by charging a fair 2 percent, with little risk, since leaving prison eleven years earlier. He found that basing in Phoenix, Arizona, gave him a comfortable "separation" from the entities he served and yet afforded him relatively easy access to his latest clients: Las Vegas casino operators wanting to move, cleanse, and hold cash in safety. It was in this nature that he met the Chicago – and New York-based absentee owners of four Las Vegas casinos at the Camelback the night Swifty encountered him.

Artie was not a "made man," nor was he ever competitive with the mob. In New York, this son of a Brooklyn jewelry store owner, who died in a train accident when Artie was sixteen, ran with street hoodlums. Whatever lawbreaking he engaged in, Artie made certain to honor his mother's wish that he finish high school, which he did just after his seventeenth birthday. Two months later, various petty infractions led to a judge's ultimatum "to serve in the army or be remanded to the juvenile authorities."

As an infantryman, Artie displayed the toughness he learned on New York streets when he landed in a replacement unit midway through the Battle of Normandy. He fought at Caen and marched into Paris with the First Infantry, August 25, 1944. In a firefight south of Cologne, Artie took a round in the knee. He was evacuated to Paris and later sent home. After rehab, Artie served the next year as a clerk in Army Intelligence at the Brooklyn Navy Yard, and in January 1946, he was discharged back onto the streets of his youth.

Artie took a few night-school classes, worked as a numbers runner and then, at twenty-one, began to function as hired muscle for one of the local mob figures. Over the next few years, Artie gained a reputation as a man you could trust. He was careful in his selection of assignments and never took sides in conflicting mob interests. He developed a particular skill at knowing how to compromise teamster drivers into making lucrative truck hijackings relatively simple. He would go to their homes, pay them up front, and stare them down with those steely gray eyes. And he was able to devise a method for counterfeiting streetcar tokens that he sold, through some of his cronies, at a discount to local commuters. The later was his undoing and eventually led to a two-year term at Dannemora Prison.

Undaunted, Artie did his time, kept his crew running from prison, and even developed a few new scams in his free hours. When he was released, in the early fifties, the heat was on organized crime. A subcontractor had to be discreet and trustworthy. Artie was that and more, he was smart and resourceful. He found himself being called upon more and more to collect and hold cash. With the acquiescence of the owner, Artie used the cash to run a loan business. His commission was never more than 2 percent, and his customers always paid up. Eventually, one of his runners was knocked over by a few street punks and his daily receipts were stolen. Artie made the loss up out of his share, but in drawing the money from his account, he attracted the attention of an IRS agent who happened to be conducting private business at the bank. The agent tipped the U.S. Attorney's Office that a local hood apparently kept a large bank account, and the ensuing investigation found Artie prosecuted for tax fraud. He had filed returns since the forties, but had failed to report most of his income. "Dumb," he thought, as he traveled by secure bus to the federal joint at Rikers for a three-year stay.

At the federal lockup, Artie met a higher class of criminal – the swindler, the con man, the skilled counterfeiter, and a few businessmen, who, like him, had made errors in judgment. By the time he was released, Artie had planned what he thought was a more legitimate business, based on need and greed. "Fence" is the popular term for someone who receives and discounts stolen property. Once received, it often requires storage, refurbishment, dismantlement, and/or redistribution. All of this is expensive and dangerous.

The Interstate Commerce Commission issued Arthur J. Leonardo, federal rap sheet notwithstanding, a license to transport goods across state lines within eight weeks of his release from prison. As a trustworthy guy, his old mob connections were happy to help him cut through the red tape and to acquire three moving vans prominently displaying the logo of a national home mover.

With eastern families moving to the Sunbelt, it was not difficult to "piggyback" fenced goods westward along with couches, refrigerators, beds, and end tables. By the end of the fifties, Artie's business was thriving.

His final trip to the slammer had nothing to do with any previous scheme. Artie and his girl, Teresa Partepellea, rode west with a shipment of household goods and electric typewriters one August. When they reached Riverside, they caught a bus into Los Angeles. After five wonderful days of shopping and sunshine, the plan was to ride the train to Chicago and then on back to New York.

Artie needed to pay his respects to a client or two on the trip. While he sat sipping a drink at the old Windsor in the Wilshire district waiting for a contact to arrive, he was swept up in a raid. Mickey Cohen, reputed to head the West Coast Mafia (which couldn't be since he was Jewish, not Italian) made his home at the Windsor, and this was at a time when his favor was fading. Whatever the case may be, Artie took exception to the rousting of the patrons by what turned out to be LA cops and feds and ended up breaking the arm of a federal officer. He received only five years' probation because his parole on the earlier offense had expired and all the patrons testified that the cops had not identified themselves. The judge had felt Artie's background should have alerted him to stay out of the action, so he provided a little more than a slap on the risk by referring him to federal court. A federal judge reasoned that he had violated his expired probation by associating with known felons and sentenced him to six years at Lompoc, out in Ventura County.

"The Man" had suggested, "Mr. Leonard or Leonardo, whatever it is . . . this stay in California will be good for you and for the people. Might I suggest that upon your release you remain away from the negative influences in the East that led you to a life of crime and stay out of California!"

By this time Artie and Teresa had the two kids, Jake and Toni Marie, so he took the judge's advice. The family moved to Nevada. By the time of his release from what was considered a "country club" prison, Artie had become a trustee office manager, a fair golfer, and a man who understood banking. They settled first in Las Vegas, then – a few years before Swifty met him – in Phoenix, Arizona, where one of his heroes, Barry Goldwater, served as senator.

CHAPTER 3

JAKE

Driving from Scottsdale to Phoenix is no big deal: west on Camelback to Seventh Street, then left a few miles to downtown. But there was just enough traffic and stoplights to make it a pain early in the morning. Swifty arrived at the office building on McDowell just after 9:00 a.m. He parked the flower delivery truck in a yellow zone, locked it up, and hiked up the central stairway to the second-floor office. *East-West Investors* was stenciled in plain letters on a plain wood veneer door, with a *2* above it.

Swifty knocked and then tried the door. It was locked. He rang the small buzzer to the left of the knob. Nothing. He looked around the floor, and then tried each door. Nothing. Next, he hiked downstairs and across the boulevard to a coffee shop, where he sat sipping one black and thought. Ten minutes went by, then twenty; he had to get back to work. He looked at the card. "Shit." He went to the pay phone, deposited a coin, and dialed the number.

After he was received the response from the service, telling him that the office would open at nine o'clock. It was 9:40. He walked outside after paying for his coffee and sprinted in front of traffic to the other side. He took the steps, right inside the door, two at a time. He banged on the door, rang the bell, and swore, "Shit!"

"What the hell's the matter with you, asshole?" A round face appeared from behind the gradually opening door.

A young man Swifty's age, with wavy black hair, a stocky build, and an open sport shirt glared back at him. "I said, what the fuck is the matter with you, asshole?"

"Sorry, sir. I was told to come here to pick up my pay. Maybe I have the wrong office. Is this East-West Investors?" Swifty was staring more at the business card he held in his hand than at the rather formidable-looking guy in front of him.

"What pay? What the fuck did you do for any pay from us? What are ya selling?"

"Flowers, sir."

"We don't need flowers . . . get outta here, I got a backache."

"Wait, no, I – "

"No? No? Noooooo? Who do you think you're sayin' no to, asshole?"

The man stiffened; his steely gray eyes bore right through Swifty.

"Oh god." He gulped. "Are you, ah, related to Mr. Leonardo, sir?"

"I am fucking Mr. Leonardo, flower boy . . . why?"

"Maybe it was your dad or brother I helped last night . . . he owes me $700 for some work I did for him." Swifty spit out as he backed away from the hiss of this shorter, bulkier, younger version of his employer of the night before.

The man opened the door wider and motioned for Swifty to come in. He gestured toward a chair. Swifty sat, hard.

"Yeah, yeah, my father said some kid helped him. He said I should pay this kid should he show up. But first he needs to do one other thing," he said.

"Sir?"

"Knock off the *sir* shit man . . . you want some coffee?" This son of Arthur Leonardo relaxed, replaced his scowl with a slight smile, and pointed toward a coffeepot on a nearby counter.

"Thanks," Swifty mumbled as he sprang from the chair and fumbled with a paper cup and the percolator. "What was the other thing, Mr., uh, Leonardo?"

"Jake . . . Jake, and what was your name again?"

"Swifty Koenig. Colin 'Swifty' Koenig, Jake." It was plain that Jake was a weight lifter. Even his potbelly seemed to be layered with muscle. Jake Leonardo had one of those extra little pots that protruded under the belt and was never becoming. Knock off twenty pounds, get rid of that undergut, Swifty thought, and he'd look like a movie star too, like his dad.

I like movies and I have been known to compare people I know to movie stars. Like with Artie looking like Jeff Chandler. Well, Swifty was a young John Derek type back then, and Jake reminded me of a fat Sly Stallone. With Swifty and Jake, the comparison got lost when they talked. Swifty sounded like a washing machine churning, and Jake had a high-pitched voice like Jerry Lewis in character. Artie, on the other hand, was smooth as silk and coulda been in the movies. KKF

"Okay, Swifty . . . here's the deal. We need one other small facet of last night's project completed . . . you get that done today, take you about two, three hours, and I'll have the seven brought right over here for you this afternoon."

Swifty audibly moaned, but as he did so he measured how easily he could get out the door should Jake Leonardo become physical, as Swifty was sure he could. Jake, was a short, pudgy version of his father, but he projected the same animal power.

"Hey, look, Jake, I did the job and he said I'd get paid. I have to work today. I'm late already. If you guys are reneging, I guess I'm just out." Swifty was trying to sound light.

"Hold it, Swifty," Jake smiled broadly. "We aren't going to burn you. It's just that we need to bring this thing to completion. Tell you what . . . hey, you in college over here at Arizona State?"

"Yes . . ."

"Well, we have something in common. I just graduated in June. Took me five years, but I got it done. The old man rode my ass until I finished."

"That's good, Jake . . . but I have to go."

"Swifty, Swifty . . . please" – Jake sidled his ample bulk up against the chair and lowered his beefy arm to Swifty's shoulder – "hear me out. Tell ya what, I'll make it a full grand . . . not seven but a thousand."

"I have to work . . ."

"Swifty, here, here's four, six more on your return. Do it after work, hell, do it tomorrow. What do you say?" All this as he plunged his fist into a trouser pocket and rescued a fistful of bills.

Swifty didn't feel good about this, but $1000 more greatly appealed to him. It was half a year's rent and groceries. It was another car for Kimmie. It was better furniture, the rest of his education, and part of hers . . . he'd do it.

"Okay, Mr. Leonar . . . Jake. What do I do?"

"Good, good . . . it's simple . . . here's an address." Jake handed Swifty a rumpled piece of paper. "All you have to do is take this package . . ."

Jake Leonardo explained that Swifty was to take a package about the size of a phone book to an address in Tucson. When Swifty began to protest again, Jake said it would be fine to do it the next day. Swifty found himself explaining this to Kimmie late that evening, after his deliveries.

"What's in it?" She asked, curiously tugging at the corners of the brown wrapping paper.

"Hey, stop that!" Swifty lightly spanked her pretty little hand. "We don't need to know what's in it, I just need to drop it off and that is it."

Swifty explained that he would do his morning deliveries early and leave for Tucson about ten thirty. He expected to be back by four o'clock to complete his day's work.

CHAPTER 4

PELTZ

DRIVING SOUTH ON Interstate 10, Swifty encountered little traffic and the usual share of wind and dust. Two hours and ten minutes after leaving Scottsdale, he was parked in front of a sprawling ranch-style residence with a low-slung roof. The house was set back on a large lot. Desert plants and trees, ocotillo and paloverde trees, and three large saguaro dotted the front yard. As he passed through the split-rail fence and followed the rock-strewn path to the large glazed double door, he could see a swimming pool sparkling in the sunlight through the broad windows that lay beneath the cooling overhangs both front and rear. "Nice house," he thought, ringing the bell while balancing the heavy package in his right hand.

"Hey . . . you the guy with the stu . . . the delivery!" It was more an exclamation than a question from the short squat man in the flowered and baggy bathing suit who stepped from the shadows and answered the door.

"Guess so . . . here it is," said Swifty, extending the package toward the opening screen door.

"Nah, nah, I'm not authorized, buddy. Wait on the porch a minute."

Swifty waited, puzzled.

A tall man with gray sideburns and a gruff demeanor replaced the fat guy at the screen door. He pulled the package inside and turned back into the shadows.

"Kid, I got an address here. You take the stuff to this place and drop it with a guy named Louis Peltz, then that's it."

Swifty looked at the address neatly written on a number 10 envelope. 6067 Desert Broom Lane, Queen Creek. "Hell, that's all the way back to Phoenix." He felt frustrated.

"Do it," the tall man ordered, thrusting the package back around the door. "An' don't call nobody, especially the guy that gave you this. You clear on that?"

Swifty saw the dilemma. If he was to be paid, he had to follow the new directions.

"Yeah, okay. I got it."

Swifty turned on his heel and headed with the package back to the delivery truck. Traffic was picking up on the way back, and he had trouble finding the turn to Queen Creek. Eventually, he crossed the Indian Reservation traveling east and found the intersection of Price and Queen Creek. From there he zigzagged across dairy land until he found Desert Broom Lane, little more than a dusty cow path.

Three bumpy miles south and east and he found *6067* on a broken mailbox. A forlorn cotton warehouse of wood lay several hundred yards along a rutted drive. Swifty drove it, bouncing from side to side. Adjacent to the wide-open doors of the building, Swifty stopped and retrieved the package. It was then that he noticed: the package was lighter and wrapped in a paper of a different texture and slightly different color. Curious.

"You Louis Peltz?" he asked the small, neat man in shirtsleeve that sat at a cluttered desk just inside the open barn doors.

"Yeah, you got it? Give it to me." A deeper-than-expected voice arose from the diminutive Mr. Peltz, who swatted flies away from his face as he stood and reached toward Swifty.

He handed over the new package, closing his nose and his mind to the rich smell that emanated from the half-dozen cows that leaned against the stacked cotton bales that filled the warehouse.

"Stay here, I'll be right back," little man Peltz boomed as he bounded up a flight of dirty wooden stairs and disappeared into a loft containing some sort of office.

A moment later he returned, holding a box about the size of the package Swifty had given him. "Take this to the room shown on this paper over at the Biltmore."

"What! Hey wait a minute. I already did what they asked. Why are you guys sending me on this goddamn scavenger hunt?" Swifty was getting hot ... hotter than the stifling cotton warehouse.

"Look, sonny, I do what I'm told. Maybe you ought to do that too. Now, I got work. So take off to the Biltmore. And don't tell anybody you were here or it won't go good for you. Go." Peltz extended an arm about as long as his body and pointed a finger toward Phoenix.

Swifty shifted from foot to foot as he tried to think of an alternative. As none seemed available, he swiped up the box with one hand and caught the piece of paper that blew off the top of it with the other hand. With this, he set off back toward Phoenix, leaving the impishly annoying Mr. Louis Peltz in his dust.

Forty-five minutes later, he pulled off of Twenty-fourth Street, turned right onto Missouri, and crept along the winding drive to the fabled Biltmore Hotel. The homes on the grounds of the Biltmore were the plushest in Phoenix, and the hotel with its unique architecture remained a showplace in the west.

Swifty pulled the delivery van passed the valet station and parked in the red zone. He dropped a red cone behind the van and brushed into the lobby with the box. He had stuffed the paper with the room number into his pocket. He fished for it and strained to read it in the relative dark of the lobby. Room 309, down the left corridor.

Swifty Koenig had been in this hotel fifty times delivering flowers, but he seldom entered the guest areas. Somewhat unsure, he followed the signs and moved to the rear of the sprawling hotel, stopping before number 309. He ignored the bell and knocked. Nothing . . . but there was a rumble that sounded like activity from within. He knocked again.

CHAPTER 5

KIM

KIM KOENIG HAD beautiful hair. She prided herself on presenting her neat blond locks in the best possible way. Though short, it was the first thing that caught your attention, the way it wound around her pretty head and fanned out into a flip in the back. Sure, she had great skin, a perfect body, large limpid eyes, and wonderful teeth, but it was the hair. Kimmie washed her hair at least three times a week and set it.

When the phone rang, she had just wrapped a towel around her head and donned a light robe.

"Hello?" she whispered into the mouthpiece in her sexiest voice, expecting Swifty, who was late, to be on the other end.

"Mrs. Koenig?" A high-pitched male voice inquired; definitely not her husband.

"Oh, oh, I'm sorry . . . yes, I was uh . . . expecting my husband."

"Yes, I am sure you would be . . . and, ma'am, that is why I am calling."

"Oh god! He isn't hurt is he?"

"No, no, no . . . he's not hurt. Mrs. Koenig, I'm Joe Seeley . . . an attorney here in Phoenix."

"Yes?"

"Well Mrs. Koenig, I'm afraid your husband has been arrested. He's in city jail."

"Oh god, oh Jesus . . . oh noo, no. What's the matter . . . what did he do?"

"Well, we're not sure he did anything at all ma'am, but the police took him into custody at the Biltmore early this evening. Seems he was apprehended with a large sum of money . . . money that might have been involved in some illegal activity."

"Oh no! Gosh, I knew something was fishy with this thousand-dollar thing. What can I do?"

"Well that's why I'm calling, Mrs. Koenig. I have been retained to help him . . . first to get him out of jail. The bail is $20,000. Do you have $1,000 in cash?"

Kimmie rummaged through Swifty's desk drawer while she tried to gain her composure. She found the bankbook, but lost the other battle. Tears streamed down her cheeks as she coughed out an answer.

"I have fifteen hundred in the account. But $20,000! We don't have that. What should I do?"

Joe Seeley instructed her to meet him, with the bankbook, at the coffee shop near the jail. Together they would go around the corner to the bail bond and arrange to finance Swifty's release.

Kim dried her hair, put a brush through it, slid into pedal pushers and a blouse, then searched for her keys.

Thank goodness the car had gas. It started, and the fifteen-year old engine sounded strong. So many things ran through her mind as she drove across town that she let the late-night music show boom loudly even though it agitated her newly developing headache. "Why was Colin so damn ambitious. He always pushed things. I wish we could go home to California . . . Oh god, Momma."

It was nearly midnight when the old Chevy coasted up to the only light blinking on McDowell. Sam's, Open 24 Hours . . . there it was.

The small counter was packed, as were the five booths. Several policemen were drinking coffee, as were a few men in suits and a couple of strange-looking women, all painted up. One man stood – a short thin man with a nice beige sport coat and tie.

He stuck out his hand. "I'm Joe Seeley. You're Kim . . . couldn't miss ya. Swifty said you were the best-lookin' girl in town. Sorry, I mean it as a complement . . . come on, sit."

"Thank you." Kimmie started to cry as she sat in the booth opposite the slightly balding, vaguely handsome lawyer.

He let her be until the spasms slowed and she started to hiccup. He handed her a couple of paper napkins. No one else paid attention.

"Here's the deal, kid. We'll take your bankbook over to the bail guy. It and some cash Swifty earned doing a job will give us what we need. The tab to you for now will just be the bankbook. I think you might even get that back sometime . . . well, forget that. Just if anybody asks . . . you put up your bankbook and some cash Swifty had. Okay?"

She wiped her tears and shook her head.

Joe Seeley steered the dazed girl around the corner to Arnie Arona's Bonds and Searches. In twenty minutes, she had signed the papers and was given a draft to deliver to the court.

"Kimmie . . . now we take this to the all-night judge . . . really just a clerk with commissioner authority, and he should sign the release form."

She could only nod and follow. "What about my car?"

"Leave it . . . nobody will care till six in the morning. We'll be long gone by then."

The two walked the three blocks to the jail building.

A fat cop stuck his face in Seeley's direction and responded to his request defiantly.

"I don't really give a damn what the judge says . . . I been told to hold this little shit till the fuc . . . the goddamn feds get over here. That ain't gonna happen before nine in the mornin'. 'Sides . . . Corner ain't a real judge . . . he's just a asshole commissioner." The fat, flat-nosed detective barked into Seeley's face, glancing at each expletive toward Kim.

She kept sniffing and hiccupping.

"Bluing, you got no manners and you're a jerk. Now you obey this lawful order or I go get the DA outta bed. He's gonna tell ya to release the kid to me . . . I'll promise to return the kid later in the day for the feds to interview, in my presence, of course. Also, since the chief loves me and my Cactus League contacts . . . you gonna be on midnights till you're off the job!"

The argument was over. Twenty minutes later, a tired, red-eyed Swifty arrived in the small visitor waiting room, led by a thin rope attached to handcuffs. Detective Bluing took the rope from the delivering officer and fumbled with the cuff keys. No one spoke until Swifty was freed.

"Come on, kids . . . we're outta here." Joe Seeley guided them through the halls and out the front door. The two youngsters held hands, but did not embrace or speak a word until they had returned to Sam's.

"What's gonna happen to me now, Mr. Seeley?" Swifty asked after he and Kim embraced and had a good cry.

Joe Seeley led them to a booth in the corner and signaled Sam for coffee. Streaks of light were beginning to appear in the eastern sky as the clock over Sam's greasy grill read 4:50.

"Well, I'll talk to the feds and the DA, try to figure out what they're really goin' to charge you with, if anything, then we come up with a plan."

"What do you think they might charge me with? I told you I didn't know there was money in the package. And . . . so what if there was? Is it illegal to deliver money?" Swifty was tired and exasperated.

Joe nodded toward Syl, the waitress who was approaching with three coffees, and waited until she had served them before answering. "You ever hear of money laundering?"

"No."

"Well, it sometimes means taking dirty cash, money that could be traceable and exchanging it, discounting it, and returning an agreed-upon 'clean' amount to the original party. It can mean other things, but that's probably what's going on here . . . I mean in the feds' minds."

"Hey, Joe! I didn't even know what was in the package Jake gave me or the ones I got in exchange. I was an . . . could I say . . . unwitting messenger . . . an innocent party? We can have Jake come in and tell 'em." Swifty slapped the table in triumph.

Joe Seeley thought for a long time, first looking at Kim, then the clock, then back at Swifty. "For now, let's not mention anything about anybody else . . . not the guy you just named or any of his relatives . . ."

"But – "

"Don't say anything about or to anybody, period!" Joe Seeley was suddenly sounding like Artie Leonardo. "You got that?" He was using a harsh whisper.

"Okay, you're the lawyer, but I'm not taking any heat for some hoods . . . I don't care how tough this Jake is." Swifty was cautious in his position and looked very carefully into Seeley's sad, experienced eyes as he talked.

CHAPTER 6

THE LAW

ALL THE WAY home, Swifty was stewing more about how Joe Seeley had spoken to him than the trouble he was in. Kim kept trying to bring him back to the point by asking over and over again, "Exactly what did you do, Colin?"

He went over it with her and in his mind several times. Dirty money, what did he do with dirty money? All he did was deliver a package or two. How was that bad?

After returning home, both kids had to get ready for work. I kind of got the impression there was lovemaking in there somewhere, but it was not my place to pry. Swifty made up for his lost day by working well into the next night. Kim was wide-awake when he got home.

"Hey, honey, why are you still up? Gee, you still got your work clothes on." Kim was dressed in the neat beige slacks and white sleeveless blouse she had put on after their morning shower. She had been crying. Her eyes were as red as her nail polish.

"They were here. Oh Colin, we have to get away from this place!" Kim started sob again.

"What? Who was here, what's going on?" Swifty stood back, trying to read his young wife. Then he realized she was upset about something more than the previous night's trouble and went to her, holding her close.

After a moment her sobbing lessened, and she blurted, "That fat guy, Leonardo and another man. They scared me. They said we could both be hurt bad if you didn't keep your mouth shut."

"Goddamit! I'm going over there now. What did he say?" Swifty let go of Kim and began running around the small apartment looking into drawers and under counters for some undefined weapon.

"They were already in here when I came home. They were watching TV and drinking your beer. They said – "

"Those bastards!"

"They said . . . 'You tell Swifty to be cool . . . tell him to stay quiet and we'll take care of him. If he doesn't then we'll have to' . . . no, 'We'll be forced to take care of the both of yaus.' Only he said *yaus* instead of *you*. Honey, they sacred me."

"Those sons of a bitches! Who was the other guy . . . was it only one?"

"He was skinnier and taller than the one he called Jake who I guessed must be the guy Leonardo you talked about, but I never heard his name. There was just the two. They were both sticky sweet and they stood too close to me when they talked. The other one kept saying, 'Yeah, sweetie, you listen to the man.'" Kimmie Koenig was twisting a Kleenex into shreds, and minute particles fell onto the rug as she paced and jiggled to Swifty's ramblings.

"Joe? Goddamit! This is Swifty. Hey, this bastard Jake Leonardo has been over here bothering Kim and she's scared half to death."

After a maelstrom of threats and rantings, Swifty slowed down and related what he knew to Joe Seeley. Seeley chuckled a bit and said he was sorry it had happened. He promised that he would "take care of it" and was adamant that Swifty make no contact with "the man" or "his mouthy kid." Swifty read this to mean Artie and Jake Leonard.

Swifty and Kim spent another near-sleepless night wrapped in each other's arms.

Three days passed, and nothing was heard from either Joe Seeley or Jake Leonardo. Swifty called Seeley's office and got a service. He told the operator it was important that Joe return his call. "He's in court, sir. He'll get back to you. Thank you." *Click*.

For two weeks Swifty worried, called Seeley repeatedly, and worked. Kim seemed to have forgotten the entire incident. She was immersed in her job and focused on studying for her real estate exam. Swifty started school and tried to concentrate on his studies. But always there was a threat looming over him. He could feel the black cloud of Jake Leonardo breathing above his neck. Every time he saw a stranger staring at his flowers, he knew it was a message from Jake. About the time he was ready to drive to the offices of East-West Investors to confront Leonardo, Seeley called.

"Kid . . . meet me at the Phoenix Country Club for lunch, tomorrow . . . now wait, make that Wednesday, noon. Okay?"

"Hey, Joe, where you been? What's going on with the feds?"

"Gotta get back, Swifty, Judge's calling us in . . . we'll talk noon, Wednesday." *Click.*

CHAPTER 7

THE TRUTH?

PHOENIX COUNTRY CLUB in the '60s and '70s was an old place full of old men who smoked too much and wore sport shirts that were too loud and too big. A few overweight younger guys hung around the bar . . . in the old days they smoked cigars and drank whisky. Swifty found his way to the ornate bar where Joe Seeley was starting his day with a vodka rocks.

"You figured I'd be in the bar, huh, Swifty? Drink?"

"Nah, the kid in the parking lot told me where you'd be. Gee, Joe, I can't drink while I work

. . . how do you do it?"

"No work today, kid . . . 'cept you. This case I been on. It wrapped up yesterday . . . except for sentencing, which is in about a month. I got this guy reduced from murder two to manslaughter. He'll do less than three years. The guy don't appreciate it. He shoulda got life."

"What did he do?" Swifty, intrigued and impressed, almost forgot his own case.

"Hunted down a guy who owed money and beat him to death. There were twenty witnesses."

"How much did he owe him?"

"Not him, the company . . . eleven hundred. He was just supposed to rough him up, but the guy fought back, so Karass took a sap to him."

"Gosh."

"Okay, let's talk about you. Now, this is all completely confidential both ways. Understand?"

Swifty said he understood and listened while Joe Seeley explained the deal to him. It seems the feds were after a ring of people who had been shuffling cash around until it was untraceable. Swifty had been recruited to courier a load of such cash. Federal authorities were not interested in Swifty, but they did want him to tell the names of the people who contracted him to carry the cash and those he encountered along the way.

Here is where the hook came in. Seeley explained that the people who hired him to represent Swifty wanted Swifty to say he didn't know any names, only addresses. He should describe the men vaguely and tell the locations and that's all. In exchange, his legal fees would be covered, his cash would be restored, including the money to cover his bail and the original thousand he had been promised. Also, incidental expenses would be provided.

Swifty protested, "Hey, that's federal stuff . . . I gotta tell the truth."

"Truth is fine, kid, but no names . . . you forget the names or – "

"What's the *or*, some kind of threat?"

"Swifty, I am an officer of the court, I don't engage in threats. However, the information I have is that relating the names, especially the one who started you on this run, would not be good for your health, or . . . or Kimmie's."

Swifty didn't like him calling her Kimmie. He started to burn, but then he figured there was probably no use. They had lunch in the bar.

"Okay, Joe, my memory goes bad, then what?"

"Well, the feds act frustrated, they threaten you, then they release you. They'll follow you for a few weeks and then it's over."

"Okay . . . I got no choice. Okay."

CHAPTER 8

THE FEDS

FOUR WEEKS LATER, after several grueling sessions with local and federal authorities, Swifty was informed that his lack of memory has earned him a formal federal criminal accessory charge. He kept telling them the addresses, including East-West Investors, the Tucson house, the farm out by Queen Creek, and the Biltmore room. He even described the individuals he met. But he could not confirm the names Arthur Leonardo, Jake Leonardo, Malcolm Ussery, Homer Batera, or Louis Peltz. He guessed Ussery and Batera might have been the men in the Tucson house.

When Swifty suggested to the feds they check the names of the people who owned or rented the properties in question, he was told to shut up . . . that was done. He heard the agents talking about the properties all being leased by an agency in Henderson, Nevada, that had up-fronted cash and subsequently gone out of business.

"You're our only conduit to these bastards, Colin. Be better if you owned up, otherwise were goin' to the U.S. Attorney on you. We can get him to lock you up indefinitely. You don't talk, kid, you either go to jail direct, or go to trial for currency fraud." The federal officers tag-teamed their grilling of him, punctuating it with this same theme.

Joe Seeley told him there was no such federal statute and that they were just trying to scare him. Swifty was so upset and confused that he just kept repeating in his mind, "No names, no names, no names."

Kim was scared to death that something would go wrong. She didn't trust Joe Seeley and was still smarting over the encounter in her home with Jake Leonardo and his henchman. Nothing Swifty could do would soothe her; rather, her apprehension affected Swifty. He began to lose his appetite and headed for the nearest bar after work each night. Finals week he was so tired and distracted he barely passed the tests. Fortunately, his earlier work carried the semester, but what could have been As were Cs.

Finally, January 15, Joe Seeley called. "I need to see you kids in my office tonight . . . say eight o'clock." He hung up without another word.

Kim wore her best wool dress and heels. Swifty put on a jacket with no tie. They stopped at a little Mexican place for a bite, but neither of them was hungry. Swifty had two beers, Kim a Coke. They arrived at Joe's office on Fifth street at 7:45. There was no one in the outer lobby of the plain but neat cubbyhole near the courthouse. They had no choice but to wait.

At 9:20 Joe came in the front door. He was dressed in a dark wool pinstripe with matching tie. Swifty noticed his pink shirt and flared trousers . . . and the black Chuckle boots. Joe's slightly balding pate was well tanned and he had let the gray edges of his sideburns grow over his ears. A man of the times, this Joe Seeley.

"Hey, kids, sorry, sorry to be late . . . here, I brought us a drink from the club." He opened his briefcase on the reception desk and produced a half-empty pint of whiskey and two pop-top cans of cola. "Sorry, no ice . . . let's go in the office."

Swifty and Kim followed Joe into his office, with Swifty carrying the bottle and cans. When they were situated, Joe said, "Look, both of you guys need a stiff drink . . . so take it." He poured liberally from the bottle and cans, using paper cups he had secured from the credenza behind his cluttered desk. "Drink up."

Swifty took a long pull on the concoction, but Kim set hers on the desk and sat on the edge of an office chair, looking expectantly at the dapper lawyer.

"Okay, well, shit . . . here it is, the U.S. Attorney has decided to indict you on an accessory charge, Colin. His guys dug out some old statute they used to use on Mafia couriers. I think we can beat it, or at least plea it down . . . I mean, even if you have to do some time, which I doubt, it will be minimum security, local and short – "

"Time! Time! What the fuck are you talking about, time! I'm not doing time for nothing. Listen, I kept my goddamn mouth shut like you said. Now I'm opening up . . . screw Arthur and Jake Leonardo, screw Louis 'whatshisname' Peltz and those other assholes! No way!"

Swifty raged about the small office, stopped to drink the contents of his cup, choked, and raged some more. Kimmie sat silently, looking at the prints of Kokopele on Joe Seeley's wall, as tears formed in her beautiful green eyes.

"Look . . . Swifty, I can only imagine how you feel. This is a bad deal all around . . . but – "

"Bad deal my ass, I'll show you a bad deal . . . it's over for those fucking jerks. Leonardo is busted! I'm going to rain all over him and his fat-assed son . . . goddamit, Joe you tell 'em, it's over!"

"Swifty . . . Swifty, settle down now." Joe stood and braced Swifty by holding his shoulders. "Look at me . . . now, listen, you do not want to mess with these guys. Listen." He shook the young man lightly and returned to his chair. As Swifty poured another stiff drink and chugged it down, tears rolled down the lovely cheeks of Kim Koenig.

Joe took the opportunity of the brief silence to add, "Both of you have to be practical. Testifying against these people is not an option. Believe me, they are covered . . . you will be out on your own. Think this through, and besides . . . well, time may be averted. Let me work on it."

"You work on . . . you work on it, but by god I want to see Artie and Jake Leonardo, face-to-face . . . Now!"

"Kid, that is not wise . . . plus, they wouldn't, shouldn't be seen within a mile of you. Bad for you and them."

"I don't give a shit! I want to talk to 'em. You tell 'em. Now! Fucking *now*!

Kim had never seen Swifty like this. He was wild, hysterical . . . out of control. She was afraid Joe Seeley would either get physical and hurt Swifty, or the other way around. She stood and tried to restrain her young husband, placing her fists on his chest, but no words would come. Both men, recognizing she was terribly upset, stopped talking, and Swifty softened.

"Tell 'em tonight, Joe . . . ," he said more softly as he pulled Kim to him and held her. She struggled at first, then began to cry loudly, with her chest heaving against Swifty's embrace.

"Okay, kid . . . okay, better take her home. I'll call you tomorrow, early. I'll give you the options then. Better not count on a meet though."

"You tell 'em, Joe, tonight."

Swifty and Kim drove home in silence. Swifty was concerned that he had raged beyond reason without learning much at all. What was this "time" business that sent shivers down his spine and what were his actual options? Would the Leonardos get heavy with him for making a fuss? God, what was happening to his life! Kim was more upset than he'd ever seen her. He wondered if she would leave him if he indeed had to go to jail. God! Jail! Shit!

Kim was cold and aloof to him for the next several days. He knew that she had been talking to her mother on the phone and that she had been crying a lot. He longed to hold her close, but she would have none of him. He felt so alone. Swifty's dad died a month before he went to the Air Force. His mother married some jerk from her work a few weeks after he and Kim moved to Scottsdale. Certainly he couldn't call her for consolation.

Joe Seeley had indeed called the next morning with some news. He told Swifty that he had reached "the party" in question and would have more news soon. Also, he explained that the U.S. Attorney was willing to consider dropping the charges if Swifty could "give" them somebody new. Otherwise, he was going on trial as an accessory to currency fraud.

He told Joe that he was ready to tell the feds about Jake Leonardo giving him the package and about Peltz and the others. "That's not who they want, kid. They want somebody 'new.'"

"What does that mean?"

"Mr. Leonardo junior has taken a trip out of the country to continue his studies. Mr. Peltz has received immunity from prosecution for testifying against someone in an unrelated case. Mr. Batera has disappeared and Mr. Ussery is recently deceased. They want another name . . . like 'the man' himself, which ain't an option."

"Jesus!"

"Yeah, hey I'll call ya in a few days when I got more." *Click.*

It was ten days, but Joe called. "I'm surprised, Swifty, but 'the man' wants to sit down with you himself . . . without me. Now this is dangerous and I told him so. But, he is his own man. He said he knows you, he can read you, and he trusts your word. It's nuts . . . don't tell him I said that . . . but, that's what he wants."

"Where and when?"

"I was not told. He will find you at a 'convenient time.' That's it. Keep your mouth shut and listen, Swifty. This could be for a lot of marbles."

CHAPTER 9

THE MEET

KIM HAD TAKEN a long weekend to visit her mom in Long Beach, where she moved after Lynwood got a little too "uncomfortable." The blacks had moved east across Alameda Street from Watts and north from Compton, displacing a white majority. The once-proud All-American City of 1962 had been "halved" by the blight along Fernwood Avenue, where the Century Freeway was planned.

It took thirty years to build the freeway but only five to destroy the quiet bedroom community. Bars went on windows, armed guards replaced red-aproned greeters at the supermarkets, and St. Francis Hospital changed from a first-class refuge to field medical facility for the Crips, White Fence gang, and DXYs during their Saturday-night "wars." The emergency room had more poor and destitute, non-paying customers than a Main Street soup kitchen. "White flight" took families first to Downey then to Long Beach and then to Orange County.

Swifty sat in the bar at the Royal Palms Hotel on Camelback, drinking too much scotch and half watching *Jeopardy*. A large man in a dark sport shirt worn outside his pants pushed onto the stool next to him. Swifty glanced his way and pushed the bowl of peanuts in that direction. "Thanks," he heard.

A minute later a fresh drink appeared before him; a beer was placed near his new neighbor. "From the gentleman . . . ," whispered the bartender.

"Hey, thanks," volunteered Swifty. "You here for some meeting?"

"Yeah," came the reply. "Finish your drink and you and me are going to a meeting down the street. No hurry."

Swifty turned his body toward the large man and was about to say "What?" when it dawned on him that this guy could be from Leonardo.

"Okay . . . but I gotta be sure who – "

"I'm sure . . . you can be sure it is the meeting you been expecting. Relax." There was a soothing quality in the rough tone of this large character. Swifty decided not to argue.

They emptied their glasses, and Swifty tried to act cool as he slid off the stool. It didn't work, and he lurched to his left. The man caught him with a strong left hand and easily righted him without a word. Swifty followed him out the side door to a black Lincoln. The man pointed and Swifty crawled into the back seat. Swifty noticed the bulge under the man's shirt as he adjusted his bulk and slid behind the wheel. Clearly it was a gun. Swifty felt sick.

Riding through the desert at night is like flying. You can't see anything. After more than a half hour with not a word spoken, his large companion turned the car onto a paved but narrow road leading up a hill toward some dim lights.

He saw lighted gateposts as the car pulled into a winding drive and stopped in front of a large home built into the side of a mountain. Swifty followed his guide onto the asphalt and nearly lost his breath as he appreciated the view before him. Black, beyond the driveway illumination, stretching out toward another planet he guessed to be Phoenix or Scottsdale. They must be in Carefree.

About twenty-five miles northeast of town, this dusty little community peopled by prospectors, cowboys, preservationists, and millionaires chose to remain isolated from Phoenix to the Southwest. Only actor/producer Dick Van Dyke violated the unspoken code of the community's privacy by erecting a small studio in which he produced his and a few other TV shows.

Black Mountain, Swifty guessed. They were on Black Mountain.

The large man directed him up two steps onto a broad patio where a lone figure sat, smoking.

"Sit down, Colin. Dom, get Swifty whatever he's drinking. Arthur Leonardo. Good to see you." Swifty saw the handsome face, even the fierce gray eyes and the even teeth, by the light of a small candle in some sort of hurricane lamp as the figure gestured to shake hands from a half crouch.

"Thanks," Swifty forced as he took Artie's hand. "Could I use the bathroom?"

"Dom, show Mr. Koenig the head please . . ."

The large man opened a screen door and motioned Swifty out of his newly taken seat. Once he had closed the door of the very Sonoran-decorated restroom, he lifted the saddlelike toilet seat and threw up. He caught his breath, flushed the toiled, urinated, waited, flushed again, then washed his face and hands. He reached in his pocket and found a mint. He popped it in his mouth and returned to the porch.

"Okay?" Arthur Leonardo was smiling and nodded slightly toward a glass of beer and some peanuts on the coffee table.

"Yessir, thank you," Swifty belched.

"Colin . . . may I call you Swifty?" He waited for the nod and proceeded. "Swifty, this problem we have is terribly distressing. I know, more for you than me even. But, if you'll let me explain the overall predicament, I'm hoping we can come to at least a halfway reasonable agreement." Arthur Leonardo's narrow gray eyes were opened wide and his eyebrows were raised in an unfamiliar questioning pose.

Swifty could only suck on the beer and nod.

"Swifty, there seems to be no way for us to avoid you taking a fall. Now wait, let me finish." He became forceful as he sensed a protest from Swifty, who sat back as admonished.

"Look, I'm sorry I got you into this mess. Believe me, son, I don't often apologize for anything, but this is my problem. Unfortunately, you are caught up in it and the feds want a token. I can't come forward and explain. Swifty, I have been in prison three times. The next time it could take twenty years out of my life. I would be an old man. It cannot be. So . . ."

"Twenty years? Geez, I can't . . ."

"No, Swifty, no they can't tag you like that. Joe figures maybe eight months to three years. Now wait . . . I'm going to do everything money can do to keep you out, but I need you to stay cool."

Swifty drank his beer and had two more as well as all the peanuts while Arthur Leonardo explained his options. In the end, Swifty, now quite drunk, understood he would have to "cop a plea" and serve a predetermined prison sentence or take his chances at a trial. Leonardo explained that Joe and his colleagues feared that a guilty verdict would net Swifty five or more years in a federal penitentiary somewhere on the East Coast. A plea would keep Swifty in minimum security near home, where Artie had friends.

I think they call it a Hobson's choice, where neither alternative is worth a shit. This was a triple. In state, out of state, or face the unspoken but very real wrath of Arthur Leonardo and unseen associates. Swifty felt fear like he had never known. In the service, he had experienced the threat of harm a few times, but never up front like this. He was too sick with fear to be sober.

He awakened with a dry mouth and a headache, wrapped in his clothes and a blanket on his own couch. There was no recollection of leaving the mountain, the ride back, or being dumped in his apartment. He struggled to his feet, feeling hot and sticky. He staggered to the bathroom. A mess faced him. Clearly he had thrown up in and around the toilet. He gagged as he cleaned it up and then took a shower.

Ready to face the day, Swifty did something he never thought he would; he drank a cold beer with bread and cheese for breakfast. At ten past nine he walked over to the shop. A fear gripped his every thought, a fear that would live with him every waking minute for the next five years.

Nobody else was around to open up. Luckily, it was Monday and no new flower deliveries were expected until the next day. Nor did he have to make a buy at the flower mart. Swifty hitched a ride to the Royal Palms from a gravel hauler and picked up his panel truck for the next day's work.

Kim was due home in the evening. He missed her, but he dreaded have to tell her his options. God, he didn't want to lose her.

CHAPTER 10

REMORSE

EVEN THOUGH THE mountain hid the morning sun, there was enough light by six thirty to cause Artie to stir. He was haunted by the vision of that drunk kid . . . that poor drunk kid. How in the shit did he let this happen? What else could he do? Shit. It just wasn't Arthur Leonardo's style to bully or bribe innocent people, especially a good young kid like this Swifty.

Fuckin' Jake. Big shot. Couldn't be bothered with grunt work. College man, too important to handle a simple assignment. Then he takes muscle with him and scares the young wife. Damn!

Well, he was in Europe now and way in the clear. Now all that could be done was being done. He'd find protection for the kid if he had to do some time. He'd find a way to get the girl some cash, maybe a better job. Why, why . . . . *WHY*! Why was this happening? Shit.

Artie arose, put on a light robe, and took his cigarettes out on the porch. He liked this time of the day . . . nice and cool. The first streaks of morning sun crept around Black Mountain and divided the shadows created by the jagged rocks. Shit!

"Mr. Leonardo? Do you want your car brought around?" Dom's considerable bulk filled his vision.

"Nah, Nah, Dom. I ain't even dressed yet. What time is it? Guess I fell back to sleep out here."

"It's eight thirty. What time do you want to go in?" Dom was clearly antsy to get to town. Probably had a broad to see.

"Hey, pal, you go on in. Take the Lincoln. I'm goin' to hang around here and annoy Mrs. Leonardo today. 'Sides, I got some thinking to do . . . okay? I can drive that shitty little jeep deal if I need wheels."

"You still worrying about that kid, huh."

"Yeah. It's a rotten deal, but I can't think of an alternative . . . can you?"

"No. You want me to look in on him today?"

"Yeah. Hey, Dom, you take today for yourself . . . in town. Check on the kid tomorrow then give me a call. Keep the Lincoln."

"You sure?"

"Yeah, call me in the morning."

"Okay, boss man . . . see ya. Don't worry too much. This kid is solid. He'll make it through."

"Yeah."

Unshaven and clad only in a cotton robe, he watched Dom Luisi, his boyhood chum, hulk down the steps in his green golf shirt and khaki shorts. What a sight! White legs, loafers with no socks, the shirt looking like a dress as it draped out over the massive rear end. Calling him Mr. Leonardo. "Shit! I'm living in a dream world," thought Artie.

Teresa left in her little jeep to do some grocery shopping. She liked living out here in the sticks, even with the snakes and scorpions. He agreed to lease this six-thousand-square-foot "retreat" halfway up Black Mountain until June. It was certainly better than the Biltmore, at least the hotel part. Maybe he'd buy a place on the grounds there and keep this place too. He could afford it.

He could afford to send his punk-assed kid to Europe to "study" too. Which probably meant boozing, gambling, and chasing broads. But Jake had enrolled in the University of Zurich to study international banking. Maybe he'd learn something while he was there . . . at least academically. What the hell ever happened to honor? Shit.

Artie tried to concentrate on something other than Swifty, but he couldn't. He had no worry about taking a fall. If the kid started screaming his name, Artie would just laugh it off. The feds had no link to him. He had no jeopardy. But he hated what he was doing to this boy. He remembered the fear he had felt when he was sent to jail . . . and he was guilty. He had known and taken the risk. This boy was totally innocent. Shit!

Artie wandered back into the house, found the kitchen, and made himself a cheese-and-salami sandwich. He took a bottle of milk out, then replaced it and grabbed a beer. This was going to be a long day.

Artie's dad, Leonard Jacob Marx, talked about honor. The old man always regretted not following his religion. He let his kids go to Catholic school because that's what his wife wanted. He changed his name to Leon Leonard because she wanted that too. He never bar mitzvahed, and young

Artie couldn't either, because his mama was not Jewish. If he had turned his back on his religion, at least he could maintain his honor. The one thing he made certain to instill in young Artie was that same sense. Artie's mother reinforced it with her Catholic values, so it was there deep inside. Damn. Why couldn't he have gotten Jake to understand? He had not done well by his son. A good home, a good education, but no true sense of honor . . . no personal value system. Damn! He had another beer.

Somewhere around midmorning he heard the little jeep return and a door slam.

"Shit, shit, shit!"

"Arthur, do you have to keep swearing! What if we had company? Why don't you think of some other ways to express yourself?" Teresa was treading on dangerous ground correcting him when he was upset. He was about to tell her to mind her own business when the phone rang. He picked it up on the second ring.

"Yes?"

"Yes, this is he. Who is this?"

"Yes, I know of you, Mrs. Kulokowski. Sorry, Ms. Kulokowski. What can I do for you?"

"He what? Oh god . . . what's his condition? I'll be right there . . . half hour or so . . .

"Thank you." He hung up and stared out the window at nothing.

"Who was that, Arthur? You look like a ghost. Was it Jake?" Teresa stood in the doorway holding a bunch of carrots.

"Dom's friend . . . he's had a heart attack. I gotta use your jeep."

"Oh my God! Take something for your breath. You've been drinking. Do you want me to come?"

He didn't hear a word she said. Within a minute he had put on a coat, grabbed her keys off the counter, and sprinted down the stairs to the jeep.

At Phoenix Memorial he found Miss Kulokowski in the waiting room of the cardiac care unit. She was a big gal, maybe five-ten and one sixty. Pretty, in a bouncy sort of way, and about forty-five give or take.

"We was playing Yatze and he jus' fell over. I called my son Kyle. He lives down the street. He called the ambulance. On the way over Dominic said I should call you at the number he had given me." Her eyes were red and puffy, but she was fairly composed.

"He was in such pain . . . I could tell. We was going to ask you to stand up with us next month. Now, I guess gettin' married'll have to wait. God, Jesus, I hope he'll be okay." Artie figured this girl was an okay match for his pal; not too bright, but kind of sincere. Good company for Dom.

A nurse came by. He asked her about Mr. Luisi. She said she'd ask the charge nurse to come by. A few minutes later, an older woman came in and said the doctor would be in soon. Two hours later, Teresa arrived. She had taken a cab after calling the three major hospitals to find out which one Dom was in.

"You could have told me where he was . . . Arthur . . . geez, he's my friend too."

"Sorry, dear, I was upset and confused . . . honey, this is Mrs. Kulokowski. My wife,

Teresa . . . ah – "

"Naomi. Hi, Mrs. L . . . uh, Teresa." The big woman collapsed into his wife's waiting arms and began to convulse while snorting like a pig. Artie figured it was her way of crying. Teresa kept patting her on the back like she had known her eighty years. Women . . . go figure.

Dr. Booker, a tall guy dressed all in green surgical gear and looking tired, shuffled in, pushing those funny slippers they wear along the polished tile floor. "Are you all for Mr. Luisi? He asked for Naomi and Artie. That you? You next of kin?"

"I'm his brother, Arthur, this is my wife, and his fiancée. How is he, doctor?" Artie was about as sincere as he could be with a dry mouth and semihangover. He was conscious of not shaving that day.

"Well, I must say he is terribly overweight . . . that doesn't help us here. He has suffered a myocardial infarct . . . a heart attack of some strength. My guess now is that there is some considerable heart muscle damage. I want to do an angiogram, but I have to wait till he is stable for a day. He's resting now. Do you understand what I'm saying?" He looked from one to the other.

"Yes, he has had a severe heart attack and you want to run a wire up to his heart from his groin and check to find out where the blockages might be. You have to wait until he can take it. If he's not alert, I'll sign whatever release you need . . . I have his power of attorney." Artie knew the drill. He had lost two uncles to heart attacks. They were too damn fat, just like Dom. You couldn't tell them.

"Can we see him . . . is he sleeping?" Naomi whispered.

"You can look in . . . he might recognize you. I have him sedated and full of blood thinner. He's there in number four." He turned on his heel, nodded, and shuffled to the nurses' station, filling out a chart. Artie followed him.

"Dr. Booker, when do you think you'll do this procedure? Shall I plan to stay nearby or will you call me? And, doctor . . . I want to know his chances . . . as you see it now." Artie's steel gray eyes bore into the taller man until he seemed to feel them and turned, a little disarmed.

"If you will leave your number with the charge nurse here, she'll see to it my exchange calls you if anything changes. Otherwise, just check in here tomorrow at this time. His condition is critical. He could expire tonight. If he begins to improve today, I would expect him to be ready for an angiogram tomorrow afternoon. He's too damn heavy . . . his blood pressure was off the charts. I'll wager I'll be cutting on him by the end of the week . . . if he makes it through the night. That enough?"

"Yeah, thanks. I appreciated your candor, considering the liability issues we all face these days. Your a good man, Dr. Booker." Artie touched the man lightly on the shoulder, then moved past him to number four.

Dom was whispering something into Naomi's ear when Artie got there. She pulled back when he neared. "He wants you." She breathed through a new batch of tears.

"What the fuck you tryin' to pull, you malingering guinea?" Artie spoke, with his lips near the sick man's ear.

"I knew this shit was comin', Artie . . . I could feel it for a week. Too much pasta and vino. What's it gonna be . . . will I make it?"

"Fifty-fifty today, gets better tomorrow. They gotta stick a wire in your vein down around your gonads and run it up to your ticker. They watch it on a TV screen. They can see where the blockages are. Probably they'll have to break open that flabby chesta yours enda the week. That's all I know, buddy." He kissed the larger man on the cheek and patted his arm.

"Shoulda exercised . . . okay. Hey, Art . . . do something for me. Take care of Naomi a little if I kick it. Okay?"

Artie squeezed the big man's arm, signifying he would.

"Nother thing . . . I decided on my own to talk to that kid, Swifty," Dom puffed.

"Relax now, we can talk tomorrow . . . sleep." Artie patted his arm again

"Kid is good . . . knows the deal . . . he can be trusted . . ." Dom dropped off to sleep.

Artie drove both women to Naomi's place. Her son was there and looked at them expectantly. He called them "Sir" and Ma'am," so Artie made a note to check him out. He had a skinny wife that took over the comforting job that released Teresa to go home with him.

After some confusion, Naomi found Dom's pants and surrendered the keys to the Lincoln. She also handed Artie a paper sack with a gun in it. He put it in the trunk of the Lincoln, opened the door for Teresa, and waved as he exited the working-class neighborhood of South Phoenix.

CHAPTER II

SCIENCE MEETS THE UNDERWORLD

LOUIS PELTZ STEERED the little Peugeot through the narrow streets of Basil, hoping to miss the afternoon-work traffic that was certain to begin precisely at 4:00 p.m. God, he hated this place. It was so unlike his home in Rancho Mirage; so cold, so bucolic, so boring. Switzerland was a necessary evil, though, and it would be some time before he saw Palm Springs and environs again, thanks to his brash young charge, Jake Leonardo.

Working as a scientist for Ciba both in Connecticut and Zurich for eighteen years after his postdoctoral work, he became an expert in oncological research. Moving to Lyceum Ltd., he became chief scientific officer with a piece of the action in the midsixties. Four years later, they go bust; and Louis, who learns to enjoy a luxurious lifestyle, is deep in debt. A friend asks him if the Lyceum miracle drug K148 that had been written up as promising in several journals can actually cure certain cancers. Louis says, "Well the clinical trials were not completed, but we saw a number of near-miraculous improvements . . . even cures of prostate and pancreatic cancers." Both of these disease families were guaranteed curtains in the '60s. Pancreatic cancer continues to this day to be a death sentence for most people.

Anyway, this friend relates to Peltz that his brother has been told that his prostate cancer has spread and is inoperable. Does Peltz think he could get some of this K148 to treat the brother? Peltz says it would be illegal in Switzerland or the United States, but he could get some. The friend says, "Where isn't illegal?" Peltz says,

"In Santiago, Chile, possibly." "Get it there, along with a physician and technicians trained to administer it, and I'll give you $100,000 plus costs."

It's done. Louis Peltz PhD, man of science, discoverer of miracle drugs, is an undiscovered felon. He keeps his home in Zurich, though he leaves his wife of twelve years and their two small children with her mother in Basil. He finds Basil better for the kids. Besides, it reduced the likelihood of Mrs. Peltz finding out about his girl friend in Zurich. He travels to Chile after contracting with a medical colleague in South America to administer K148. Six weeks of chemotherapy and the patient, who meets them in Santiago, has improved. Two more rounds of chemo over a six-month period and the man is in total remission. Peltz is a success. The word gets around... Peltz becomes an underground medical contractor. Terminal patients flock to Chile for K148. Some make it, some don't. But, there are no refunds.

Eventually, Louis sets up housekeeping with the girlfriend in the desert city of Rancho Mirage and takes up golf. He travels to Switzerland to help manufacture K148 in an illegal laboratory. Shipping it to South America is no problem. It is packaged as an allergy drug and shipped overland to Genoa, Italy, then to Santiago.

Political problems in Chile cause Louis to move his operation to Mexico. He doesn't like it, because he has to pay large bribes to local and national officials . . . and the rules are forever changing. KKF

The cool wind that blew across Lake Zurich when he finally reached his apartment chilled him to the bone.

"My life was perfect until I met Artie Leonardo. Sure I needed him to clean up the money thing and to control those damn Mexican bandits, but now he's got me babysitting that rotten kid of his!"

Ute, his Swiss girlfriend, gave him a puzzled look as he muttered up the stairs to their luxury apartment overlooking the lake.

"What it is you say now, Louis? Why you are so late? The old witch wanting more money?"

"No, no . . . I'm just tired after the drive . . . help me off with these boots."

CHAPTER 12

UNFAIR CHOICES

KIM KOENIG LISTENED to the two attorneys bantering back and forth. Most of what they said made little sense to her. Jeffrey Domres, the expert in federal crimes that Joe Seeley had brought in to defend Swifty, seemed to be more on the government side than theirs. He chatted and whispered with his counterpart on the prosecution, and they exchanged words like, *racketeering, currency fraud, nolo contendere,* and *mail fraud by public conveyance.*

Finally, after four confusing hours before the federal judge, Jeffrey and Joe presented them their options: Swifty could plead guilty to receiving stolen property – evidently the money he delivered to the hotel – and receive a light sentence. Or he could take his chances with a jury trial. This proceeding was evidently what was called a preliminary hearing. A full trial would cost a lot of money and might not take place for a year. They recommended making a deal with the feds because they read the judge as "hostile."

Swifty wanted to go the whole route. He was not guilty! Why should he take a plea bargain agreement? Joe said he saw his point, but Jeffrey said they wanted a scapegoat. All the others had disappeared. One man even died. If Swifty wouldn't confirm whom he had been dealing with, he would have to be "punished, so to speak." They reiterated that it would be soft time – not much worse than Swifty's stint in the service, and not nearly as long. He could petition the court, after three years, to have his record expunged, his rights restored.

Kim pulled him aside. "Colin, I know you didn't do anything wrong. This isn't your fault. But I'm afraid. If you fight this thing, these men will come back after us. If you tell, the federal government won't protect us. Look at how Jeffrey gets along with the prosecutor and the Judge. Honey, we can't win here."

She started to cry. "If you have to go away for a while, I want you to know I love you and I'll wait. You'll have a home to come back to." She held him by the arms, her nails piercing the fabric of his coat. He knew his forearms would be bleeding. Her face was against his, but she wasn't kissing him . . . she was biting his chin.

Swifty loved this woman. He did not want to lose her. Up to now he was certain that she planned to leave him. Now she had declared her loyalty. He felt joy and pain, both nearly unbearable. About five drinks would've gone good. Instead, he bit his lip, broke free of Kimmie, and strode over to Jeffrey and Joe. The clerk and bailiff rose as he came through the gated railing as though he was breaking some cardinal rule. The two lawyers ignored him momentarily, then glanced up, annoyed.

"Hey, okay, you guys. I'm ready to take the deal. What do I have to sign?" Swifty barked this out with more volume than he intended, causing the bailiff to waddle in their direction. The clerk stood, hands on her hips.

"Colin, go back over there and sit down!" Jeffrey ordered, and then winked. The bailiff stopped, turned, and then returned to his seat.

"But – "

"Yeah, we heard you . . . Jesus, wait till we get outside," Joe whispered.

In a week it was done. The judge approved the deal and sentenced Swifty to three years in the federal minimum-security compound at Safford, seventy miles southeast of Phoenix. Joe and Jeffrey said with good behavior he'd be out in eight months. There would be no bars – just a fence – and no "hard-ass" types.

Artie Leonardo heard from Joe Seeley that afternoon. "Three years, Arthur, it could have been worse. I figure parole in a year, maybe. Unless they want to keep playing hardball, then the kid is there until it runs its course."

"My God, Joseph, this cost me a fucking fortune . . . for this guy Domres. I thought he was supposed to be an ex-assistant U.S. Attorney. I thought he could get the kid probation or something!"

Artie knew he was being unrealistic, but being the ultimate cause of this clearly unfair sentence was totally frustrating. He was not used to guilt.

Joe said, "Look at the positives, he could've walked if he named names, Arthur. He didn't. Now even if he could put you in the picture with fingerprints and an audit trail, it would be too late. You are all clear, and if Jake stays away, he is too."

CHAPTER 13

MEANWHILE, IN THE SNOW

JAKE LEONARDO MOVED slowly through the chilling air. He hated this weather . . . he hated all weather: Phoenix was too hot, this was too cold. One time he was in New York in October, that was okay. His father let him bring that "yacky" broad, Amber Trainer, with him to Zurich. At least he had somebody to keep him warm at night and to make a fuss about his muscles when he worked out with the locals.

"Purgatory! That's what this place is, purgatory. Two years of this and I'm goin' nuts. Studying and class takes four hours a day, working out, maybe two. Then it's boredom. Maybe I'll learn how to ski when it starts to snow. Yeah, skiing . . . skiing." Jake had almost reached the small private gym that was used by the local weight lifters. Amber would be there from shopping pretty soon.

The noise of a small car broke the silence. He looked around. "Fucking Peltz! Why can't that little asshole leave me alone . . . geez."

"Hey, Jakie . . . come over here. I got a message from your father." Peltz was a twerp. "Why did he get the deep voice . . . why not me?" thought Jake.

"Yeah?" Jake stomped over to the car and rubbed his hands against the cold.

"Get in."

Jake climbed into the little car with some effort and closed the door. It was warmer inside. "What, Louis . . . what?"

"Your father sent me a message through one of our people. It seems that kid who couriered for you is going to be convicted. He'll probably spend some time in prison," Peltz said evenly.

Jake shook his head in disbelief. "He didn't do anything. What do they have on him? Does the old man think he'll talk?"

"It's some kind of currency charge. They tried to force him to tell who gave him the original package and he won't say. So they figure to put him away unless and until he talks. Your dad says not to worry. See, Jakie, they only looked to the money. They have no idea of what was actually involved. We're home free." Peltz didn't look as though he believed himself.

"Well, does that mean we can go home?" Jake asked meekly.

"No, we have to stay here until we are certain the boy doesn't change his mind. He has your name and mine, as well as your father's, but for some reason he has agreed to keep quiet." Peltz seemed puzzled as he related this to Jake.

"Well, he probably doesn't want to have to deal with me . . . or Dominic. Geez, Dominic would scare me too!" Jake gave a short snort.

"Oh yes, that's the other thing. Dominic has had a heart attack and needs immediate heart surgery. The prognosis is questionable," Peltz recited.

"Goddamit! Dominic! Shit, he's Pop's best friend. Hey, we gotta get back there!" Jake pushed against the door of the Peugeot.

"No, he says . . . you stay here with me. He'll keep us informed. Nothing you can do to help." Peltz was back being confident and in charge.

Jake said he'd see Peltz later and struggled out of the small car. He resumed his climb up the hill to the gym. At the front door he could see Amber sitting inside at the counter, talking to the blond kid with the big arms. He was from Germany someplace.

"Hi, baby!" Amber scooted off the stool where she had been showing the shape of her legs, through a black leotard, to young Wolfgang and threw her arms around Jake's size 20 neck. She kissed him full on the lips and began her usual chatter.

By the time Jake had stripped down to his workout shorts and sweatshirt with no arms, Amber had related every fabric, aroma, texture, and flavor she had experienced since breakfast. She also rattled off the names of Wolfgang's sisters in a place called Russelsheim and asked Jake for ten thousand Swiss francs.

He peeled off some bills and stuck them into the scooped neck of her leotard. Then he carefully hung up his clothes in large pine locker and called out, "Hey, Wolfie . . . spot for me! You come watch, baby . . . you make me feel stronger. But, honey . . . not so much talk while me an Wolfman are workin'. Okay?"

She smiled and plucked the bills from her neck, counted them, and put them in her purse. "Oh, okay."

They moved to the gym floor and Jake began to stretch, thinking of Swifty Koenig and his father. "If the kid gets time he's bound to blab out everything he knows, which is nothing. As long as my name isn't mentioned we're all clear. Pop's dealing with him was legitimate. Yeah, I'm the linchpin here . . . my name."

PART TWO

CHAPTER 14

REALITY

                                                                    SITTING SILENTLY, SIDE by side on the long wooden benches, he had tried to imagine what he was in for, what it would be like without Kimmie. She had said she would wait. God, he loved her. He didn't want to go. He could still feel the little bumps from the scars left when she pierced his coat and brought blood to his forearms two weeks before.

    Soon, the names were called. Eleven men had preceded him, mostly Hispanic. He had kissed her; she held him briefly and said, "I'll come see you as soon as I find out where and how . . . brush your teeth every day." She turned, and he rushed through the door, fearing another moment would shatter them like glass.

    Now. Now. Now. He had to live in the now. From the court, he moved to processing. Four hours of sitting in a holding cell gave way to a brief lunch break. They were given box lunches and bottled water. Now they were back in fingerprinting. What would be next? It was a group shower with no drying off. They stayed wet while officers in rubber gloves inspected every orifice, then fumigated them everywhere but in the face. They were given gray one-size-fits-all jumpsuits and clogs and told to put them on still wet.

    According to the clock on the wall, they sat another four hours in a new holding tank across the earlier one. They could see the trustees cleaning up their old cell and eating the leftovers from their lunches. A few Mexican swear words were shouted, and fingers waved, but it meant nothing.

An old school bus had been converted to a prison vehicle, with bars and metal mess doors welded in to separate each row of seats. Swifty had been pulled from the holding cell first and marched to an empty room where handcuffs and leg irons were fitted to him. Then he was led to an open yard where the buses sat. He was pushed into the first and oldest of the transports. It was gray, with flecks of yellow showing through . . . it was a converted school bus all right.

Two large male guards entered with shotguns and positioned themselves at either end of the bus. A third guard stood next to the wheel and barked, "Listen up! You people sit down and keep your eyes front. Keep your hands in your lap. If your feet are in the aisle or your hands hang outside the gates, they will be smashed when we close them . . . which is about now." A guard moved quickly down the aisle, checking for compliance. He seemed satisfied and screeched, "Clear!"

With a responding "Clear" from the guard up front, the barred gates closed on each row. They were individually padlocked, and the three guards took seats. A driver mounted the vehicle and took his position. Swifty couldn't see where the guards actually were sitting, but he could see a shotgun barrel sticking up near the front. The motor started, backfired, and then chugged smoothly. The accordion door closed, and Swifty finally became aware of his seatmate.

Connor Grove was an embezzler who had been convicted of mail fraud and stealing from a savings and loan where he was an officer. His case had been a mainstay in the Arizona Republic for nearly two years. Grove was a handsome man of fifty-five with graying temples, slickly combed black hair, and a winning smile. His sentence of six years was on appeal. Having been in and out of jail for the past several months, Grove didn't seem too rattled about his current incarceration. "I'll be out in a month," Swifty had overheard him tell another man in the holding cells. Swifty thought about saying something to him on the ride to their new home, but the guard had told them to shut up with their eyes to the front. He decided to wait. KKF

The old bus bumped along the double-lane asphalt surface of Highway 18 for three hours before reaching Safford. It was just past six and Swifty was hungry. Stopping at the gate of a chain-link fence where he could see a group of men policing up wastepaper, the driver exited momentarily. He returned and spoke to the two guards, who were now standing in the front of the bus. The third man, shotgun at the ready, slowly paced the aisle. In a couple of minutes, the driver closed the door and swung the bus into a drive where a gate had been opened. Two cars marked with some official seal sped past them and headed up a dusty road. Following the cars, the bus rounded a bend and dropped into an arroyo. Swifty could see an inner and an outer chain-link fence with barbed wire barriers on top of each one. A full metal gate and a subsequent chain-link gate rested imposingly on the twelve-foot fences. So much for minimum security, he thought.

Grove was audible in his disapproval. "Shit. These cowboys must think we're Luke and the boys." Swifty guessed he was referring to the popular Paul Newman movie, *Cool Hand Luke*.

After clanking through the two gates, the bus crept to the front door of a one-story building marked Administration, Bureau of Prisons, Safford.

Ghosts. All the new guys, because of the gray jumpsuits, were called ghosts. There were catcalls and whistles, shouts from the guards, and the clanking of metal doors.

"You shitheads are ghosts until you get your room assignments and new uniforms. All rooms are two man, except we're full up . . . so you ghosts are gonna be added on to two-man rooms where one man is soon to be released. We don't have any more uniforms so you're gonna stay ghosts till somebody leaves and hands you down a uniform. Work boots we got. So you'll get them when your work shift starts. No questions. Put your goddamn hand down."

Sergeant Ackerman, in charge of processing in, was speaking.

Connor Grove slowly pulled his hand back to his shoulder and shrugged. "How in hell are we supposed to know what's going on if we don't ask." He whispered to no one in particular.

"No goddamn talking!" Two guards moved near Grove and glared in his direction. He smiled and nodded.

Swifty was moved with eight other men to a holding room. Grove was in his party. All the men were white and had relatively fresh haircuts.

"Segregation?" Grove wondered aloud.

"Yes," said a burly bald man with a handlebar mustache. "I heard about this from another guy. They minimize trouble by putting like types together. My guess is they will put us in with some other white guys convicted of soft crime."

"Soft crime?" asked another man.

"Yeah," said the mustache. "You know, 'white collar,' victimless, etc."

"Sounds good to me," said Grove. "Last thing I want is to defend my body, or worse, my virtue, against some 'brown bandit.'"

"What makes you think you're safe from us?" joked another man. The group quietly laughed, then relapsed into their own thoughts.

In his first two days, Swifty was approached by two gay prisoners insisting he align with them. His first cellmate, a convicted drug dealer, threatened him if he didn't run product for him. He resisted both approaches. Day three he was muscled around by a counselor who told him he would have to "play ball" or "be dead." By the time he was thoroughly frightened, day four, he was moved to a holding cell and told he was being reassigned.

Day five, Swifty was surprised when he was assigned to a room with Connor Grove and a man named Nelson Leigh. Leigh was about fifty-five with dark red hair and a thin mustache. His uniform of navy blue looked tailored, and he wore expensive-looking loafers and no socks. By contrast, Swifty and Grove slouched in their gray stained jumpsuits.

"Welcome, gentlemen, please don't sit on the beds with that crap you're wearing." He pushed a chair and a stool in their direction. "I like things clean and neat."

"So, you are the famous Nelson Leigh," said Grove, taking the plain wooden chair. "How did we luck out with you?"

"Because I made arrangement for you to join me, you and young Mr. Koenig here." Swifty sat down hard on the stool.

"Why'd you want us in here with you?" he asked.

"I didn't, Colin, may I call you Colin? Of course I may . . . I was instructed to make such an arrangement with the authorities here. Personally, I would rather be in here alone, but it was not in my hands. Since I have certain influence . . . it wasn't difficult to arrange for you and Mr. Grove to join me." Leigh's eyes were green and shined when he smiled. He smiled almost constantly.

Grove asked, "Who instructed you . . . ?"

"Let's put it this way, mutual friends felt that my experience could be helpful to you and that your safety could be in my interest. Let's leave it at that." He smiled.

"Safety?" Swifty said inquiringly.

"I know what you have been through in your first three days. Minimum security means just that, my young friend. We have counterfeiters and embezzlers . . . sorry, Mr. Grove, but we also have drug dealers, weapons smugglers, and bank robbers. You two are so tender, you would be 'dead meat' without some protection. You will be safe with my influence." Leigh smiled brightly, but with little sincerity.

"You said friends, mutual friends. Just who . . . ," Swifty began to ask.

"Shhhh. No talk about that. Just accept gifts graciously when offered." He smiled broadly again, and Swifty decided to let it be.

Two trustees and a guard carrying clothing and bedding interrupted them. Leigh showed them the small bathroom they would share, which included a shower. They changed from the jumpsuits and donned neat blue uniforms and black bedroom slippers. While they were changing and Leigh used the bathroom, Swifty asked Connor Grove who this man Leigh was.

Grove explained that Nelson Leigh had been the mastermind of a major con game that had gripped the Southwest a few years earlier. His real name was Sidney Silverstein and he had a record dating back to childhood.

It seems that Leigh had employed a number of swindlers to act as salesmen in a mutual-fund scheme. The fund represented to buy a basket of high – and low-risk stocks that paid dividends as well as enjoyed appreciation. Purchasers could follow their stocks in the paper as well as tracking the fund there. Since dividends were paid on time, nobody suspected that premiums were not being invested, but rather skimmed off to a Bahamas bank. Eventually, someone wished to sell their fund and discovered there was no "there" there. Mexican authorities boarding planes to a variety of European and South American countries apprehended Leigh and most of his people. He had been serving time against his fifteen-year sentence for three years.

Well, it wasn't long before three became a crowd. Connor Grove was an aristocrat of his own design. Neither he nor Nelson Leigh could stand the arrangement. Within a week, Leigh had found a way to have Grove reassigned to the next room, where a very old con, Billy Belger, was serving out the final years of his thirty-year counterfeiting sentence. Billy was glad for the company and welcomed Grove with a smile, but very few words.

During the day the room doors were left unlocked. Inmates, prisoners, or whatever you want to call them, were free to move about within their particular block. At meal times they were walked, not marched, to a common dining room. On movie nights, Wednesdays and Saturdays, they were walked as well. Those not wishing to watch a movie were locked in the block, but not in the room. Guards were easygoing in the block buildings. It was only in the dining areas and administration buildings that they were a pain in the ass. Rooms were locked down at 10:00 p.m. and opened at 6:00 am.

Most rooms did not have showers, but used a common area. The Leigh quarters were larger than most of the others and, in addition to the shower, had a TV and radio. There was also a tiny writing desk, throw rugs, and some cheap drapes on the two glass and mess windows. Swifty figured Leigh had a lot of pull for a crook. He would learn later how much.

Swifty wrote Kim every day. He told her how much he loved her, how he had met a couple of nice men who had been helpful, that he had been assigned to work in the library, how the food was, and how he was counting the days. Sunday, visiting day, was the hardest day of his life. There she stood, beauty in motion, except she wasn't moving.

Sunlight formed a halo, an aura, all around her body. She wore black form-fitting slacks and a beige short-sleeved top with a scoop neck. She wore no jewelry, as it was not allowed in the prison proper. Her lips were red and her hair recently clipped and rinsed. "God, she is beautiful . . . ," he heard Nelson Leigh murmur as he slipped to a nearby table where a lawyer-looking guy waited.

At Safford, they could touch, as long as it was discreet. Kimmie hesitated. Swifty motioned for her to come to the table. He knew he could not cross the line. She moved cautiously to him. They embraced and cried silently together. A female officer whispered to them to break and sit. They did.

She told him of her good fortune – passing the real estate exam and having an interview with the big real estate mogul Norm Cellestine himself. He told her that the man at the next table was his roommate. She smiled toward Nelson and, as if he could feel her glance, he looked up and nodded affectionately.

When they parted, his heart fell. When the bell rang the second time, she walked slowly to the door. She turned and made a little wave. He stood in shock, rubbing the small bumps left where she had pierced his forearms with her nails two weeks before. He heard the female guard say, "Come on, Koenig . . . she loves you, she'll wait."

He walked out of the room in a trance and followed Nelson and the others back across the grounds to their block. In the room, he broke. Nelson, Connor, and Billy all patted him on the shoulder. It did little good.

"You gotta toughen up, kid . . . it'll kill ya if ya don't. Shit, Leigh, he's your guy. Help him out." Billy said little, but he was clearly moved.

Swifty brooded and sobbed for two hours as he paced the hall. Finally, Nelson Leigh could take it no more.

"Come in here, Swifty, you too, Connor. Billy, you can listen if you wish." Leigh was firm but friendly.

Billy and Connor brought chairs. When they were seated Leigh spoke:

"Okay, son, stop the fucking whimpering, now!" Swifty looked up.

"You can get your ass kicked for losing it in here. But, more importantly, as Billy says, you'll kill yourself with anxiety. You have to get a hold of yourself and get busy. You must use your time wisely and productively," he lectured.

"Like you do, Nelson? I don't see you doing much," Connor said mockingly.

"You'll learn soon enough what I do and how I do it. By the way, Connor, it is my shower you use while the others lather up in that common trough," Nelson Leigh snapped.

Grove sat back.

"You'll do that pretty young wife no good either. She'll get tired of the whining and look for the comfort of a real man."

"You son of a bitch!" Swifty sprang to his feet before Nelson and drew back a fist.

"That's it! Good lad. You have to get strong. We have to find a way to get that energy channeled into something productive. Sit back down now . . . I was only trying to get your attention. Sit down." Nelson was firm again.

"Shit, I'm sorry, I . . ." Swifty started to cloud up again.

"Look, son, this is hard enough without feeling sorry for yourself. We've all been there. Since you were royally screwed on this deal, I will give you more than the usual fifteen minutes to feel sorry, but tomorrow, we go to work." He looked at Connor Grove.

Grove looked back. "What makes you think I'm going to take orders from some con man, Nelson. I have been a CEO for twenty years. I have a master's . . . I've controlled a billion dollars!"

Nelson Leigh smiled broadly and set his green eyes on Connor. "You stupid shit. I control your very existence in here. I own you. You are mine. Your intellect is mine. Your education is mine. And you know full well I can influence your life when you get out. You will obey me. Get off your high horse and listen."

Grove said nothing, but Swifty saw him wilt in place.

Swifty was thinking, "Who the hell is this man, Nelson Leigh? Why does he have so much interest in me? Did Artie Leonardo put him on me? What's it going to cost me later? Do they just want to be sure I won't open up on them? Yeah, this guy is my babysitter. Babysitter."

He began to lose his pain and to think again.

The next morning before work, Nelson did not work. He strolled about at will with no apparent controls. Nelson said, "Swifty, when you break for lunch stay in the library. Connor and I will be there at noon. There will be no guards or trustees. The librarian will be otherwise occupied as well."

At a quarter to twelve, Angus Mooney, the librarian, said he had a meeting and locked Swifty in the library stacks. At noon sharp, Nelson and Connor arrived with a basket.

"Lunch!" Grove said enthusiastically. He began to spread a plain cloth over one of the tables.

Nelson opened the basket and removed sandwiches, Cokes, and napkins, as well as assorted chips and candy. Swifty had not seen such things in his ten days at Safford.

"Now, we eat and work," said Nelson.

As he munched away, Nelson spat out a few sentences.

"You need to finish your education, boy. My friend Connor, here, and I will be your professors. Also, it seems that in a few months you may be eligible to attend Arizona State extension classes in the town of Casa Grande. More on that later. Connor."

"Yes, yes, Nelson. Swifty, we are going to lie out an education plan for you that includes finance, liberal arts, etiquette, and the principles of leadership. We know you can take correspondence courses that will be credited toward your degree. Couple that with what you already have, according to your records and our coaching, and you can finish college and your real-life education right here at Safford by the time you are released." Grove was acting like an employer outlining a development plan for a management trainee.

"My records?"

"Yes, I'm assigned to administration. A few phone inquiries and a check of your file and . . . well, that's all it takes." Grove stood, beaming.

"We're going to keep you so busy you won't have time to think of Kim or anyone else!" Nelson was triumphant.

THREE YEARS EARLIER

Connor Grove sat, uncomfortably, in the rear of the Lincoln town car, chatting with his attorney, Morton Karp, about his upcoming trial.

"Goodness, Mort, it's not like I broke the law. Heck, I just fudged a bit on the potential outcome. Actually, I still believe we have a shot at making this thing go. Sure, bravado, but no crime. Can't we cut a 'hand slap' deal?"

"Connor, we should not be speaking this way on the phone, especially that car contraption. We are facing a very serious problem here. This is a federal charge. The U.S. Attorney is very ambitious. He wishes to make an example of you. I can cut a deal with him . . . but, I doubt you'll like it." Karp was very professional.

"Well, check it out and call me at home. I'm steering clear of the office. Every time I approach the place, old people attack me with signs. My own people look at me like I'm a crook. Shit, Mort, you're my friend. Help me."

"I'll get back to you," said Karp, still businesslike.

Grove stopped at the club for lunch. He ordered a Johnnie Walker Black on the rocks. "Double, Jerry," he fired at the bartender. Halfway through his drink, Norm Cellestine slid into the chair next to him.

"Good, good, drinking your lunch. Glad to see it, Connor." Cellestine smirked. "You got big trouble, I read."

"Fuck you, Norm," Connor slurped through his drink.

"Jerry, two more over here and a menu . . . ," Norm Cellestine ordered to the bartender.

"Norm, I'm not in the mood for your unfortunate style of humor today. Please go away . . . please," Connor pleaded.

"No. No. No. You don't want to get rid of me now, old buddy. I have an answer to your problems. It'll cost you, but you have plenty to offer . . . at least for now you do. Hear me out." Norm Cellestine was unusually spirited today.

"What makes me think I'm about to get further screwed. Every time you come to me with a deal it costs me. Remember, it was you who originally talked me into this deal." Connor took a stiff belt of scotch.

"Ah, but it was your creative genius that took my germ of an idea and made it a reality: 'Pharaoh's Paradise'! Remember, I'm a shareholder. I stand to lose, old buddy," Cellestine said mockingly.

"That's the only bright spot, seeing your sorry ass lose. Okay, what's your deal?"

Five years before, Norm Cellestine had suggested that Connor Grove's Desert Empire Savings and Loan acquire two thousand nine hundred acres of desert land, with water rights, northeast of Scottsdale to develop a "multiple golf course" residential community. Norm said he was not big enough to market the concept, but he figured he could invest and ride the project to success. He said that with Connor Grove's Savings and Loan, plus his architectural and development contacts, he could put together a team that could make this "desert paradise" a reality.

Connor Grove liked the idea, and since Norm Cellestine had optioned the land and completed the surveys, he could take it from there.

He had put together a team of the finest designers and planners in the country, including pro golfer Bud Wendell to design the two courses. Within a year, Connor Grove had begun the largest real estate marketing campaign ever endeavored in the Southwest. Nine hundred residential units – four hundred custom homes and five hundred developer units – a two-hundred-thousand-square-foot office complex, a tennis facility, and two clubhouses were all designed. Four model homes were put in place and decorated to the nines.

Economic fortunes ebb and flow. At the height of the Pharaoh's Paradise marketing campaign, interest rates began to climb. Sales stalled. A large number of loans, mainly those that had made Connor Grove a hero in the early seventies, began to default. Desert Empire Savings and Loan became the subject of an in-depth series in the Arizona Republic questioning its viability. Concerns snowballed, and the company was rumored to be in jeopardy. Despite Connor Groves's efforts to dispel concern, reporters continued to press.

Finally, someone discovered irregularities in the Pharaoh's Paradise marketing campaign. Statements made by Connor Grove about water rights were determined to be questionable. There had been no approval for water usage beyond the first phase of residential development. Indeed, there was no guarantee of any future golf course water. People who had invested in the project, either through the savings and loan or independently, demanded restitution. Those who had purchased homesites demanded their money back. It snowballed into a crisis that threatened the continuation of Desert Empire Savings and Loan. Then, the last shoe dropped: Connor Grove and two of his officers were investigated on federal charges of false representation and the unlawful use of federally insured funds for the promotion of private projects. The other two officers, including a young woman Connor had been sleeping with, agreed to testify against him if no charges were brought against them. Connor was skewered.

Norm Cellestine suggested they eat lunch first, and then take a golf cart ride out on the course, where they could not be overheard. As they finished their drinks and light salads, Norm grabbed two cold beers and an opener from Jerry. "Sign my name, Jer . . . *206* is my number, but you know that."

"Sure thing, Mr. Cellestine."

They drove the cart path passed number 6. Very few golfers were out at midday. Norm stopped under a tree, where they could hear the distant echo of a mower. They sucked on the beers for a minute and then Norm began.

"Okay, pal, you are going to go down on this deal. We all know it, most of all you. If you actually have to do some time, it could be at some convict country club or maybe a 'hard-assed' pen. Anyway, you are finished in business whether or not you're convicted." Cellestine paused to sip some beer.

"You're so fucking blasé about my life," Connor injected.

"Yeah, sorry, but we have to face facts. Let me shed some sunshine on this thing, now. If some 'white knight,' say me, comes forward with a discounted buyout plan that recoups some of the shareholders' money, the courts may take that into consideration when you are sentenced. Assuming you are convicted."

"How much recoupment, two cents on the dollar? They won't go for it."

"No, I'm talking about fifty percent for the whole damn thing!"

"Where in hell would you get that kind of money? Shit, Norm, we're talking eighty million dollars . . . no way."

"I can offer seventy-five million cash. Nobody else will touch it."

"Assuming you can find some idiot to do the deal, in an interest-rate environment of eighteen points, why would they? No way the project can go without water. Even if we get Colorado River water, there is no guarantee we'd be able to draw it. Anyway, it's going to be in the courts for ten years."

"My people are willing to wait. They believe in the future of the desert. Besides, they need a place to park the money."

"Why come to me with this? For god's sake, if I'm indicted you can go direct to the receiver or special master if the court appoints one, which they are certain to do."

"Because, my friend, you are still chief executive officer of Desert Empire Savings and Loan and all of its subsidiaries. You can sell me the real estate companies, the insurance companies, the title companies, and the buildings. You can also strike a deal with me and my friends that is too good to be challenged, even though there would be no bidding." Norm Cellestine had become very serious, looking into Connor Grove's round, brown eyes and spitting beer foam on his chin.

"What do I get, assuming Mort Karp agrees this is a legitimate thing for me to do?" Grove had let his beer, which had gone warm, tip to a point where it dripped from the neck of the bottle onto his brightly shined shoes.

"A guaranteed easy time in a cozy federal lockup, one of these 'country clubs.' And three million in a Swiss account when you get out in a couple of years, maximum." Norm finished his beer and burped. "Karp stays out of this, Con, you gotta make a decision by tomorrow without benefit of that slick fuckin' counsel of yours."

"What if I say no?"

"Your broke ass will rot for ten years over at Terminal Island while another good-looking executive has his way with that cute little MBA girlfriend of yours. Shit, Con, you got no choice." Norm Cellestine stepped on the accelerator of the electric cart and wheeled it back toward the clubhouse.

Connor Grove sat transfixed. His life was ruined. Two years? He could handle that. He had two million put away. After lawyers eat up half, that would leave one. Another three would be very nice. He could take Dixie, once she divorced that slacker husband, and move to Europe, or South America. They could live like royalty on four million! He'd forgiven her for agreeing to testify against him, but he better not tell her about this. She might get scared and run to the feds.

He had a headache. He was hot and tired. He'd take a nap and then call Norm later.

Cellestine wished him a nice afternoon as they arrived at the clubhouse. "Be good, Connor, and don't be calling me or that prissy asshole Karp. Somebody will call you at home tonight."

Dixie didn't wait. She was in bed with a partner at Karp's law firm before Connor was found guilty. His ex-wife and kids were in Salt Lake. He'd already taken care of them. His two million became one in a hurry, and a rash of lawsuits would probably take the rest. Karp had advised him to consider filing for bankruptcy, after paying his legal bills, of course.

He was sentenced to six years in the federal penitentiary and fined nine hundred thousand dollars. That took care of his home, his cars, and most of his cash. He was able to keep only his golf clubs and coin collection. But he wasn't worried. He had confirmation that the three million from Norm and his friends would await him in Switzerland when he was released. After eight months in Lompoc, in south central California, Connor returned to Phoenix for his appeal hearing. Karp's litigator was able to get him free on some trumped-up medical issues, at least until his appeal was heard. He played a little golf and tennis, soaked up the sun, and waited.

Thirty days later, his sentence "adjusted" to three years on appeal, with a promise by Karp of some hope for another medical release, Connor Grove was reassigned to Safford.

CHAPTER 15

KIM ALONE

AT FIRST, KIM was lost without Swifty at home. Their little dog, a mutt named Puffy, kept looking for him everywhere in the apartment. Swifty had usually taken the mutt with him on morning rounds. "Why'd ya call him Puffy, Colin?" Kim's Mother had asked. The dog had short hair, like one of those Jack-somebody Terriers. You'd think Puffy would be a poodle or something.

"Because she has big cheeks," Swifty would answer.

"Huh?"

"Oh, Mama, he's only teasing . . . we just liked the name," Kim would giggle.

So Kim had to decide what she and Puffy would do without Swifty for a few months. It was only two days before some ideas would come her way. Along with confirmation that she had passed the real estate exam, a letter from the biggest broker in Scottsdale arrived in the mailbox. She was being invited to a seminar for new agents to determine who might be selected to join the firm as an associate. Kim was excited, but disappointed she couldn't tell Swifty right away. She called to make an appointment for the seminar and was surprised to learn that her call was expected.

"Please hold on, Mrs. Koenig, Mr. Cellestine has been hoping you would call." Norm Cellestine was a legend in Phoenix and Scottsdale. He had started after WWII in a small one-man office and since had built a massive array of real estate and insurance businesses in the Southwest. He maintained his headquarters in Scottsdale, but had offices in Los Angeles and Dallas. It was rumored that he would be developing golf resort complexes in Phoenix and Tucson, besides office buildings in Texas and Los Angeles. He had purchased the Pharaoh's Paradise project east of town from the failed Desert Empire Savings and Loan. Rumors had it that he had secured additional water rights and would begin selling lots again soon.

"Hello, Mrs. Koenig, glad you got my invite. Any chance we could get together before the seminar to talk about things?"

Norm Cellestine himself! Yes, she would be happy to meet with him. "Monday at ten would be just fine. Thank you, sir."

She had made herself as beautiful as possible before driving out to Safford for the first visit with him. She took off early and had her hair done and her nails. She needed to do it anyway for her meeting with Mr. Cellestine on Monday, but she wouldn't tell Swifty that.

After the visit, she was depressed. "God, he looked so lost, Puffy. Daddy is very, very sad." She tried to keep her mind off the visit so she would be bright for the interview at ten the next morning. She hoped Norm Cellestine would not ask about her husband.

"Mrs. Koenig, I am so happy to meet you. A mutual friend told me about you, how bright you are and such. Certainly you are just as pretty as my own daughters, and that's saying something." Norm Cellestine's two daughters, now married and living out of state, had both been debutantes (at least the equivalent for the Southwest), and the youngest one had been Miss Arizona in the midsixties.

"Oh thank you, sir. I have heard so much, all good, about the great Norman Cellestine. It is an honor to meet you." Kimmie blushed.

"Let me get right to the point, Kim . . . may I call you Kim?" She nodded, embarrassed. "I need some bright young people to help me with my new projects here in Arizona. Later on, I plan to take the cream of the crop with me to LA. But, for now I'm organizing at team of high-powered, highly trained 'go-getters' to sell my Desert Prince project at Sweetwater, then tackle Pharaoh's Paradise! Have I got your interest piqued yet?"

"I just passed my exam . . . I'm a bookkeeper. I could learn, but . . . gee, don't you think it's a big step for me?" Kim was unsure as to whether she should act confident or express her true feelings.

"Honesty. That's what I like, honesty. No, darling, it's not too big a step for you. You're bright, you're eager, you look great, what a combination. Hey, I was your age when I went to war. By gosh, I handled it. Even got wounded. By the time I was twenty-six I had my own business. Sold eighteen houses my first month on the job. Kim, you learn from me and I'll have you makin' more money than you ever dreamed of." Norm smiled, almost leered, at the young woman before him.

While he went on, Kim took the measure of Norman Cellestine: over six feet, about fifty-five, long nose, wart on his right cheek, white hair, broken veins in the bridge of his nose and cheeks, watery brown eyes. Cellestine spit when he talked, and his mouth flapped like he had false teeth. His skin had patches of red and brown and was leathery, like he spent most of the time outside. His shirt was fancy and monogrammed and his tie was hand-painted. She could see his suit coat hanging on a hanger behind his mahogany desk, as they sat in padded chairs at a table next to the desk. It was a very expensive-looking Italian cut.

Swifty would call this guy a BS artist, but he sure was a success. He had to be sincere. She had never heard anything but good things about him. She wondered, she watched, she hoped.

"So, Kim, what do you think? Willing to give it try and change your life? Norm sat back, proud of his work.

"Yes, sir, I am! I'm ready." Kim heard her own words and hardly believed them.

The next Sunday she went to Swifty with a new energy and was met with a surprise. Swifty was upbeat; said he was going to make the most of this bad deal. He was going to finish school while he was in this place. She shared the information about her new opportunity and found him congratulatory, but a little reluctant to cheer. He wanted to know more about Norm Cellestine and his intentions.

When they parted, he wasn't so morose. She hugged him extra long, until the female guard made them break it up. He smiled when she turned to wave. Her drive back was more pleasant than the other time. She wasn't so depressed and there was the new car Norm Cellestine had assigned to her.

She had to figure a way to make classes on Sunday and still go see Swifty. The first time she had begged off at noon and still made it to Safford by two. Next week she would have to stay. She decided to call Safford and see if she could visit one night during the week instead of Sunday.

Class was exciting. There were eight of them and Norm. Buck Janis was the sales manager. He conducted the session, with Norm pontificating at will. Most of it was motivational. They talked about goal setting, positive imaging, even a preferred diet and exercise regimen. Buck said, "Kids, were going to outwork, outthink, outrun, and outsell everybody who ever lived!"

Four of the others were her age, all men. Three were women in their thirties. They were stunning. The guys were really good looking and bright. Most of them had a good deal of experience, except for Kim. But she kept up. Both Buck and Norm were very encouraging. By the time the next week's meeting arrived, she was eager to attend.

She called Safford and was informed visiting hours were on Sunday, except for lawyers, who could come in anytime.

She called Joe Seeley and explained her dilemma. He agreed to drive out there with her on Thursday night. Swifty had been surprised and puzzled, but she explained that Sunday was work for her and she didn't want to miss seeing him. Joe said he would get her on the list as one of his associates. Nobody would check it. She could come out anytime. Swifty sort of agreed it was a good idea.

Her second weekend with the Cellestine Enterprises was even more exciting. Buck took the group to the development sites and explained the strategy for marketing desert land. "Show them the 'sizzle' – our model homes, the renderings of the clubhouses, the tract maps, the interior finish plan. Let them feel the fabric, breathe the fresh air, and drink in the panorama. Then, let the 'sizzle' sell the steak!" This, she decided, was going to be fun.

Monday, she spent her lunch hour with Buck and two of the new associates. Buck said to the three of them, "Kids, why not design me a plan for setting up an office on-site at Pharaoh's Paradise? If it's good, I'll try to sell it to Norm. It looks like I'll be bringing three of the others on right away to help me with the Desert Prince project in Sweetwater. Norm needs Bill and Sandra over in California, so it's just the three of you left."

This change came as a shock to Kim. She had thought they were developing a team for Arizona. Now, two of the others who had been plucked from Norm's California operation were going back, and all but three of those left were breaking off to work on an existing project. She, Pam, and Walt were the only ones left in the seminar. Each of them had other jobs. In fact, they were the only ones who had not been depending on real estate for a living. Kim was disappointed by these unexpected changes.

"Buck," she asked, "what about our weekend seminar? Is it over?"

"Oh no, kitten, the four of us will keep going until we get everything smoothed out. I'll be running a parallel class at night with the kids over at the Prince." Buck had his sincere smile focused directly on her.

Walt asked, "Buck, do you think we should quit our jobs? I mean, are you guys going to start paying us?"

"Not so fast, buddy, hey, we're still in class here. Better hold on to that paycheck till we see how it goes. Okay?"

After a few minutes of small talk, the three had to get back to their jobs. They agreed to meet the following evening to go to work on their plan for Pharaoh's Paradise.

Kim was confused and a little depressed by this new development. She kept busy the rest of the day with filing designs and replacing sourcebooks that had been used during the day. At 5:00 p.m., Kim locked up the office, since the others had left, and slowly walked to the car Norm Cellestine had loaned her.

As she fumbled in her purse for the car keys, she was shocked to see a large man sitting directly in front of her in the passenger seat. She turned to run when she heard a voice. "Mrs. Koenig! Please! Sorry to frighten you. I have a message from Mr. Cellestine."

Kim stopped and turned toward the voice. He was a large man with a fatherly smile. He had both hands raised in the air. "Honestly, miss, I'm but a simple messenger."

She cautiously walked in his direction. "What message?" She asked.

"I left a package on your front seat. His office will call you in the morning. Sorry to scare

you . . . sorry. Have a nice evening." With this, the man backed away, then turned toward the street and disappeared around the corner of the building.

Kim waited a moment, weighing her options. She could run back to the office and call someone or quickly open the car and jump in, lock the doors, and speed away. She chose the latter. The car was open; it started immediately, so she sped out of the drive without locking the doors. As she made the right turn from the drive, she saw no other traffic. The man had disappeared. She started to shake and could barely maneuver the Chevy sedan to her home.

She parked in the drive and carefully opened the car door, wondering if it was safe to go in the bungalow. Looking toward the building, she reached for her purse and instead came up with a carefully wrapped package. It was square and about three inches thick. She looked at it curiously, forgetting any thought of possible danger awaiting here in the house. She tore open a corner, but it was so heavily wrapped she could not tell anything about its contents.

She retrieved her purse from the floorboard of the car and exited the vehicle.

Upon entering the bungalow, she busied herself with Puffy, then let the dog out in the back where a small patch of grass lay stranded in the midst of a rock-and-cactus garden. She found a pair of scissors in a kitchen drawer and began to cut through the thick layers of paper on the package. Money! It was full of money! She pulled the thin stacks of bills from the paper and a typed note fell out on the table.

Kim read it slowly:

> *To friends from friends. Thought you could use some extra help. By the way, we hear desert real estate may be booming soon. Good luck to you both.*

A FEW WEEKS BEFORE NORM AND CONNOR MET ON THE GOLF COURSE

Artie has been planning to make a break for quite a while. Things were getting more risky than he liked. Federal officers had seized control of two Vegas casinos, and there were promises of more to come. He had put away a good deal of money, over six million. He had his thing with Peltz, which held a lot of promise with little downside.

So when the Japanese approached him with an offer, he bit. He didn't know or care where the money came from. A very well-spoken Japanese lawyer from San Francisco called him to discuss a land transaction. At first Artie thought it was about the Carefree house. He agreed to a meet. It was bigger than a house deal.

Yoshi Hankawa was as American as he was: cool manner, hand-tailored suit, street-level vernacular. "Glad to meet you, Mr. Leonardo, okay if I call you Artie?"

"Usually people call me Arthur, what business are we talking about?"

"Okay, Arthur, I'm Yoshi. Look, I have a law office in San Francisco and even though I'm a born-American citizen like you, I have lots of contacts in Japan. My folks came here in the thirties. We had to go through all that relocation crap during the war – moved to a camp in Utah when I was a kid, et cetera, but I got sent to Japan when I was in the army. Spent eighteen months in Tokyo right after the Korean deal. Naturally, it was soft duty in the judge advocate general's office 'cause I'd already passed the bar – "

"Fine, Yoshi, I'm happy to get a rundown on your history. I'm sure you're a flag-waving American like me, but what business are we talking about?" Artie was becoming impatient.

"Yeah, well I just want to give you some background. Anyway, a Japanese American client of mine asked me to travel with him to Japan to talk to some businessmen about an American investment. I did, and basically, these men have a lot of cash, American dollars, they want to put someplace. Your name was mentioned to me by a client in Las Vegas." Yoshi smiled.

"So?"

"So, Arthur, so we would like to use your bank in Grand Cayman as an intermediary. My client has 105 million American dollars . . . I'm talking hundreds, fifties, and twenties . . . it fills fifteen large suitcases . . . that he wants to invest in U.S. real estate. It has to be 'converted' to another form of currency, we presume, as that volume of cash would raise eyebrows . . . certainly be investigated. Are you with me on this?" Yoshi smiled again.

Artie thought, "A good looking little sucker for a Nip . . . smart too."

"Yoshi, I don't know if I'm 'with you,' so to speak. But I do know what you are asking. Naturally, you and your client would have to be checked out.

I don't want to involve myself in anything that could be viewed as illegal." Artie returned the smile.

"Naturally, Arthur. But, hypothetically, is this something that could be accomplished here in the desert?" Yoshi grew serious.

"Yoshi, there are opportunities of all varieties everywhere in this great land of ours. The Valley of the Sun is no exception." Artie stood to signal the initial meeting was over.

"You can reach me at my office in San Francisco, Arthur. My card."

Yoshi extended an embossed card printed in English on one side and Japanese on the other. "I'll be in touch . . . and, Yoshi, do you play golf?" Artie inquired.

"I hack around, Arthur, why?" Yoshi was duly self-deprecating. His handicap was eight.

"Well, if you are back this way, bring your weapons and we'll arrange something." Artie raised his eyebrows and smiled.

"Hey, thanks. Very enlightened out here in the desert. Nonwhites get to play with the big boys?" Yoshi shoved in the needle.

"Anybody with me is welcome at my club, Yoshi. Some of the members probably even have prison records and beat their wives." He didn't smile.

Norm Cellestine was struggling with his eight iron on the practice range when Artie Leonardo ambled up in a white polo shirt and beige slacks, set off by a white belt and matching golf shoes.

"Hey, Grandpa, you swing that like a cane. Don't you ever loosen up first?" Artie laughed.

"Oh, it's the Don Corleone of the desert . . . what are you doing now, muscling in on the golf instructors?"

"Just trying to help a fellow crook. How's the real estate business?" Artie questioned absently.

"We're makin' a living . . . serving the public . . . at least the honest citizens. Of course you don't associate with many of them."

"No, I don't. That's why I'm inviting you to join me for nine holes, followed by lunch, which I am willing to buy." Artie stood flat-footed, watching Norm struggle with his swing.

"Rob a store or somethin', mafiosi?" Norm teed up a practice ball and smiled with satisfaction as his swing finally worked.

"Knocked over an insurance office this morning . . . could have been one of yours." Artie picked up two wedges and began swinging them to warm up.

The two traded barbs for a few minutes while a range assistant loaded Artie's clubs on Norm Cellestine's golf cart.

They took mulligans on the first tee after slicing their shots onto the parallel fairway. The second shots were relatively straight and about two hundred twenty yards out.

"Tell me what I did to deserve this courtesy, Your Eminence," Norm barked as they sped down the cart path toward their balls.

"I have a very favorable business proposition for you . . . one, as we say in your favorite paperback, that 'you can't refuse.'" Artie looked forward as he drove, but smiled.

As they finished their second shots, which were short and to the right of the green, Norm said, "What's the deal? We gonna rob a bank?"

"Exactly, my friend, exactly," Artie said with grim finality.

They played two bogey holes each before he reraised the issue. Finally, Norm couldn't wait any longer.

"Shit, Artie . . . sorry, Arthur, will you get to the damn point! What is the deal?" Norm stood in his yellow plaid golf pants and multicolored pullover, looking like a circus clown.

"Norm," Artie paused for affect, "we're going to get that crazy Ivy League buddy of yours to sell us Pharaoh's Paradise and anything else you think he has of value before his ass goes to the slammer."

"Deal . . . why hell, I thought you were smart, Arthur, that would be a fucking disaster. Desert Empire Savings and Loan is going down and Connor Grove is going with it. My dream of Pharaoh's Paradise is not viable in this interest rate climate. We can't even get the water. 'Sides, the project's a hundred sixty million in hock. You crazy? Anyhow, where would we get the idiots with that kind of money to invest?" Norm was enumerating and dismissing any thought of Artie's idea.

"Listen a minute, big mouth. I already thought of all that. Here's what we do."

Artie Leonardo described his plan to Norm Cellestine. It was very straightforward. Artie would bring in the money. No one had to know where it came from. In fact, he would arrange for a dummy offshore company to be formed that would be the acquirer. That company would be in his brother Simon's name, as were his banks, since Artie was precluded from such transactions as a convicted felon. He would take in the Japanese money, purchase low-risk instruments from various European countries, hold them for ninety days, sell them, and buy U.S. Treasury bills. Norm would pressure Grove into selling Pharaoh's Paradise and whatever miscellaneous assets they may find of value, at a huge discount, before he was indicted by the feds. Norm could have a point on the Pharaoh's property as it went forward. Norm only needed to know his own assignment and remuneration, not the details.

Artie planned to take the interest on the seventy-five million plus four percent on the project as his end.

"Well, tell ya what," said Norm. "I need something in this for Connor, 'else he'll be up on his 'high horse.' Also, my conniving friend, I want all the

Desert Empire side assets for myself. I'm talking insurance, Title Company, real estate division. How's that ?"

"Grove's getting three million in a Swiss account. You and I will split the ancillary companies. I will be your silent partner in the real estate business. Fact is, I'm going to provide you with a substantial infusion of cash to revitalize your organization." Artie beamed.

"I don't need a partner. Just give me the three million. I'll take care of Connor." Norm tried.

"No, Norman. I like the real estate business. You're such a skillful old dog, I'm going to trust you with my future. As far as Mr. Grove is concerned, I want to be certain he doesn't redevelop his memory while he is away. Once he touches the account we're setting up for him, his complicity will be so documented he won't dare sing." Artie waited for a further response.

"Shit. You got me in a stranglehold, you greasy bandit!" Norm was speaking slowly and quietly, almost mumbling.

"Yes, yes I do. Neither of us will ever forget how difficult it was for me to get you out of your trouble a few years back. But we should never mention it, should we?"

"No . . . no, you bastard."

Artie had helped Norm out of a very sticky situation before his wife's death. Norm had involved himself with a classmate of his youngest daughter who had become pregnant. Norm's wife was terminally ill, and he was at wit's end worrying that the poor woman's last memory of her loving husband would be his tryst with a coed – not to mention having to face his daughters. He appealed to Artie, whom he knew by reputation only. In exchange for a sponsorship in the country club, despite his dubious background, Artie would "fix the problem."

A professional aborted the young woman's pregnancy, and she was mysteriously awarded a scholarship to an out-of-state college. Norm was grateful and, along with Connor Grove, sponsored Arthur Leonardo into Ocotillo Country Club – and later, into Phoenix Country Club.

"So, what about the water rights? That you can't fix," Norm said meekly.

"Yeah, I can. The courts will decide in Arizona's favor on the Colorado River thing, but that's years away. For now, we will have well water for the first three residential phases and the clubhouses. The nonpotable stuff for the courses will be recycled. My operatives in state government tell me it is for sure we will be included in the awards for participation in the new recycling plant's distribution next year," Artie explained.

"How'd you do that?"

"Friends in Las Vegas agreed to delay annoying a couple commissioners about their overdue gambling debts." Artie shrugged.

"That's the first time you have ever confided to me anything about your business. You ain't going soft?" Norm was trying to pep himself up with a little humor.

Artie looked at him icily and replied, "We're going to be partners, Norm. I have to feel I can trust you."

Most of what I knew about Norm Cellestine and Connor Grove I had read in the papers. They were celebrities to a guy from my neighborhood. Later, I got to know them both pretty well. Neither was a bad man. Norm was a smart, hardworking, grassroots kind of a guy, while Connor, also smart, was full of himself most of the time.

Connor had his good points though. He was charming, softhearted, and he had a hell of a sense of humor. Both had worked their way up from the bottom and, in their own way, appreciated what they had achieved.

Norm Cellestine was born in a dirt-floor shack in southern Oklahoma. His parents brought him to Arizona during Depression, hoping to find work. His mother found early death through childbearing, and his father found love for a bottle. Norm had no way to go but up. He worked as a messenger for a land company, and when WWII broke out, he joined. Five years later, with a load of shrapnel in his hip and shoulder, he emerged a man ready for success. He married a local girl that he had charmed with his natural gift of gab and had two daughters. His wife's father was a land developer who took Norm in. He was so successful his first year he quit and opened his own office in Scottsdale. Hard work and shrewdness made him one of the largest real estate brokers in the Southwest.

Connor Grove – or, more correctly, Grover Alan Condit – worked his way through two years of community college in Wyoming before being awarded a baseball scholarship to Colgate. He graduated with honors and was accepted to the University of Pennsylvania's Wharton School of Business. The wife of a Colgate alumnus who found him irresistible aided his unlikely rise. In order to control the wife and to suppress young Grover, the man arranged for the unusual Jaycee transfer. Neither he nor his wife was disappointed.

The affair continued apace for two years. Connor, or Grover, earned his way, athletically (both ways) and scholarly! Within a year after graduation, and having legally changed his name, a Midwest bank hired Connor Grove. He excelled. Two years later, a recruiter introduced him to the chairman of Desert Empire Savings and Loan. The man was taken with the young Turk from Colgate and gave him a free reign. Connor succeeded him upon his death.

So both of these guys were self made and decent in their own ways. They just had appetites for greater things and were willing to work hard to satisfy them. Neither was a habitual lawbreaker, but both sometimes saw the law as an antiquated impediment to their goals. In short, they were both "players." That was their nexus . . . nexus. KKF

CHAPTER 16

THE GENIUS

PELTZ WAS HAPPY to be going back to Palm Springs, especially since he didn't have to continue "babysitting" Jake. Palm Springs, we all call it that, even though it's several communities. Actually, Louis Peltz had his little place in Rancho Mirage. He wasn't a golfer or a tennis player, though he planned to learn when he had time. It was the warm desert air and the absence of snow that attracted him most.

Ute kind of missed the snow, but it was nothing money wouldn't cure. This girl found El Paseo and its expensive shops irresistible; and as long as she had cash, she was happy.

A few years earlier Louis had begun to experience problems with his operation in Santiago. Inflation had ballooned to 300 percent. Salvadore Allendé and his Marxist government had run roughshod on private – especially foreign-owned – business, and taxes were virtually doubling. Even though the embargo by the United States and its European allies had little effect on his products, as they were classified as medical, Louis needed to find another base of operation for K148, and the newly developed drugs he was contracting for on the international medical black market. He approached his banker, who also had arranged transportation to Chile for his products, Artie Leonardo.

"Sure, Louis, I can make that happen – probably in northern Mexico. But we are talking partnership here. The level of risk I must take warrants 30 percent of your operation." Louis had begun to protest when Artie added,

"But the good news is I'm going to double your revenues by expanding your customer base into other markets."

Louis protested further until Artie reminded him that he could be out of business immediately if certain authorities learned of his activities.

Within two years, revenues had tripled; the product array had increased; happily, medical results were even better; and Artie had taken 52 percent of the operation. Peltz fretted, but his risk had lessened and he was making one hell of a lot of money. Of course, he sheltered his assets in a Cayman bank controlled by Artie Leonardo, through Artie's brother Simon.

Cliniquè de Obregón was located in the beautiful Umbria valley eighteen miles south of Nogales. It had all the appearances of a top-drawer health spa, and it employed an international staff of medical experts and technicians.

A slight man, about five-eight with short gray hair, Louis Peltz did not stand out in a crowd. There was something so plain about him and about the way he saw himself that becoming someone else would almost be preferable to Louis.

When he put on the white coat and hung the stethoscope around his neck, he looked like one of the doctors, which was his intent. Louis loved walking the wards, nutrition centers, and lecture halls, spewing technical data that made him sound like the boss, which he was.

The physicians, mostly from Mexico – but several from Canada, western Europe, and the United States – tolerated Louis' proclivity for pedanticism because he paid well.

Artie had arranged with local authorities to enable the smooth transfer of products in and hazardous medical refuse out of the clinic. Artie really didn't want the discarded needles, bodily fluids, and such dumped in a local river, so he had it burned in a local high-pressure oven normally used for extruding aluminum. Mobile-home window frames all over the Southwest contain some interesting particles.

Expenses were much less than in Chile and the outlay for bribing local officials, in comparison, was negligible. Artie had talked about the clinic with Norm Cellestine. Norm's wife's disease was too far along by the time he had become closely associated with Artie Leonardo for the clinic's services to be of help. Norm often lamented this, and when he and Artie's became partners, he suggested a marketing plan that might help expand the clinic's clientele.

Artie Leonardo and Norm Cellestine sat on the verandah of a rented villa near the clinic, drinking Jack Daniels straight with a cold beer back.

"This guy Peltz says there's doctors all over the goddamn world who might have better techniques for curing disease than those commonly accepted. He also says there's lots of drugs that are effective against life-threatening diseases that aren't ever gonna get approved by the FDA 'cause they have bad side effects. Well shit, who cares about bad side effects if it saves your life!"

Artie shrugged. "Nothing much we can do about that."

Norm shook his head in disagreement. "Arthur, I figure we can contact all these docs and let them know we got a clinic in Mexico where they can send their worst patients and where they can come and share info about their techniques."

"We do that and the Mexican government will come down on us like a hammer, Norm. Our feds would threaten to cut off their financial support if they didn't," Artie said.

Norm shook his head again. "Sometimes I wonder how mankind ever survived itself! Okay then, we go to the Mexican government up front. We make 'em believe this will make 'em look good in the eyes of the world, then we buy their asses off!"

"That might not be too easy . . . maybe you better stick to real estate and insurance," Artie chuckled.

"No, damn it! This here is going to be a crusade for me. Artie, listen, my wife mighta been saved by that stuff Peltz invented. Maybe someday it could be Teresa or one of us. We should do whatever we got to do!" Norm was standing, flapping his gums so that his teeth seemed to clatter.

"You passionate son of a bitch, Norm. I'm impressed. But Peltz and I are in business. I'm not screwing that up. Tell you what. Tomorrow, we'll talk it over with Louis and see what he thinks." Artie took another shot and chased it with a gulp of beer.

Eighteen hours later Norm pitched Louis Peltz with his basic idea. Peltz responded unpredictably. Artie had expected he'd say it was too risky. Louis surprisingly liked the idea. He said that he had enough pull with the Mexican medical hierarchy to pull it off. He would appoint a couple of key Mexican docs to the clinic board, pay them some exorbitant consulting fee, and gain agreement to do whatever they wanted. It was that simple.

Within a year, oncological physicians (cancer doctors) from all over the world converged on Cliniquè Obregón for consultation. Artie made arrangements for a hotel to be expanded to accommodate visitors. The local authorities were delighted as revenues both above and below the table more than doubled.

Louis was in clover. He started his golf lessons and applied for membership at the prestigious Morningside Country Club, where he and Ute had moved. Even though he had to travel frequently to Switzerland, it wasn't as though he had to spend months there. He had even convinced Ute to accept his kids when they visited. Life was good. Then Malcolm Ussery arrived at his front door.

CHAPTER 17

SAFFORD U

SWIFTY WAS IN the swing. He would study his college correspondence topics most of the day in the library. Old Angus would help by setting up quizzes on the various subjects and then coaching him on the answers until he had it. At night, Connor would lead him through the complex world of finance.

By day it was political theory and logic; by night it was balance sheets, income statements, and cash flows. Once he got going, Connor would wax eloquent about Wall Street, IPOs, investor conferences, road shows, and quarterly earnings. He would set up business models for Swifty to shoot holes in and build scenarios about current companies and have Swifty guess what kinds of business strategies they should be using. To hear Connor talk, he should be in great demand as a consultant to the Fortune 500.

Nelson Leigh saved his coaching to the weekends. Since Kim visited Tuesday and or Thursday nights and Nelson seldom had a visitor, Nelson and Swifty spent most Saturdays and Sundays together. Nelson wanted Swifty to catalogue his strong and weak points. At first Swifty was reluctant to open up, but after a couple of sessions of "kick-ass," he let it out.

Swifty was short on focus and motivation, but strong on hard work. He was great at memorization, but didn't have a clue what any of it meant. Nelson explained over and over what it meant to stay on topic and reason out answers to knotty problems. He took Swifty from Socrates, through the greatest of them all – Aristotle. The Age of Belief, St. Augustine, Aquinas,

Abelard, all the way through to Machiavelli. Then he moved to the more current ideas of Friedrich Nietzsche, Immanuel Kant, William James, George Santana, and Baruch Spinoza. Swifty could spout quotes from *The Prince*, *The Mystic's Way* and *The Idea of Divine Purpose*, but he had no idea how one idea interacted with another. He just couldn't focus. Nelson reasoned that he "didn't want it bad enough."

Swifty said, "Bullshit, I want to learn . . . I do."

They were in the prison kitchen picking out some fruit when Nelson said, "Swifty, you have to want this. Remember the lesson Socrates taught one of his students about knowledge?"

"No, what was it?"

"Come over here."

As Swifty approached the sink where one of the cooks was soaking soiled pots, Nelson sprang at him, folded his arm in a hammerlock, and thrust his head into the greasy lukewarm water. He held him there as Swifty attempted to kick free. Seconds passed, then minutes. Swifty's struggling became so intense, Connor thought he might allow his arm to be broken in order to get loose. Finally, Nelson pulled him out of the water by his shirt collar, then pinned him to the floor with his diminutive body.

As Swifty gasped for breath, Nelson asked in a thick, raspy voice, "What was it you wanted most when your sorry head was under that water?"

"Air, you fucking bastard! Let me up! I'm going to kick your ass!"

"Precisely, air." Nelson released his grip on Swifty as Connor sat on a fruit box, astonished.

"And Socrates went on . . . Now listen, Swifty, calm down. This is a lesson. Sit there." Swifty was flabbergasted. He rubbed his arm and neck, kept breathing deeply, and let the color return to his face. Connor threw him a soiled towel.

"Okay," Nelson went on, "Air . . . you wanted air, just as Socrates' student wanted air. And Socrates went on, 'When you want knowledge as much as you wanted air when your head was under the water, it will come to you!'"

Nelson smiled broadly. "Now let's have lunch."

Swifty slowly struggled to his feet, confused but with his lesson learned. After washing his face and drying off, he joined Nelson and Connor in the dining room.

Swifty had to marvel at Nelson's knowledge. He could compete with Connor on almost every topic, even though he admittedly had not completed junior college.

"A great deal of time spent in institutions similar to Safford allowed me to enhance my knowledge base. Of course, it was in the field that I was able to test my newfound learning. Usually, it stood me in good stead," Nelson would muse.

"Swifty, you need to stretch when you get out of here. Don't just learn and hold it in, but test what you think you know. Fall on your face a few times, get back up, and win!" Nelson could not emphasize enough the need for confidence – the sense of being in control.

Nelson gave Swifty a broad array of "pop" books to read, learn, and memorize. The variety included Wayne Dyer's *The Sky's the Limit*, Michael Korda's *Power*, Og Mandino's *The Greatest Salesman in the World*, Frank Bettger's two books on's salesmanship, Joe Karbo's *The Lazy Man's Way to Riches* and he also gave him the tapes of business school guru Warren Bennis on management. As mentioned, the classics weren't ignored in this eclectic prison education. Swifty received as much philosophy from Nelson as he had picked up in college courses, but Nelson's were steeped in practical application.

Connor introduced Swifty to various management methods, including the art of brainstorming: writing down whatever comes into one's mind on a subject until a long list is compiled, then sorting it, refining it, and coming to a conclusion.

Nelson played the game like a business-school star.

Connor chided Nelson, "You're good, Nelson. You could have done extremely well in legitimate business. Why did you choose the dark side?"

"Same reason as you, you arrogant asshole, greater profits!" Was Nelson's enthusiastic response.

Swifty thought it odd that these two very bright men had found their way into prison; Nelson several times. He never wanted to return and would do whatever was possible to avoid such a fate in his future.

It was two days before Swifty got over the Socrates incident. He chose not to speak to Nelson during that time, and when Kim came to visit, he mentioned that he and Nelson had had an altercation.

"Well, you're bigger than he is. How can he push you around?" Kim brought things home.

"I guess he's just smarter than I am and got the best of me," Swifty sniffed.

"Well, dummy, don't let it happen again. That would really be stupid." Kim was smiling.

Swifty didn't like his wife treating him this way. He wanted sympathy and support. After all, he was in prison, through no fault of his own. Why was Kimmie turning on him? He noticed her new clothes, that her hair looked even better than normal . . . he wanted her to be happy, but not too happy. God! Why was this happening!

Then it dawned on him: If he didn't take complete charge of his own life from here on out, he would be no good to Kim, himself, or anyone else.

"Yeah, you're right. I won't let it happen again. He was just trying to teach me a lesson and I think I just got it," Swift said, pulling himself together and smiling too.

"What lesson?" Kim asked curiously.

"To go after what I want with everything I've got," Swifty said firmly.

"Well, silly, what do you want?" she said coyly.

Swifty didn't bite. He squeezed her hands in his and looked whimsically out the mesh-covered window. "So how's your plan coming?"

"Slow . . . I can't seem to get the others started."

"Have you tried 'brainstorming.'?"

"What's that?"

Swifty explained.

"Okay, Nelson, you got me. I'm going to focus till my ass can read in the dark. Nothing is going to stop me from getting these goddamn lessons, from getting the hell out of this place, and from becoming a success when I'm out!" Swifty stormed in on Nelson as he carefully shaved around his mustache in the tiny bath area of the secure room they shared.

"Well, congratulations, Swifty. But now that you have it, can you maintain it? That is the question. That is always the question." Nelson continued to carefully groom his mustache without looking at Swifty.

"Huh?"

"It isn't difficult to become enthused about something new and then lose interest after a while. Like AA. A drunk goes there for a while, confesses to his fellows, and is a born-again sobering drunk. But, after a few days or weeks, the lure of silky smooth drink, cigarette smoke, and cheap perfume beckons. Alas, he falls on his ass and is drunk again. I speak from experience." Nelson winked.

"I don't hardly drink, Nelson. I'm talking about being focused on what I said. What does that have to do with drinking?" Swifty queried.

"You dumb shit. I am the drunk and I would kill for a fifth of Jack Daniels right now. It was only a metaphor, an example of what can happen. One must stick to his guns through thick and thin. Let's see how you feel about things in a week." Nelson looked at him carefully, as if to assess.

CHAPTER 18

THE ESCAPE

IT WAS THE next morning, after Kim's Thursday night visit. The prison supervisors were taking some of the inmates on a field trip to the nearby Indian Trading Post. Nelson and Connor were considered trustee counselors and valuable as liaison outside the fences. Swifty had no business going as a library assistant, but he was called out anyway. All the others held various trustee administrative assignments at Safford. The plan was to see if a joint project between the Indian community and the prison was feasible, with the objective of improving the images of both with the town.

Sergeant Ackerman and two other guards, Lewis and young Slattery, rode along on the bus, with weapons held to their sides. That testy counselor Swifty had bumped heads with his first week, Gil Stoops, was in charge. He'd told Ackerman that no shackles or cuffs would be needed.

The ride was less than ten miles, around curves and up and down a few narrow hills. Six miles out of the fences, the bus encountered a road crew apparently repairing potholes. A flagman waved them slowly to a stop. Both guards and Ackerman leaned forward from their positions – two in front and one in back of the bus.

It happened quickly and without warning. Swifty heard a loud *crack!* The bus filled with smoke, and he felt something sharp splatter on his face. He became weak and his eyes began to burn.

"Don't rub 'em. It'll make 'em worse. Get on the floor." It was Nelson from behind him, in the next aisle, pulling on his shirt collar and whispering hoarsely. "Get the fuck down!"

Swifty slid to the floor. It was better down low. He heard several more cracks, and he sensed feet shuffling next to him. Connor, who had been his seatmate, seemed to be dragged from his position.

Gradually the haze cleared, and Swifty could see other men on the floor of the bus around him. He waited. It must have been ten minutes of complete silence. Finally, he heard Nelson say, "Swifty, your panel seems to be open. See if you can find some keys and get the rest of us out of our cages." The rustling of men trying to get to their feet followed this quiet comment.

He stood up, wishing desperately to rub his eyes, but mindful of what Nelson had said. Years before, when he was in basic training, he remembered gas drills. Using his thumbs and forefingers, he opened his eyes wide and allowed the breeze to clear away the gas.

Walking to the front of the bus, he could see Ackerman, Stoops, and the other two guards, plus the driver, lying lifeless in the road. He froze. He had never seen dead bodies this close. He walked cautiously toward them. Ackerman was nearest and his keys were hanging on his belt. When Swifty snatched them loose, he heard the steady breathing of at least two of the prone men. He hurried back to the bus.

"Hey, it must have been a break. Some of the 'screws' are still alive out there! Connor's gone!" His hands were shaking, and so was his voice.

Nelson reached through the bars and pulled the keys from his hand.

In a matter of seconds, all eight of the remaining men were out of their cages. Swifty was sitting in the driver's seat, shaking badly.

Nelson said, "The radio isn't likely to be effective in these hills, so lets load the 'screws' on board and head back to the farm."

The men slowly filed from the bus, checked each of the sprawled bodies for wounds, and carefully loaded them onto the floor of the bus. Swifty continued to sit, shaking badly.

"Move your ass, kid." It was the bald man with the handlebar mustache, Curt Rhymes.

Swifty moved to his cage, climbing over Ackerman and one of the guards. Rhymes started the bus, turned it around with some difficulty, and slowly started back toward the prison.

One of the other men called out, "Hey, why the fuck can't we go to the Indian store? We could buy some shit and call the 'screws' from there."

"Shut up. This is the best move," Nelson said firmly, and everyone else remained silent. Later, Swifty marveled that no one thought to try an escape.

Three miles out, Rhymes tried the radio. No response. Two miles out, no response. One mile, "This is Rhymes on the bus. Somebody ambushed us down the road. Your officers is hurt, but nobody is dead. They took an inmate by force." Static. "We're about a mile out. The radio wouldn't work any closer." Static. "Okay, we're stoppin' on the road."

Rhymes said, "All you guys get out and place your hands on the side of the bus. Eyes front, spread 'em out. The 'screws' want to play cop."

Swifty started to get off, but Nelson pulled him back. "Son, you didn't see shit. You hear me? You were overcome with some kind of gas and you may have lost consciousness for a few minutes. Got that?" He shook his head and allowed Nelson to guide him, by the shoulder, off the bus.

Sirens shrieked, red lights flashed, four cars skidded to a stop at odd angles. Eight or nine uniformed officers, guns drawn, leaped from the vehicles and rushed toward them, shouting. No one moved.

Two or more cautiously climbed on the bus. "Jesus, they're shot or something."

Guards began to poke at each of the men and demanded they "assume the position." In reflection, it was quite comical, since they had already assumed the position voluntarily. Soon, the correction supervisor, Darryl Cobb, arrived and took charge.

They were settled into the cars and driven back to the prison and placed in isolation. There they remained, each man alone, until interrogators could get to them. When it was his turn, several hours later, Swifty did as Nelson had instructed. "I was overcome by the gas. I didn't see anything or hear anything but a few loud bangs."

In a day he was back with Nelson, in their secure room.

"What the hell do you think happened, Nelson? Were those guys 'hit men' or something? Why would they want Connor?"

"Don't know. Maybe someone felt Connor needed some fresh scenery. I doubt that he's been hurt."

Nothing more was said until Swifty was called into another interrogation a week later. This time it was an assistant U.S. Attorney named Breck.

"Mr. Koenig, we have been pretty easy on you, you know. Your offenses could have netted you over ten years in prison. Instead of that, it's only three. Frankly, it could be much less if you help us with the identities of the men who worked with you on the money laundering caper. Also, we want to know the truth about the escape of Connor Grove from Safford."

Adam Breck, was a tall, powerful-looking man of forty with thick black hair, an athlete's build, a finely tailored suit, and an aggressive bearing.

He braced his large hands on the table where Swifty was sitting and thrust his face toward him. "It's your decision. You can help us or you can spend the next two years, ten months, and three days right here at Safford. In fact, Mr. Koenig, we can arrange to have you transferred to Terminal Island, where it is a little less pleasant."

Swifty repeated what he had been saying to the other authorities; he had seen nothing and may have been overcome by gas. He had no idea who the people were who had handed him the packages last year and had him running between Phoenix and Tucson. He was an innocent victim, just doing a job. The questions came from every direction, over and over again, and his answers were always the same. He was innocent.

Breck repeated his questions and threw in a reference to Swifty's close "friendship" with Connor Grove. Swifty didn't confirm or deny his relationship with Connor. He just stuck to his story.

Eventually Adam Breck eased up, smiled, and said, "Well, Swifty, that's it. You've sealed your fate. Don't blame us for your problems in the future. Just hang here twisting slowly in the wind . . . expecting the worst, which will happen, I guarantee it!"

Swifty was worried sick. For three nights he was confined to a small room, with only a toilet, in the solitary dormitory. A guard who did not speak brought his meals to him. On the Thursday after Connor's strange disappearance, he was released back to Nelson's secure room in the main dormitory.

"Well, did you 'squeal?'" Nelson joked.

"Shit, I didn't know what to say to them, so I just kept repeating the same thing: 'I didn't see anything, I was overcome by gas.'

"I got to tell you, Nelson, that Adam Breck is one scary bastard. He threatened me with a move to TI and said I'd serve every day of my time. I was planning on getting out of here in a few months."

"Well, let's not get too excited about this boy Breck. He's a bright star in the Democratic Party. With all this Watergate shit going on, I'm betting he'll get pulled in to help screw Nixon," Nelson shared.

"How do you know all that?" Swifty asked.

"Swifty, my boy, presidents get elected and hung with money and contacts. Kennedy and Johnson had money and the right contacts and were 'helped,' you might say. They were not grateful, so they were afforded no further aid. Nixon did it on his own, but he faced no specific opposition from the 'powerful factions' who helped JFK and LBJ. Remember, the Teamsters, certainly the most corrupt union since John L. Lewis died, endorsed his tight ass. So it is clear, that while he had no friends on the dark side, he was preferred to the backstabbing Democrats."

"You think these 'powerful people' will let him get hung on this Watergate Hotel deal?"

"No, those dumb shits have screwed that up on their own. Now the Demos, with a strong, larcenous network in place, plan to crucify Mr. Nixon for beating them. They'll get him . . . but it will take every ambitious, ruthless, partisan prosecutor in the land. Mr. Breck is one such fellow."

"Nelson, how do you know this?" Swifty wasn't convinced.

"Because he is the young man, he and his boss, the late Mr. Kennedy, the younger, who nailed my ass. He also directed the prosecution of Connor Grove. It is his considered belief that anyone who has made money, legally or otherwise, should be persecuted. That is the way of the Democrats." Nelson said the last part with finality.

"Gee, we're Democrats," Swifty said naively.

"See, Swifty, you don't even try to learn. You're not anything anymore but a felon. You sure as hell can't vote, but you can be a well-informed observer. Why not find out why you support or don't support a party by understanding its position? Do you even fucking know what they stand for, any of them? Or is it, as I suspect, an emotional response to bullshit? Don't answer." Nelson shook his head in disgust and strode out to get a Coke from the officer's private refrigerator.

Swifty did not tell Kim of his ordeal with Adam Breck. He called from Angus's private line in the library and told her he was isolated a few days because of Connor Grove's escape.

"Oh my god! You were on that bus?"

"Yeah, but I can't talk about it now. There was a bunch of us. We put the officers on the

bus . . . they were sort of unconscious . . . then we drove back to the ranch . . . to Safford."

"Oh my god! Did you see them? Did they have guns?"

"I couldn't see anything at all and, honey, I can't talk about it now. Okay?"

"Yes, okay, I understand."

She told him that it had been all over TV, but his name was not mentioned. "They called it a 'daring daylight jail break planned and executed from the outside.'"

"Did they mention anybody else was on the bus?"

"Yeah, they said four prison officers were overcome by several armed and masked men who disabled them with tear gas. They said one trustee prisoner, whom they declined to mention for his own safety, helped them get back to the prison. I'm reading here in the paper. Was that you, honey?"

"No . . . no more talk about that. Coming to see me Thursday?"

Twelve months earlier, Dominic Luisi, Artie's best friend aside from Teresa, died on the operating table. Naomi Faust was hospitalized and treated for shock.

Afterward, Artie and Teresa got drunk in Naomi's little house in South Phoenix and had to ask her son, Kyle, to drive them back to Carefree.

"Thanks, young man. You take my car back home and we'll pick it up tomorrow."

"That's okay, sir, you might need it in the morning. I'll catch a ride home."

"Bullshit! There's no traffic this time of night. Take the car."

"Well, okay, but I'll pick you back up tomorrow, how's that?"

"That's good. Call me at the number on this card . . . say after ten." Artie was a little rocky, but fished out a card and passed it to Kyle.

Thus began the relationship between Kyle Faust and Artie Leonardo.

In the following days, Artie began to enjoy Kyle. He was a bright kid, full of energy and quite resourceful. In a way, he reminded Artie of Swifty. Kyle was a little older, not as smooth, and maybe a little heavier, but the similarities were there. The kid picked him up in the morning and continued to drive him for the next eighteen months. Much to Jake's consternation, Artie eventually treated Kyle like a son. Though he treated Jake no less favorably, it just seemed odd to Jake that his dad would pick up a stray like Kyle and treat him so well. KKF

EARLIER, ON THE BUS RIDE

Connor heard a loud bang and snapped out of his shallow sleep. His head came up into some kind of haze within the bus. It hurt his eyes. He began to rub them. He saw shuffling figures around him through the mesh. There were more bangs, and his cage opened. Two men who said nothing pulled him from the bus. Someone wrapped tape around his eyes, and he felt himself being hoisted into the air. Then, some kind of cloth was placed on his nose and mouth. It choked off his breathing. He felt himself falling, falling, and then landing on a soft surface. Dreams flashed before him, nonsensical dreams.

"You're going to feel uncomfortable for a little while. As soon as the plane lifts off, we'll get you out of here. Don't say anything." It was a strange-sounding voice; deep and resolute. He felt the cloth again, then nothing.

"Okay, sir, wake up . . . you can get up now." This time it was a young voice; his face came slowly into view. A smiling young man with a round face, crooked teeth, and curly dark brown hair was dabbing something on his face. He was wearing one of those WWII leather flying jackets. "This is alcohol . . . for the tape residue. You feel okay?"

"Huh? What the hell happened? Have I been kidnapped?" Connor gasped.

"Well, technically, sir, you been temporarily rescued. Let me get the boss man." Suddenly Connor was aware of a loud swooshing sound. He seemed to be lying on a mat on the floorboard of a flying airplane.

Suddenly a small man was bent over him. "You are now awake, Mr. Grove?" It was the deep voice. "You have been out for almost six hours. Perhaps you should slowly stand. You'll need to urinate, then we'll get you something to eat." The two men helped Connor to his feet. The younger one led him into a small toilet and held him while he fumbled with his pants. He felt nauseated and began to black out. The man pushed his head toward the small metal sink and began to wipe his face with a wet towel. He regained himself and urinated for several minutes. He felt better.

"Where are we going?" Connor rasped as he sat down hard in a comfortable airline seat.

"You will see when we get there. No more questions, Mr. Grove. No harm will come to you. Your food and coffee will be here soon." The small man with the deep voice slid across the aisle to another seat.

"Here it is, sir, bacon and eggs, toast, and coffee." The smiling young fellow with the crooked teeth stood over him with a tray.

"Thanks, say . . . can't I ask anything?"

"Sure . . . what do you want to know?"

"That man said I couldn't ask?"

"Oh, Mr. Peltz? He gets bossy, but he isn't the boss, he is." The boy pointed to the front seat near the cockpit.

A large man – Connor's age, with a deep tan and graying hair, wearing a ski sweater – sat sideways, reading a newspaper.

"Who is that?" Connor asked, stuffing eggs and toast hungrily into his mouth.

"Mr. Arthur Leonardo, sir. He's the boss. Finish your meal and I'll tell him you're ready to talk. I mean you can communicate okay."

"What's your name, young man?"

"Kyle, sir, Kyle Faust."

"Well, Kyle Faust, you tell Mr. Leonardo that I am looking forward to finally making his acquaintance."

CHAPTER 19

THE QUICK TURNAROUND

ARTIE LEONARDO SAT surrounded by a huge leather chair, in a room with a vaulted ceiling before a glowing fireplace somewhere in the Swiss Alps. He drank from a large cup. A scotch bottle rested on a side table. Connor Grove sat across from him in a straight chair, sipping from a smaller cup.

"Wow, this stuff gives a new meaning to the term *hot coffee*! Scotch and coffee . . . I never would have thought of it back at Safford." Connor was transfixed by the idea, perhaps heightened by his jet lag.

"Glad you like it, Mr. Grove. My son tells me you will enjoy the skiing as well. Make the most of it, you only have three days," Artie suggested.

"I will, I will. But, I'm still not clear on why you took the risk to pull me out of Safford and bring me all the way over here." Connor looked expectantly at Artie.

"Simple, Mr. Grove. We wanted to check on our investment and we wanted you to have an opportunity to verify that the money was in your numbered account, as agreed," Artie explained, leaning slightly forward in the overstuffed chair.

"Well, I am more than satisfied. It's there, all of it, and as you can see, I'm here . . . your investment, so to speak," Connor said cheerily.

"Yes, but in three days you will be on your way back to Safford." Artie let the words drift slowly out as he sipped his laced coffee.

"What? Oh, you're making a joke. Ha! Ha! Wouldn't that be something . . . to have to go back with the memory of this!" Connor rubbed his eyes and took a long pull from the cup.

"But, it's not a joke. You are going back and I expect the memory of this . . . what awaits you in two years . . . will keep our investment soundly intact." Artie lit a cigarette and fixed Connor Grove in the sight of his steel gray vision.

"You can't mean it! You couldn't have actually taken the risk to this only to let me go back. No, please don't do this, please!" Connor Grove began to sob, tears spilling into his cup. Chest heaving, he sobbed loudly.

"Drink up, Mr. Grove, you only have three days." Artie picked up a newspaper and began to read.

Connor drank too much, and the altitude enhanced his horrible hangover. He spent the next day trying to ski, drinking moderately, and eating voraciously. In the afternoon he took a nap, and by evening, he felt halfway decent. He was joined at dinner by a beautiful Swiss ski instructor who gave him a few tips, promised to provide him with the best lessons he'd ever had, both that night and the next day. He was not disappointed. Her name, he remembered, was Maya.

"Hey, Kyle, who is this Maya? Does she work for the organization?" Connor asked as they drove to the airport on the last day.

"She's a pro, sir, a very highly recommended pro. I heard the boss tell Peltzie that. Peltz is always so nervous about anybody seeing anything . . . or saying anything. I don't know why."

"Who is Peltz?"

"He's some kind of scientist . . . I don't know exactly what he does, 'cept he has a clinic of some kind in Mexico. I heard them say they have a cancer cure that works real good." Kyle turned into the private aircraft gate and drew to a stop before a medium-sized business jet. "Hawker . . . ," Connor mumbled. "Long-range tanks . . . God."

"Kyle, how did you guys get me out of that bus? Were any of the guards hurt?" Connor asked as they loaded onto the plane.

"We didn't do it. Some specialists from over here or Israel I think. No, the guards weren't hurt . . . maybe just roughed up. If you're worried about your story for when you get back . . . well, you are going to get briefed on the way back . . . I heard." Kyle held his finger to his lips to indicate they should quiet down.

Indeed, Connor was briefed; first, by Artie prior to takeoff, since he would be returning commercial a few days later; then, by Augie Bash, another long-time associate of Artie, on the trip back.

They would travel from Zurich to London Gatwick, then to St. John's Newfoundland, and then to Akron, Ohio. From Akron, where they would clear customs, they would take another plane to Joplin, Missouri, then to a small dirt strip near El Paso, Texas. Connor would be smuggled into Mexico in the trunk of a car, driven to a small village where he was to let his beard grow for two weeks. At the appointed time, he would be taken out in the desert and released. He would walk to the nearest public service agency and ask for help.

When repatriated to the United States he would maintain that he had been drugged and kidnapped for ransom. He would say that he escaped from his abductors by cutting through his binding with broken glass while they slept. When both Mexican and U.S. Officers raided their hideout, they would find evidence to verify his story.

Connor had been afraid to ask Artie, but Bash seemed so docile that he ventured to ask, "How do you guys know I won't make a deal with the feds and talk?" He sort of smirked as he said it.

"Mr. Grove, we know you have verified your account in Switzerland. You have experienced what freedom can be like. We trust you. Oh yes, we also know that you are aware how easy it was to get to you. The slightest question of your loyalty and, well . . . someone, wherever you are will know and . . . let's not even think of the unpleasantness that might ensue." Bash could see in Connor's eyes that he got the point.

Nineteen days after his "kidnapping," Connor Grove was tucked safely back in the folds of Safford's secure block. Four Mexican nationals were in custody south of the border, but since they would not waive extradition, a trial was planned in Sonora. All four were sentenced to twenty years at hard labor. Of course they were out leading the good life in less than eight months.

CHAPTER 20

TIME MARCHES ON

THE WEEKS PASSED and Swifty continued to learn. Since the library had no current newspaper subscriptions, Kim would bring him three-day-old newspapers so he could scrutinize the details of the search for Connor Grove. By fall there was no further mention of the "Flamboyant Financier" and his puzzling kidnapping from the minimum-security prison.

Nelson began to praise Swifty's resolve to focus. Exercise, running, and weights helped both of them pass the time and served to heighten Swifty's concentration. Nelson was pleased that after a lifelong battle with the waistline, he lost several pounds.

By Christmas, Swifty was considered to be in his senior year of college, though he was not permitted to leave the prison campus for class since the Connor Grove incident. His muscles were bulging and he too had lost some pounds. No doubt he was making progress in his studies with Nelson as well. He had been at Safford for nine months. Kim had expected him home by now.

Curiously, Swifty was enjoying his days. Study, work, exercise, rest, and visits with Kim, while keeping emotions in check, kept life bearable.

Kim was excelling at her new post. She had been with Cellestine Enterprises for three months, having decided to accept Buck Janis's offer to "come on board" as a trainee associate. Her duties were not much more than clerical, but she had time to study and the pay was slightly better than at the mart. She sold Swifty's old Chevy and put the $500 in the bank. Every two weeks, when she cashed her check, she added $50 to it. Now, with $1,000 in the bank, a good job, and no bills, everything would be perfect if Swifty was home. Well, soon.

She had put the stack of bills, wrapped in brown paper, the large man had put on her car seat, out of her mind. It was still there, in a Christmas card box under her night table, where there was just enough space below the bottom drawer. He had said that it was a message from Mr. Cellestine, but she hesitated to go to her big boss about it. She assumed he would say something. But whenever she saw him, he was very polite and businesslike but not too familiar.

She hadn't told Swifty and had only briefly toyed with the idea of telling Joe Seeley. She decided she just wouldn't think of it until later.

Work on the plan for Pharaoh's Paradise with Pam and Walt was slow. Walt tried to take charge, but it was clear to both young women he had no idea what he was doing. Finally, they just sat back smoking and let him talk.

One Sunday morning, Kim arrived early at the cramped office Buck Janis had allowed them to use in a partially leased office building in Scottsdale. She set up two chart pads, a stack of marking pens, and laid out two rolls of masking tape. She had been thinking about this all night. She was taking charge.

When Walt and Pam arrived with coffee, she broke it to them. "Guys, I'm going to try something new today. We're going to 'brainstorm.'"

"What's that?" asked Pam indifferently, lighting a cigarette.

"You sit there and spout out anything that comes to your mind about the project and I will write it on the chart paper. I'll hang the pages on the wall. When we fill the room with paper we'll see what we've got!" Kim said triumphantly.

"Well, who the hell died and made you queen?" was Walt's response.

"Walter, you have not made a contribution with your blithering. We are no further ahead than we were the first day. I think we need to open up with our ideas and see what new stuff we can come up with to make this project unique." Kim put her foot down.

"Sounds like a plan to me. Let's do it . . . get me some coffee, Walter" was Pam's response.

It was at that time that Kim knew that her suspicions about Pam and Walt were correct. They were an item. Confirmation came as Walter bowed his head and proceeded to fill a Styrofoam cup with black liquid from a thermos and then carefully added sugar and cream.

"Okay, let's start. Pam, what's the best way to go about marketing this project?" Kim said decisively.

"Well, I think we have to figure out what kind of project this ought to be, who we should try to sell to, where we are going to find the potential buyers, how we qualify them and when before we start trying to blindly sell!" Pam spit it out with machine-gun speed as she slurped the coffee Walter had lovingly placed before her.

"Good, now we're on the move . . . keep going . . . Walter . . . you too," Kim encouraged as she scrawled rapidly on one of the chart pads.

"Shoot, I don't know that Buck is going to let us change everything, but . . ."

"But what?"

"But, I hate that goddamn name . . . it sounds like Vegas. I mean Pharaoh's Paradise . . . geez."

"Gimme some names." Kim kept scribbling on the charts.

"Desert Oasis, Desert Destiny . . . uh, Desert Destination . . . uh, Windsong West." Walter spit out a dozen names.

Pam gave him a perplexed look and began to correct him when Kim interjected: "Everything counts. Let's get it all down before we shoot holes in ideas . . . this is a brainstorm. Good going, Walt, what else."

Pam broke in, "Marketing 101 says we need to build a brand. The name thing is good, but we have to get customer satisfaction at the point of hearing about the project and then when they move in and join us in marketing it as satisfied customers."

"Yes," said Kim, "and we need to get both a tangible response and an emotional response when they hear the name."

"You mean like XYZ means quality to them, or maybe even 'feels' quality to them," Walt added.

"Guys," Kim hummed, "we are getting good!"

By the end of the day, with only a brief break for lunch, they had a plan.

This was at the height of the "warm fuzzy," "matrix management" era in business; a time when a new openness began to permeate boardrooms and frustrate the old guard of leadership. It was a time when young women showed up in pantsuits and, worse, demanding more restroom space and the right to smoke at their desks. As a guy who knew nothing about nothing then and has by now had lots of business and other kinds of experience, I think it was more good than bad. Maybe it's now time the pendulum swung back toward the middle. But what do I know? What did Swifty know then? What did any of us know then? You'll see. KKF

Swifty was glad that Christmas had come and gone. He had given Kim a few things that he had made in the prison shop. She brought him some new slippers and a cake. They had been allowed to spend unlimited hours together on Christmas Day, under the surveillance of only one female officer.

New Year's Day he and Nelson watched football from morning until night: Sugar Bowl, Rose Bowl, Orange Bowl. Swifty mentioned that he missed Connor.

"Yeah, me to, kind of. He'll be back over here before long."

"What do you mean, 'back over here before long?'"

"Just what I said, my young friend. Now that your Mr. Breck has been tapped to help persecute our errant president and his 'accomplices,' I suspect they'll stop browbeating poor Connor and send him back home to us," Nelson said matter-of-factly.

"What? Breck's been transferred? No shit! You mean they caught Connor?" Swifty was so excited he ignored a Nebraska touchdown.

"Not caught . . . not caught, he returned on his own several months ago. The feds have had him in solitary over there in the black building . . . putting pressure on him, I suspect." Nelson turned up the volume on the TV.

"Wait a minute! How do you know all this? Are you sure, I mean what's the deal?" Swifty was all over the room, but Nelson further focused on the TV.

"Sit down and watch the game . . . you are quite aware that I know most everything," Nelson said resolutely, as he smoothed his pencil-thin mustache. "It shouldn't surprise you that I have information about what's been going on across the walk" – he turned slightly away from the TV and casually waved his hand toward the window – "there in the solitary block."

It was as Nelson had said. Connor Grove returned to them February 1. He had lost a good deal of weight and declined to talk about his ordeal, except to say that the months in solitary block were much worse than his days in captivity.

February 6, Swifty saw a box in the previous Sunday's *New York Times* Kimmie had brought him that described the addition of Assistant U.S. Attorney Adam Breck to the Justice Department team evaluating events following the break-in at the Democratic National Committee headquarters the previous June.

PART THREE

CHAPTER 21

THE REBIRTH

SUMMER CAME ON with its furnace heat and Swifty kept busy. Fall, followed by the mild winter, came and went. He looked back at the year and how he had grown – physically, mentally and emotionally. He was pleased, but restless for release. He was approaching his second anniversary at Safford. Connor had readjusted after his ordeal and was spending a reasonable amount of time teaching Swifty. Nelson continued to treat him as a major project. But he missed Kim, and his friends just were not enough.

All three men were annoyed that Swifty could not gain accreditation for all of his courses; therefore no university would graduate him. Even Correction Supervisor Darryl Cobb wrote Arizona State University asking for reconsideration, to no avail. Eventually, Cobb suggested that he write the Federal Department of Corrections, asking for leniency. Swifty asked Joe Seeley about it and received a cool response: "Frankly, Swifty, you could piss them off, especially if Adam Breck is contacted. Let sleeping dogs lie. Keep it as local as possible. Maybe Cobb could convene a special Corrections Board Meeting without contacting the U.S. Attorney, but I doubt it. Let me check."

Seeley came back to him in a week and said it was best to "cool it" for a couple more months, then Cobb would be within his authority to affect a "provisional release." What was a "provisional release"?

An inmate, under certain circumstances, could be released under the supervision of a parole officer for work and school only. He would have to report back to Safford each weekend until his normal release date. Swifty said he was interested.

Nelson didn't like the idea. "Break clean, no ties, that's the way to do it. You get outside and it will kill you to come back on Saturday. Remember how depressed poor Connor was after his brief sojourn? And we didn't even see the bastard for several months."

"But, I could be with Kimmie . . . you don't know how much I miss her," Swifty fretted.

"Bullshit! You have to be strong. When I was your age I once got a conjugal leave . . . my first wife. Well, one night in bed, I'm hooked and totally frustrated at the thought of going back. So I drink . . . and drink . . . and drink until I can't perform. The eventual result was, I lose my freedom, my wife, and 20 percent of my liver. It was good for me to spend the following eighteen months in lockup so I could completely dry out. Take my word for it, stay until it's all over." Nelson seldom had been so frank, so definitive.

Swifty usually took Nelson's advice, but he couldn't stand the thought of being able to get out and then staying in. As it happened, it was all moot. Cobb was transferred, and all hope of a "provisional" died with his departure.

His next opportunity came at the normal Parole Board hearing in May. His first review was favorably received because of his exemplary behavior, his focus on educational rehabilitation, and the glowing review left by former correction supervisor, Darryl Cobb.

Swifty was devastated when he learned that the board never released on the first favorable review. "Two consecutives . . . ," Sergeant Ackerman told him. "Shoot for August, Koenig . . . you'll make it."

"Swifty," Nelson said, "Connor and I have been talking. We think you need some coaching for your big show in August."

"What? You guys think I'm not smooth enough?"

"You're smooth . . . but what you need to be is believably contrite. These idiots have a great prejudice against you. You are a con. They have to believe that all the fire, hate, and poison has been sapped from you . . . so you're no threat to them." Nelson smiled.

"Well, I told them that I wanted to be a good citizen and I showed evidence with my school and all." Swifty was defensive.

"They don't give a shit about that. Most of them would prefer you to be a plow horse with your intelligence completely destroyed. If you were black they'd expect a 'Yasah, boss . . . I gets ya shoes. Thank ye.'" Nelson was clear in his disrespect for the Parole Board and all such civil servants.

"What should I do, develop a shuffle?" Swifty was incredulous.

"Good thought, but why don't we try a few other affectations." Nelson looked to Connor.

Connor suggested Swifty speak very slowly, look directly at each board member when answering questions, then bow his head. They practiced. After a few iterations, it worked.

Next they worked on answers. Why did Swifty continue college? Was he trying to become a "jailhouse lawyer"? The answer was "No, sir, I just want to get a job I can handle to support me and my wife. I figured college would help me to partially overcome the stigma of having been incarcerated. If it wasn't for my record I'd try for the fire department. Maybe a job in warehousing. I been studying the list in the correction supervisor's office." Connor suggested Swifty shorten his sentences and avoid multisyllable words in their final draft.

Swifty practiced moving in and out of character until he could do it in his sleep. He could be humble at will. By the time August 4 rolled around, he was prepared.

Only three members of the board attended, along with Correction Supervisor Mervin Swink. Swink enjoyed hearings and relished in presenting parole candidates with a lengthy preamble. At 2:00 p.m., Swifty was called in, and Swink, with a broad smile, presented his top candidate for parole, Colin Koenig, "A young man who made a mistake and has learned his lesson. Colin is a model inmate here at Safford. Along with keeping our library humming, he assists my office with clerical support. You see, Colin has more than three years of college. Upon release he will finish up at Arizona State. His young wife visits here once each week . . . she's very devoted. She has been supporting herself in real estate while her husband has been paying his debt. Colin, tell the board why you should be released at this time."

Because only two men were being considered for release, the board devoted a full hour to Swifty. He was polite, subservient, and remorseful. Each member lectured him briefly after questioning, then nodded toward Swink.

He did not sleep that night. Two issues kept him awake: the resignation of the president of the United States and its corollary – what effect would the Nixon departure have on his parole.

As it occurred, there was no effect at all. The morning brought the news: the board voted unanimously for "provisional release"!

Ackerman slapped him on the back and exclaimed, "Told ya, two consecutives!"

Connor said, "Take it, kid, take it."

Nelson said he should turn it down. "Provisionals are bullshit!"

Monday came slowly, but it came and, with it, his release. Swink said, "I'm glad to lose you . . . your record at Safford shows you earned this. I'll see if we can reduce your reports to us to monthly. Perhaps the chief of police in Scottsdale, or the Maricopa county sheriff will be willing to take over your supervision under the provisional release. Next board meeting I will work on them to make this a full parole. Good luck, son." Next meeting his sentence would be up anyway.

Swifty hugged Nelson and Connor, shook hands with Curt Rhymes, Billy Belger, who was still awaiting release, hugged old Angus, traded fake punches with Ackerman, and let the young guard Slattery and Mervin Swink lead him out. Kim was waiting outside in the heat. She looked beautiful in her white sleeveless blouse and beige walking shorts. She was wearing little white sandals and carried a white-and-beige purse.

She didn't say a word, but held him for a moment as Swink stood with his arm on Swifty's back. Then, she took him by the hand and pulled him toward the car. Swink called, "Take care . . . see you Friday, late." Slattery waved and smiled.

It seemed so strange. He was leaving prison where he was serving a sentence that wasn't just, and yet, he felt he was leaving a part of his family. He knew he couldn't share this feeling with Kim as she would not understand. On the drive home, she talked airily about their new apartment in north Scottsdale, beyond Camelback, and about her job with Cellestine Associates. Swifty couldn't help thinking it would be tough for him to move back in to what he was already considering Kim's place.

When they arrived at the new place, Swifty asked about where she parked his car. "Oh, honey, I got rid of that old thing. We're going to buy you a new one."

Swifty had been under supervision for over two and a half years . . . he would just go along here too. The new place was not comfortable. He took off his shoes before entering and hung back, wondering where he should put his overnight bag. He had left most of his meager possession at Safford, not sure if he would even keep anything once he left for good. While Kim went out to the store, he took a shower and put on a robe. He carefully cleaned and dried the floor and the sink with his towel, then hung it up again.

When she returned, he helped her put things away. They ate a light meal of chicken and salad, watched TV for a while, and went to bed. It was not as either of them had expected or planned. Swifty would require a period of adjustment . . . they both would. They talked most of the night and finally fell asleep in each other's arms.

Two days later Swifty enrolled at Arizona State for his final semester. He saw a counselor and requested a waiver to take eighteen units. After reviewing his transcript and reading his file, the professor agreed. To wrap up his degree, all Swifty needed were classes in his minor, communications: Oral Presentation, Audio-Visual, Media Training, Debate, Applied Logic, and Organizational Development; the latter two being crossover classes that counted in business as well, though he had all the credits needed in that area.

His first day at school, he received a note advising him to stop after class to see his counselor. He did and was told of a job opening that might fit his schedule. It was a book-publishing warehouse in Phoenix near the airport. With no car, he wouldn't be able to get there. The counselor mentioned that another student worked at the warehouse and he might be able to catch a ride. The other student's name was Kyle Faust, a graduate marketing student. Swifty waited for him after his classes and caught the young man coming from a Sales Theory class.

"Hey, glad to meet you, Colin. Sure, I can run you over to Miller's. It's really a good place for a student, because there's lots of free time between loads when you can study." Kyle Faust was a chunky young fellow, about Swifty's age, with a cheery demeanor and crooked teeth.

Getting their books together, the two walked to Kyle's black '72 Ford with wire wheels and tuck-and-roll upholstery. The black sucked up the heat, and it was like a furnace in the car. Kyle clicked on the obviously retrofitted air and slid down the electric windows until the car cooled a bit. Then, with a flourish, he put the windows up. It was beginning to cool in the overpowered car.

They rode in silence for a while, listening to the throaty sounds given off by the souped-up Ford. Eventually, Swifty asked if the job paid well. "Sure, for the work. You start at four dollars an hour . . . 'bout twenty hours a week . . . it's a good deal."

Eighty bucks . . . not much, but it would help. Kimmie was doing good, making over two hundred. The foreman was a guy about thirty named Sheldon. He asked a few questions and said, "Good, then. If Kyle recommends you, you sure know filing and stuff. You got a lot more library background than us. When can you start?"

"Hey, well great, right now. But you know I just met K – "

"Hell, Colin's a great guy, Shel, he's reliable and smart. No problem," Kyle cut him off and pushed Swifty aside.

"Okay. Show him what to do, Kyle, and I'll get the paperwork together." Sheldon ambled off toward the office.

"Gosh, Kyle . . . thanks." Swifty put out his hand.

"You can pay me back someday, Swifty. I know you're a good guy."

"How'd you know my nickname was Swifty?"

"An important part of marketing is research . . . . I always check people out."

Swifty wondered what was going on, but let it drop and went to work.

Kyle said he would be happy to have Swifty ride with him Monday through Friday. He would be moving off to another assignment for the company, but he needed to stop by Miller Publications each afternoon and evening, so it would work out great until Swifty bought a car.

Swifty didn't find out for several years that Miller Publications Warehouse was one of the ancillary businesses acquired by Norm Cellestine when Connor Grove made the deal to sell off assets in an attempt to save Desert Empire Savings and Loan. When he asked Kyle about the ownership his first day of work, the response was, "I guess it's a conglomerate."

CHAPTER 22

THE ADJUSTMENT

WHEN THEY TALKED, Kim chattered on about Mr. Cellestine, Buck Janis, Walt, and Pam. Swifty could repeat rote what they wore, what they said, and how they smelled. God, he was sick of it. All he could talk about was class and Kyle; an oxymoron if there ever was one. Class and Kyle were not synonymous. Swifty was aware of the peril of discussing Safford or referring to Nelson, Connor, or anyone there but Mr. Swink. Kim clearly had no use for the opinions or preferences of convicts. She wanted to put that "awful experience" out of her mind and their lives.

What Swifty did find interesting was Kim's plan – or the shared plan of Kim, Pam, and Walt – for the real estate development they were working on. Kim had grown and matured in the nearly three years he had been away. She had a more sophisticated way of talking, and her dress was decidedly more "upscale." Swifty felt awkward by comparison.

Kim described her intent to recommend that Pharaoh's Paradise be renamed Desert Oasis; that the project be scaled back from nine hundred to six hundred units: four hundred developer units and two hundred custom homes. She would propose that they limit the community to one clubhouse, two golf courses, and a moderate-sized tennis facility. The project would be built in three phases, the first with one hundred developer units and fifty custom homes. A temporary sales office would be constructed, along with two new models; the first golf course and the tennis facility would go up immediately, and a temporary clubhouse would be put together using modular buildings. The original heavily Southwestern finishes would be replaced with a combination of modified Southwestern and contemporary materials, finishes, and colors. He thought she had some great ideas.

Swifty could only help in the areas of business and finance. Kim was mesmerized with Swifty's knowledge of financing and economic projections. He assured her that "interest rates and political stability have more to do with real estate business's success than how pretty the renderings are." She cranked this thinking into her plan presentation.

Friday night came too fast . . . just as Swifty and Kim were getting reacquainted with living together. After work, Kyle was dropping him at home when, surprisingly, he asked if he could meet Kim. Swifty was taken aback, but saw no harm and took him up. Kim was waiting and seemed a little annoyed to have a guest before the long trip to Safford.

"You know, I am so happy to meet you, Mrs. Koenig . . . Swifty told me how pretty you were, but I had no idea!" Kim blushed.

"Thank you, Kyle."

"Hey, buddy, we got to go . . . got a long drive ahead." Swifty tried to encourage his departure.

"You know what, if you want, I can drive you where you're going. I got nothing else to do," Kyle blurted. "Fact is, if you want my car . . . take it. I just live over here and I will be using my boss's car all weekend. Go on, take it . . . or I'll drive you. I insist on helping." Kyle became very forceful.

Swifty protested, not wanting Kyle to know where he was going. Finally, in an effort to get rid of him, he agreed to use Kyle's car.

Kyle handed him the keys, said good-bye, and disappeared quickly.

"What in the devil was that all about?" Kim asked, astonished.

"Don't know . . . he's just a tad nuts, I guess. Anyway, it saves you having to drive out there. I'll just use his Ford and be back Sunday as soon as they'll let me out." They embraced, and he faded into the hot, dark night. Kim locked and bolted the door. Twenty minutes later, she remembered the hidden money. Next time she would tell Swifty and maybe they could buy him a car with it.

Swifty listened to the radio as long as there was a signal. The Ford ran smooth. Outside of the rather gaudy upholstery and "too flashy" appearance, it was a heck of a car. He fumbled with the tape deck – he had never used one – and pushed a cartridge in. Music played. A group. Not bad.

Nelson and Connor were installing a new TV antenna the next morning when he awoke. The block had been locked down when he had arrived, so he slept in a transit barracks and arose late, dawning a uniform and hanging his clothes in an empty locker. No one bothered him.

"Hey, what are you guys doing?"

"Ho . . . it's the provisional releasee. Don't get near us, you're tainted," Nelson said in mock disgust.

Connor said, "Somebody sent Nelson a color TV. The screws are letting us put an antenna on top the building and helping us string a cable down the side of the block to Nelson's window. He promised to let them watch it sometimes."

"If these philistines would ever get the cable out here, we'd have some decent channels too. I believe we can get reasonable reception with this high-gain antennae, we'll see," Nelson said, struggling to pull the cable through the mesh on the window.

They watched the NBC affiliate most of the weekend, since there was nothing worth watching in color on the two other channels. Nelson waited until Sunday afternoon to ask him how he liked the outside.

"Is it what you expected? Be honest now. Are you fulfilled?"

"No. No it isn't. I feel like an outsider in Kim's home. I feel like I'll get her dirty if I touch her. After we . . . well you know . . . I feel I violated this nice young woman. I feel like shit . . . like a fucking dirty con!" Swifty started to tear up.

"Stay strong, boy. It is destined to be like this. Believe me, I know the feeling. See, you still have a chance to wipe all this crap out of your life. A guy like me . . . a fifty-six-year-old has-been con has no goddamn chance. A 'legitimate' woman'll' never love me again. I'll never vote . . . never hold a real job . . . never collect social security . . . never see what family I have out there somewhere. I can handle all that. It's what I did to myself for the sake of . . . of action."

"Geez, Nelson."

"Not 'Geez, Nelson' . . . No, goddamn it! 'Honest, Nelson, I will never be back here full-time again. I will lead a good life . . . a decent life . . . the life of a fucking citizen.' That's what I want to hear from you, Swifty. Not that you can't take help or cut corners . . . but that you won't fall into the trap of looking for the easy way . . . the con's way. Promise me that all the time I spent educating your young ass was not wasted. Promise me!"

"I promise . . . you can take that to the bank. I promise. I promise."

Nelson was standing before him, round-shouldered, thin pencil mustache, tears streaming down his cheeks, and his nose dripping. Swifty loved the man. He was like a father . . . but better. He knew that moment there would always be secrets kept and not shared; alliances made and not always approved. It had nothing to do with his ferocious love for Kim. She couldn't be expected to understand.

Sunday night Swifty tooled home in his civvies. He really liked this Ford.

Kim was waiting for him. She had pizza and beer. Swifty knew he wasn't supposed to drink, but what the hell. Nobody was going to break into his house and watch him. It had been over two and a half years since he had had alcohol. It was okay. He only had two, but it made him feel a little giddy.

Kim said coyly, "I thought if I got you a little drunk, you could relax. You don't talk much, except late at night and you keep to yourself so much."

"Yeah, I guess I have been a little tight. But, it's taking me some time to readjust. Honey, this is all so different. I've been in jail, for god's sake!"

"Well, you're home now. You have me. You have your life back. You can forget all that other stuff and those guys."

"Jesus, I wasn't dead! I was alive and learning and loving and hoping . . . it's a permanent part of my life now . . . including 'those guys.' They were a family to me during the times you weren't there. They cared about me and they still do!"

"Oh, Colin, you need therapy. That is ridiculous. Those are convicts, not family . . . not people. You're upset. I'm going to talk to somebody about a counselor for you."

Swifty rose from the table and felt rage for the first time in years. He took two deep breaths and looked toward the window. His inclination was to run, but he took another breath and looked down at her. She looked apprehensive, but seemed like she was trying to be in charge.

He sat down again. "Yes, Kim. Yes, I probably need some kind of readjustment therapy. Maybe we can look into it together."

"Okay then, we're getting someplace. Now help me with the dishes."

He knew even more than he had in the afternoon that his inner life was his alone, not to be shared.

Kyle had left a number and Swifty called just before midnight. A woman answered. "Yes,

oh . . . Kyle is here. Just a moment, he'll be right here. We were playing canasta and he's in back watching TV. Kyle! Phone! Say, you're Colin Koenig, aren't you?"

"Yes, ma'am."

"Well, I know that nice little wife of yours. I'm Kyle's mom, Naomi. I work for Mr. Cellestine over at Phoenix office. Kim and I talk on the phone sometimes. I hope to meet you two sometime. Oh, here's Kyle."

"Hey, Kyle, got your wheels . . . thanks . . . where do you want them?"

"Hi. Just bring her to school. My mom will drop me off tomorrow. How'd she run?"

"Perfect. Great car."

"Want to buy her? Make you a helluva deal. We'll talk."

"Yeah, we'll talk. Small world. Your mom knows my wife."

"She said that. Small world. See ya mañana."

Click

Strange days . . . strange days. Prison was easier. Swifty couldn't sleep. Kim dropped off after sex and purred like a kitten. He paced the living room, wondering what was happening. His circle had gotten too big too soon. He couldn't find the walls to lean on. The floor was dropping beneath him. Perspiration surfaced, and he couldn't catch his breath. He sat on the couch for a minute and leaned back. Next thing he knew, sunlight filled the room and he had a stiff neck. Kim was in the bathroom . . . the water was running.

"Morning," he said, leaning into the bathroom and spying her in the tub.

"So, you sneak out at night and don't want to sleep with me anymore, Mr. Mysterious," she said in mock anger.

"Couldn't sleep . . . didn't want to wake you."

"Get in here with me and make up for your bad behavior." He did.

CHAPTER 23

KYLE AND JAKE

ARTIE SAT ON the patio, drinking coffee and reading the paper. Jake was doing push-ups in sets of ten. Teresa bumped around in the kitchen, getting something together for them to eat.

"What is this shit, you kids can't keep your women. Your mother and me, we don't have problems like that." Artie was referring to the recent departure of Jake's wife, Amber, and Kyle's wife, Janice.

"Pop . . . Amber will be back . . . whew . . . wait a minute . . . nine . . . ten." He sat heavily on the deck. "She will be back, I guarantee it. When she runs out of cash . . . she'll be home."

"Why'd she go? You playin' around again in full fucking view?"

"I got a little careless, yes. I will be more careful in the future."

Artie took a sip of coffee and looked out toward town. "God this is a beautiful life . . . Jakie, why do you want to screw it up? Look, call the girl . . . tell her you're sorry . . . you're a fool . . . you're madly in love with her, you can't make it another day without her. Do it today."

"Pop . . . I can't do that, she'll come crawlin' back."

"You stupid asshole. I am not making a suggestion, I am giving you an order. You do it or I'll personally kick that overmuscled ass of yours! She's a good girl. She deserves good treatment. Besides, she knows too much about our business . . . because of your big fucking mouth!" Artie pinned his son to the deck with his steel gray eyes.

Teresa waddled out from the kitchen. "What's the noise . . . what's with such talk to your

son . . . my son?"

"Tell your mother, Jakie."

"Mama . . . I . . . uh, behaved badly. That's why Amber left to visit her mom. Pop suggested I give her a call and tell her how much I miss her and maybe ask her to come back right away," Jake fumbled.

"That sounds nice, but why such language?"

"Emphasis, my dear, emphasis. Go make your call, Jake, then I will listen to your business proposition." Artie was firm.

Call made and coffee drunk, the two Leonardo men sat, talking business. Jake explained that his research showed that a new level of discretionary income was becoming evident in the younger ages of the middle class. He felt that this gave the health business potential. While it was unclear how the Leonardos could get into the food or clothing end of it, exercise was a good bet. Jake wanted to open a chain of fitness studios using the latest equipment. He would sign up as many subscriptions as possible and use young, beautiful people to promote the project, maybe local celebrities. He'd expect more people to sign up than would use the facilities, so oversubscription was not a problem. He'd start with three units in Phoenix and Scottsdale and then move to LA and beyond.

Artie pointed out that Vic Tanny, Jack La Lanne, and others had capitalized on this idea earlier. Jake said he knew that, but that neither had continued to personally promote the businesses and that's why it fell off. He wanted to develop centers that did not rely on specific celebrities so he would change out his "stable" as their popularity waned. He wanted the studio to be the "brand," not the person name that was attached. Jake said that TV and radio advertising were still cheap in the Greater Phoenix area . . . so he would focus on that. He left the business plan with Artie to read. Artie never read the projections because they were "pie in the sky." He did go with the basic idea and then listen to his "gut."

Kyle was late picking him up, but the kid had a good excuse.

"Had to get Swifty over to Phoenix for a lab deal, then get back and change cars. I'll be glad when he buys the Ford from me and I don't have to do all the double-running around, I mean so I'll be where you want me, when you want." Kyle was always a little nervous when first encountering Artie early in the day.

"Yeah, well, if he doesn't buy that hot rod of yours, we'll channel him into another car. How's he doing?" Artie asked very seriously, those gray eyes scanning Kyle for meaning.

Kyle squirmed a little inwardly. "Good, he might be still having trouble making the adjustment

". . . but pretty good. You know Mr. Leonardo . . . un . . . he is really a smart guy. He figures things out. He sure did pick up on the coincidence of my Mom working for Cellestine and all."

"Do you like him, Kyle?"

"Swifty? Hell yes, I mean . . . uh he's a great guy . . . very funny, full of devilment, and a good person . . . real deep sometimes. Sure I like him." Kyle asked the last with inquiry in his voice.

"Just wanted to know if he's likable . . . uh, is he going to graduate?"

"Yeah, with honors, I suspect."

"Good. One other thing . . . different subject."

"Sir?"

"What do you know about fitness?" Artie bore in again with the eyes.

"Me? I know I need to be more fit . . . but nothing, sir."

"Well, I want you and your pal Swifty to find out about it for me, without him knowing it's for me and without Jake knowing it at all. Are you with me?"

Kyle sat down in rapture. A real assignment in his field from the "man!"

Artie explained that Jake was interested in fitness as a business. He wanted Kyle to use Swifty's good offices and his own ability to find out if Jake's idea made sense. Sort of to double-check Jake and his people by examining the feelings of the young people at school in the bars, etc.

Kyle didn't know where to start, but he figured Swifty would. They were on their way to work when Kyle posed the question to Swifty:

"Hey, bud, I got a project from class to find out how the market is for an exercise-studio thing. You go any ideas how I could start?"

Swifty thought for a minute and brought up demographics . . . income levels, preferences, ages, distances from work, singles versus marrieds, etc., and then suggested a survey.

Things were slow at work, so they spent four hours talking over approaches. By the time the evening was complete, Swifty had convinced Kyle they could both get class credit for such a project and get the information Kyle needed by using their classes as the measurement base. Kyle had to think fast. He suggested they use only Swifty's class because he didn't want his marketing class to know what he was doing. It was easy enough to sell. Swifty was certain that his "flaky" Organizational Development instructor would fall for this idea in a minute.

He was right, and within a week, the two young men had a market survey constructed and began to administer it to Swifty's class. Before long, they became aware that they would have to broaden their examination. Another professor, one Kyle had engaged in conversation about the topic, suggested his grad school class in Marketing Demographics might be a good laboratory for their effort.

Most of these students were out in the workforce and took the seminar at night. It proved to be the answer. Of the eighteen students, eleven lived in singles apartments, and the others shared dorm rooms or houses with friends. None were married. Within two weeks, after researching county statistics on incomes, marital status, and travel patterns, the various classes had come up with a solid report, coupled with their anecdotal feelings, that suggested the community around the university was ripe for the idea of a "toney" fitness studio. They also surmised that Paradise Valley and a few other upscale communities were good bets for a slightly modified version of the studio concept.

Kyle reported his progress to Artie daily. By the end of the month, it was clear that, independent of Jake, Kyle and Swifty had verified that the fitness studio was not a bad idea.

Jake couldn't believe it! Sure the old man would give him . . . loan him the $200 hundred "k" he needed for the fitness studio kickoff, but he had to let that shithead Kyle work with him on it! He felt stupid. At first he felt like telling the old man to shove it . . . he'd go elsewhere for the cash. But that made no sense. He'd have to eat the insult in order to get the backing.

He even whined to Peltz about it. "Look, Jakie, don't cry to me about your father. He has pissed me off for years. I was pissed at him when I was poor and I'm pissed at him when I'm rich, but it was what pissed me off about him that made me rich. Shut up and go with his feelings. He's smarter than us. Kyle, he's harmless . . . let him tag along."

It was so. Jakie swaggering around giving orders and acting important with vendors; Kyle taking notes, asking probing questions, and keeping the records. Jakie didn't like input from his inferior, Kyle. But he had to admit that all the suggestions were good. In two months they had a place in Tempe not far from the campus. Their initial marketing campaign included leotard-clad grad students in the quad passing out fliers and overmuscled weight lifters giving demonstrations in bars and restaurants off campus.

When the spring semester started, they had over one thousand subscriptions and were forced to open a second center two blocks from the original. The athletic teams, with ample equipment in the field house, began to use the studios instead of the school gym. Young girls flocked around, from Arizona State, the local community college, and the high schools. Jake began to lease space where Kyle told him to . . . Kyle following the demographics reflected by the attendees at the original studios. Jake was a success, on his own. Amber came back. Swifty graduated. There was no one to go to the ceremony, so Swifty went to work.

CHAPTER 24

THE GRAND PLAN

KIM WAS EXHILARATED! Buck allowed her to present the new plan to Norm and the senior staff. Pam and Walt helped, but it was her show. Swifty kissed her good-bye when she left for work and wished luck before he headed off to look for a full-time job.

He had graduated from college, but still he had a record; he was a felon. Who would hire him? In April, unless there was some unforeseen setback, he would be completely free. Until then, he was still restricted as to what he could do and where he could go. If he did find a job away from the Phoenix area, he couldn't take it. Kim wouldn't leave her job, and he was bound to Safford.

Norm Cellestine said nothing as the group listened to the initial phases of Kim's presentation. Buck annoyed him by interrupting, so he lightly waved him off, as if to say, "Let her go on." The others looked nervously toward Norm each time Kim or Pam or Walt punctured one of his sacred cows. Of course, the name-change recommendation sent a gasp throughout the room. The reduction in phases and toning down of the design brought waging heads. For more than an hour, Kim – assisted by Pam and Walt (Walt mostly changing the charts and advancing slides) – talked on, with authority.

Abruptly, she stopped and said, "Okay, feedback time. We need to know if the rest of you think we're on the right track."

No one said a word, they just looked toward Norm. He smiled. Shook his head and began to sigh. "Oh it is sooooo hard to let go of old, dead ideas.

The rest of ya think I'm insulted. I'm not. All the other assets we acquired four years ago from Desert Empire have thrived. This one has sat and sucked up time and money. Pharaoh's Paradise is tainted . . . has no chance of bailing itself out as it stands. The kids have some great ideas. Let's open up, use our expertise, and see if we can't help 'em smooth this plan out an maybe make a go of this thing."

That did it. Everyone talked at once. Each member of the senior group, all vice presidents of Cellestine Enterprises, claimed they had always thought major changes were necessary in the project, but the timing wasn't right.

Afterward Buck said, "Well, Kimmie, you sold the old man. He wants to sleep on it and we'll get back together on Wednesday to about a new marketing campaign. You guys did exceptional. Damn good!"

Kim, Pam, and Walt went to lunch at a little Mexican place nearby to celebrate. Pam asked how Swifty was doing. Pam said he had graduated and was looking for a job. When Kim was looking away, Pam rolled her eyes at Walt, who smiled.

The next several weeks were a whirlwind for Kim. She worked twelve hours a day getting a new marketing plan together: brochures, advertising, media buys, press releases, and a major press conference for Norm to announce the grand reopening of the project under its new name.

During that time Swifty looked, looked, and looked for a job. No one would touch him with his record. No bonded jobs, no city, county, state or federal jobs, no department stores, government contractors, insurance companies, banks, car dealers, or public utilities. He was dejected.

Four more weekends at Safford. He was sick of it. Borrowing Kyle's car and relying on him for transportation was a pain in the ass. Kim was too busy to talk about buying him a car. He didn't have anyone to talk with, so he confided in Nelson.

"Swifty, Swifty . . . you are too damn smart to let this get you. Use your talent, start your own business. You don't need to work for some assholes. Think about what old Connor and I have taught you. Go it on your own. Owe nobody, depend on nobody but Swifty!"

"But what can I do?" Swifty looked bewildered.

"How 'bout running one of those fitness deals you worked on with that other kid?" Nelson suggested.

"I wouldn't know how to start and besides it doesn't sound like my thing." Swifty shook his head.

"Ask the other kid, what's his name?"

"Kyle . . . but I don't really want to do that . . . that kind of work."

"What do you want to do?"

"Don't know."

"Start making a list . . . start now. Inventory your like and dislikes. List your skills. Get at it. Here, we'll chart it like we used to when we first started getting you straightened out. Hell, I knew this would happen. We didn't finish with you before you accepted that stupid provisional. Shit." Nelson pulled open a small closet door and reached for a chart pad.

"Connor . . . CONNOR! Get your ass in here!"

Eventually Connor arrived, drinking a Coke. He raised eyebrows high and asked, "What?"

"We work . . . we find a business for old Swifty here . . . so he can get rich and take care of me in my old age," Nelson chuckled.

"What are you working on, honey? Did you get any good leads on jobs?" Kim was, as usual, in high gear, getting ready for a long workday.

"I'm designing my own business . . . 'cause nobody will hire an ex-convict. What's your day going to be like?" Swifty lightly responded, his head buried in the papers he had strewn about the dining room table.

"Honey, please don't call yourself that . . . God, I'll be glad when you are away from all that stuff. What business?" Kim stopped and looked.

"And, I need a car . . . soon. How much money do we have?" He kept looking down at his work.

"Huh?"

"Money . . . how much can I spend on a car. I can buy Kyle's for eight fifty . . . it's a steal." Swifty looked up at Kim, standing before him.

"Oh . . . that silly car. Why not get a good one? We have the money."

She was looking down, smiling at him sitting there in his underwear.

"We do?"

"Wait . . . I want to show you something. I should have told you a long time ago." Kim marched toward the bedroom.

She had moved the money in the brown wrapper to a lower drawer when she relocated to this apartment. She had only looked at it periodically over the past two years, having repackaged it about six months before. It was there. She plucked it from the drawer and walked straight to the dining room and dropped it on the table amongst his papers. "There."

"What's this?"

"Open it up."

Swifty carefully removed the top layer of brown paper and pulled back the next corner. He saw the money. He dropped it back on the table. "What in the hell is this?"

She told him about the big man in her car two years before. She showed him the note. He was white as a sheet.

"Kimmie, this is what sent me to jail . . . this money thing. Goddamn!

It could be a setup . . . it could be marked . . . trying to catch me in something. Shit! You should have told me." Swifty jerked up and began to pace. He couldn't catch his breath.

"Well it's not marked now. I used some and then put money back. By now all that's there is money I put in. It's five thousand dollars. Possession is nine-tenths . . . it's ours," Kim spoke with finality.

"We haven't paid taxes on it. I'm already a felon. I could go away for twenty years for this kind of thing. Did you tell anybody?" Swifty could not keep his balance. He sat down and began to tremble.

"Honey, get a grip. I haven't filed any taxes since you went away. I know I should have . . . but I didn't." She sat watching him, perplexed.

"Well, in a way that's good . . . 'cause it can't be fraud then. Oh geez . . . have we got any beer?"

"No. No. It's morning. No drinking. I have to go to work. You take that money and buy your damn car. We can fix the taxes later. Now get a grip, Colin!" She had no idea what he felt at that moment.

Later that day, after three bottles of beer and a sandwich, he paid Kyle eight hundred dollars for the Ford and made an appointment with a tax attorney.

He bought another six-pack and continued to write out his plan while he drank. Kim came home and looked disgusted. "What are you doing? God, Colin, is this what you learned in jail? My god!"

"Hope you had a nice day too," he said.

She changed clothes and slammed out, yelling, "I'm going to a meeting. I'll be late! Make your own dinner . . . or drink it!"

He was asleep when she returned. For three days, little talk passed between them.

When Swifty left for Safford Friday night, things were beginning to get back to normal. He was excited to show Nelson his plan and to get some feedback. He drove the Ford carefully along the old road, listening to Barry Manilow on the eight-track. Life was getting better. When he checked in, the night guard told him to find his own way to his block, Swink was out of town and Ackerman was off. Only the young guy, Slattery, was on, working on his law books, said he was "prepping for the bar." When the cat's away. Nelson and Connor were playing chess at midnight . . . the lights were still on.

"Hey, the prodigal returns! Qué pasa, Swiftman." Nelson was jovial. Connor smiled and shook his hand.

"Not much, how's with you dudes?"

"Dudes? My God . . . they've got him, Con . . . dudes indeed."

"I'm retiring now that you're home," said Connor, yawning. "Let's finish tomorrow, Nelson."

"Good night, my friend. No cheating tomorrow." Nelson turned his attention to Swifty.

"Well, what do you have to say for yourself?"

"I've got a plan, Nelson. I need your criticism . . . your judgment on it," Swifty spoke proudly.

"Good, first thing in the morning we'll go over it. Now, we get some sleep."

Swifty was a little disappointed. When he found the two awake, he wanted to share immediately. But tomorrow would have to do.

After breakfast, they sauntered back toward the block. Nelson said, "Say, let's go in the library where we won't be disturbed. It happens that I am your replacement, Swifty, old chum . . . I have been entrusted with the keys. Actually, I took old Angus's extra set and no one missed them."

They entered and took seats, Nelson and Connor on the left, Swifty on the right.

"I don't have chart pad pages, 'cause I didn't have any at home. But, I'll pin these eight-and-half-by-elevens on this corkboard. I did them in marking pen . . . so I think it will be clear," Swifty began.

"First, I want to start my own business." Nelson nodded and smiled, Connor listened. Swifty continued.

"People, most people need help. There's lots of talent out there lying untapped because we expect our smart success stories to come in six foot two, eyes-of-blue packages. Short, fat guys stand no chance. I think it's a waste. What's a chunky girl with warts going to do unless she has a law degree?" He looked inquiringly.

"Go on, go on," Nelson nodded.

"My plan is to offer personal advice to those who need help in gaining confidence, getting their act together, and asserting themselves. I plan to find two or three guinea pigs . . . bad analogy

. . . sorry. I plan to find two or three test cases. I'm going to charge them a small fee to start and then collect one-fifth of their second-year salary, after I help them get their dream jobs. If I can get two examples . . . do a kind of before-and-after profile on them . . . you know photos, résumés, et ceteras, then they can give testimonials about the great Swifty Koenig."

"King," Nelson pronounced.

"What?" Swifty paused.

"Swifty King . . . your new name. Your old one pretty much means king in German anyway . . . change it to what it should be, Swifty King."

"Oh I like this one, Swifty King . . . good one, Nelson," Said Connor.

"But, what about my identity? Who I am?"

"Oh sure . . . Colin Koenig, convict, felon . . . man who did time . . . must protect that ID. Get real, son . . . you're a natural Swifty King. Now go on . . . you've got something good here," Nelson directed.

Still puzzled, but encouraged by the positive statements, he continued.

"I'm going to prepare résumés, put these people on diets, make them run, buy new clothes, improve their speech. Naturally, their finances and personal time will have to be reorganized. I am going to take some losers with potential and make them winners, then give them their lives back." Swifty was triumphant.

"You will have to help them with education and personal habits . . . even what they drive. Your initial selections will have to be carefully made . . . can't screw up with the first batch," Connor chimed in.

The three went on for six hours with Swifty taking notes feverishly. By evening they were all exhausted. They had dinner, watched a Perry Como special, and went to bed.

Sunday morning Swifty heard a page. "Call for Swifty King . . . Call for Swifty King. Pick up at the office."

"See, I told you your name was King," Nelson yelled from the bathroom.

"Hello?"

"Mr. King . . . formerly Koenig?"

"Yes."

"My name is Augie Bash. I once met your pretty young wife. I was hoping we could spend an hour chatting on Monday. It could be very valuable to you."

"What about . . . and how did you know this King thing?"

"Why Mr. King, I was there at your birth . . . your rebirth, even though you were not. I'll explain tomorrow. Say, ten at José Bender's?"

"Well . . ."

"Fine, good day." *Click.*

"Okay, Nelson, who in the hell is Augie Bash? My first customer?" Swifty demanded when he returned to the block.

"Augie, heavens no. There is no possible hope for that old warhorse." Nelson was trimming his mustache.

"Well, who the fuck is he?"

"An old and dear friend. Someone who is carrying a message that can help you. Listen to him and stop asking so many questions. When things are good, go with the flow." Nelson smiled.

The next morning Swifty was drinking his third cup of charged coffee at the local breakfast place, Bender's, when a large man, probably sixty or so, ambled in, stomach first.

"Hello, I'm Augie . . . your genie . . . sort of." The big man extended his paw and Swifty took it.

"How'd you know who I was . . . uh?"

"Give me some credit . . . I am a detective . . . private . . . not the police kind."

"Okay, well what do you want?"

"Coffee and a roll. I'll buy. I'm on an expense account right now." Augie Bash had his roll and coffee and another roll and more coffee. Swifty was getting impatient.

"Say, let's take a ride . . . not the movie kind . . . a ride into the desert so we can talk. By the time we get where we're going, it will be lunchtime. We can eat lunch on my expense account." Augie smiled.

"Should we take my car?" Swifty asked.

"No, I have a great car . . . a Caddy. You'll like it. How's that pretty wife of yours? Good I hope. Gee, I scarred her when I left a message a couple a years back . . . I felt real bad about that. Please tell her I'm awful sorry still." He pushed his mass off the stool and dropped a ten on the counter. "Let's go."

A Cadillac indeed. A new one with power-everything. As they drove east on Scottsdale Road, Augie Bash asked, "How is my dear old friend, Nelson?"

"He's fine. How long you known him? Years I bet," Swifty answered.

"We have been friends for thirty years. We were in a similar business once. I was a cop and he was a crook. The lines crossed. I quit when he got railroaded. He was sort of a helpful informant and got burned. He's a con man, but harmless. Really, a fine man . . . fine man."

Thirty minutes later they pulled into Rancho Palo Verde golf club near Cave Creek. Augie stopped but didn't turn off the car.

"Swifty, I bring news from a friend . . . along with some . . . a . . . additional living expenses. Take this package." He reached into the glove box and produced a package wrapped in brown paper similar to what he had gotten from Kim.

"It's clean. Spend it easy though . . . don't want people to pry into where you got a bunch of extra cash." Augie smiled.

"Mr. Bash, I don't need your money or anyone else's. What did I do to earn such a thing?"

"You are an investment that has been paying off right along. You will not be forgotten. I have another bit of news . . ."

"What would that be?"

"My employer, who is also your benefactor, would be pleased to offer you employment as well . . . a good paying job." Augie smiled again.

"What, as a money runner . . . who gets his ass thrown into federal prison again?" Swifty spoke it as poison.

"Now, now. The man is concerned about you. He has a legitimate position in a solid, clean business that would fit your skills and education. The man has lots of interests that are not connected to anything . . . . questionable. My advice: listen to the man. He can help you a lot." Augie Bash couldn't help his smile.

"You and Nelson are part of the same thing, aren't you?" It was more of a statement than a question.

"Nelson is truly fond of you . . . the man and I know it. You started out to be a project . . . an assignment. Now, you're like a son to him. We're impressed with his dedication to you." Augie kept nodding with his smile.

"Okay, look. I'll take the cash, because I need it. But, I want to do a legitimate job to earn it and I want to have my taxman aware of it. But, as far as working for the Leonardos . . . I know who it is . . . no deal. Last time it cost me three years. I want to build a life and forget jail and what got me there. My lips are still sealed. I'm no threat."

Swifty stopped and looked out the window. Jake Leonardo was walking in front of the car with a slim, attractive blonde woman on his arm. He was wearing golf shorts and a sport shirt. His muscled bulged everywhere, but the extra below-the-belt pouch was still there.

"Shit."

"No, that would be Mr. and Mrs. Jakie Leonardo. We was going to join them for lunch. Jake wanted you to join his fitness business as a manager . . . a junior partner too, I think. But, you got better things . . . I don't know." Augie stopped smiling.

"Mr. Bash, Augie, please thank Mr. Leonardo senior, but don't ask me to associate with the guy that put me in the mess . . . I mean Jake Leonardo . . . God." Swifty was final.

"The boss thought you might feel this way. So, take the cash as a bonus for the great work you did at the book place. Put it in your taxes for this year, not last. If you haven't added that other amount into your taxes and you want to . . . just have your guy handwrite an amended return and send in a personal check for taxes and penalties. Nothin' will ever come of it. I've done it. Let's go someplace else for lunch." He straightened and put the Cadillac in gear. Gravel sprayed as they sped out of the lot back toward town.

They ate at Michael's at the Point. It was enough for two days, but Swifty figured Augie would need a refill by eight o'clock.

Two days later he met with the tax attorney and arranged for a handwritten late return for each of the previous three years that included the five thousand Kim had received. The following week he paid the attorney by check, four hundred dollars. His additional taxes, on his and Kim's income, plus penalties totaled less than eighteen hundred dollars. He paid that gladly, by check, and sent it "special delivery, return receipt requested."

He didn't know if he had made a correct choice. A job with Jake Leonardo might not be too bad. Now, he knew how he got the book warehouse job. Oh yeah . . . what was the story with Kyle?

"Kyle . . . Swifty . . . got an hour?"

They met at a little coffee shop near ASU.

"You no-good son of a bitch! Why didn't you tell me who you worked for? Why did you let me make a fool of myself! Damn!"

Swifty was hot.

"Whoa, ho, ho . . . whoa, my friend . . . hey I was helping, is all. No harm intended, only good things." Kyle backpedaled toward the wall.

Swifty slowed down and moved back toward a booth. In a minute Kyle sat down in front of him. A waitress came. Kyle ordered Cokes and fries for both of them. Swifty sat silent. After the fries and Cokes were served, Kyle spoke.

"Mr. Leonardo . . . he's a great man, Swifty. When my mom was in trouble he helped us out."

"Oh god, your mother too."

"No, she was engaged to Mr. Luisi . . . Dominic . . . he died. He was Mr. Leonardo's best friend. Mr. Leonardo promised Dom, on his deathbed . . . Dom's . . . that he would look after Mom . . . and me." Kyle looked very sad.

"So she works for him too?"

"No, she got a job with a man he does some business with . . . you know, Mr. Cellestine . . . where your wife works. She's okay now. Lost weight, got into a club playing cards and all."

"And you?"

"He lets me drive him around . . . do errands . . . made me promise to go to school. He asked me to help Jake. Jake doesn't like me, but he knows he needs somebody or me . . . I suggested he get you involved with Jake's deal. Hell, it was you and me who did all the research for it."

Kyle rested.

Swifty felt like a fool. Even poor Kyle tricked him. He needed a long run and a workout. It was hard to hate Kyle, with his pudgy body and snaggled teeth . . . what a deal.

"Swifty . . . Mr. King . . . I heard you was changing your name . . . uh, if you don't work for Jake, what are you going to do?"

"King . . . King . . . you know everything too, eh? Well, Kyle, I'm going into business for myself. I'll show you sometime."

CHAPTER 25

THE OTHER GRAND PLAN

SHE WAS "HIPPY" and her sweater was too tight. It was not that she was big busted . . . she wasn't, particularly, but she seemed "tucked" into a size too small. Her black hair was piled too high on her head and there was too much facial fuzz and arm hair too. Otherwise, not such a bad-looking girl. Not his type, but somebody's. Toni Marie Leonardo was really prettier than her mother, Teresa, but she didn't carry any part of it well. Swifty sat in the reception area outside Cellestine Enterprises. One of the young women in reception told him Mrs. Koenig would be with him soon. He asked her who the other girl was . . . she looked so much like Mrs. Leonardo. It was confirmed, she was the Leonardo daughter, Toni Marie.

"Hi, baby, waiting long?" Kim broke Swifty out of his thoughts.

"No, no . . . just got here. Honey, that girl Toni . . . how long has she been here?" Swifty asked as they went out the door.

"Toni? . . . she just started. I guess you know whose daughter she is. She just finished college in the East. She's really very nice. She wants to be a nurse, but her mom doesn't want her around blood."

Kim was full of information and not even trying to make the connection between Cellestine and Leonardo. Of course she had much less reason to live a life of suspicion than he did.

They reached the car and Kim threw up her hands. "Forgot my purse . . . got my briefcase . . . but no purse. I know where it is . . . be right back." She ran back to the office while he loitered about the car. When she returned, Toni Leonardo was keeping stride with her.

"Honey, Toni Marie heard you were asking about her and wanted to meet the handsome man who was so interested," she giggled.

"Toni, this is the famous Swifty Koenig . . . well I guess his stage name is Swifty King." She laughed out loud.

"Happy to make your acquaintance, Mr. King. You are certainly as handsome as all the girls said you were." The voice, thick . . . New Jersey, oh god . . . poor kid.

"Thank you, Miss Leonardo. I am honored to meet you. Won't you please join my wife and me for lunch?"

The girl almost fainted. Her knees visibly buckled and she reached for the car fender.

"Ha ha," laughed Kim. "I already invited her, Sir Galahad." Kim didn't seem to notice the young girl's dilemma. Swifty quickly opened the car door and helped her in the back. Her tight skirt nearly split from pressure as she crawled in.

Lunch was uneventful – all small talk. Notwithstanding her appearance and voice, Toni Marie was a very nice person. She seemed fascinated by Swifty's plan to offer personal services. Kim joked about it. But Toni Marie thought it wonderful. Swifty saw the young women back to the office and headed off to the library.

Nelson had instructed Swifty to gather some information about proper grooming. Most of what he found in the stack was useless, so he bought a few men's magazines at the newsstand. *Playboy* had a lot of fashions, as well as some great skin flicks. He was still quite pissed at Nelson for not telling him the whole truth over the past three years, but to sulk would mean he would have no friends.

Since he could not confide too deeply in Kim for fear she would scoff at him, he continued to rely on his relationship with Nelson and, to a lesser degree. Connor. For god's sake, Kim just laughed at him when he said he wanted to change their name to King. He explained how important it could be to the future with credit and other things, but she didn't even try to get it. He didn't push anything with her because she already felt he was jealous of her success. Of course he was. But she didn't have to scoff at everything he was doing. It hurt.

Friday he sped out to Safford, listening to Sinatra. He had seven magazines and two books to share. The Ford was running great. He really liked the car, but he was feeling he better think about something more in line with the station he aspired to. Maybe a Cad or a little

Mercedes . . . a Corvette? He'd consult Nelson. This was his last weekend at Safford. No celebration planned there . . . or when he got back home. He wondered if he would be in Kim's way on the weekends.

Nelson and Connor were asleep. The block was dark, so Swifty stayed in the transit dorm. Saturday morning the three quietly breakfasted alone. Nobody else bothered them. They retired to the library and studied the books. Connor was quite taken with *Playboy*, a technically off-limits publication at Safford. "How did you get this in here?"

"Nobody says a word to me anymore . . . you'd figure me for a screw or something," Swifty laughed.

"Swifty, I know you needed transportation, so I can't fault you for the Ford. But now you have to dress and drive the part. Get yourself a plain Pontiac or Buick sedan. Look reliable. When you're a big hit, go sporty, but not now. You'll scare people away. Look prosperous, but not frivolous."

"On clothes . . . stay light on the shirts and dark on the ties. A blue blazer and tan trousers work just great in Phoenix. Keep your shoes quiet . . . slip-ons and blue shirts. For goodness' sake make sure the socks match!"

Sunday they played chess until lunch. After eating, Swink showed up to wish him well on his last day. He said good-bye to Nelson, Connor, and the others, then idled out of the parking lot with his windows down, playing Sinatra loud enough for the guys to hear on the other side of the fences. Kim wasn't home when he arrived.

CHAPTER 26

SWIFTY KING, ADVICE

JAKE'S ARMS GLISTENED and the sweat poured from his forehead as he worked his fist back and forth like pistons. The other man struggled to stay upright and pulled left and right like an animal caught in a trap.

"You stupid shit. You ever say anything about my sister again and you're dead! Get that . . . dead!" One last punch and then a slap across the head put the man on his knees. He covered up, expecting a kick or a flurry of punches. None came. Jake turned and walked to the car as a small, fearful crowd looked to the injured man.

"That was not smart, Jake. What if some good Samaritan jumped in or a cop came. It's no good to do that sort of thing." Augie pulled the car quickly around the corner, hoping no one had taken down the license plate number.

"Fucker made a crack about Toni. I ain't allowing that. Amber heard him say it yesterday. When I spotted him coming out of that joint, I went kind of crazy." Jake inspected his bleeding knuckles.

"You know, you are an educated man, Jake. Why is it you want to look, act, and talk like a street punk?" Augie smiled wide.

"It's in the blood, I guess," Jake said gruffly.

"Your dad was never like that. Whenever he roughed anybody up, it was for business. I know. I rousted him enough when I was a cop."

Augie smiled again.

Swifty was working on his ad when Kim came in with Toni Marie. She kissed him and went in to change. He offered Toni a chair. She watched him with rapt attention as he crafted his ad on a blank piece of paper.

"What are you doing, Swifty? Making a plan for something?"

"No. Remember I told you about my idea?" She shook her head affirmatively. "This is my ad for the paper."

She looked.

> SWIFTY KING, Advice.
> Confidential career and life assistance. Qualified
> Applicants only. P. O. Box 5658 Scottsdale.

"Hey, I like that. How would you start if somebody sent in their résumé?" Toni asked earnestly.

"I'd go ahead and lead or facilitate a self-assessment first. Find out what the person thought of themselves and . . . uh, what they thought they could do to improve."

"You think they will be honest with you?"

"Probably more honest than they have been willing to be with themselves," Swifty said firmly.

Kim came out in a yellow sunsuit and took a quick look. "Nice. Let's go, Toni. We'll be home by five, honey. Bye."

"Bye," Swifty said with little enthusiasm as he watched the two women bounce down the stairs and head for Kim's Chevrolet.

Swifty cleaned up and headed for the local office of the *Arizona Business Journals* in Scottsdale. He stood in line for half an hour until a pimply-faced young man finally waited him on. "What kind of advice? You ought to say it here if you want a response."

"People who need it and are motivated will get it, believe me, Clarence," Swifty said sharply.

"How'd you know my name? You a psychic? Those ads go under – "

"No, Clarence, I saw it on your desk plate. Put it under business personals. It'll work."

"Your money . . . fifty-two fifty please." Clarence stood, looking dumb as Swifty wrote out a check. "It won't run till the check clears."

"Gotcha, Clarence . . . it's okay." Swifty left.

Swifty drove to Phoenix and looked for a movie. He had nothing to do but wait. Might as well see a flick. *The Wild Bunch* was playing. He went in, ate popcorn, and enjoyed William Holden and Ernest Borgnine shooting up the place. Robert Ryan, in one of his last roles, was phenomenal.

That night he suggested to Kim they go out to eat. That was fine with her. During a Mexican dinner, he heard all about Desert Oasis, again. She also told him about some man making a nasty crack about Toni when she was shopping with her sister-in-law. "It was that big man that acts like a bouncer over at Wild Jack's Bar, I think."

"Yeah, he's a piece of work . . . so to speak. Matter of fact, I saw him across the street there when we came in," Swifty observed.

When they left, they noticed a small crowd across the street. As they watched, Swifty saw Jake Leonardo hurry to a car on the corner. He could clearly see Augie Bash behind the wheel of his black Cadillac. A man sat flat on the sidewalk, holding his ribs. It was Gordon Macaw, the co-owner of Wild Jack's Bar . . . a real jerk.

He didn't mention Jake to Kim and pulled her toward their car. Later that night, she said that the man behind the wheel of "that big car looked like the man that gave me the package with the five thousand dollars in it."

"Yeah, could be . . . it was Jake Leonardo that got in his car . . . I guess, after kicking the shit out of Gordon Macaw. Couldn't happen to a nicer guy," Swifty chuckled.

Kim said, "Funny . . . funny that someone was hurt? Swifty, when are you going to work? You still have all that prison mentality in you."

She turned off the light and pretended to go to sleep. But not before she stabbed him in the heart.

The next morning Kim said little as she prepared for work. Swifty wondered what he could do to make things right between them again. It was clear that Kim had lost respect for him since his jail stay. Nothing he could say these days came out right. It used to be that he could make a quip and Kimmie would laugh or give him an endearing look. Now, she seemed impatient at the least or disgusted at the most, no matter what he said. Inside he said, "This shit must change."

Saturday it was raining heavily. Kim was at work – she usually worked at the office every day but Monday, the day she did laundry. Swifty was expected to clean the apartment and do the ironing, except for Kim's fine stuff. He did it – not well, but he did it. So, with little to do after cleaning, Swifty decided to make a "rain run" to Safford.

It was not a pretty drive, with rocks and branches strewn about the old highway, but he made it in less than two hours. Nelson was surprised to see him, and both were annoyed that Swifty couldn't get beyond the visitor center.

"Good of you to come . . . did you bring me a gun or hacksaw? Without you here I have little to do. I'm even getting sloppy about my workouts." Nelson had his wry sense of humor in gear.

It was crowded and noisy in the visitor center, but they had no choice. Swifty tried to express himself without talking too loud, and Nelson, as usual, was able to grasp his drift and to summarize:

"Sounds like she doesn't regard you as 'the man' anymore. Understandable. You have lost your power . . . she has seen your soft interior. Swifty, my boy, welcome to true married life. It will never be the same."

"What does that mean?"

"You will never be 'Mr. Mysterious' again. You are a known quantity and she 'has' you. She still loves you . . . but, you are her property now. Get used to it . . . or get out, with women, there are no other choices." Nelson gave him his most sincere, sympathy smile.

"You mean even if I hit it big I'll still be the asshole who forgot to take out the trash?"

"Correct. Just be sure to take out the trash."

"That's not fair . . . I – "

"Fair, fair . . . you silly ass . . . nothing's fair. She knows you love her. If you become a supersuccess, it will be because she inspired it and you did it, on command, for her. If you didn't give a shit about her you'd tell her to hit the bricks . . . but, we both know she has you by the proverbial balls. Lament not, we have all been there." Nelson closed his eyes and looked at the ceiling.

Swifty, feeling some inapparent intrusion, glanced to his left and noticed a bearded Mexican guy from "A" Block smiling at him and shaking his head in the affirmative, as his wife chattered on about kids. The wife, oblivious of the visual exchange between the two men, yapped on, yet Swifty felt his face turn red with embarrassment.

"Nelson, I never thought anybody could get the best of you. You mean there was a woman in your past that got to you?"

"Three, minimum, boy. My first still preys on my mind every night. Why do you think I brush my teeth so meticulously? I fear she will haunt my dreams if I let one day go by without flossing," Nelson chuckled.

"Where is she now?" Swifty asked confidentially.

"Married to a fucking lawyer in LA. Someday I'm going to kill him and take her away. But first I have to look up at least two more and break their hearts the way they broke mine . . . ah, life is such a trial," Nelson sighed.

They made small talk for a while, and Nelson wrote out a list of books and toilet items he wanted Swifty to bring him on the next visit.

Swifty drove back in the rain, no wiser and no more satisfied.

Kim was livid when he told her he had been to Safford. "Well, why in the hell don't you move back there with your jailbird buddies. Shit! I worked so hard while you were away to make a home for you, and all you care about is some damn con man and a bank robber!" She stormed into the bathroom, slamming and locking the door.

Four days later, Swifty's ad ran. He didn't show it to Kim, but Toni Marie Leonardo did.

"Well, how much did this cost?" Kim asked caustically, throwing the local *Business Journal* down on the table, where he was working on what Kim assumed to be another one of his "obscure" plans.

"Fifty-two fifty for three issues in five states."

"So, what if somebody responds? What are you going to tell them?" She stood, hands on hips, head cocked to the side, waiting for an answer.

"What I showed you in my plan . . . tailored to their specific needs . . . like I been saying." Swifty ran out of air and began to choke on his words.

"Uh-huh?"

"That's it," he whispered.

"Do you really think anybody will pay you money for this stuff?" She was skeptical and impatient to the point of disgust.

"Yes . . . I do . . . but, I don't think I can defend it to you right now. I am just going to have to prove it to you . . . to everybody." His eyes welled up with tears.

"Oh, is the baby going to cry now? Well Mama's sorry . . . damn!" She stormed right out of the door without closing it. He heard her say as she stomped down the stairs, "I have never been so embarrassed in my life!"

The next Saturday it rained again. Swifty gathered up the items from Nelson's list and called Kyle. "Hey, bud . . . want to take a ride in your old car? . . . Where? . . . to visit a friend in jail, that's where. Okay, pick you up in fifteen minutes."

"Swifty . . . what jail are we going to?" Kyle asked.

"Don't give me that shit, Kyle. You know damn good and well where I was incarcerated. Your employer surely made you aware of when, where, and with whom!" Swifty slapped the dash.

"Now, now, don't get pissed at me . . . I just wasn't sure if you maybe knew somebody in another prison . . . shit. Hey! I saw your ad in the paper . . . both yesterday and today. Neat! My mom saw it too. She said they were talking about it in the office." Kyle tried to change to what he hoped was a more palatable subject. Wrong.

"Oh, I bet they were talking . . . talking about the pathetic asshole Ms. Koenig has the misfortune of being married to . . . at least at the moment." Swifty slapped the dash again.

"You aren't having a good day, huh?" Kyle said meekly.

"Fuck no, I'm not having a good anything, day, week, month or life!" Swifty was outyelling James Brown, who was playing on the eight-track.

As they drove, Kyle tried a number of conversation breaks, looking for a subject that would calm Swifty down. Finally, Swifty asked him a stark question, out of the blue: "What happened to your wife, Kyle?"

"My wife . . . Janice?"

"How many have you had? Yes, your wife Janice."

"She took off back to Mama in New Jersey. Said I was irresponsible, couldn't hold a decent job . . . always catered to my mother . . . an spent too much time with Dominic . . . she said he was a fat, illiterate gangster. Hauled ass right after he kicked it . . . said I was spending too much time 'babysitting' my Mom," Kyle rattled on.

"Did it hurt?" Swifty asked.

"Yeah, shit yes it hurt. I loved that girl . . . but she wanted more stability than a guy like me was likely to provide." Kyle hung his head.

"Why'd she marry you in the first place . . . you some hidden great-lover type?" Swifty was cruel in his questioning.

"She loved me . . . even said she was pregnant . . . then when we got married, false alarm. 'Nother reason for leaving . . . was that . . . wanted kids. I just wasn't ready for that . . . too much of a kid myself." He sheepishly smiled.

Swifty thought quietly for a while. Kim wouldn't have a baby because he wasn't stable either. Besides, she wouldn't want her kid to have a "jailbird" father.

Nelson was surprised to meet Kyle, but he had clearly seen him before, from a distance . . . it wasn't clear when. They chatted for an hour, then Connor came in. Connor and Kyle talked quietly together like old friends.

On the way back, Swifty wanted to know when Kyle had met Connor Grove. Kyle was vague, but said he really liked Mr. Grove. Swifty also asked about Kyle's father. Kyle said he never knew him. His mother always had some man around – some he had even called Dad – but he never knew his own father. Dominic was the only one he was ever close to. He had been around, in New Jersey and Phoenix, for about seven years, until he died three years before.

Swifty really liked Kyle. As he spent more time with him, he appreciated that behind those snaggled teeth and the slight rolls of fat lay a fine mind, though Kyle seldom displayed it.

"You ever think about working out, Kyle, maybe at the fitness studio? Certainly with your involvement with Jake Leonardo, it wouldn't be a problem," Swifty asked, already knowing the answer.

"Naw, I wouldn't know how. Jake and the others would make fun of me anyway. I like to deal with him on a basis where I'm competitive . . . business. It really confounds him that I'm as smart as he is. I mean he is smart, but he gets all flustered when someone else knows the answers . . . Ha! I love that part . . . ," he giggled.

As they chatted on, driving through the rain, Swifty felt he had at least one friend he could share with, outside of Nelson. Kyle felt something too; that he could confide in Swifty, and it would be held to him only, without ridicule.

Maybe you are wondering why I haven't pointed out which of these characters reminded me of famous persons. Well, they all did, and Swifty and I used to play a game deciding who they reminded us of. I always won. Nelson was a red-haired Paul Newman, Connor a dead ringer for Lyle Waggoner, from the old Carole Burnett Show. *(He runs motor homes for the movies now.) Kim, of course, was a very young Ann Margaret, with short blonde hair; Norm Cellestine was a thin Lyndon Johnson with a red face; Swifty said Darryl Cobb was a perfect Dennis Weaver, and Swink could pass for a thin James Cromwell; Teresa Leonardo looked like a large, dark Bette Midler; Augie Bash a huge version of Alex Karras, the old Detroit football guy, actor; and Dominic Luisi a copy of Orson Welles, with lots of black hair and a big nose. Toni Marie and Kyle (me) we'll get to later. KKF*

CHAPTER 27

WHEN A PLAN WORKS

SWIFTY'S FIRST RESPONSE letter went unnoticed in the wake of Kim's recognition as "Producer of the Year" at both Cellestine Realty and Cellestine Enterprises. Swifty never understood the difference, but he knew winning both was a good thing. Kim had listed or sold eighteen properties alone and another twenty-six in partnership with Buck, Pam, or Walt. She began work on her broker's license as well. There was a party and a bonus. Swifty sat quietly while everyone celebrated his wife. He was proud, but jealous.

Toni Marie Leonardo made her way to his table while Kim was floating from spot to spot, sipping Champagne and laughing at bad jokes.

"You must be so proud, Mr. Koenig. Okay if I sit with you for a while?"

"Yes and yes . . . I would be honored."

"You are such a gentleman . . . I wish I had the courage to answer your ad." Toni turned red at the sound of her own voice.

"I would give you a special rate . . . since there is so much to work with . . . so much latent talent." Swifty smiled and laid it on thick.

"Shoot . . . Too much Champagne." Toni Marie fanned herself with her hand. "I'm too fat. I have too much facial hair. My nose is too big. The only reason the boys want to take me out is to go to bed with me!" She started to sob.

Swifty ducked his head, embarrassed at her outburst, and looked around to see if anyone was paying attention. They were all too busy having fun. He put his finger to his lips and handed her a napkin. She nodded and turned even redder as she dabbed her eyes and blew her nose.

"Did you get any?" she whispered loudly.

He ducked again and looked around.

"Did anyone write to you in response . . . you know . . . to your ad?" she said between sobs.

He could barely discern what she was saying in her New "Jerseyese" through the napkin. Her father was so articulate and smooth. Kyle said the mother had only a slight East Coast accent. Jake had none in his high, squeaky voice; but Toni had spent time with her aunts and cousins while she went to school at Rutgers. Evidently, she was the only one within whom the thick accent stuck.

"I received one . . . From a young man here locally. I plan to meet with him in a couple of days. No way to tell what it will lead to yet," Swifty said gravely.

She came close and clutched his sleeve. Swifty could smell the combination of lipstick, cologne, and alcohol as she spoke, breathlessly: "Please keep me informed, Mr. Koenig. I'm very interested in your work."

Kim was a little friendlier the next few days, he thought, because of her newfound success. At the first of the week she brought in the mail and shouted, "Yippee!"

Swifty looked up from his book and raised his eyebrows.

"I got my first big check . . . and my second . . . and my third! Honey, we're rich!" She kissed him loudly.

With all of Kim's success, she had not actually received payment for any of the year's sales, as the properties had not closed escrow. The first three closed the prior week and she got her share: 1.5 percent of the purchase price; fifteen hundred, eleven hundred, and nine hundred dollars. She was rightly excited.

"You did good, baby. I'm very, very proud of you." He held her while she cried for joy.

They went out that night and spent fifty dollars for dinner.

Two days later, on a Wednesday, Swifty met with his first potential client. On his way to the Camelback, where they were to meet, he stopped by his post office box. There were nine more responses to his ad!

Peter Phenet was thirty, blond, and short. He was pudgy, but not fat, and wore a tight double-knit jacket and unmatching trousers. His Chuckle boots squeaked when he walked. Swifty thought, "Oh . . . I can work with this."

The young man had a weak handshake and mumbled when he talked. He never looked at Swifty, but averted his glance toward the window. Swifty said, "Glad to meet you, Peter . . . now look at me when I address you!"

Peter Phenet came to attention and faced Swifty in fear.

"You've been in the service . . . that's a good start. Now relax, Pete, and look at people when they talk. Hey, you have nice teeth. Let's get a drink." Swifty had the boy's attention.

Peter's story was typical. He had not been getting promoted at work. His girlfriend had little interest in him, he judged she was always shopping for a new guy, all the usual.

"Okay, we can work on this stuff. You're a vet and a college grad. You look good, speak well . . . we'll make some changes, but we have a good nucleus to work with. This is going to be fun, Peter . . . if you feel you want to go forward." Swifty ordered a couple of drinks and some chips.

"How much will it cost?" Peter asked.

"For my services: one thousand dollars in advance and one-fifth of your pretax second year's salary. No results or you're not happy, we'll keep it at the thousand. But the real cost to you up-front will be the investment in yourself. Clothes, car, haircut, maybe facials, gym work, diet counseling . . . still with me, Peter?" The boy nodded uncertainly, and Swifty went on. "Don't pay me the grand until you are sure I'm legitimate, Peter, but do follow my advice about your grooming."

"Where do we start?" the boy asked tentatively.

"What do you say we eat . . . have a few drinks . . . get to know one another, then we'll start an inventory and set a schedule." Swifty felt confident as he got into his pitch.

"Okay, let's do it!" Peter Phenet had made the best decision of his life . . . and maybe Swifty's.

They talked for hours. Peter was on vacation. His parents and girlfriend thought he was fishing in Mexico. He had come back early to meet with Swifty. He worked for General Alliance Insurance Company San Diego as an operations supervisor. He earned fifteen thousand dollars a year. Peter was smart. He was industrious. His degree was in business from San Diego State, and he knew a lot about business that wasn't being utilized by his employer.

When they parted, they were on the road to becoming friends. Peter agreed to return with a personal inventory of his strengths and weaknesses on the following Friday. They met again at the end of the week, went over the inventory, and set some goals for Peter. They also laid out a schedule, for meeting and for Peter to achieve certain milestones. Before Peter left town, he gave Swifty a check for five hundred dollars. Swifty was in business.

After the first meeting with Peter, he rushed home and opened his mail. Three of the nine applicants were bogus on their face: jokes. Four were from real losers who couldn't even spell, but two were very promising. Swifty returned all letters with a polite written response and called the two promising ones and two others. The last two were duds . . . but the other two were "hot!"

Becky Strahman, twenty-eight, skinny, bad legs, stringy brown hair, overeducated, and too pushy. He had read that bad breath mostly came from the teeth. Becky's teeth looked okay, but her breath was real bad. "Why," he thought, "wouldn't a woman recognize she had peach fuzz all over her face?" Becky was ready to go, but she didn't like to take orders from a man.

He had to finesse her into the necessary changes. She demanded a written report each month. Swifty agreed, if she would do the same. "Who for?" she asked. "For us, my dear, for us," he responded.

"You can knock off that 'my dear,' patronizing shit right now, buster!"

"Sure, Becky . . . but you're my accountant, say" – she was an associate with one of the old Big Eight firms – "wouldn't I be expected to rely on your professional judgment? Sure I would. Same deal here . . . only I'm the pro. Let me do it the right way . . . my way."

She looked skeptical.

"How long you been waiting to make partner in the 'old boys' club? How long since you had a date with a decent guy? Huh?" Swifty smiled and batted his lashes.

That did it. Becky tossed down her rye on the rocks and started to cry.

He handed her a handkerchief (he was getting used to that) and patted her on the shoulder. Becky and Swifty would be close pals for over twenty years, and she would become his accountant. It all started that day with her thousand-dollar check.

Chet Levine didn't seem to need any help. He was good looking, tall, and very well educated, with a master's from UCLA. He had been an athlete, a varsity basketball player at UC Santa Barbara, before transferring south to get the advanced degree. At twenty-nine, he had progressed normally in the bank where he worked. As an assistant vice president in the loan department, his future was promising.

"Chet . . . why do you need help? You seem to possess the whole package," Swifty probed.

"Swifty . . . Mr. King . . . I . . . um . . . I'm not what I seem. See, I want to meet some girls . . . get married . . . so I can show my employer I'm a normal guy." He began to sweat.

"What the hell, Chet, you queer or something? Geez, you have everything . . . any girl would be wild about a guy like you." Swifty slapped him on the back.

"Yes . . . I – "

"So you got it all. Maybe a little tune-up and that's it. Nothing could be wrong with you?" Swifty saw something in Chet's eyes that told him otherwise.

"I'm a homosexual, Swifty . . . or at least a bisexual. Guys like me aren't likely to go very far in banking. You kind of need a wife to move up the ladder." Chet didn't cry, but Swifty wished he had.

"Oh shit, I'm sorry . . . oh Chet . . . I didn't mean to be insulting. I didn't know . . . nobody could tell by looking at you." Swifty could have crawled under the carpet.

"Yeah, nobody wants to believe it, even me. That's why I need help. I've been everywhere, psychiatrists, hypnotists, rabbis, nobody can help. I . . . I . . . have a compulsion to have sex with men, women sometimes, but more often men."

Swifty must have looked apprehensive because Chet quickly followed with, "Don't worry . . . I don't throw people down and pounce on them in hotel lobbies . . . usually anyway." He smiled . . . a very nice smile.

"Chet, I'm not worried . . . but you said you want to meet girls or a girl . . . to get married. This would have to be one hell of an understanding girl. Why don't you just change jobs, move to San Francisco or someplace, and be who you are?"

"Because I want to be normal, that's why. Can't you help me?" The big guy looked lost.

"Shit . . . nobody ever said the 'advise' business would be easy. Sure, I may have to consult with a couple colleagues, but yeah . . . I can help. If I can't I won't take your time or charge you. In fact . . . I'm not going to charge you at all, unless you want to pay me later."

"That's not fair, Swifty. Here, I'll give you the thousand on account . . . on account of you're willing to try." Chet looked relieved and Swifty didn't know why.

So Swifty had three clients just like that. He was already helping two of the three. He didn't talk about any of it with Kim until he had the twenty-five hundred.

He sprung it on her over breakfast, matter-of-factly mentioning he had collected nonrefundable advances from three clients. "I'll set up a business account at the bank, like you, hon, then we won't get everything mixed up. We can draw on each account for our living expenses . . . I guess pay ourselves a salary . . . then use some for expenses. We can keep track for taxes. I guess that will work for now . . . if you agree. Later, I guess we'll need an accountant."

Kim was dumbfounded. She had worked hard for three years – studied night and day – to get to this income level. Now, here comes her "jailbird" husband, who can't find a job, making as much as her for one's weeks work. "Work! A scam . . . it was a scam he learned from that Nelson Leigh at prison. Oh! Damn it!" She cried to the bathroom mirror.

Kyle was very proud of Swifty. He couldn't help but tell Artie and Toni Marie. "He's really doing good. It has to be your influence, Mr. Leonardo . . . having Nelson Leigh give him all that coaching . . . and Mr. Grove too."

"Kyle, the man did it on his own. Those fellows just kick-started him a little. He has lots of moxy though. Got to hand it to him. You stay close to him . . . learn from him, teach him what you know that he don't . . . 'scuse me . . . doesn't. I want you to stay close to Jake too . . . he needs you . . . all you boys need each other. I just wish I could put you together. But Jake and Swifty wouldn't get along. How you doing with Jake?" Artie smiled knowingly.

"Jake's the boss. I let him be . . . I just put in a word here and there. We're okay, together." Kyle shook his head in the affirmative.

Toni Marie and Teresa pretended not to hear anything being said, as they busied themselves with some sewing.

"Hey, Toni . . . do you think I should let Swifty take a crack at improving me?" Kyle raised his tousled mop and tried to imitate a Shakespearean character.

"Mr. King in the magic business now, Kyle?" Her New Jersey idiom fit well with the sarcastic response.

"Yeah, Toni, maybe he is, maybe he is."

Toni Marie dropped a résumé in the mail addressed to Swifty's box. "I am very serious, Mr. King or Koenig . . . I need your help."

Swifty groaned when he read it, but placed a call to her at work.

"You're not going to meet with her!" Kim was astonished.

"How'd you know she sent me a letter? She tell?"

"No, the receptionist told everybody who would listen that my husband was calling Toni Marie Leonardo. How do you think I felt?" Kim was back on her high horse.

"I just called her to ask for suggestions about a gift for you and that is the truth. The fact that we have business is incidental and nobody else's affair," Swifty offered.

"So you are going to meet with her." Kim stood feet apart, hands on hips – her fighting stance.

"I must respond, even if it's to reject her request. It's only common courtesy."

"Send her a letter . . . I'll take it to her."

"Honey . . . honey, please relax. We'll talk to her together. We can help her together." Swifty hit the right cord.

"Okay. I'm free tomorrow from twelve to two."

"I'll set it up . . . or you can." Swifty looked inquiringly.

"No, you do it."

Toni Marie was not happy that Kim was going to be involved, but she wouldn't back off. Ten minutes into the conversation, she forgot Kim was there. Kim sat in a trance, seeing a part of her husband she never knew existed. She thought to herself, "You idiot. If you ever stopped thinking of yourself, you might have seen him growing up. God he's good."

"I'm fat. My bust is too small for my big shoulders and hips. My face looks like a man's. I feel like I need a shave. My brother used to tease me about it. Look at my arms . . . all hairy. My nose looks like I'm a prizefighter. My voice makes me sound like that girl in the movies who snaps her gum . . . like I come from a low-class area in Brooklyn. I don't know where I got all this. My mama is so pretty and Papa is like a movie star. Even Jakie . . . even he is good looking. I guess I'm the ugly duckling." Toni buried her face in her hands.

"Toni . . . you have an inner beauty that is so evident. All we have to do is bring more of it to the surface. You're very bright . . . you are pretty . . . and the other stuff is cosmetic. We can fix it. What I need to know, Toni . . . is . . . is . . . what do you want to do with your life?" Swifty opened with his modified standard pitch.

"I don't know."

"Well, we'll do an inventory. I'm going to give you an assignment for next time. You have already given me my assignment . . . to figure some ways to help with those cosmetic issues . . . not hard. Your job is the tough one . . . to find out who Toni is and who she . . . who you want to be." Swifty smiled.

"You'll take me? You'll help me?" Toni was excited.

"Sure he will," said Kim. "Sure he will."

Two birds with one stone! His own wife finally bought in to him. He was real again.

Toni Marie insisted on giving him a check. He tried to refuse, said, "Pay me later if you're happy with the result." But Toni wouldn't have it. She cut a check for one thousand. Kim raised her eyebrows.

Later she said, "My husband . . . the talking gigolo . . . doesn't even have to take his pants off. My, my, I am impressed."

"Just doing my job, ma'am, just doing my job." Swifty smiled.

"What can I do to help? I mean those awful clothes she wears . . . that ugly hair . . . she needs a cute haircut. She could get a nose job . . . voice lessons . . . electrolysis . . . and . . ." Kim saw Swifty writing it down.

"You just helped. Give me some clothes ideas . . . maybe take her to a nice store and to the hairdresser. I'm going to make a personal plan for her to build her confidence. See, honey, this is what I do. This is my new life's work." Swifty looked up at her.

"Yeah. Yeah and I must admit, you got potential, kid. You really have developed the 'gift.'" She bent over and kissed him.

Swifty wanted to drive right out that moment and share with Nelson. That would have to wait.

CHAPTER 28

THE WORKS

"LOOK, NORM, IF the kid is this good, one of us should hire him. He won't work with Jake . . . he doesn't want to be associated with me, but you got a lot going on. This boy can help you. I want you to talk with him." Artie leaned over in his patio chair and stretched to let the droplets of sweat roll down his back. He held the phone loosely to protect from the loud outburst from Norm Cellestine. Norm, hard of hearing since his war days, had no idea how to modulate his voice.

"Arthur, the young girl is doing wonderful. She was our top producer. Why would we want him in the fold too? We already have a hook in him," Norm barked.

"Keep it down, Norm. You're busting my eardrums. Can anybody hear you there?" Artie stretched against the heat of the evening and wiped his face with a towel using his free hand.

"Nobody is here. I'll try to talk quieter, but these damn phones are no good." Norm said, adjusting his hearing aids.

"Okay, well look . . . just talk to the boy. It would be good to have him completely with us. No telling when a guy might get religion. Nelson says he is full of himself over this business he's got going." Artie stood and let the towel fall from his naked body.

"Yeah, Toni Marie probably told you. He's helping her do some kind of a makeover. Hell, she's a cute little girl . . . doesn't need nothing," Norm barked again.

"Well, kids always think the answer is in a bottle or makeup kit. Her mother says it makes her feel better, so what harm can it do. Anyway, I got to go in the pool and cool off, Norm. Just talk to the boy." Artie didn't wait for a response, but hung up and stepped into the warm water.

Norm Cellestine put on his nicest, "honey-sweet" demeanor and ambled up to Kim's cubicle. "Ms. Koenig . . . Kim? Hi. Busy I bet . . . but got just one second?"

"Yes sir, Mr. Cellestine," she said standing, with the phone tucked under her chin. "Call you right back, Suzy . . . the boss needs me. Bye."

"Oh, you didn't need to do that. I could have waited." He bowed his head and broadened his ever-present smile. (I swear he looked just like Lyndon Johnson – a skinny version – when he did that!)

"No bother, sir."

"What I was wondering . . . uh, is your husband available, do you know if he could meet with me? At his convenience, of course." Norm looked, face pushed forward with his eyebrows raised.

"I could call him, sir. I expect he's home. Most of his appointments are in the afternoon and evening this week," Kim said flatly, wondering what in the world her boss would want with Swifty.

"If you think he'd take my call, I'll dial him up now, if that seems appropriate," Norm squeaked.

"Yes, sir . . . here's the number." She wrote furiously on a notepad and thrust it at him.

"Honey, I am old enough to be your daddy, but this is an informal office . . . please just call me Norm. Shucks . . . you're the one feedin' us all these days." With that, he turned and ambled double time to his office.

Kim saw Swifty before he saw her. He was dressed in a smart blue blazer, beige trousers, cordovan loafers, a soft yellow shirt, and a dark striped tie. Bouncing up the two flagstone steps and into the sunshaded glass door, he looked like a fashion model. Even his tan and haircut were perfect.

"Good morning, Mrs. King, he whispered in her ear." He had pretended to sneak up behind her, knowing full well that she had seen him come in and purposely turned back to her listing file on the credenza.

"Oh, it's Cary Grant . . . my, what are you doing here?" she fluttered.

"Your boss wants me to turn him into Ronald Reagan. He told me you gave him the number. Lunch after?" Swifty was supremely confident these days – especially when in his "business mode."

"Guess so . . . if you can spare the time," Kim said with a note of sarcasm.

Norm Cellestine rained charm all over him. After hurling superlatives, mostly unwarranted, he asked Swifty if he was interested in joining Cellestine Enterprises as a district manager, after a brief training program. Swifty reminded him that he had no real estate license. Norm said he had another type role, outside of real estate, in mind for Swifty . . . one more in the area of business development. Norm asked him to think it over, get back to him, and if he was interested, they could talk specific, "duties, money and all."

At lunch Swifty told Kim about the meeting, which he found quite curious. "Betcha it has something to do with the Leonardos. Sounds like the old man is getting nervous about me."

"Oh, honey, you can't be serious. You don't even know for sure there's a connection between Norm and Leonardo," Kim said skeptically. Inside she was feeling insecure about how she got her job, where that ten thousand they had received actually came from, and what would be required of them in the future. Swifty was thinking the same thing.

"Look. You're a pro now and in demand. You can go anyplace. If Cellestine's operation makes you nervous . . . hell, quit. We'll move to LA or someplace. We can do our thing anywhere. We're good! C'mon, baby, lighten up!" He smiled and they finished their meal in silence.

Three days later Swifty called Norm Cellestine and thanked him for his interest, but explained that he was developing his own business and wished to pursue that endeavor. Norm said he understood and wished Swifty luck. "Maybe when it's going good I'll buy it from you and get the benefit of your skills that way."

"Never can tell what the future will bring, Mr. Cellestine." Swifty rang off and began to plan his next move. He had resolved the day he and Kim had lunch that he would need to meet with Artie Leonardo to tell "the man" to back off.

Peter Phenet was beside himself. "I lost eleven pounds. All I did was give up desserts and start exercising. Hell, I just went back to my army workouts."

"You're doing very well, Pete. Are you doing the affirmations? Have you written down your short – and long-term goals?" Swifty looked Peter in the eye and was met with a good, sincere gaze. He reached out to shake hands and felt a firm, decisive grip.

"Good man, Pete. Let's look at those goals."

Peter had written too many short-term goals, many of which would be so difficult he would be disillusioned by not achieving them. His long term goals were good: to be president of General Alliance Insurance Company by age forty; to be married with two kids by that time; to own, outright, a house at Coronado; to own a thirty-foot fishing boat; and to belong to a first-rate club. Good goals for a thirty-year-old.

Swifty got Pete to cut down the short terms to some "easy wins," followed by three stretch goals. He was to change his wardrobe; wear only suits and white shirts to work; get his shoes shined every day; stop by the big boss's office once a week to ask how he was doing; and read one book per week. The stretches were to get promoted to department manager by the end of the year and to hit the twenty-thousand-dollar-a-year barrier at that same time. Pete had already cut his hair, shaved the fuzzy mustache, and trimmed his sideburns. Pete wrote him a check for another five hundred.

Becky Strahman had an eight-hundred-dollar experience at Wonderland (which, incidentally costs upwards of five grand now), where she had her hair done, learned to work out properly, was given a nutritional regimen, and had the fuzz removed from her face. A dentist and a daily tongue comb were put on her agenda, and smoking was eliminated from her life. She gained seven pounds and had something round on her body for the first time since babyhood.

"Hey doll . . . you a feminist?" Swifty joked.

"If I didn't need your smart ass I'd kick it, boy. Do you think I look better?" Becky, probably for the first time in her life, wiggled like a real girl.

"You look fantastic. Too bad I'm married. By the way, I really want you to meet my wife." Swifty shocked Becky with this one.

"Why, she have a thing for skinny girls? I would have thought a 'babe' like you would be nearly enough." This time her smart aleck attitude didn't seem quite so shrill.

"We have a need for some accounting help. I thought you could give us some ideas. Would you mind? Of course I'd pay you." Swifty felt a little sheepish about asking once the words came out.

"Swifty, if it doesn't bother you to mix and match . . . sure, maybe I scratch yours, you scratch mine, eh?" Becky poked him in the ribs.

Kim might find Becky just a little too much a "piece of work." He'd have to see.

"Now, on those goals. You sure got the appearance stuff done. Great-looking suit . . . nice shoes. You are a killer, Becky. They should make you partner just on your looks . . . 'course as a feminist you'd have to turn the offer down," Swifty joked.

"Only if I have to screw the old bastards . . . now let me show you these goals. Swifty, I'm stoked. I want to get right to the meat of it. These idiots don't deserve me and I don't want to be a partner in that stuffy joint for the rest of my days. I want to run my own business! Goddamn it! I know I can do it. You help and I'll do your books gratis . . . for fucking ever!" She poked him in the chest.

"Becky . . . short-term goal." She nodded and looked questioningly. "No more profanity in public . . . no more loud talk . . . at least until you make your first million, okay?" She nodded and stuck her tongue in her right cheek.

Then she smiled, leaned over, and kissed him on the cheek. "Yes, sir, you chauvinist SOB." No more bad breath.

Chet Levine was surprised, but not upset. Swifty had just told him to quit his job. "The leadership at the bank has left you feeling you have to go against your nature to get ahead. Chet, you can't live a lie and feel good about yourself. It's going to come out sometime, some way. Get out of the situation and go someplace where being Chet and reaching your career goals work together."

"So I should maybe open a gay bathhouse, Swifty?" he chuckled.

Swifty had not really understood the term *gay* before, but he got the drift.

"Sure . . . that would work . . . or maybe a consulting business in your area of expertise. You are so damn smart, you have endless contacts, and you have some cash. Seems a great time to get into something of your own that doesn't crowd your 'inner self.'" Swifty pushed it a bit, but Chet didn't blink.

"Never thought of it. Let me kick it around with my dad. You know anybody that's gone into their own thing lately, Swift? Like somebody that could push me in the right direction?" Chet was intrigued.

"Matter of fact I do, me for one and another person I work with. Let's both do some checking." Swifty was thinking of Becky's recent pronouncement.

CHAPTER 29

SWIFTY AND ARTIE

PELTZ HAD JUST taken his teenage children to LAX for their return to Switzerland. He felt guilty about them. Ute had become the complete American "chick." He earned, she spent. His divorce was final now for three years, and Ute was pressing, pressing, pressing for marriage. Peltz was struggling with his golf swing. His nose kept itching. Artie was on him for better profits. Annoyances. He hated annoyances.

He pulled the rental car into the lot at Santa Monica Airport, dropped the keys and contract in the box, and legged it over to Jim's Air. He punched the code into the keypad, slid the gate back, and thrust his hands into his pockets. Why was it always colder and windier inside an airport gate than outside? Someday he'd run a study.

Learjet. Good, he'd be in at the clinic before ten. He'd sleep, then hit the lab before the staff got in. This would be fun.

Takeoff was on time, weather was good, and they were down and buttoned up at nine fifteen. Customs was a breeze, so he arrived at the clinic at ten of ten. A tamale, a beer ... some coffee, and to bed in the guest suite. At five forty he was in his white coat, pacing the lab, waiting for coffee to brew. The dogs began to cry for food when they smelled the coffee. He buzzed the kennel boy. The kid was there in a minute and began walking the animals and feeding them.

At six the scientists and physicians began to arrive. By seven the presentation had begun. Thirty-one months of trials, twenty-four patients . . .

all surviving. Fourteen kidneys, two bladders, three livers, two lungs, and three hearts. Prognosis was good on all but the hearts. The lungs and livers required constant enzyme bathing, but the bladders and kidneys were only supported with antirejection drugs. Not bad. Not bad after that first fiasco. Shit. Nine of them had died back then.

He thought, "Now Artie will get off my ass. We are in the legitimate transplantation business for real and we have a virtually endless supply source. We'll pull people from all over the world to this center. We'll be internationally famous. I'm going to be on the front page of *Time*, *Newsweek*, *Match*, *Fortune*, and the *New England Journal* all in the same month."

After the presentation, he called Artie.

"You will not believe the success we are having here. You need to come see for yourself. I can't talk about it on the phone, but you must see it. Uh, no . . . none of the problems of before . . . just a few rejections . . . normal. Look, Arthur . . . we are saving lives here. How can it be antireligious . . . forget your Catholic sensibilities . . . think Jewish . . . oh, that's even worse. Well, God would love you for this . . . it's a good thing to save lives . . . come see it anyway. Okay . . . Okay. Bye-bye."

"Philistine. The man doesn't comprehend anything but finance. I prepare to share greatness with him, and he . . . he doesn't get it."

Louis Peltz was mumbling audibly and the others began to look up from their tables. "Fine work, ladies and gentlemen, you are all to be commended for this keystone accomplishment!"

Accolades meant more to these people than paychecks. He knew that. They also understood that they had been entrusted with one of the most far-reaching scientific discoveries in modern medical history, albeit in secret.

Artie hung up the phone and leaned back in his chair. He looked at the clear blue sky and blew air from his cheeks.

"What's the matter, Pop?" Jake was lifting a twenty-pound barbell up and down in a piston motion with his right arm and sipping coffee with his left.

"You know, Jakie, you are starting to look like the Incredible Hulk. Seems appropriate that Kyle calls you 'Mr. Bixby,'" Artie snorted, but with a smile.

"That little asshole calls me names? What's this Bixby shit supposed to mean? I'll bend him in half . . . he makes smart remarks!" Jake said indignantly.

"Bill Bixby is the actor on TV who plays the guy before he turns into the Hulk, who is Lou Ferrigno, or something like that," his Mother said. "And don't be using bad language around here. Also, Jacob, you leave Kyle alone or you will have to deal with me!"

"Jake, listen to your mother," Artie said. "Besides, you have a master's degree . . . why must you continue to talk and act like a street punk? My god, man, you are almost thirty-five years old . . . you're married, soon to be a father yourself. Act it."

"Mama, Papa, how come when I visit you I get treated like a kid? Toni Marie, now she's to be treated like a young woman, but me . . . naw, I'm to be ridiculed, and in front of my wife too," Jake whimpered, half-kidding.

"Your wife sleeps till noon. She hears nothing. When she wakes, on goes her mouth, off goes her ears. Your sister works. She attempts to improve herself," Teresa offered.

"Now, now . . . enough of that stuff, the girl is with child. She needs her rest. Jakie, come out on the patio with me. Bring your barbell if you want. I'll brief you on what the call was about." Artie lifted his sixty-year old frame from the chair, beginning to feel the early signs of arthritis.

"Pop, if what Louis says is for real, my god, this is a breakthrough in medicine like the cure for polio. The FDA or whoever regulates this stuff won't allow it, but we can harvest organs out of Mexico and sell them for millions. Let me take a run down there and confer with Peltz. This thing could be big, very big, and we don't want it screwed up." Jake was very serious.

"Jakie, it just doesn't sound right to me. What was that weird book that Jules Verne wrote . . . *The Island of Dr. Somebody*? I mean it's sacrilegious. Maybe we both better take a run down there." Artie didn't relish getting around medical facilities, but he felt uncomfortable letting Jake go by himself.

"*Island of Dr. Moreau* and it was H. G. Wells who wrote it, Pop. Look, we use animals for research. This is just the next step. John Wayne had a pig's valve in his heart for a while . . . it's just science."

Unlike his father's moral concerns, Jake was interested in only the financial aspects of the Mexico business. He noted that most of the other "expats" down there that used to be competitors are now in the drug business. It was his contention that their medical practices would be left alone as long as the right hands were "greased." What his father had heard from Peltz made his hair stand on end.

"We'll see . . . ," Artie said. "We'll see."

Artie was getting a haircut on Main Street when Augie Bash found him. It was just a quick walk around the corner from his office . . . the small one, in the unmarked building on First Street, that Norm Cellestine had leased him at twenty-two cents a square foot.

"Hey, Arthur . . . glad I found you. This morning I got a call from the kid. He wants to meet with you. What do you want me to tell him?"

Augie was out of breath just from the short walk.

"Good morning, Augie, and just which kid are you talking about? My kid, your kid, the barber's kid?"

"The kid . . . King, he calls himself now. Wants . . . he wants to meet with you." Augie sat down in a chair to catch his breath.

"Okay, I have an office. Tell him to come and see me during office hours," Artie said matter-of-factly.

"Might I suggest you meet away from the office, perhaps out on a golf course or something," Augie belched.

"Might I suggest you lose some weight before you and Dominic become bookends. And, I accept your suggestion, which is a good one. Please arrange it." Artie stepped from the chair and admired his trim. "God, I'm old," he thought to himself.

"Your suggestion is good too. Maybe Jake can help me," Augie gasped.

"Jake would kill you in fifteen minutes. He works out a tad too hard for you, Augie. But you might ask Amber for some nutritional help. She has some kind of degree in that stuff. Jesus, a degree in eating! I hope she has some education in motherhood too . . . 'cause she is only about a month away." Artie paid the barber, tipped him liberally, and let Augie hold the door open for him.

Toni Marie sat picking at a fruit salad while Pam lapped up the last of a burger and fries. "You're so lucky not to have to worry about your figure. Every time I take a bite it goes right to my hips."

"Yeah, well . . . your diet, is umh . . . umh, 'cuse me . . . is working good. How much have you lost?" Pam wasn't thin, but her frame, at five-nine, could carry a good deal of weight.

"Nineteen . . . I'm shooting for twenty five. Thank you for noticing."

"Are you taking voice lessons? You sound different." Pam finished her fries and took a pull on a Coke.

"Yes, Mr. King has me with Professor Dague at ASU. Next month I go to LA to have my deviated septum repaired. My life is getting more and more exciting." Toni Marie smiled.

"So, anything going on with Mr. King and you? I mean you spend so much time together," Pam asked confidentially.

"Of course not! I am surprised you would say such a thing, Pam. You know how I feel about Kim. In fact, she sits in on some of our sessions. They are true professionals." Toni was trying to seem even more naive than she actually was.

"Yeah, well . . . don't let me get a shot at him. Kim's my friend too, but all's fair as they say." Pam smiled.

"That's something I wanted to talk to you about . . . stuff like that," Toni said.

"Like me and Walt?" Pam asked.

"No, like you and my married brother, Jake."

"What?"

"Look, Pam, I know you have been seeing my brother for over a year. I don't know if Walt suspects or if you're even that serious about poor Walter, but that's your business." Toni pressed in on Pam.

Pam turned red and appeared to be trying to find some way to respond. Before she could conjure something up, Toni bore on.

"You realize that my brother's wife, Amber, is about to have a baby. You also know that when she caught you and Jakie last year she left him for two months. That should have sent the message to you that you were and are just a dalliance to Jake . . . just another 'floozy,' just another cheap 'lay,' just another 'two-bit wh – '" Toni moved closer when Pam cut her off.

"Toni, please don't do this. I'm sorry . . . I should have been up-front with you. I feel like shit. It's just that . . . that it's hard to give Jake up. I try and then he calls. He always seems to know when Walt is gone to California. He's your brother, but I can tell you he really knows how to treat a woman. Amber doesn't appreciate him." Pam buried her face in her hands and appeared to cry.

Toni moved face-to-face with her: "I am not so naive, baby, so don't give me this crap. You drop Jake now or I'm telling Walt, Norm Cellestine, and my father . . . I know you don't want that." Toni's brown eyes flashed with the laser strength of her Dad's gray pupils.

Pam took her hands down. Her eyes were dry. She looked defeated.

"Okay, hey . . . hey now, don't do that, Toni. I'm just having some fun with Jake. He buys me things. I know he gets Buck to send Walt to LA. I'll beg off him, I promise. Please don't tell anybody . . . please." Pam seemed slightly more sincere in her pleading.

"First and last warning, Pammy . . . I'll get lunch." Toni smiled sweetly.

At the very time Toni Marie Leonardo and Pam Hurst were meeting over lunch, Artie Leonardo was entertaining Swifty King on the golf course at Carefree Ranch.

"Your swing isn't that bad . . . you just need some lessons. Your turn is good." Artie had just outdriven Swifty by forty yards. "Be sure you get those wrists cocked, keep your head down, and follow through. Next hole I'll show you."

Swifty put his driver in the bag, sat hard in the cart, and waited for Artie to drive. "It's cart paths only?" he asked.

"Yeah, but I cheat. Nobody is ever out here. The old members can't walk it anyway. What did you want to see me about, Swifty." Artie was casual in his question.

Swifty was surprised that Artie Leonardo would wear shorts. His legs were tanned and as well formed as the rest of him. He said he played twice a week. It showed.

"Well . . . it's about a lot of things. Number one" – Swifty started slowly as Artie leaned toward him, driving the cart on to the fairway toward his ball – "I am growing uncomfortable with our involvement."

"What involvement? We met three times in five years. How is this involvement?" Artie said lightly.

Swifty hit a respectable second shot with a five iron that landed a few yards short of the green.

"Nice shot!" Artie pulled up to his ball, hit on the green, and watched his ball run to within ten feet of the hole.

"Now, that was a shot," said Swifty. He hit on and three-putted for a six. Artie easily pared the hole.

"What I mean is, the help you provided me by putting Nelson Leigh in as my jailhouse 'guardian,' your having Kyle Faust steer me into a job with a company in which you have interest, my wife's position at Cellestine . . . that I suspect you own a large piece of – "

Artie interrupted. "Look, Swifty, Nelson was there. We just asked him to keep an eye on you. Geez, they'd have eaten you up in there. All that 'coaching' shit he did on his own. Far as the job . . . we needed a guy, Kyle was driving me and suggested it . . . he had some knowledge that we might have met. Your wife . . . now your wife is Norm's top producer . . . God, man, you and she are doing us a favor. Fact is, I do own a piece of Norm's operation. How is an ex-con like me supposed to make a living? You know about that!"

"Sir, you don't have to justify helping me . . . I truly appreciate it . . . as well as the job offers and the cash, but I'm just getting uncomfortable with all of it. I guess I'm asking you to back off . . . . a little." Swifty stood on the tee box, looking up at the laser gray eyes of Artie Leonardo.

"Hit your ball," Artie said gruffly.

Swifty hit a better shot . . . about 220 yards just off the fairway.

"Much better." Artie took an easy swing and put his ball fifteen yards beyond Swifty's and on the fairway.

"Course management . . . that's the key, once you have the basics down." Artie walked to the cart, dropped his driver in the bag, and sat in the driver's seat looking at Swifty.

"Do you know what I mean, sir? About backing off?"

"Time was, I'd kick a man's ass for being ungrateful and, or, telling me to back off. Look, son, I owe you . . . I'm grasping for ways to display my appreciation . . . to pay my debts and – "

"To protect your investment?" Swifty tried to ease the words he had just spoken.

"You better close your eyes, kid, because I am going to kick your ass," he said quietly. "If what you said wasn't true, I'd do it in anger!" Artie threw his head back and roared. His laughter stirred up a nest of quail nearby that burst into the air, momentarily, then settled back into the brush to feed.

Swifty waited until Arthur Leonardo settled down to see what his final demeanor was likely to be. Once he saw Artie was truly in good humor, he relaxed.

"One thing you better be aware of is that Phoenix, I mean Greater Phoenix, is a small place. It's not like LA or New York where there may be rocks to hide behind. This is open desert . . . and the oasis is small. Certain people know which way the water flows and who is swimming in it. Nothing goes on politically without Goldwater's knowing it. Nobody makes a move in business without me knowing it. It's live and let live if nobody crosses the other guy's path . . . but if there is a cross-up, well, there better be a quick apology and correction. If not, things become unpleasant."

"I'd never cross you, sir . . . I believe I have already proven that," Swifty said.

At the turn, Artie said, "Okay, Mr. King. I understand your concern. I will move back a few notches. It's clear you don't want to work for me. Fine. You go it alone. I hear from my little girl you're doing pretty good too . . . even though her nose job and new clothes are costing me a bundle. But, understand, I will always be here if you need me . . . and . . . and this is a big AND, *I RESERVE THE RIGHT TO KEEP AN EYE ON YOU*. There is no negotiation on that one. Understood?"

"I think so, sir."

"Good. Does backing off exclude you and me not playing a game of golf now and then?" Artie smiled.

"No, sir. I'd like that. I like playing golf with you. I like you," Swifty said.

"Will you take a suggestion?" Swifty nodded affirmatively. "Go to court and change your name legally. Later it may make it easier for you to erase your record and get your voting rights back. Look into it."

They played on. Swifty shot ninety-seven, Artie eight-one.

CHAPTER 30

THE REAL MR. KING

SWIFTY BROACHED THE subject of the formal name change gingerly. He couched it as necessary to petition to get his voting rights back . . . to erase the stigma of prison and, "Hell, *King* sounds good." Kim said, "What's wrong with *Queen*? Remember Ellery Queen?" (Jim Hutton was one of the last ones . . . remember the dad of Timothy?)

Swifty remembered Ellery Queen, but he liked the name *King* better.

Kim reminded him that all of her licenses and his were in the name of *Koenig*, as were their bank accounts, social security numbers; all their friends in California knew them as Koenig. He said, "Paperwork, I'll do it all. We'll send a Christmas card announcing our new identity. We'll make it fun." She said, "Oh, okay . . . I guess now that you're Cary Grant instead of Archibald

. . . uh." She struggled to remember.

"Leach . . . Archie Leach."

"Yeah, him."

Eight months and nine hundred dollars later, they were Mr. and Mrs. Colin S. King. He liked it. She remarked that she had only slept with one man in her life though she had been married to two.

PART FOUR

CHAPTER 31

SUCCESS

THE YEARS WENT by and business got better and better. Swifty amassed nineteen paying clients. Kim was top producer at Cellestine Enterprises three straight years. Artie and Jake visited the Cliniquè de Obregón and were amazed at what Peltz and his team had wrought. Jake convinced Artie, at least superficially, that what was going on at the clinic was not immoral – though quite illegal, even in Mexico. Norm Cellestine's business empire expanded and flourished. Pam and Walter married and joined the commercial sales team in Los Angeles.

Toni Marie entered nurse's training at UCLA and graduated with a bachelor of science degree to add to her BA. She continued her work with Swifty. Her accent faded with her hips. By thirty, she was a svelte one hundred twelve. Thanks to medical science and a great makeover, her facial and arm hair disappeared, her nose got smaller and turned up, and her hair became a short, black bonnet that wreathed her pretty face. "I owe it all to that sexy husband of yours," she told Kim.

"All the girls tell me that!" Kim smiled.

Connor Grove was released from Safford and moved to Switzerland. Before his departure, he gave Swifty his golf clubs and Nelson his stamp collection. Nelson planned to use it as his "stake" upon his parole.

Artie's wealth began to be more relevant in the Phoenix area. More and more, his fellow club members, especially Norm Cellestine, hit him up for charitable contributions. Before long, he was chairing as many fund-raisers as Norm. He and Teresa began to enjoy the limelight. Of course, there were whispers that Arthur Leonardo had once been in prison, but no one pursued the issue. He was such a nice man.

Jimmy Carter was a nice man too and smart. But, unlike Artie Leonardo, circumstances did not favor him. A second worldwide oil crunch, a hostage crisis in Iran, and a follow-on recession saw interest rates balloon out of sight. Home sales stopped and businesses failed. Jimmy Carter lost his reelection bid. Artie and Norm just tucked in to wait for the cycle to turn. Kim's commission income was hit hard, but she busied herself with resales and remodels. Swifty didn't even notice the problem. His people were the ones who profited from the unrest.

Peter Phenet not only became a department head at General Alliance Insurance Company, he was promoted to vice president of business development, reporting to the president. A year earlier, already one of the company's youngest department heads, Peter had taken his ideas to the "old man" and received a surprising response. "I've been waiting for somebody in this stodgy old company to think of something new . . . your real estate ideas may be just what we need. I'm bringing you into my office to work directly with me on this."

Peter had called Swifty to tell him the old man had raised him to $50 "K" a year! But one problem: with interest rates so high, he had no way to find an appropriate partner willing to throw in with General Alliance on the Southern California development project he had in mind. Swifty said he'd look into it. He called Augie Bash to set up a meeting with "the man."

Becky Strahman was a super tax consultant, and her partnership with Chet Levine was, if not a marriage made in heaven, a great business deal. Swifty had introduced them. Becky almost fainted when this tall, handsome guy smiled at her. What intrigued her further is that the "jock" was smart . . . smart about business. It wasn't until their fourth meeting that Becky raised the idea of partnership. Chet said he liked the concept. Later, after dinner and too much wine, she hoped they were about to consummate their "union" when Chet abruptly announced, "Becky, baby, I'm a 'switch-hitter.'" She pulled back momentarily, then smiled and moved into his arms. "Screw it, Chetty boy, so am I!"

Swifty didn't really need the details of their intimate behavior, but he got it anyway . . . from Becky. "Shit, I don't care what he does, he doesn't care what I do . . . with same sex . . . but we're going to be true to each other with our opposite sex and – "

"Okay, Becky, that's cool . . . your business. But, how about your real business deal? Is it going to work or blow apart the first time one of you finds the other 'bopping' a client?"

"No sweat, Swift . . . we talked it out. We're going to make the whole deal work. If we fight a little, that lends spice to it. Main thing is . . . we have a plan . . . we're going to take advantage of the new good times on the horizon. 'Strahman and Levine' . . . Swifty, we are your new financial advisors! Now you get great tax advice, plus the best investment – and money-management team in the business. You can't lose, boy!" Becky was hopping around the room. People in the Beverly Wilshire Hotel lobby were beginning to notice.

"Great . . . great, but what's that going to cost me?" Swifty smiled nervously.

"Plenty, but we're going to make you so much money you won't care!"

And so they did.

CHAPTER 32

NO IMMUNITY FROM TRANSFORMATION

SWIFTY HAD STRUCK up a relationship with a young Beverly Hills plastic surgeon who had answered his ad in *Forbes* magazine. Stuart Rosenfeld was shy, cerebral, and totally focused on his medical specialty. Stuart couldn't understand why he wasn't more successful in solo practice. Five years of understudy with a noted practitioner, who was phasing out toward retirement, had left him with a good reputation, but something wasn't clicking. A friend had shown him the ad and suggested he write Swifty. He preferred not to say who the friend might be. (*I know. It was Chet Levine. – KKF.*)

Stu didn't realize that his shyness translated to the client. Swifty told him, "Stu, you have to loosen up. Sure, they want you to be 'Mr. Doctor Rosenfeld,' the pro surgeon, but you also have to be a friend. For god's sake, you're going to know the sex symbol's tits aren't real and the leading man had his removed. You're going to see the aging screen siren's beefy hips while you lipo under them . . . and the muscle man's real *swanze*, not the one that gets pasted on for the sexy close-up. Think about it, buddy, you gotta be their hairdresser . . . their therapist." Swifty could see it so clearly. Stu couldn't.

"Hairdresser . . . fifteen years of training and I'm a hairdresser?"

"Not trying to insult, Stu . . . look, I have a friend, a nurse . . . okay if I bring her in on a confidential consult?" Swifty smiled his most supportive smile.

"Why do I need to meet another nurse? I have two here . . . and a nurse practitioner?" Stu asked skeptically.

Toni Marie walked in wearing a prim business suit and a Judith Leiber purse, smiled once, and stole the celibate surgeon's heart. "Hello, Dr. Rosenfeld, do you remember me? You assisted on my surgery."

"Ms. Leonardo, I had no idea you were a nurse. I see Dr. Maelstroff's work has held up well

. . . I mean, you look good." Stu was stammering about.

Stu had assisted him on several surgeries in the seventies as he and his boss, Benjamin Wadell, attempted to perfect new techniques using lasers. Wadell had become so wealthy that he decided to write, teach, and play golf rather than continue with the business risk associated with surgery. Stu bought him out. Maelstroff continued to be an associate, but not a competitor. Stu's heavy financial burden – the rent at an upscale Beverly Hills address, the high-priced technicians, and debt service to the loan he obtained to pay out Wadell – kept him strapped. His revenues were falling rather than rising. He needed all the help he could get.

"Yessir, I completed nurse's training two years ago and have been working on a Physician Assistant Fellowship at UCLA. My purpose here, though, is to help Mr. King help you. And, and . . . thank you for the compliment. You look good too." Stu blushed so that his ears matched the color of his thinning hair.

For four hours, Swifty and Toni tag-teamed Stu on how to relax . . . how to probe the most vulnerable reaches of his patients in a way that would bind them closer together. Before the evening was over, it was Stu and Toni that had been bound.

Stu told Swifty that he couldn't afford to pay his fee: ten thousand up-front and 20 percent of the second-year increase in his revenues. Swifty said, "Stu, pay me what you can. I'll come up with a plan that will serve us both well. First, let's get your income commensurate with your talents." Stu liked that.

Within eighteen months, Toni Marie was working in Stu's office as a surgical nurse, while attending UCLA's Physician Assistant program. A PA is almost a doctor: having taken all the required classes, but without passing the exams, doing the internship and residencies to be an MD. Toni found out later that the leap was more psychological than academic. Her addition and the weekly coaching by Swifty had helped Stu increase his practice by 40 percent. He was on his way to financial stability. Emotionally, however, a certain toll was taken. Stu had left his religion, become "nonobservant" soon after bar mitzvah. His parents were disturbed, but also proud of their son, "the doctor." Now Stu had fallen in love . . . for the first time . . . and with a *shiksa* princess; and it didn't sell well with his psyche, never mind his mother!

Swifty arranged for several clients to "see" Stu Rosenfeld. In return, a share of their surgical fee, classified by the accounting and financial consulting firm of Strahman-Levine as "special consultancy," found its way to Swifty's bank account. All of Swifty's fees were channeled to the same firm. All of his clients eventually used the same firm. Even Cellestine Enterprises and the Leonardo Companies (Jake's multitude of companies) were soon using the same firm. Becky was true to her word; Swifty paid dearly for her and Chet's services, but they made him wealthy.

When Ronald Reagan became president, interest rates went down and the real estate business gradually got better. Kim found herself traveling back and forth between Phoenix and the California cities of Los Angeles, San Francisco, and San Diego. She divided her time between residential and commercial properties. Swifty's schedule was equally challenging. He worked the coast and the eastern seaboard, having dropped his simple ad into *Forbes* and the *Wall Street Journal*. The Kings saw their incomes skyrocket.

Swifty was very proud of Kim and her success. He was nearly equally proud of his "children": Peter, Chet, Becky, Toni Marie, Stu, and the three dozen others. All but two "duds" had achieved varying degrees of success. They all owed at least a part of their success to Swifty. All remained friends and confidants. Only Stu exhibited any guilt. He had become Jekyll and Hyde. On the job, he emerged as "Mr. Charm," schmoozing his way through. Alone with Toni, he anguished over what he felt was the compromise of his professional ethics and abandonment of his religion. She "soothed" his guilt in every possible way. Before long, the squat, balding "Dr. Look Good," as the Hollywood crowd referred to him, was wearing Armani suits and squiring the chic Toni Marie Leonardo to all the hot West Side eateries. They were married in a civil ceremony in Beverly Hills. Artie Leonardo threw them a first-class reception at the Beverly Hilton. Teresa cried. Stu's mother cried. Stu cried. Swifty, who was best man, laughed out loud.

Artie was dubious about the marriage, but "anything for the angel," that's what he called Toni Marie back then. He had stalled Swifty for a few months about a proposition with General Alliance that he had proposed on behalf of Peter Phenet, but at the wedding he was ready to talk.

"Mr. King, thank you for being here. By the way, that deal we talked about earlier . . . the land development thing in Orange County. I think I have an interested party for you. Can you get your guy to Hawaii in about a week? My people will be there if you can." Artie bore in on Swifty with those gray beacons of his.

"Yes, sir. Just say where and when, and we will be there." Swifty smiled back.

"Give Augie your guy's name. He'll know where and when. Excuse me. I must dance with my daughter." Artie moved toward the bride with some effort. Swifty was aware that his arthritis was getting worse.

It was at this time that Kyle Faust (me, of course) let the alcohol get the better of his taciturn nature. Not responsible for driving "the man," he glued himself to Swifty and Kim, getting them drinks and not sparing his own. "Swifty, ole buddy . . . I got a favor to ask . . . ," a slightly drunk Kyle slurred.

"Anything you want, my friend. Anything you want!" an equally tipsy Swifty King responded.

"Careful, hotshot," cautioned Kim. "This bumpkin has a master's in business."

Kyle had taken courses religiously at Artie's direction until he held two undergrad degrees – one in business management and another in English literature. More recently he had taken a master's in business, having completed his thesis in Focused Resource Allocation.

"I know the sucker is smart, but he looks so docile . . . I can't deny him," Swifty chuckled.

"What can I do for ya?" Swifty steered Kyle from the noisy table toward the hall.

"You won't laugh."

"Sure I'll laugh, but I'll listen. Listening is my specialty and advice is my game."

"Okay . . . okay. See, Swift, I'm way over thirty." The slightly tipsy Swifty lifted his eyebrows. "I'm tired of just being a runner for Artie and a shadow manager for Jake. I want to be my own guy. Do my own deals. Hey, I don't even have a girlfriend . . . not a permanent one anyway. I was hoping you could give me some advice. Shit . . . I don't make enough to pay you the big bucks you get from guys like Stu . . . but hell, Swifty . . . I want to be more like you are."

Swifty saw the tears before his friend felt them well up. Maybe it was the booze, but the two men embraced and had a good cry.

Chet Levine inched up behind them and offered in his deep bass, "Good . . . good, I see you guys are joining my team. Welcome."

Kyle broke away and began to wipe his eyes while Swifty alternately laughed and cried, choking until Chet had to pound on his back.

When the emotions cleared, Swifty threw his arms around both men and said, "I love you. guys . . . Dick Vermeil, move over!"

(*You might remember Dick Vermeil for coaching the Rams to a Super Bowl Championship, giving up a solid broadcasting career to reenter the grueling world of pro coaching to lead a team for which he was once an assistant. But this same Vermeil, a one-time LA Ram assistant and UCLA coach, had led the Philadelphia Eagles to the 1980 Super Bowl against the Raiders. Upon resigning, he said, crying, "I love these guys . . ." People made fun of him for years after. KKF.*)

Four days later, Kyle flew Swifty from LA to Scottsdale in Jake's Cessna 210. Jake and Amber were on their way to Hawaii, leaving their children with her mother. Jake allowed Kyle to fly and maintain his three-airplane fleet. Jake himself was a skilled pilot and had an order in for the new Cessna Citation II that was due out in about a year. Kyle couldn't wait to get his hands on it.

Over Banning, Kyle switched on the intercom and said, "Funny that Jake and Amber are going with Artie and Teresa to Hawaii. They usually don't swim in the same circles."

"Lucky they didn't follow Stu and Toni to France!" Swifty responded.

"Yeah, but what I meant is, there must be a deal brewing. Artie depends on Jake more and more when it comes to business. He thinks he's losing a step because of his arthritis and such."

"The man still plays golf in the mid-eighties . . . he should worry so much. How old is he? Sixty-three maybe. My read is he wants Jake to get sharper on the details. But, you know better . . . you work for them." Swifty sort of stuck the needle in.

"Yes, yes, I know. Swifty, that's why I wanted to talk to you . . . I have to get out of this thing. I'm little more than a driver. Shit, I'm going to be forty and still a chauffer!" Kyle added a few knots by adjusting his manifold pressure and looked at Swifty.

"We'll talk, my friend, we'll talk." Swifty closed his eyes and began to run through pending issues:

Kyle wanted to talk to him about his future. Kim had stayed in LA to get a routine checkup at UCLA. Their rapid-paced life had its charm, but it was taxing, especially for Kim. Artie had arranged a deal meeting for Pete Phenet and himself in Hawaii. Presumably, Jake would be there. Not good. Jake didn't like or trust him. He knew that drawing Peter and his company near to Artie Leonardo was very risky. But, it was a way to help Pete. They could always say no. He kept asking himself why he wanted to associate with the man that put him jail, stole three years of his life, and put a permanent mark on his name. He couldn't answer the question. No Artie, no Nelson, no Connor, no Kyle . . . no sweet life. Maybe that was it. Maybe he liked the bittersweet thought of living on the edge a little, being in the game, going for the "action." He fell asleep.

Kyle poked him and he started awake. Kyle tugged at his shoulder harness. They were on final to Scottsdale. He heard air traffic control hand them off to the tower. Kyle's request to land was sharp and clear . . . funny, it was not like Kyle's normal language. Maybe that was one of the answers for his buddy. He nodded at Kyle and tightened his harness. "Gear down and locked . . . three lights. Prop full, flaps twenty. Field in sight . . . Clear to land.

Flaps thirty. Speed reduced to seventy-five . . . seventy . . . sixty-five . . . over the fence . . . sixty . . . fifty-five on the numbers . . . flare . . . touch down and roll out. Just like it had a brain, Swift, old man." They taxied off the runway and toward their hangar.

"Hey, you got time for a drink?" Kyle asked as he buttoned up the aircraft.

"Sure, nothin' else to do, but let's make it coffee. I'm boozed out." Swifty responded. He knew Kyle wanted to talk about his own development, and he dreaded it.

They stopped at a coffee shop on Shea and Scottsdale road. After they ordered – Swifty a black coffee, Kyle a jelly donut and coffee with cream and sugar – Kyle said, "Will you take my case, doctor. Oh, and will you give me a friend's discount?"

"Kyle, you don't need any help you can't give yourself. You have three college degrees . . . you can do anything you want. Just look in the mirror," Swifty said earnestly.

"You be my mirror. You tell me. I've seen what you've done with Toni Marie, with Pete Phenet . . . Becky . . . you got some magic in you, buddy. Please help me?" Kyle was serious.

"Cost you."

"How much?"

"Lifetime friendship, ten grand, a fifth of your second year salary, and strict adherence to a plan. Can you afford it?"

"Yeah . . . yes, sir!"

"Okay, then start by drinking that coffee black and sending the donut back!" Swifty was abrupt.

"Why?"

"Because I said so."

"Didn't you tell me that you were married when we first met? What happened to her?" Swifty demanded.

"She took off back to Mama, like I said before. She got married again to some lawyer that worked for her old man. We were just too young when we got together," Kyle muttered.

"Why did you get married in the first place?"

"She got pregnant in high school."

"I thought you said it was a false alarm."

"Nah, I lied. She had twins."

"Oh my god, Kyle! Where the hell are they?" Swifty slapped the table.

"Back in Pennsylvania with her and the lawyer."

"Do you talk with them?"

"Yeah, on birthdays and such. Them and Phillip."

"Who?"

"Phillip. He was born a year after the twins when I was 20. He's real smart." Kyle looked at the ceiling.

"You mean to tell me that you have three little kids and you don't see them! Kyle, no damn wonder you are so screwed up." Swifty sounded disgusted.

"Geez, buddy, you are a hard-ass," Kyle moped.

"Damn betcha. Get some paper out of your briefcase. We're going to make a plan." Swifty was in charge.

They (we) sat over coffee for four hours. At the end, they had a plan that would transform a man's life. My life!

Kyle would take a leave of absence from the Leonardo Companies. He would sell his cars and his gun collection. He would use the money to have his teeth capped and to break both his smoking habit and his eating habit through hypnotherapy. He would spend thirty days at a "fat farm" in southern Utah. He would undertake a lifelong exercise and balanced nutrition plan.

He would immediately contact his former wife and arranged to have regular visits with his three small children, both in Philadelphia and in Phoenix. He would begin savings accounts in each of their names. Even though their maternal grandfather was flush, it would be their father who provided for their educations.

Upon his return, Kyle would propose to Jake that he be made executive vice president of the Leonardo Companies. Once that was accomplished, he would realign the organization, set up a five-year plan, and propose an ownership share for himself. If Jake rejected his plan, Kyle would quit and pursue employment elsewhere, with the new commitments to the children, a frightening prospect.

"One thing, Swift, I'm going to have to owe you on the ten grand."

"No way . . . you have four cars . . . all some kind of weird hotrods. One of them has my name on it," Swifty joked.

"You got my best car ten years ago. Okay, you take my Mustang and call us square?" Kyle looked hopeful.

"No . . . I take the Mustang and hold it until you pay me the ten and the second year one-fifth." The deal was done.

CHAPTER 33

THE GREAT CHALLENGE

KIM'S CALL WAS more than a shock, it was a thunderbolt! Just those words, "They want to run some more tests." She had come back from LA a few days after he had and moped around the house, only going through the motions of working. He'd ask what was wrong, she'd say, "Nothing, I'm tired that's all." He had gone with Peter to Hawaii and proceeded with a series of the most bizarre meetings he had ever attended. Thank God Pete was a first-class businessman.

Now here he was, in the middle of these meetings, and she was telling him the tests had shown there could be something seriously wrong. He hadn't even known she was feeling poorly. She had lost some weight, but women always complained about their weight. He had to get home.

Yoshi Hankawa was an anomaly to Swifty: a slick, good-looking Japanese-American who could shift from Hollywood jive talk to respectful bowing and scraping, Japanese style. Peter wasn't fazed by Yoshi or his associates. When Swifty let him know that he needed to get back to the States, Peter explained that he intended no disrespect, but his associate had grave concern for his wife's health and would have to depart. Yoshi understood and made the apologies. Artie sat quietly as Peter, Yoshi, and Jake discussed numbers and values. Swifty smiled and bowed, backing out of the door as Yoshi's three stodgy Japanese associates bowed in return and looked concerned.

Flying east is usually faster than flying west because of the jet stream, but this time it didn't work. Five hours went to six before he landed at LAX. Again, Kyle was there to pick him up and fly him to Scottsdale in Jake's burly 210. Less than two hours later, they were taxiing to the hangar.

"It was good of Jake to let you use his plane to pick me up again. I'll be sure to thank him," Swifty said sarcastically.

"What he doesn't know, et cetera. I take care of all the records anyway. More important, buddy, Kim is really upset. She will try not to show it to you, but my mom has been over at your place today, and she said Kim is shaking like the proverbial . . . don't mean to worry you more, but you better take something to cover the booze." He handed Swifty some mints to mask his breath. On the plane, Swifty had two drinks and some wine with dinner. He didn't realize it was still evident.

"God, get me there as soon as you can, Kyle, shit!" Kyle let the '67 Mustang do its job. Swifty noted the car's performance and realized it was about to become his charge for a year or more.

Kim was pacing the living room when he arrived. Their living quarters had expanded substantially over the years. They had knocked out the adjoining walls of two three-bedroom condos on a quiet street near the edge of Paradise Valley. Kim had converted two of the bedrooms to office space and one living room to their master suite. It was quite striking.

She began to cry and ran to his arms before he could enter. "Honey, they're going to take my kidney out! I have a rare disease . . . I can't even say the name!"

He held her. "We'll fix it, baby . . . we'll fix it . . . we'll fix it."

When she was able to talk, Swifty found out that she had not wanted to worry him. Her side had been aching for weeks and she had noticed substantial blood in her urine. A local physician had suggested she go to UCLA for further review. They found the cause almost immediately. The documents said *glomerulonephritis, or Goodpasture's syndrome.* Swifty went to his copy of *Medical Digest.* It described Goodpasture's as a rapid deterioration of the glomeruli in the lungs and kidneys, manifesting itself by bloody urine and spitting up blood. Had she spit up blood? Yes, she had.

In near panic, Swifty tried to call the doctor at UCLA. It was fruitless – after midnight, no one there. He put Kim in a warm bath and washed her as though she were a child. He shampooed and conditioned her hair, dried her carefully, and wrapped her in a large terry robe. November had brought a chill to the desert. He lit the fire and put her on the rug before it. There they remained, holding each other and crying until sleep overtook them.

A ringing phone can cut through the most pleasant of dreams and the most fearsome. Swifty's was the later, so the sound of Mr. Bell's alarm brought a welcome relief. It was Kyle.

"Artie called to see about Kim. We're all wondering. Can I do something?" Kyle didn't seem to notice that it was six in the morning.

"What's Artie doing up? It's two a.m. over there!" Swifty asked, drowsily.

"He couldn't sleep. His arthritis . . . it kills him at night. How's Kim?" Kyle pressed.

"Well, it ain't good. She's asleep. As soon as I can rouse somebody at UCLA, I'm going to find out more. Right now, it is real bad. She had to lose a kidney in the next several weeks and then, I don't know. It's called *Goodpasture's syndrome*. There's a more technical name, but it boils down to a bad kidney and lung disease. Shit, Kyle . . . she's peeing and spitting up blood! I don't know what the fuck to do." Swifty's voice started to shake.

"I'll call Artie. Hold up, man. She needs you now . . . more than ever." Kyle hung up.

What the hell could Artie do? Must be old habit from Kyle. He'll call Artie. What's Artie going to do? Wave a wand?

Kim ate sparingly and moved with great effort. It was as though the news and his return gave her permission to be ill. Swifty filled three prescriptions for her, after getting the local doc to rewrite what they had given her at UCLA. Naturally, the doctor's license didn't allow him to write in Arizona. Shit! Bureaucracy!

CHAPTER 34

EMERGENCY

Artie understood everything that was being discussed in the meetings, but he was bored. Why did the Japanese have to take so much time to decide? He could see it clearly; this Pete kid was smart and had a plan to corner a significant amount of Southern California real estate. He knew what he wanted to do, but needed the expertise and additional financing to pull it off. He explained there were all kinds of regulatory hoops to jump through, but it could be done. General Alliance would put up 30 percent, amounting to two hundred million dollars. Yoshi's Japanese people would put in 65 percent, or $434 million, and he and Norm Cellestine would make up the 5 percent balance of thirty-two million. Phenet would handle the regulatory and paperwork, Artie and Norm the expertise (mostly Norm), and the Japanese the much-needed additional cash. It was a good mix.

Jake ran the numbers and worked well with Yoshi and Peter. Artie was proud of him. This big lug of a bodybuilder really knew his "ins and outs." He didn't miss an opportunity to insert an advantage for their side. He had learned a lot from himself and from Kyle about lying back before committing. Kyle was by far the better operational guy, but Jake really understood the big picture. Too bad Swifty had to bail out. He would have enjoyed watching him operate. Artie hoped the wife was okay.

Artie took frequent breaks. His arthritis was killing him. The medication didn't help much. Booze helped, but then the next day it didn't seem worth it. His level of patience was waning as well. Shit, he was close to sixty-five. None of the men in his family had ever lived so long. He was in good shape financially, so he'd let Jake carry the load. Jake, Peltz, Norm . . . Kyle. Yeah, he needed to pay Kyle more. The kid was really important to the stateside operation and Jake wasn't taking care of him. How old was Kyle? A year older than Jake? God, he must be almost forty. Got to pay him more.

He and Teresa kind of enjoyed the afternoons. After a couple of drinks and his medication, they could walk on the beach and take in the breeze. Artie had purchased the place below Diamond Head three years earlier. The access was good and the expense was easy to write off. Jake liked Maui better and kept a place there, but it was too hard for Artie to get there . . . all that plane-change shit. Not such a bad place to retire, Hawaii. But, he loved the desert too, especially his retreat out in Carefree. Hell, he'd have coffee with Dick Van Dyke in the morning and dinner with Don Ho. He even found Tommy Sands running a little club in Honolulu. Sinatra had deep-sixed that kid so bad when he and Nancy junior had their problems, Sands was lucky to still be breathing. He was breathing hundred-proof as it was.

That night, when the meetings broke up, they always involved lots of booze as the Japanese were major-league drinkers. Jake took the guests to an after-hours club. Artie got on the phone. Kyle was playing cards.

"Don't you sleep? It has to be five in the morning. Oh, yeah, almost six." Artie was feeling his drinks.

"It's Monday . . . my day off. I always play cards all night on Sunday after we check out the receipts . . . the games and all. Please tell Jake we had a really good week, last week. Sir, have you been drinking a lot?" Kyle asked

"Yeah, yeah, these Japs hit it hard . . . I go along. We got us a good plan here . . . a very lucrative deal. Kyle, please call Norm for me and tell him to call me at noon, my time . . . that would be what? Three in Scottsdale, or four?" Artie slurred.

"Four. I'll tell him. You okay?" Kyle asked.

"I'm fine, shit I'm drunk. How is the girl . . . Swifty's wife? How's he dealing with it?" Artie inquired.

"Swifty's okay, but Kim is not good. Kidney has to come out and more serious stuff after that. It sounds like short-term comfort and long-term curtains to me. She's got to be the sweetest gal in the entire world too. It pisses me off . . . sir." Kyle might have been a little drunk too.

"Ah shit. Well you tell Swifty that whatever she needs, we'll get it. I'll put that asshole Peltz on it . . . all of his white coats . . . anything that is needed. You tell him." Artie was losing his battle with conscientiousness.

"Yes, sir, I'll tell him. Please tell Jake things are better than good. Get some rest, boss," Kyle said softly.

"Okay . . . okay. Hey, Kyle, I'm telling' Jake to give you a raise or something. He doesn't deserve you." He hung up.

Norm Cellestine called on time that afternoon. Artie couldn't remember exactly what he wanted, but he made it sound important.

"This thing is going to knock your socks off, Norm. It's a deal to end all deals. We have to scrape up thirty-five million. How soon can we get it?" Artie demanded.

"Thirty-five? You crazy? We don't have thirty-five! We have eleven at the most . . . in free cash. Why is this such a good deal?" Norm said, kind of bored.

"Listen, goddamit, Norm . . . find thirty-five now! You'll get the detail later. Have Kyle run some numbers out of Jake's shop and see what that does. We need thirty-five in a month." Artie slammed down the phone.

"Hello there, Kyle Faust? Good. Say, this is Norm Cellestine. I was just talking to Mr. Leonardo. He asked that you and I get together to see if our combined operations can come up with a certain amount of cash for a project." Norm was sugar sweet as usual.

The two met in Norm's office. Kyle carried two briefcases full of receipts, ledgers, and forecasts into the conference room. Norm watched as Kyle laid out every asset, line of credit, and cash source of the Leonardo Companies. Norm opened his own ledgers and began to scan. Four hours later, they had secured thirty-four million eight hundred dollars. Most would come to them within thirty days . . . some would take six weeks. Norm placed a call to Artie.

"Arthur, I have the numbers you asked for yesterday. Even though you were very rude to your long-suffering partner, I have slaved to meet your express needs . . . and thanks to Mr. Faust here, Jake's number-two man, together we can cross the finish line on time," Norm chuckled.

"You're full of shit, Norm, but good work. Yeah, Kyle is a hotshot. Jake is the only one that doesn't recognize it," Artie said.

"Well, I'll happily take him over here for twice what that skinflint son of yours pays him. He's good." Norm was serious.

Kyle beamed at the words and committed then and there to follow through on the plan he and Swifty had developed for him. As mentioned before, it completely changed his life.

"Swifty, this is Kyle. I'm at the 'fat farm' in Utah. How is Kim?" Kyle called every other day. This particular day Kim had her surgery.

"She came through fine. The doc hopes to arrest the progress of the disease now that the worst kidney is out. He's not sure if he can hold it until they find another kidney for her. She has to go in the queue . . . then they'll pull the other one and put in the replacement. We just have to pray it's on time," Swifty poured out.

"Swifty, I lost eight pounds my first two days. You know, I have the worst toothache from the caps, but that'll be gone in a day or two. Please give Kimmie my love. And, buddy, don't worry . . . I've got some ideas." Kyle rang off.

"Ideas? What the hell ideas?" Swifty said to the dead phone.

Artie Leonardo sent a huge spray of flowers and a note. Norm Cellestine sent some as well. They took the flowers, candy, and cards to the Beverly Wilshire Hotel, where Kim would rest for a week before going back to Scottsdale. She felt sore, but not much worse than before surgery. Swifty remained by her side every minute, though he had hired twenty-four-hour nurses to attend her.

Kyle called to give her his love, and sent flowers too. He said he had lost twenty-three pounds. Kim said she had too, but hadn't tried. She chuckled, and he didn't know what to say.

On the third day, a man named Louis Peltz called. One of the nurses took the message and gave it to Swifty when he came back from a haircut. He carefully dialed the number. It seemed to be Riverside County.

"Mr. King, you may not remember me, but we met many years ago . . . in Chandler, Arizona."

"I remember, Mr. Peltz. What can I do for you? My wife is here recuperating from surgery . . . I – "

"I know all about it. That is why I called you. Can you prepare your wife for travel by tomorrow morning? I want to take her to my clinic in Sonora," Peltz said in his acquired European tone.

"What?"

"Mr. Leonardo has directed that we evaluate her case at our clinic . . . to see if we may improve upon her prognosis. We have some very advanced systems and modalities. Our algorithms are state of the art . . . in fact in advance of the art. Can she be ready?" Peltz asked.

"I'll call you back in an hour." Swifty hung up, then placed a call to Jake Leonardo.

"Hey, look, Koenig . . . or King, don't look a gift horse . . . the old man wants us to spare no effort. Take it. Peltz is a pro. He has a dozen of the best oncological, renal, coronary, and even anal specialists in the world. I ought to know, I'm fuckin' payin' for 'em. The old man wants it . . . you get it . . . or your wife does." Jake was rude and, as usual, crude.

"I'd like to talk with your father . . . I – "

"You just talked to me . . . you don't need to talk to him. Get her ready to go." Jake hung up.

Swifty called Augie Bash.

"Look, Swifty, Arthur is very concerned. He wants the best for your wife and for you. Take her to Mexico. What can it hurt? Anyway, I'll ask Arthur to call you down there. Go, Swifty . . . it's a good thing. And by the way, you have a very good friend in Kyle." Augie hung up.

Swifty called Peltz. "Mr. Peltz . . . Swifty King . . . she'll be ready."

Kim didn't understand what was happening, but she was too weak to fight it. Swifty didn't know much more. When he asked Peltz in the ambulance, "What about our passports?" Peltz had answered, "Next time . . . this time we will be in an out in a day . . . a three-day visa will do. They will be waiting for us."

Curiously, they didn't stop on the U.S. side of the border. Landing at Sonora Grandé Airport, they were quickly processed through immigration and customs by two courteous young women . . . the local Federales.

Swifty knew from Kyle that Artie and Jake had some kind of medical business in Mexico, but he had no idea of the details. Here, in the lush Sonoran desert, between two saguaro-covered hills, lay a sprawling complex of white stucco buildings with red-tiled roofs. A small sign, in English and Spanish, painted in neat black letters, identified each building. Most of the dozen-or-so buildings were attached to one another with red-tiled, covered, paved, walkways. A smattering of desert plants and trees were positioned around each structure, and a small elliptical pool, with spa, adorned five of them.

Kim was taken, by gurney, through the side entrance of the main building. Swifty jogged alongside.

He was not permitted to join her in the exam room, where no less than five white-coated men and women crowded around Kim's supine form. He caught a glimpse of Peltz – in a white coat, scrub cap, and green scrub gown – entering the long hall of the low building as Kim's door closed. He turned as the slight, now goateed, figure approached.

"So, Mr. King, how is the patient?"

"I can't say . . . I don't know what you are doing. Those better be real doctors in there . . . Peltz."

"So, you do remember me after nearly fifteen years . . . relax, she is in good hands. The best. Four are Physicians, one is a medical technician. All are scientists of the highest order. Fortunately, we here at the clinic are familiar with your wife's disease. While usually fatal, we have made great strides in arresting it in lab animals and a few humans. You want this girl to live, don't you?"

"What kind of a fucking question is that? Of course, I want her to have whatever it takes, whatever it costs! What's this shit about animals?"

"No need to worry about cost. This one is on us, so to speak. Shall we say payment for an old debt? Believe me, Mr. King, if she can be saved, she will be saved here at Obregón. As far as the animals are concerned, they are an important part of medical research. And, we aren't going to do anything, apply any therapies, etc., without your knowledge and approval. You will get a full education on the subject when we know all we can know."

Nine hours of pacing and drinking coffee left Swifty wired and tired. When an attractive young woman in whites touched him on the arm, he almost jumped to the ceiling.

"Sir . . . sorry to startle you . . . you have a call. You may take it here in the office." The girl smiled.

Swifty followed her to a door where she motioned him in. There was a small desk, two chairs, and a phone stand. Lights on the phone were blinking. "Line nine, sir."

He nodded as she exited and closed the door.

Swifty sat down heavily and punched *9*. "Hello, King here."

"Swifty, this is your friend Arthur, Arthur Leonardo. How is the girl?"

"Damned if I know . . . I haven't seen her for nine hours." He bristled. "If this fucking Peltz of yours is playing Dr. Frankenstein on my wife, I'll kill him and you too, goddammit!"

"Swifty . . . Swifty . . . hold on a moment. I am not frightened of you . . . but I am frightened for you. You are upset. But try to understand that that irritating little bastard Peltz is a fine scientist and he has a team of unparalleled professionals down there. If anyone in the world can help your wife . . . Kim, they will. I promise you that. Do you believe me, son?" Arthur was on the brink of pleading, not a characteristic trait.

Because of Artie's unfamiliar tone, Swifty fought back the emotion, let the tide pass, and said, "Yes, sir . . . I'm sorry. It's just that I don't know which way to turn. Jesus, this happened so fast. She's so damn young. It isn't fair."

"No, it's not fair and we're going to rectify the situation. I promise you, son . . . I promise you. Now go to your wife. Let Peltz do his work. It will be all right." Artie paused.

"Yes, sir . . . thank you, sir."

"Okay then." Artie hung up.

Two hours later, Peltz found him in the coffee room. He smiled gravely and said, "She's quite a girl. She was awake through most of the tests. Even told me a joke. You are a lucky man."

"So, what do the tests show? Can you help her?" Swifty said weakly.

"Hey, I'm a scientist, not a doctor. I will give it to you very straight. She has a deadly disease. It will kill her in two to three years if we don't intervene. My people say we can give her a new, disease-free kidney as soon as her blood count improves. I'd say two weeks, maybe three. Also, we believe injection of certain hormones taken from the same host will allow the disease to be overcome and defeated. Her cells will grow back to health in a year. By then her permanent kidney will be ready." Peltz waited for Swifty's response.

"Where do you get the new kidney, some poor Mexican farmer? What is the temporary kidney, a machine?"

"No, Swifty, no. Initially we will transplant a kidney from a recently deceased person; probably someone fatally injured in an auto accident. We have withdrawn certain cells from the excised kidney and we've extracted bone marrow from her leg. We will chemically cleanse the cells and marrow then introduce them into a host. Within a year, the host will be carrying complementary cell packages and a new kidney that is basically Kim's. We'll transfer them to Kim and she will be well for ten years or more . . . perhaps a normal lifetime." Peltz waited for the inevitable question.

"Who is this host who is willing to trade his or her life for Kim's?" Swifty said skeptically.

"Come, I will introduce you." Peltz led Swifty through a series of doors, then across a walkway to a secure building. Peltz used a card key to enter. The minute the door closed, Swifty heard it . . . the barking.

"Dogs?"

"Dogs and other animals . . . come on." Peltz led him into a laboratory where several dogs and a few cats were caged.

"Here we are . . . little Kimberly." Peltz opened a cage and extracted a brown bundle – a beautiful, wide-eyed cocker spaniel.

"This pretty little bitch will host your Kim's cells, grow her a new kidney, and provide a genome fix that can defeat her disease for a very long time. Maybe for good." Peltz smiled up at an astonished Swifty. "It's a biosynthetic process called chimerics. We will apply for approval in three countries next year. I believe the United States will accept this within a decade. Sweden, Finland, and Australia are ready now."

"You want to introduce cells from an animal into my wife?" Swifty looked at him incredulously.

"No, we will remove cells from your wife, allow this especially prepared female animal to nurture them for her, then reintroduce the product of her own cellular development into her body. This process works, Swifty. We have over 180 adults walking the streets today who have benefited from this process. Sixty-nine of them have chimerically cultivated kidneys. The host animals generally lived normal lives afterward as well. Those who became ill, or died, were autopsied and the data used to improve on our processes." Peltz gave him a grave smile. "It is a wonderful piece of science."

"My beautiful wife, the girl I love more than I love myself, is going to be your science

project," he spoke to the window and the saguaros in the distance. Peltz looked with him at an unseen answer in the Sonoran desert.

"She will be fine, Swifty. You will have her as she was before."

"For how long?" he said to the window.

"I am not God, young man . . . I cannot predict longevity. But, I would say up to ten years . . . or more . . . much more." Peltz looked back at Swifty and saw the pain in him.

"Would you do it?" Swifty was still talking to the window or some object beyond it.

"For me, yes. For my children, yes. For my wife, Ute . . . yes, yes, and yes," Peltz said with finality.

"Let me talk to her . . . I'll get back to you." He walked to the open door. Peltz caught up with him and steered him by the elbow to the wards.

She didn't seem to be in pain. Her smile was warm, and he felt love well up from his heart.

"How are you, honey . . . tired I bet?" she said it before he could. They always read each other's thoughts and usually finished sentences that were left incomplete.

"You?"

"I feel very serene. They are so nice here. These doctors are comforting and gentle. Honey, it's like they're on a mission. Does that make sense?" She smiled and looked at peace.

Peltz stepped forward and instinctively began to take her pulse. "She has had a mild sedative. Let her sleep overnight. Take her back tomorrow," he whispered to Swifty. "I'll come back in a few minutes and we'll have dinner." He turned and disappeared, followed by two young nurses.

"Did they tell you what they did?" Swifty asked hesitantly.

"Every step . . . they're going to save my life. Honey, they showed me a puppy that is going to save me. Isn't it wonderful?" she said dreamily. "I had a dream sometime while I was in there. I asked God if this kind of thing was all right. An angel touched my hand and said, 'Yes, it's fine.'" She pulled him by the arm with surprising strength. Swifty bent down to her waiting lips.

He saw his tears fall on her pink cheeks as she kissed the tip of his nose and then his lips. "Go get something to eat and some rest. Let me sleep." He stood upright and looked for a Kleenex to wipe her face. When he turned back, she was sleeping.

The trip back was quiet. Kim sat up most of the way, drinking tea and talking quietly with the attendant. Every few moments she would squeeze his hand and rub her cheek on his shoulder. Swifty felt love and bewilderment the entire ride to Scottsdale. Peltz dropped them and went on to Palm Springs. He said he would call to schedule the next appointment within two weeks. He suggested Kim continue all prescribed medication, plus the herbs given her at the clinic.

"This shit is illegal, Kyle. Why didn't you tell me what was going on?" Swifty demanded of his friend.

"Look, bud, you just said why. Piss on the law . . . if it saves her life, I mean shit, Swifty . . . her life!"

"Look, I can't think straight. The bottom is falling out of my world right now. When are you coming back?"

"When you say to."

"When are you scheduled?"

"Two weeks . . . in two weeks I'll be the new man you want me to be . . . Then I was coming back."

"Okay. Look, think about this for me. I need your help. And Kyle, . . ."

"Yeah."

"Lose the bad grammar and New Jersey fog before you get here or I'll kick your ass!"

"Yes, sir, I will follow our action plan . . . sorry, my mentor."

"Good, bye."

"Take care of yourself, my friend." Kyle rang off and fell into a period of deep thought as he gazed out at the Utah mountains.

His friend Swifty sat shaking in the living room of his condominium in Scottsdale, Arizona.

CHAPTER 35

GLADDIE

GLADDIE AMES HAD only seen her sister at family Christmas get-togethers since Kim had moved to Scottsdale fourteen years earlier. At thirty-nine, she was still beautiful, where Kim was cute, pretty, sexy, and fun. Regal Gladdie had two kids in school – one at Andover, the exclusive prep school, and the other at University of Illinois – and she was divorced from the football-playing stockbroker. When her kids had first started school, she enrolled in college and eventually took an advanced degree in education. She had become head mistress of a Montessori-style school in Brentwood, across the freeway from Beverly Hills.

Swifty could not believe his ears. He had spoken to Gladdie only occasionally at his in-laws' house since they broke up twenty years before. Each time he had felt awkward.

"Hi, Colin, this is your first love calling . . . remember me?" Ah the sweetness . . . the lingering aftertaste.

"Sure I remember, Gladdie, how are you?" He tried to sound aloof as he searched for a rapier that would cut through her heart the way she punctured his so many years before.

"I'm missin' my guy, that's how I am. I want him back. Does he want to come back?" Oh god, she knew how to dig into his soul.

"Gladdie, I'm still very much in love with Kimmie, you know that." He thrust the point home.

"Oh sure, be mean. I know little sister stole you away for a while, but betcha you'd like to come on home to Gladdie by now."

"Gladdie, you got knocked up by a football player while I was studying for finals . . . remember?" Swifty twisted the blade.

"Oh Paul? He was just to make you jealous . . . how do you know Trisha wasn't yours anyway? Coulda been . . . you must admit," she cooed.

"Gladys Ann Ames, I have dark hair and brown eyes . . . little Patricia, who I have seen more than once, is as blonde and blue eyed as her hotshot daddy. Now let's get real. Your sis is a sick girl and my job and I would hope yours is to get her back to perfect health as soon as possible. So, you ought to stop trying to tease me with some olden-time stuff." Swifty stumbled over the last of his words, and he knew Gladdie understood there was still something way down deep inside him that she could control.

"Okay, you silly boy, and that is just what I am going to do. I have a break coming up next week and I intend to come over there and do my own assessment of my little sister's health . . . and yours too. You're still my guy, ya know. Little sis would want me to look after you if anything happened to her . . . not, of course, that it would. Can you pick me up at the airport, honey . . . I mean Colin or Swifty, or whatever I am supposed to call you now that you are this big successful man."

"I can pick you up. Is your mom coming? She should, you know. We have lots of rooms . . . lots." Swifty stumbled again.

"Momma will come for two days. That's all she can handle. I will stay eight days, if you'll have me. By the way, honey, little Trish is now twenty years old and a junior at U of I, Champaign. Ha. I'll call you back when I have a flight booked. Bye-bye . . ."

"Bye." He thought, "Shit, shit, shit!"

Nelson Leigh had completed his morning paper and was about to brew a third cup of coffee when his phone buzzed.

"Yes, Nelson Leigh."

"Nelson, Captain Ackerman here . . . I just cleared you for an incoming call. It's Swifty. Pick up two and I'll hang up."

"Why thank you, Captain, very nice of you." He put the first button on hold, and then punched the second. "Swifty, my boy, wonderful of you to call. How is the girl?"

"Oh, Nelson, you slay me. Now the Captain of the Guard is your personal phone operator!"

"Only on Sunday, now, how is your wife?" Nelson sniffed.

"She's better each day . . . weak, but better. Nelson, I have two or three things I really need your advice on. Could I come over?" Swifty asked.

"Swifty, you are a citizen, I am a criminal. You can come visit any old time... It is your right. However, I might suggest you come pick me up and I'll ride back to your place for a few hours. Seems I have a twelve-hour pass coming... several in fact."

Nelson insisted on Swifty putting the top down for the ride back. For several hours, as Kim slept, the two men sat in Swifty's study and conferred.

"Swifty, I have read of chimerics and I know of Peltz's work. It is credible. In fact I know two men whose lives were saved with those chimeric kidneys. One at Peltz's place and another in Switzerland. They are quite normal now, though given up for dead before. I'd give it a shot... for god's sake... you must do whatever is possible for the girl. But, one suggestion."

"What's that?"

"After she has the initial kidney transplant, take a ride over to Switzerland and let our old friend Connor Grove tour you around to some of the clinics there. He has all kinds of contacts. Surely you'll find researchers there who will verify this Professor Peltz's processes or give you a clue to another alternative," Nelson reflected.

Swifty also told Nelson about Gladdie's call. The older man laughed and laughed. "Oh, Swifty, I knew you were just like me, the girls can't resist us!"

"Best steer clear of your sister-in-law, old buddy. I think she could be extremely bad news. You love Kim. Be nice to her sister. Don't let Gladdie get mad at either of you, but don't let her get her claws into you... or it's all over." Nelson continued to chuckle.

Then Nelson sprung a surprise.

"Swifty, I have a problem you can help me with. It seems the federal government has grown weary of caring for me. I am to be released next month... released to a world I have not seen for thirteen years, except twelve-hour sojourns such as this. I need an anchoring point." Nelson opened his face into the familiar smile.

"An anchoring point?"

"A place to be, some contacts... wheels... a way to make a living, without, immediately at least, running afoul of the law. Can you set me up in LA?" Nelson asked.

Swifty thought for a moment. He owed this man more than he could ever repay. He knew that Becky and Chet could set something up. They had plenty of office space. It would be easy for Becky to put Nelson in a furnished apartment and find him a car. He'd call her. He'd ask her to find a role for Nelson... take the whole thing off his account.

"Not a problem, my friend. Beverly Hills okay? Maybe Brentwood?"

"Lovely... lovely. I knew I could count on my boy, Swifty. Remember, I have a guy to kill over there... then I'll recapture the girl. Neither will be difficult. I've had years to plan. But enough of that. Better get my old ass back to jail. Ha! Ha! I'm going to miss that dump."

As Swifty checked on Kim and made certain the attending nurse was on top of things, he escorted Nelson to the car. As they approached the garage, Swifty spotted a familiar figure hulking toward his rear entrance.

"Ho, Swifty . . . just coming up to see how Kim was doing. What's this! Fucking Nelson Leigh has escaped from jail! How grand. Nelson, you old dog! How the hell are you?" Augie Bash thrust his big paw toward them.

"Officer Bash! My god, I'm arrested again. Last time I saw that big paw it had a thirty-eight special in it. Good to see you too!" The two men shook hands, and then embraced.

"This is the bastard that arrested me, Swifty. He's a hell of a fine man. Good investigator too." Nelson laughed.

"Well, actually, we've seen each other in court and twice out at Safford. Plus, we've talked on the phone a bunch. He's a good one, Swifty. Too bad old Nelson went into crime. We could have used him on the cops . . . and in business. He's the reason I left the cops and joined Arthur's organization. I have never been sorry." Augie was still holding Nelson's hand in his big paw.

"How is dear Artie? I am the only one who dares call him that." Nelson kept chuckling.

"He's got a bit of arthritis, but not bad. He's backed off a lot . . . lets Jake and Peltz run their things. He and I watch the other business . . . though banking is not what it once was. I'll tell him you asked. Say, when do you get out of the Graybar Hotel?" Augie grew serious.

"All free and clear, no parole, nada . . . next month. I'm off to LA to seek my fortune, recapture my wife, kill the jerk that stole her from me, all that shit." Nelson smiled.

"Wonderful. Hope you can see Arthur before you leave the state."

"I'd like that." Nelson shook hands with Augie and turned to the car.

Augie whispered to Swifty, "I hope he's kidding about killing a guy."

"Me too." Swifty slipped into the seat of his new Cadillac and started the engine.

As he backed out, Swifty saw Augie climb the steps to his back door.
]
AND THE NEXT DAY . . .

Jake watched his father swing the golf club. It was precision, quite unlike his own jerking, hacking style. Jake tried to do it with brute force while his Dad used finesse.

"Nice shot, Pop. You're getting better with experience. One of these days you'll shoot your age," Jake said lightly.

"If I live to be seventy-nine, I might have a shot. You're doing better. You should come play with Swifty and me next week. Jakie, you'd like the kid if you gave him half a chance." Artie struggled to the cart and reinserted his driver in the leather bag.

"Maybe . . . maybe. Hey did you take your medicine today?" Jake looked concerned.

"Forgot . . . damn thing is murder today. I could use a drink and about nine aspirin." Artie tried to stretch as Jake drove across the fairway, ignoring the Cart Paths Only sign, to their balls.

"Wait'll the turn. I call Augie to bring you your stuff. There ought to be some aspirin in my bag . . . I'll check," Jake offered.

The two men had been discussing business. Jake advised Artie that "that fuckin' Kyle" had demanded a title, executive vice president, and wanted a point of the business, plus a raise to a $150,000. Artie said, "The kid is good, maybe you should pat him on the back and tell him you were just about to do it anyway . . . maybe give him two points. Jake nearly went berserk. "Two points! Two points! Pop, I killed myself for this business . . . I sweat my balls off and I should give it to this jerk for nothin'?"

"Well, let him buy in then . . . give him more cash and let him buy in . . . maybe a bonus. Jake, the guy has helped us a lot. We don't want to lose him."

"I don't need the asshole! He annoys me. He and that slick punk, Swifty King. They talk about me behind my back . . . you too."

"Paranoia, son, they call it paranoia. You may not need them, but you should use them. That is management. Let both those guys do your job for you. It'll free you up for more important stuff . . . like with Peltz and such." Artie tried to reason with his son.

"Bullshit! It's my business. You let me run it my way. Kyle is out and Swifty sucks wind! That's my decision." Jake slammed at his ball, which flew about ninety yards along the ground and stopped.

"Shit!"

They reached the turn; Jake calmed down and called Augie. The big man met them at eighteen with Artie's medicine. The three of them sat for an hour, drinking and eating peanuts.

"Augie, talk some sense into Jake here. He doesn't want to give Kyle any title and a piece of the business. I suggest the guy is good and deserves a shot. What do you think?" Artie asked, looking to see if Jake was willing to listen.

"Kyle is good . . . he" Augie started as Jake snatched the empty peanut bowl and stomped to the bar for a refill.

AND THE NEXT DAY . . .

"No kidding? Leonardo must be nuts. You have a place over here anytime you want it," Pete Phenet offered to Kyle.
"Thanks, but I'm going to talk to Swifty first. That's why I called . . . see if he was with you. I'll get back to you, Pete."

AND THE DAY AFTER THAT . . .

"Hi there, Kyle. This here is Norm Cellestine. Any chance we can talk today? I heard you weren't with Leonardo Companies anymore. Thought maybe you might consider comin' in with me."
Kyle was with Norm Cellestine for three hours. They agreed on the title of Executive Vice President, Cellestine Enterprises. A salary of one hundred seventy thousand dollars and a ten-thousand-dollar signing bonus. Norm also offered "phantom" options that would become real if and when they took the company public. In the interim they would pay a percent of profits each year. Buck Janis was upset at first, but settled in when Norm made him president of the company.
"Buck, I want Kyle here to focus on mergers and acquisitions . . . plus the potential for us goin' public. Judging by what he did the Leonardo, he can help us a lot." Norm looked for agreement.
"Yes, sir, Norm. Great move! Welcome aboard, Kyle." Buck's toothy grin was accompanied by a firm handshake.
Before commencing his duties with Cellestine, Kyle accompanied Swifty to Switzerland for some research. Kim was resting comfortably in Scottsdale after her kidney transplant, which was deemed a success. Her mother and Gladdie had hovered over her to the point where Swifty could not even enter the room. He had her flown back from Beverly Hills four days after surgery, which was done at the new kidney center at UCLA. Gladdie, who had made three trips to Scottsdale in the past six weeks, had driven her mother over the same day as they had arrived.
"She's doing good. Next year at this time she'll be down at Obregón for the big one. The docs who did the pre-op on her said they were impressed by her improvement after the last operation. I guess Peltz's stuff did it's job. We can only pray the same will be true with the next procedure." Swifty briefed Kyle. "That's why we're here. To see what the next procedure ought to be."
Kyle smiled, his new teeth and facial structure sending a message of strength and confidence. "I believe we'll find confirmation for the Peltz plan, Swifty. But let's check everything out."

Swifty marveled at the new appearance of his friend. A svelte 178 pounds on his six-foot frame, new dental caps, a restructured jawline, and the hint of muscle emanating from several points of his physique.

"What did Jake say to you? Why didn't he counteroffer?" Swifty asked.

"Fuck you."

"Huh?"

"He said, 'Fuck you,' end of story. Then he slammed out of the office. The secretary came in and said, 'Jake told me to tell you to get your ass out of the office. Leave the keys. If he sees you here again he'll physically eject you, sir.'"

"You left."

"I left."

"Didn't want to run physically afoul of Jake, right?"

"Very perceptive . . . right."

BACK IN SCOTTSDALE THE DAY AFTER . . .

Gladdie slid her hand under his shirt and ran it across his stomach. "Oooooow, flat and nice. You've got muscles there. Let me feel some more." Swifty pulled away and brushed her hand back.

"Gladdie, stop that shit. Your sister is in there asleep and you have no respect?" Swifty sputtered.

"Come on, baby, it's just me. Can't hurt to have one kiss . . . come on." She pulled his arms and slid close to him, rubbing her lower body on his hip.

"Jesus, Gladdie, knock that shit off. I'm going in to check on her." He ducked away from Gladdie and pushed into Kim's room.

She was half-awake, watching some inane show on TV. The nurse sat quietly reading in the corner of the room. Both looked up as Swifty came in.

"Baby, you awake?"

"Yeah, kind of. I will be so glad to get out of this bed. Daytime TV is so bad. Honey, please feed me some cool juice." She struggled to sit up. The nurse leapt to help her, but Swifty was there first. The nurse handed him the juice.

"When we get you on your feet, we are going to Hawaii and lie on the beach for two weeks. No TV at all. How's that sound?" Swifty bent over and kissed her lips.

"Sounds good . . . next month, maybe." She sipped the juice and nodded.

Gladdie stood in the doorway, smiling that knowing, evil little smile of hers.

"Please leave us for a moment," Swifty asked the nurse. Gladdie reluctantly pulled away from the door as Swifty closed it behind her and the nurse.

"Honey, Kyle and I traveled one end of Switzerland to the other. We looked at eighteen different processes for kidney regeneration and talked to every authority there on this chimeric hosting. They all say it can work . . . the only problem is the ethics of it." Swifty looked into her eyes for understanding.

"Ethics?"

"Yeah. See, people worry that scientists will use this biotechnology to develop some kind of 'man/animal' hybrid as a novelty or to be a stronger soldier . . . that kind of science-fiction silliness. For hosting human organ and hormone development, it looks pretty good. Bottom line, I think it's our best shot. We should do it." Swifty started to tear up.

"Oh, honey, don't worry. I know it's right. The minute I saw that little puppy, I knew it was the right thing. And, the angel said it was okay . . . the one in my dreams. As soon as I'm strong enough . . . I want to go back down there and have it done." She hugged his arm and he stifled his sobs.

"In a year . . . in a year."

CHAPTER 36

CONNOR GROVE

CONNOR GROVE HAD been glad to see them both. He looked older, he was sixty or so, but very fit. "Ski all winter, chase girls around southern Europe all summer, that's my regimen!"

"No golf or tennis?" Kyle asked mockingly.

"Oh sure, that too . . . and soaring. I have three sailplanes. Then there is my boat on

Lake Geneva and, of course, the yacht down in Cannes. I share that with a friend . . . the son of an uncle of the king of Saudi Arabia. Name's Al Bell, I'll introduce you. Great guy. Lots of great people over here!" Connor gloated.

"You have such a life . . . beats the shit out of Safford, huh?" Swifty needled.

"Yeah, but you know, I really miss the guys . . . Nelson, you. But, this does beat jail. By the way, Kyle, you look marvelous . . . as they say on TV. I do get recycled U.S. TV reruns over here. You look, well, just like I used to!"

It hadn't struck Swifty until Connor mentioned, but with his new body shape, jawline, and caps, Kyle did look a lot like Connor . . . a lot.

CHAPTER 37

DESERT OASIS

"YOU KNOW THAT son of a bitch is blabbing all our business around. I may just have to fix his wagon. That bastard King . . . Swifty knew all about our Mexico project. That's why he knew to have his wife taken there!" Jake was beet red and sweating.

"Jake, sit down!" his father ordered. "Kyle knows all your businesses well. Now he knows Norm's end. He is the logical guy to manage our investments with the Japanese. For god's sake he has to know the source of our financing if he is going to make that huge development work. Plus, with the market the way it's going, I think the old Pharaoh's Paradise project is going to get hot."

"Desert Oasis," Norm corrected

"Yeah, Desert Oasis," Artie agreed.

With interest rates the lowest they had been in a decade and discretionary income at an all-time high, it was clear that real estate was going to boom.

Kim had returned to work and, with some adjustment, began to recognize Kyle as an important member of the executive team. Those who had known him gossiped about his new look: the caps, the strong jawline, the muscular body – even the deep, authoritative voice, with little remaining trace of his New Jersey origins. He was quite pleased with the transformation.

Kim's weight began to return . . . the lines that had temporarily appeared stretched and faded. By November she was as cute and bouncy as before.

Kyle said, "Her inner beauty has escaped and surrounds her with a spiritual aura."

"Kyle exaggerates a bit," Kim said. "I just feel special these days, thankful to be here and confident I'm staying for a while."

Her tenacity had not waned. Desert Oasis was ready to explode with success, and Kim rolled out all her marketing strategies. She, Buck, and Kyle spent hours each day focusing on various markets around the country where new dollars were emerging. They sent out spiffy marketing brochures, targeted facsimiles to key prospects, and made personal calls in response to every inquiry. Kim was listed as Vice President of Marketing and President of Desert Oasis Properties. When she called and got a hot response, she followed up with a video of the project and called twice a week, offering a free trip to view the property. The first season, no less than eighty-five couples visited the property, spent up to three nights, and enjoyed the amenities. Thirty-two of them were supplied with round-trip airfare. The cost was cranked in to the overall project budget. It paid off with twenty-seven high-end sales that winter season of 1985, more than the total sales up to that date. With fifty-two lots sold and nineteen custom homes under construction, Kim decided to begin construction on the first forty "developer units" – two – and three-bedroom condos, basically. The second golf course was put into design. The project was designed to make money at each juncture: property sale, monthly dues, home design, resale, and property upgrades. Appreciation was the key to longer-term success, and that was assured as the water began to flow. The Supreme Court ruling upholding the lower court's decision that ceded three-fifths of the Colorado River winter flow to Arizona assured that the desert would continue to bloom.

Shortly after Swifty celebrated his forty-second birthday, Artie Leonardo sent Augie Bash to him with a suggestion.

"Swifty . . . listen to me. You changed your name . . . this was good. Now, with a friendly president about to leave office in a short time, you should apply for a pardon. You don't know who's going to replace Reagan. This may be your last chance for eight or more years. Arthur says you should talk to Joe Seeley and that connected partner of his, Jeffrey Domres." Augie was out of breath. He was getting fatter by the week, Swifty noted.

"Will you call Joe for me, Augie . . . and come in with me? I feel better when there is an extra pair of ears in the room."

"I will, of course, but understand, I do a lot of work for Joe and Jeff. My guy, 'Bluey Bluing,' runs down stuff for them all day, every day," Augie shared.

"Bluing? Isn't he that asshole detective that booked me at Phoenix jail twenty years ago? He works for you now?" Swifty asked incredulously.

"Was it that long ago? Gee. Ole Blewey retired in eighty. Had thirty years. Been with me since. Not a bad guy . . . follows orders . . . good detective. Lots of local knowledge there, believe me," Augie volunteered.

"I bet . . . I bet."

"Still want me there?"

"Set it up . . . don't need Bluing there . . . just you, Joe, and Jeff . . . any time when Kim is working."

Joe and Jeff were dubious over the possibility of a pardon. Neither had ever heard of the exact filing procedure, but Jeff knew a number of people at "Justice" who would know. Young Slattery, who had been a guard at Safford, sat in with them. He had become an associate at Seeley's firm. Naturally, it would cost a great deal of money. They would try.

After the meeting, Swifty asked what Augie thought.

"I think they can get it done. They, especially Jeff, were just being coy with you. My bet . . . you'll get a Reagan pardon. He has two cabinet members who are sympathetic to some of Mr. Leonardo's projects. Also, the opposition . . . the Democratic leadership . . . they are almost all on board. They'll lobby Reagan like hell. Remember, he is heavy in the corner of the "little guy," which you were when this happened. Our insiders will know you got set up by the guy who is now a judicial pain in the ass. You knew that Adam Breck, the former assistant U.S. Attorney for the Southwestern District, is now a federal court judge? Bastard got appointed by Carter after his work on Watergate. Reagan's people in Maryland didn't think it wise to touch him because of his connections, so he stayed seated."

"That bastard on the federal bench . . . no wonder this country is getting so screwed up. Hey, won't he try to block my attempt for a pardon?" Swifty wondered aloud.

"Not as long as Reagan is in. If Carter comes back or some new Democrat gets in . . . new story. That's why, according to Arthur, you better get it done now," Augie said grimly.

With Desert Oasis flourishing and her health at 100 percent, Kim nearly forgot about her next operation. As the months went by, she and Swifty spent their best year of the twenty they had been together. Their work world forced a furious pace, but they found time for a day here and there for themselves. When Swifty had to travel to Hawaii to meet a client, Kim used the time to pitch several wealthy Japanese couples that had made inquiry about her project. They stayed six extra days lounging on the beach at Kona and playing golf at the Mauna Lani. They grew closer and closer over that time.

"Kind of like a second honeymoon, huh?" Swifty joked.

"Remind me about the first one? I don't quite remember . . . or was that camping trip supposed to be a honeymoon?" Kim said skeptically.

"Well, there have been other times . . . other times."

"Yes, dear . . . there have been wonderful times and rough times, but they were all our times, together. We have always been together."

"Yeah . . . yeah . . . you and me, kid." Swifty thought for a second about confiding about sister Gladdie's approaches to him, but stifled the thought. Why drive a wedge between the sisters now? And besides, Kim might wonder about his . . . well, his loyalty. Even if he had had a weak moment with Gladdie, which he didn't, it would have nothing to do with how much he loved Kimmie. She was his whole life!

They rushed to the theater when in New York and to the races when in California. They fished the Keys in Florida and cruised the Rhine twice when visiting Europe. Neither had made the trek to the Grand Canyon, so they drove north one Monday morning and enjoyed the awesome grandeur of nature's wonder, then drove on to Vegas for shows and some gambling.

Soon . . . too soon, it was time to make their way to the lower Sonoran Desert and the Cliniquè de Obregón. Peltz sent a plane to Scottsdale airport. Kyle joined them on the thirty-five–minute flight.

"Not to worry, little sis. Louis Peltz is some kind of genius. His people have this thing down pat. I have spoken with three of his patients who have had the same thing . . . Goodpasture's . . . they are all fine after more than five years." Kyle and Kim had grown very close over this year. They had truly become like brother and sister.

Working on Desert Oasis, Kyle had discovered how much Kim could help him with the Southern California housing development, now called Anza Beach. He and Peter Phenet had also become close and were now talking of merging General Alliance and Cellestine Enterprises under a holding company. Yoshi Hankawa had been pushing the concept because his clients had considerable capital in both and felt it would be easier to watch under one umbrella. Artie liked the idea, and Norm . . . well Norm was becoming detached since Kyle had come aboard.

Buck and Kyle got on well, though Buck was intimidated by Kyle's superior education. His "ace in the hole" was his twenty-five years in real estate, which was primarily in the central Arizona market. Only, Kim had the handle on Arizona; it left Buck feeling a little less important. Norm had said to him, "Hell, boy, you're the president! Rejoice in the fact that you have such great people working for you. I never could have made it without you and the others . . . don't bother me a wit that y'all are smarter than me!" He lied.

Kidney surgery is major surgery – any procedure so invasive is major. But Dr. Steiger and Dr. Espinoza said it would take less than four hours. Peltz said they were very pleased with Kim's condition. She had been working out regularly and had gained nine pounds over her pre-op weight the year before. At five-two, Kim's normal weight was one fourteen. She had lost weight before the previous year's surgery, down to one hundred two. Today, she weighed in at one eighteen and looked fantastic.

Peltz, usually unemotionally clinical, remarked at how "she radiated energy" and "emanated a spiritual quality." Swifty started at this, never having heard Peltz say anything beyond facts and figures.

As the nurses wheeled her into the surgery suite, Swifty held her hand and walked alongside. "Put on a gown and scrub, you can watch, Steiger had suggested." Swifty declined, but he did stay with Kim through the tranquilizer phase and held her as she drifted into a dreamy state.

Five hours and forty minutes later, an exuberant Steiger bounced in to the waiting room in his greens, mask hanging from his chin. "Wonderful . . . it went just great. I stayed in there to supervise the close . . . she will sleep for a few hours . . . then you can see her. Espinoza says the bitch . . . the puppy . . . is also fine. You may want to take her home with you. Kim seems to have developed something of a spiritual relationship with her."

"No problems at all?" Swifty asked hesitantly.

"Best patient I ever had . . . so young . . . so beautiful. She will recover quickly. And, while I don't make predictions, well . . . I believe she has a full, active life ahead of her."

Swifty smiled and thanked the doctor who turned on his heel and disappeared. "A dog?" They hadn't had a dog since Puffy died, eight years earlier. "Yeah, a dog might be nice. A one-kidney dog . . . wonder if she is easier to clean up after . . . wonder . . . do you take her out more often?"

When she awoke, Swifty was there. "Hey, baby, how you doing?"

She coughed, grimaced, and then smiled. "It only hurts when I cough," she whispered, a slight smile on her lips.

He stroked her hair. She reached for his hand and squeezed lightly, then slept.

Four days went by and Kim recovered miraculously. The second day she was on her feet, the third she strode the halls, and the fourth she announced she was ready to go home. Steiger said, "Two more days. Sit by the pool . . . enjoy the sun. Make it a vacation!"

Kyle, who had stayed through the operation, had returned to Phoenix. He called twice a day. Artie sent flowers and a note. Buck and Norm sent a spray from the office, and Gladdie reported that their home was a "flower shop and a post office all rolled into one!"

As they lounged near the pool, Swifty occasionally cooling off by diving in, they heard dogs barking from within. Suddenly, the door to the compound opened, and a light brown ball of fur scampered out and raced to Kim's side. "Oh, here's my baby! No, no, don't jump on that side. Honey, lift her on the chair beside me. Don't hurt her tummy." Swifty obliged. The happy little dog drenched Kim in kisses then snuggled down beside her, where she would spend much of the rest of her life. Spirit . . . Kim called the puppy Spirit.

It was only three weeks before Kim was back in the office half days. Within two months, she was back in full charge again, rushing through twelve-hour days and pushing herself at the gym. Swifty worried that it was too much, but calls to Peltz and Steiger drew chuckles. "Let her do it . . . let her enjoy her new freedom. She will know when it's too much. How's the dog?"

"Same . . . same as Kim, perfect . . . I can't believe it."

"Believe it, boy. It's the future. You can't imagine what is on the medical horizon. The only roadblocks sit in the congress and parliaments of the wealthiest nations. Under a shroud of trying to protect the public, they will do everything possible to stop medical progress," Peltz said bitterly.

"But why?"

"Swifty, you of all people should know how things work. A problem solved is an opportunity lost for a politician. No one votes on the downbeat, only the upbeat. People vote on hope, never on problems solved. If I sound bitter, I am. But you should be happy. Kim is restored. Enjoy," Peltz said quietly. "Enjoy!" Steiger echoed.

I got tired earlier of telling you which famous person everybody looked like. But believe me, this was a cast of characters. Chet Levine was a tall, muscular Alec Baldwin, with lighter-colored hair, and Becky had gotten to look like a very skinny Glenn Close. Toni, well, she always reminded me of a Linda Carter . . . Wonder Woman. Kyle, well Kyle went from Bo Hopkins (remember him from the first year of Dynasty*?) to maybe an Ed Harris, with hair, thanks to Dr. Stu's skill at shaping jawlines. Fun huh? Oh yeah, Pete Phenet was a squared-away John Lovett . . . you know, the yellow-pages guy from* Saturday Night Live*! More later. KKF*

CHAPTER 38

THE PARDON

PRESIDENT REAGAN DID not pardon many, and Colin L. Koenig, a.k.a. Colin King, was not one of the lucky ones. However, his day did come at the end of the first Bush administration. The media treated him very lightly, since Caspar Weinberger and Admiral John Poindexter were the headliners. Swifty threw a small "thank-you party" for those who had supported him. Jake Leonardo and his wife, Amber, surprisingly, sent a large spray of flowers and a fruit basket. Jake personally signed the note. Artie presented him with a diamond pinkie ring at the gathering, hugging him and kissing Kim's hand. Joe Seeley, dapper as always, arrived with a Hollywood starlet, and Augie Bash spent the evening dancing with Naomi Faust Kulikowski etc., etc.

Swifty felt so good about his new status that he rushed to the post office to register to vote. He called Bluey Bluing and asked how he could get a Concealed Carry Permit for a handgun. Bluey took him to Shooter's World and signed him up for a class. He applied to the VA to see which of his veteran's benefits could be reinstated. He was no longer a felon!

Six weeks later, shooter's course completed and FBI files complete, Swifty received his permit. Kim bought each of them a handgun. She had completed her permit requirements two years earlier, but had never actually carried a gun. For Swifty there was a 380 Beretta semiauto and for Kim a .32 SIG SAUER auto. Swifty voted in a municipal election for the first time in twenty years. It felt good.

So Kim was well and heading the surprisingly successful Desert Oasis project while aiding Kyle in the Anza development. Swifty's business flourished, with more than fifty clients depending upon him for advice and paying handsomely for it. Artie, though his arthritis bothered him a great deal, was aging gracefully. Nelson had gotten out of Safford and moved to Brentwood, California, where he was acting as technical advisor on a movie and a TV show devoted to exposing con artists. Norm had left the business in the capable hands of Kyle Faust and Buck Janis, retiring to his ranch in Prescott. Peltz's clinical operations continued to bring large revenues to Artie's operation, and both had become rich in the process.

As the years passed, Pete Phenet and Kyle merged General Alliance Insurance and Properties and Cellestine Enterprises under the holding company of Cellestine General Alliance, Inc., with Kyle as president and Pete as chairman of the board. Buck Janis accepted his new role as a subordinate to Kyle with grace, since he was making a fortune in the blossoming Arizona real estate market. Yoshi had retired from the law to manage the portfolio of his Japanese clients. Connor Grove continued to live comfortably in Switzerland. Jake . . . good old Jake, continued to run his fitness and nutrition businesses. He grudgingly admitted he had made a mistake letting Kyle get away, but he still managed to "muddle along."

Wait until I tell you what happened next to completely upset the apple cart!

PART FIVE

CHAPTER 39

BRECK

WHEN A NEW administration takes office in Washington, there tends to be a lot of job rotation and a few false starts. Bill Clinton tried three times to name an attorney general. Finally, Janet Reno was selected. One of her early choices for associate deputy attorney general was federal judge Adam Breck, who would head the Criminal Division's Organized Crime Unit. This was bad news for those who couldn't keep out of sight. Breck was a "headhunter" with a long memory.

"You see this in the paper?" Kim pushed the front section of the *Wall Street Journal* toward Swifty, bumping his coffee cup and sending a few drops on to the kitchen table. They were enjoying an unusual breakfast together on a rainy Monday morning in Scottsdale.

"Hey, watch it ... what?" Swifty picked up the page and his eyes focused like lasers on the right-hand column below the fold:

Judge Breck Forsakes Bench for Justice Post

Distinguished former Watergate prosecution aide, Adam A. Breck Has accepted the position of Associate Deputy Attorney General in charge of the Organized Crime Division in the new Clinton administration. President Jimmy Carter appointed Breck to the federal bench as he left office in January of 1981 and has served the mid-Atlantic region since that time.

The article went on to mention the Watergate figures Breck helped put away and the well-known cases tried in his court over the past several years and that he had served as Deputy U.S. Attorney prior to his tenure with Watergate.

"Jesus . . . to this guy 'organized crime' probably means any tax-paying business. Talk about a zealot . . . he is one scary guy." Swifty didn't think beyond the moment on the issue, but Kim did.

"What do you think he is going to do about your case?"

"What case? I'm out of the picture . . . served my time. Pardoned." Swifty shrugged.

"I hope so, honey, I hope so." Kim looked out the window.

Swifty knew the look and the mood. She had something brewing in there and he would have to pry it out.

"What are you thinking, dear? What's going on?" Swifty probed.

"Nothing."

"Honey?"

"I said, nothing."

"Honey?"

"Well . . . you and your buddies . . . Artie Leonardo et al., better keep your heads down." She sighed.

"Honey! Honey! Artie Leonardo is not my buddy! Where do you get that?" Swifty slammed the paper on the table, spilling more of his coffee.

"Oh, then what is he to you? What is Nelson Leigh? What is Connor Grove? What is Louis Peltz? I didn't mean it in the pejorative. I meant it sincerely, you guys better be careful. My instinct tells me that this Breck guy is trouble."

Swifty cooled down and stared at her. "You think he'll come after that old situation . . . with Leonardo?"

"Yes, if he thinks of it or if someone or something calls it to his attention." Kim rose from the table and headed to the bathroom.

"You see that asshole Breck is back in the action?" Augie Bash was driving while Artie sat beside him in the front seat of the Cadillac.

"Yeah . . . yeah. He was on TV last night too. We better hope his eyes stay focused on New York. I never want to see that snake out here again." Artie reached for the car phone and began to fumble for Jake's number.

"Leonardo . . . . oh hi, Pop, finally got you using the car phone, I like it! What's going on?" Jake was pleased that his father had overcome his considerable reluctance to use the newly installed mobile telephone.

"Jakie, did you see where that creep Adam Breck has taken over the Organized Crime Unit of the Justice Department? He was on the Cable News last night. You know, CNN . . . where the guys were on the Iraq war." Artie yelled into the phone, assuming car noise would impede his transmission.

Jake pulled the phone from his ear and responded, "I saw it, Dad, not so loud. What are we supposed to do, put a hit out on him? Hey, only kidding!"

"Don't joke like that. You can't tell who listens in on this stuff. I just wanted to know that you saw it. We have to keep low. Guilty or innocent, guys like this don't care . . . they're 'headhunters.'" Artie continued to yell.

"Pop, the auditors, the IRS, the State Department of Corporations . . . they all check us out religiously. We are a clean operation . . . pillars of the community. Not even a speeding ticket . . . except for Amber . . . she got two last year . . . but, me, I am good. Don't worry. What is past is past." Jake continued to hold the phone away from his ear as he spoke.

"Come out to my place tonight . . . bring the boys . . . and Amber too, I want to talk to you about this. Besides, your mom wants to see you. You get that?" Artie boomed out.

"Yeah. Yeah, Pop. We'll come out . . . but it's got to be tomorrow night. I got business with the Frozen Yogurt people tonight. Tomorrow night?" Jake waited.

"Okay. By six. See ya tomorrow night." Artie pushed the quit button of the instrument and hung it back in the rack. "These things aren't perfected yet, Augie . . . I don't like 'em."

"They'll get better, Arthur, they'll get better." Augie smiled and drove on.

Two months after these conversations, Swifty and Kim received an invitation to the grand opening of Jake's Frozen Yogurt in Old Town. Jake has opened nine other Frozen Yogurt shops in Phoenix, Glendale, and Chandler. In one season he had created a local brand name and had begun to franchise the business, hoping to take it to Los Angeles next. The Scottsdale shop would be upscale and the first outside a shopping center. Jake hoped to entice the visitors to the Art Walk in Old Town to cool off with some yogurt. Naturally, the low season, in the summer, was a better bet; but there were plenty of warm days in the winter and spring. As it happened, this was an unusually warm April, which boded well for Jake's enterprise.

"I can't go . . . I'll try the yogurt later. Kyle and I have a big presentation that night – a whole convention of out-of-state clients at the Boulders. You go and tell me how good it is." Kim wasn't that excited about anything to do with Jake Leonardo anyway. The only reason she tolerated that family was because of Toni Marie, a good friend.

"Okay, I'll go stag with Augie or Joe Seeley. Can't get into too much trouble with them." Swifty, shuffling a few papers, felt uneasy about going to even a Frozen Yogurt shop opening without Kim.

The evening arrived and Swifty drove over in his new Mercedes, a gift from Kim for his birthday the previous fall. "It wouldn't be too long before he hit the 'big one,'" he thought.

A moderate crowd of city dignitaries, potential patrons – adults and children – and Jake Leonardo's employees gathered to suffer through the brief speeches and ribbon cutting. Jake and Amber, their two teenage boys, Artie and Theresa, Augie Bash, and Joe Seeley were amongst the throng. Norm Cellestine, who was invited, could not drive alone (Alzheimer's was feared) and remained at his ranch in Prescott.

Banners were strewn across First Street, and two colorfully dressed clowns worked the crowd. Jake looked more like the bulky businessman he was than the thug he enjoyed portraying, and his speech was self-deprecating, smooth, and effective. The mayor and the president of the chamber of commerce lauded Jake's foresight and contributions to the community. In ninety minutes, after mounds of free yogurt cones and videos for the kids, the group began to break up. Swifty hung back with Artie and Augie, while Teresa accompanied Amber and her boys to their home in Paradise Valley. Jake gave his father, Augie, and Swifty a tutorial on operating yogurt machines that all could have lived without. Finally, with some congratulations and backslapping, the group of men agreed to walk up the street to the Corral for a drink. They were likely to avoid the nearer Wild Jack's Bar, because there had long been bad blood between Jake and the owner of Wild Jack's, Gordon Macaw.

Augie and Artie walked up Scottsdale Road, with Jake and Swifty slightly to the rear. "You think my idea is good, Swifty?" Jake inquired at his squeaky best. Swifty noted that it was the first time in ten years Jake had addressed him directly.

"It seems right in line with the rest of your health-oriented enterprises, Jake. I'd say 'an idea whose time has come.' I applaud you."

"Thank you, Swifty. Say, you seen Kyle lately?" Jake never mentioned Kyle to anyone, since he had let his right arm get away.

"Yeah, I saw him yesterday. He's doing well." Swifty responded.

"Good. Good. I gotta tell you, man . . . that was the biggest mistake I ever made . . . lettin' that guy get away. I never gave him credit for his contributions . . . I learned after he left . . . I learned. Please wish him well for me." Jake actually seemed sincere.

"I will, Jake . . . Kyle will appreciate that," Swifty said.

"That guy has a real knack for figures and he works like a dog," Jake continued as Swifty shook his head affirmatively.

As they approached the Corral, he concentrated on what Jake was saying, but from the corner of his eye, Swifty saw the familiar figure of Gordon Macaw, co-owner of Wild Jack's Bar, crossing the street about a fifty yards in front of them. A part of his mind said, "This is normal"; another part sent a warning signal throughout his body. Something wasn't right. Something was definitely wrong. He could hear Jake's words, but they didn't matter . . . his mind was telling him to act.

The figure approaching had something in his hand . . . it, it was . . . it was . . .

As this was happening, his mind caught up and helped him focus, in disbelief.

It was a gun . . . a gun. But, why . . . why was this happening? The first shot downed the figure in front of him . . . Augie . . . he made a slight head fake then moved to his left, but too late!

Swifty acted. To Jake's surprise, he extracted the .380 automatic from his belt holster and raised it with both hands, clicking off the safety instinctively as he leveled it and fired.

He felt the searing heat in his chest, then the pain. He couldn't breathe. The images before him faded. Something struck his left knee, then his right . . . next came his face. It was the hard pavement. He tried to retch but he couldn't make it happen. The street became a sea of burning oil and he was in it. Then . . . nothing.

Jake was flabbergasted! He was talking to Swifty – something he normally did not do – and the man was drawing a gun? Why? Then, he heard the shots: first from ahead, then next to him, then another from ahead. He knew he had left his gun in the car. He always did when kids were around. What was going on? He stood for a second, frozen, as Swifty went down, in the street before him. His father and Augie were facedown on the sidewalk at his feet, and a few yards ahead, lying on the pavement before him, was Gordon Macaw – hands on his neck, with blood spurting between his fingers. Jake sprung forward.

Macaw, on his knees, gasping loudly, clawed at the gun he had dropped when Swifty's round caught him in the neck. Jake kicked the gun aside and slapped Gordon's bare face with an open hand. The man drew his head back with the blow and seemed surprised as it bounced against a light post. With the rebound, his face met Jake Leonardo's right fist, followed by the left. Two minutes later, when the police arrived, a blood-soaked Jake Leonardo was still driving vicious blows into the mass of pulp that was once the face of the now-dead Gordon Macaw. Four policemen pulled Jake off and secured him with cuffs on his wrists and plastic ties on his ankles.

Two ambulances arrived a moment later and backed up to the bodies as a paramedic worked feverishly on Swifty. Jake sat in a daze, watching from the sidewalk. "Save my father, save my father! Work on him! I owe you, King, I owe you! I owe you again!" If anyone heard him, they paid no attention. The three bodies were far more intriguing than the bloody maniac in the business suit sitting against the light post, howling incoherently.

Kyle put his hand lightly on Kim's cheek. Her color began to return and her lashes fluttered. Naomi handed him a cool cloth and he dabbed it carefully on her neck. Her eyes blinked open. He held her down as she tried to rise. "Stay down, babe . . . wait a minute."

"Swifty . . . Swifty . . . !" she sputtered.

"Swifty is okay. I just talked to the hospital. He's conscious, but sedated. Stay down!" She struggled to rise against Kyle's grasp as he whispered to her.

"What happened?" Kim said faintly.

"Honey, you fainted dead away," Naomi said from behind Kyle. "Kyle, let's try to get her in a chair."

Kyle and Naomi carefully helped Kim into a chair, and Naomi put a glass of cool water to her lips. She shook her head and blurted, "I want to go to him now!"

"We will. We will. Just get your blood circulating again and we will," Kyle said reassuringly.

"Who shot him?" Kim demanded.

"I guess Gordon Macaw shot Artie Leonardo and Augie Bash. One of the rounds went through Artie and struck Swifty in the chest. He has a broken collarbone and a bullet lodged under his chin. He's going to be okay," Kyle related what Bluey Bluing had told him on the phone. "I guess it's touch and go with Artie and Augie."

"Oh my god! Kyle, let's go now. I'm okay. Help me to the car. And, for hell's sake, turn the air on high. Naomi, please stay here and call Norm Cellestine. He probably won't know what you're saying, but call him anyway . . . and call Buck to tell him where I am." Naomi shook her head affirmatively to Kim's directions.

Kyle helped her to the Lincoln, put her in the front passenger seat, and scooted around to the driver's side. He started the engine and kicked the air on to high, lowering the windows until the car cooled.

Kim fanned herself. As soon as they were underway, the cooling system in the big car did its job and Kyle raised the windows.

"Why would Macaw shoot Swifty? We hardly know him!" Kim gasped through the cup of water she nursed.

"Bluey thinks he was after Jake. Augie sort of threw himself in front of everybody and caught the first round. Artie actually raised his arms, trying to shield Jake and Swifty. The next three rounds hit him, with one going through and bouncing off Swifty's collarbone and lodging in his jaw. I guess Artie is bad off. One bullet ruptured an artery. Augie has a collapsed lung with fragments in his liver. He is on life support. Jake . . . not a scratch."

"Who stopped Macaw? The police?" Kim asked as Kyle wheeled down Scottsdale toward Memorial Hospital.

"Swifty had his gun. He shot Macaw in the neck. Jake . . . I guess . . . beat him to death after that," Kyle mumbled.

"What? Swifty shot him? Oh Jesus! Swifty?" Kim cried out.

"Yeah . . . he did . . . he saved them . . . Jake went nuts and beat the guy to death. And, Kimmie . . . you better be prepared for this. It isn't fun. Both Jake and Swifty are being held until bond is posted."

"But why? It was self-defense! What's going on?"

"Bluey says the DA is suspicious of what occurred and is considering charges at least against Jake . . . maybe Swifty too. But Seeley told Bluey that Swifty was completely in the clear. There were eight or nine witnesses who say Macaw shoot before Swifty drew his gun. He is licensed. He did what he should have done. Jake . . . well Jake kind of overreacted . . . not unusual for Jake." Kyle turned into the parking lot and parked in Doctor's Parking.

Kyle walked Kim slowly toward the entrance. He enjoyed being this close to her. She was his best friend's wife, but down deep he loved her too. He relished her aroma and the feel of her body against his. He knew it was wrong and nothing would ever come of it, but he envied his friend. To him, this was the ultimate woman. What a lucky guy . . . that Swifty . . . and deserving. Nobody deserved the love of a woman like this more than Swifty. Kyle still envied him.

Swifty was sleeping. His jaw was wrapped in gauze and blood was soaking through. A nurse was checking his pulse.

"Are you his wife?" Kim nodded. "You?" Kyle said, "Brother." The nurse stepped back.

"He's in and out . . . sedated. The bullet was working its way out, so the doctor removed it right here a few minutes ago. He stitched it. The blood will stop soon. He will probably have a sore jaw for a while." The nurse spoke first to Kim then to Kyle.

The short, thin policeman hovered nearby, but did not interfere.

Swifty's eyes began to flutter. Kim moved closer. His eyes opened slightly and he first began to curl his lip, then winced. His eyes widened.

"Don't smile, honey . . . your jaw is broken . . . And your collarbone. Stay still," Kim quietly admonished.

"Am I the only one shot?" Swifty managed to spit out.

"No, no . . . Mr. Leonardo and Augie . . . They're here too." Kim stroked his forehead.

"My chest hurts," Swifty whispered.

"The bullet hit your collarbone and broke it . . . it will get better."

Swifty nodded and closed his eyes.

Kyle left Kim with Swifty and walked past the policeman into the hall. Bluey Bluing was leaning against the opposite wall.

"How's he doing?" Bluey pushed off the wall.

"Sore, but he'll live. What's the deal?" Kyle shot back at the big ex-policeman.

"DA says self-defense on Swifty. Possible mayhem on Jake. If Artie croaks he'll lighten up. Says he got a call from Washington. They want to send an investigator out because of the 'notoriety' of the victims," Bluey reeled off.

"Washington who and why?" Kyle pressed.

"Justice, Organized Crime, fuckin' Breck. Wants to put Jake away, Artie too, if he lives . . . Swifty if he could. Otherwise make 'em all very uncomfortable with lots of press. Show he's doin' a great job all over the nation to rid us of these unscrupulous gangland types who run Yogurt Stores and beat up killers. Typical Liberal bullshit." Bluey rested.

"Yeah . . . yeah. Well, let's get these guys back on their feet first, then we'll worry about Breck and Clinton." Kyle waived and moved toward the elevator.

"Where you goin'?"

"To intensive care . . . see how Augie and Artie are doing. Coming or going?" Kyle did not turn around.

"Going. I'll be back in a couple hours. See if I can get more." Bluey left.

CHAPTER 40

MATURITY

SWIFTY SAT UP in bed and read the headlines:

LOCAL MEN TARGETED BY ORGANIZED CRIME HEAD

The *Arizona Republic* pretty much paraphrased the *Washington Post* story. Adam Breck had granted an interview outlining his plans in several states to put pressure on organized crime. He led with his intent to investigate the "mob hit" in Arizona where "two convicted felons and a rogue ex-cop were wounded and a mob boss's son was being held for murder, in broad daylight." Neither article corrected the errors about "mob hit," "mob boss," "two convicted felons," "rogue ex-cop," or "broad daylight." Swifty repeated the same expletives over and over.

"I guess it wouldn't do much good to send a letter asking for a correction." Kim looked at Joe Seeley.

"No, no, Kim it wouldn't do any good. They wouldn't publish it, and if they did, it would be on page thirty. What we need to do is prepare for a frontal assault from Mr. Breck. Swifty, you have to get another lawyer. If I'm representing Artie and Jake has New York representation, you'll need somebody good . . . maybe LA. I'll check to see who'd be willing."

"I guess it sounds stupid to ask what I'm being defended against since I am not charged with anything." Swifty looked a Joe.

"Yeah, it sounds stupid. No, you won't be charged, but you will be probed beyond your imagination."

"Why us?" Kim worried out loud.

Joe responded: "Politics. Breck and his handlers see a great opportunity to take a shot – pardon the reference – at the Republicans for Swifty's pardon. It looks like Bush didn't know what he was doing or his people are in league with some crime figure. Two months after Bush is out . . . his pardonee is in a 'shoot-out' while in the company of 'organized crime figures.' Artie and Jake, well, they're fair game. Artie because of his past and the suspicion that he still 'dabbles' in dirty stuff, and Jake because it is presumed as his father's son to have his fingers in the mud too. Fair or not, that's the way it goes."

"Joe, how do you think Breck is going to approach this thing? Do you think he will send investigators to check out all my clients and to generally harass me?" Swifty asked.

"Yes and yes, plus he will find a way to get the IRS all over you. Also, I'm sorry to say, Kim will be checked out."

"Me?"

"Yes, bank on it. Cellestine . . . Kyle Faust, all you folks will be under a microscope. We'll have accountants all over the Leonardo Companies and Cellestine General Alliance and all of its subs . . . we'll have them with us for years. This 'Keating Five'[3]* deal and the Savings and Loan scandals will be wrapped up and the staff will just move to our things. My guess is they will try to tie the two unrelated issues together in order to keep the press interested. It will not be fun." Joe seemed to be counting his billable hours as he spoke.

"Isn't all that Savings and Loan stuff behind us? I mean they've already pinned all this on Keating, haven't they?" Kim asked.

"Look, it's in this administration's interest and that of the Democratic Congress to keep painting this 'Republican Problem' with red ink. It's the way of our political system. Like the man said, 'Politics ain't beanbag.'" Joe sighed.

For two years Adam Breck and his team of lawyers, accountants and investigators tore into Artie Leonardo's and Jake Leonardo's businesses. Fortunately, the Leonardos had employed attorneys who wisely separated their business activities and scrupulously reviewed their income and tax documents. Both Artie and Jake were audited each year from the seventies

---

[3] 'Keating Five – Alan Cranston (D-CA) Dennis DiConcini (D-AZ) John Glenn (D-OH) John Mc Cain, (R-AZ) Donald Riegle (D-MI). The five senators were accused of corruption in 1989 for intervening on behalf of Charles Keating, Lincoln Savings and Loan boss, who was under regulatory scrutiny at the time.

forward, so they had already been found as clean. However, Breck traced foreign income sources to a Mexican holding company. While he had no authority south of the border, he used his influence to pressure the Mexican government to close down Cliniquè de Obregón on the pretext of expiration of license. Peltz, while not pursued personally, scrambled to find a new location in Asia.

Artie, his health greatly impaired by the bullet wounds he had sustained at the hand of Gordon Macaw, was bound to a wheelchair most of the time. It was also rumored that he was suffering with pancreatic cancer.

Jake Leonardo, though found not guilty of "mayhem," was directed by the court to "lower his profile." He hired a president for his organization and stepped out of the limelight.

Augie Bash lost seventy-five pounds and moved to Flagstaff where he bought half interest in a 7-Eleven. He would walk with a cane the rest of his life . . . only another six years.

Kyle Faust and Peter Phenet opened their doors wide to federal investigators and disclosed all audits to the analyst community by press release. While they had a great deal of explaining to do about the resultant stock dip, both to shareholders' groups and clients, within twenty-four months Cellestine General Alliance stock had regained its momentum and moved from the NASDAQ to the New York Stock Exchange. CGA traded throughout the mid-nineties from thirty-six to fifty-four, with an average going-forward PE of 17. Peter and Kyle owned over a million shares each, outright, and both held options for another million.

Swifty, as a sole proprietor, took a major hit. The *Arizona Republic* ran a four-part series on the Leonardos with three full columns devoted to Swifty. They documented his time in jail, every time he played golf with Artie, every time they were seen together, the fact that Artie owned a large block of Cellestine General Alliance stock, that his wife, Kim was employed as an executive at Cellestine, and that he had "saved Jake Leonardo's life in a 'mob hit' attempt." A number of clients left him abruptly. Several did not pay. His old reliables were interviewed extensively, and his income records were reviewed, checked, and rechecked. Though he had been audited regularly and the files for seven earlier years had been certified as closed, they were reopened and reviewed again. He was presented with tax bills for each of the years, whether he had already settled, including interest and penalties. His lawyers recommended paying, then filing appeals with tax courts. He complied and paid over nine hundred thousand dollars. The Clinton Tax Increase, retroactive to January of 1993, increased his liability to one million two hundred thousand dollars. Swifty sold stock at a loss and paid the bill. (His case was not heard in Federal Tax Court for three years. He settled the next year in state court. He eventually won his cases, and eight hundred thousand was refunded and credits for two hundred thousand were applied to his state taxes.)

In reflecting back on the shooting incident, Swifty could not recall the entire event. He remembered thinking it "was not real . . . other people . . . another time . . ." "Not us, not

now . . ." kept running through his mind, as though he had seen it all in a movie. The doctors said it had to do with shock. Actually, the entire Breck persecution incident never seemed real to Swifty. He wanted to ask Breck why he was doing this to him, but he knew it made no sense.

Breck, like most Washington careerists – whether in office or on the bench – had no personal feelings about hurting people. He regarded it as his "right" as an official to follow his instinct. If someone was injured, "He deserved it."

The '94 election slowed things a bit. With the Democrats out of the leadership, there was less Breck could do to manage attacks on legitimate businesses. He actually had to focus on true organized crime in New York and Boston.

CHAPTER 41

THE FUTURE

THROUGHOUT THIS UNCOMFORTABLE period, Kim continued to excel. Her interest in Cellestine, including substantial stock options, brought her enough to overcome Swifty's lost income and tax outlay. Interest rates were down, sales were great, and Desert Oasis thrived. She had once hoped they could have a baby, but with all the trouble, that was out of the question.

Swifty, back to square one – or at least two – decided to "make lemonade from lemons." The experience of IRS audits, business setbacks due to baseless criminal investigations, and unwarranted attacks in the press gave him a new, if limited, market. He put the word out: "Swifty King, Advice . . . No Matter What Your Challenge . . . Swifty Has Been There." The going was slow, but he began to get a few bites. Smooth and confident, Swifty could charm the chin off of Jay Leno. He looked so good: just tall enough, slim, but not skinny, dark hair and eyes, and an assuredness about him that made you feel safe in his presence. He had a great sense of humor and could joke even about a person's handicaps and make them laugh. Two of his clients were in wheelchairs, and Swifty would sit for a half hour and exchange "gimp" jokes with them. Swifty was easy to take, easy to love.

One of the early "bites" was from a former State Department official who had faced a unique challenge when he served in the Clinton administration. Cedric Bain, a graduate of Princeton and a practicing Liberal, grew increasingly uncomfortable with the "truth shading" that ran rampant in his department. He served in a number of overseas assignments and saw the facts on the ground, in the Middle East, in Africa, and in Southeast Asia. Often he was required to go against the facts in order to comply with the foreign policy of the administration in power. This was true during Nixon, Ford, Carter, Bush, and Clinton. However, in the latter, he knew some of the men who died because of the posturing. When he retired, he resolved to rectify some of the "mistakes."

But the adventures with Ced Bain are for another day and I promise to report on them soon. KKF

CHAPTER 42

SPIRIT

SPIRIT HAD BEEN the liveliest little guy you could imagine. She brought joy to everyone she encountered. At thirteen, she began to slow down. At first, it seemed to be age. She had never been ill – never missed a meal, a run, a swim – but suddenly, she was an old dog, not a pup. It happened over weeks, not months. Arthritis, accidents in the house, whining when left alone. Swifty found blood in her water dish. He didn't tell Kim. He took Spirit to the vet. "Old" was the diagnosis. "One kidney . . . nature. Take the dog out of her misery before the pain really sets in . . . probably cancer."

Swifty called Kyle. They conspired. "Maybe get a 'look-alike' dog."

"Maybe take her to another vet." "Call Peltz . . . find those dog docs from Obregón." They covered it all. Peltz was in Bangkok, trying to get his new clinic up to the level enjoyed at Obregón. Steiger was with him, but Espinoza had lost his license and had fled to Andorra.

Peltz suggested, "Thirteen years . . . a good life . . . let her go."

Kim had noticed Spirit's downhill plunge. She understood. It was time. She had felt a few "tugs" in her own side and noticed a little blood when she flossed her teeth. She didn't tell Swifty . . . but she did confide in Kyle.

"Well shit, little sis, we're going to run Peltz and Steiger down in Thailand and see what the deal is. Swifty has to know, honey . . . he's your husband. He loves you more than life. We all need to put our heads together on this. Want me to go home with you tonight? We can tell him together," Kyle offered.

"No . . . thanks . . . thanks so much for being you, Kyle. I love you. But, I have to tell him, alone."

"By god, we're going in the morning! Screw Desert Oasis. Kyle and Buck have that covered. We're out of here!" Swifty alternately stormed the room, stopped, hugged Kim, and then marched back and forth again.

"Maybe I should go to UCLA first . . . get them to check me, like before," Kim suggested tentatively.

"Maybe, yeah, but I have to call Peltz. See what he and Steiger say. I'll call now!" Swifty was hyper.

"Honey, it's three in the morning over there. Let's give it a few hours. I'll call UCLA just to get things rolling. I feel good. Maybe this is just a false alarm. I have no blood in my urine . . . at least that I can see. No fatigue . . . not much . . . just a little tired." Kim began to realize that she felt awful and had for weeks. Her weight was slipping – usually a welcome occurrence.

Kim King was a beautiful woman. She had started out cute and got beautiful. The little personality lines that had appeared at the corner of her eyes, the few extra pounds, the sophistication of her walk made that cute little girl an impressive-looking woman. Swifty knew it. He was so proud of her. Some of us thought Swifty tried to stay in shape – he gained a little weight like we all do – and keep himself up because of Kim. They were a striking couple, even with all of their challenges.

Artie Leonardo was another story. He was in constant pain. The arthritis wouldn't let him play golf or walk more than a few paces. He drank in the evening and suffered all day, each day. All three bullets had taken a toll. His kidney function was impaired and his liver didn't cleanse well. His spleen, ruptured in the shooting, had been removed, as had one lobe of his right lung. Life was no longer pleasant. He missed Augie. He missed seeing Jake. His grandsons had gone away to college and never came back. He missed hearing about Swifty. He even missed that damn Peltz. Once in a while, Toni Marie would come over or call. That was it.

Breck's people had taken him apart and put him back together in several ways. Much of his fortune was depleted by lawyer's fees. He still held millions in Cellestine General Alliance stock, but that was for the kids. He had plenty of "walk around" cash, but he couldn't walk around! Auditors had combed through all of his records, and investigators had probed him and Teresa unmercilessly. They insisted that he and Peltz were operating an illegal medical business in Mexico. Artie pointed out that he owned a portion of a business on foreign soil and paid taxes in the States on all of it. He said that Peltz was a legitimate research scientist and that the clinic's physicians were all duly licensed in Mexico and their practices approved by the Federal Medical Standards Boards of that nation and the State of Sonora. Breck found a way to get their licenses pulled and to shut down the clinic. He, curiously, didn't pursue Peltz, other than getting the IRS to audit him.

Jake's records were pristine. No one questioned the current documentation, but the focus was on business processes in the seventies. Jake told them, "All those records are closed, destroyed and history." But they pressed on. Names from the past reappeared.

"What do you mean our passports are rescinded? That's ridiculous! Who . . . how?" Swifty had called the travel agent to arrange for the flight to Bangkok. The next morning, the agent called back to tell him their reservations could not be confirmed as the State Department had rescinded their passports. Their recourse was to appeal the rescission to a federal judge. Swifty called Joe Seeley.

"Swifty, I know that time is of the essence, but 'State' tells Jeff Domres that the Justice Department requested the rescission based on the 'Fleeing Felon Rule.'" They say you and Kim are material witnesses who might flee to avoid testimony in lieu of prosecution. We have to go to the Department of Justice and find out if this is from two years ago when they were harassing you or something new we don't know about. It will take three days."

The three days turned into two weeks. Spirit still displayed some energy, but she was fading fast. Kim continued to hold her and stroke until she would sleep. Swifty could see the strain on both of them. Kim was clearly losing weight again, and her face looked haggard.

Joe Seeley finally called. "It's Breck. He wants both of you to testify before a grand jury against the Leonardos. It's a fishing expedition. But, if you don't do it . . . no passports. Jeff says his contact was told to leak this to you if you hadn't come asking."

"Well shit! Doesn't he know the bind we're in? I have to get Kim to Thailand . . . have Steiger look at her now! She's sick again, Joe . . . help me," Swifty pleaded.

"We know, kid, we know. I got an idea. Maybe if you called Breck . . . asked him off the record what he wants. It's a long shot . . . But you need a quick decision." Joe seemed unusually pessimistic.

"Mr. Koenig, or King, I guess that is your alias now. Uh, why do you think I would meet with you without counsel? That just is not proper for you or for our case. Why don't you go back to your lawyer, go through channels. We'll get to you in due course." Breck was his usual pompous self.

"Mr. Breck, my legal name is King now. Look, I am pleading with you, sir! My wife is desperately ill and the only possible cure for her disease is in Asia. We must get her there now. If you won't release me, certainly she has no involvement here. Release her passport so she can go. Please!" Swiftly was not used to begging but he would do what it took.

"I am sorry about your wife and you are understandably distraught, but we have the finest medical care in the world right here in the United States. What could possibly be the advantage of some untested procedure . . . developed illegally I might add . . . by some unlicensed practitioners? Besides, your wife is a material witness in a major federal criminal case. We need her testimony and, frankly, we can't afford to have her leave now . . . and perhaps . . . due to some unfortunate and improper treatment . . . be unable to return." Breck was smiling on the other end, Swifty knew it.

"Breck, you son of a bitch! What do you want? I'll give you whatever it is now! You want Artie? You got him! You want Jake? He is yours! Please let me save my wife!" Swifty felt himself burning. He paused.

"Mr. K . . . King . . . King. Sir, you are upset. So, I won't respond to the personal attacks. However, if you have information material to a federal case . . . regardless of the potential defendants, I would advise you to confide in counsel and have him contact my investigators. That is all I can offer. Good day, sir." He hung up.

"You pissed him off, Swifty. Why in the hell did you swear at him? This could hurt us. What was this about Artie and Jake? What did he say?" Joe Seeley had been listening in from across the room. Jeffrey Domres, appearing disinterested, studied Swifty's new weight bench. They were calling from Swifty's combination office and gym in the new home Kim had designed for them at Desert Oasis.

Swifty told them of the conversation, in detail. Joe whistled. "This bastard has something or wants something we don't know about. Any thoughts, Jeff?"

"Huh? Oh, yeah." Jeffrey Domres, who never aged, took off his coat, exposing his lanky frame, and hung it on a metal peg extending from the exercise unit. "Breck clearly has a target . . . one of the Leonardos, probably Jake. Arthur is too old and sick . . . no advantage to nailing him. Maybe his target is Swifty. Plus, somebody's feeding him . . . some witness with great information. Only thing else he needs is corroboration, I think. Our question is who and what do they have. I can find out the target . . . but we all have to think who might be the witness."

"Can your guys at Justice find out for us . . . the target I mean . . . quick?" Swifty asked nervously.

"Today, Swifty . . . I can find out today. This whole call thing was part of their plan. They know they have you. You gave up Artie and Jake on the phone, but they doubt you know anything that could be used in prosecution. I think, and I believe I will know for sure this very day, they want you to go get them something on Jake and Artie. Probably they want you to take some kind of fall yourself."

"Shit. They call this government. Find out. I have to save Kim."

"Yeah, we'll find out and then we will mount a defense. Remember, lad, we are counsel for the Leonardos, not you. We may be on opposite sides come morning," Joe Seeley sighed.

"How's Kimmie today?" Kyle asked as he poured a diet Coke into an ice-filled glass on the bar.

"It's an up day. Both she and Spirit seem good. Yesterday was shitty. She was throwing up, the dog was crying. If I ever felt like going back to drinking, it would be now, buddy." Swifty was wiping down after his workout. He had stopped drinking abruptly three years earlier when Kim told him he was getting too fat. Drinking had always been a temptation to Swifty, as it was to Kyle. They both avoided it now.

"Tell me again what Jeff said. It just didn't sound right on the phone." Kyle took a swig of Coke, wishing it were a beer but knowing why this was better for him. He had held his weight steady for nine years and had no intention of going back to his old regimen – the one that kept him overweight.

"Over twenty years ago, the reason I did that time in prison, I was a messenger. I had no idea what I was carrying. But, I took a package to a guy in Tucson whose name turned out to be Malcolm Ussery. There was another guy named Batera with him. They gave me what I thought was the same package, but turned out to be another one that looked like the same one I gave them. I took that to Chandler . . . to Louis Peltz. He gave me another package to take to the Biltmore. I did, and they arrested me. The feds said I was a courier for laundered money. They wanted me to testify against whoever gave me the money in the first place. I didn't. I got jail time as an accessory."

"Yeah, I know that stuff, but what did Jeff say?"

"He said that this guy Ussery died and Batera disappeared, which the feds told me back then, but now they have evidence that illegal drugs were involved then and that Artie, Jake, and I have been involved in the drug and money laundering business for years, as partners. Ussery's daughter has volunteered this to the feds, and another witness, who knows me well, has verified her testimony. Breck wants to prosecute Jake Leonardo and me under RICO, you know, the racketeering laws. He demands that I give him everything he wants, before a grand jury, or he won't release Kim's passport." Swifty shook his head.

"Who is this witness?" Kyle asked.

"I don't know. Nobody will say. Jeff's contact guy intimated it's a woman," Swifty said quietly.

"What are you going to do?"

"Whatever Breck wants . . . as long as he'll sign an agreement of immunity with Kim and release her passport."

"You'll lie?"

"Shit, Kyle . . . what else can I do? I don't know anything. The only part I left out twenty-two years ago was Jake Leonardo's goddamn name! I just never told them it was him that gave me the package. Nobody ever much pushed me on Peltz. I'll answer, embellish, whatever, to save Kim." Swifty pounded the table.

CHAPTER 43

JUSTICE?

Jake Leonardo paced back and forth across Joe Seeley's imported carpet. "Why would King open his mouth now? Shit! We've been good to him and to his wife. Shit!"

"Well, Jake, come on. His wife's life may be at stake. The guy is emotional. We have time to talk to him. After all, what does he actually know?" Joe shrugged.

"Who knows what my father told him over the years? I mean, they were like bosom buddies, playin' golf, drinkin', the old man might have said anything . . . 'specially since he's gotten old." Jake alternately frowned and grimaced. "You'd think he was the son, not me."

"What about the wife? She have it in for you?" Jeff asked from a chair near the window.

"Why'd ya ask that? Shit, I only saw her maybe five times. Once, another guy and I sort of pushed her a little . . . nothin' rough." Jake squinted at Domres. He didn't like Domres.

"I asked because it's a woman that Breck has tucked away. A woman who is close to King and is spilling her guts. I just wondered if Mrs. King would be the one. Unlikely, sure, because it seems to be hurting her worst of all, but I wondered. How did you rough her up?" Domres stood and walked toward Jake, seemingly unafraid.

Jake didn't like people who appeared unafraid of him, it made him nervous. "Another guy and me, Paul, went into her house and waited for her to come home from work. We teased her, is all . . . didn't touch her, just suggested Swifty forget who gave him this certain package . . . maybe twenty-three years ago. You remember all that shit. And don't stand so close to me. I can smell your breath." Jake leered at Domres.

"Sorry, Mr. Leonardo. Is my breath offensive? Did you stand this close to Mrs. King? Did you scare her? Scare her enough to hold a twenty-year grudge?" Jeff did not let off.

"Hey, who the fuck works for who around here! Back your skinny ass off or you'll be sitting on it!"

"Jake! That is just the kind of behavior that gets you in trouble. You cannot act this way before a grand jury! Sit down and be a professional. And start talking like a businessman with an education. That's what you are . . . not some cheap hood. Jesus!" Joe Seeley stood between the two men and pushed Jake toward a chair.

Jake sat and looked at the ceiling. "Okay. Okay. No, I do not believe Mrs. King holds a grudge. She has always been polite to me. I apologized to her about that incident. I told her I was drunk and irrational. She accepted my apology. No, I don't believe she is the type of person who would do this. Plus, she is one sick girl . . . not the kind of behavior a sick person engages in."

"Anybody have it in for King? Anybody you can think of?" Joe asked.

"Swifty? Everybody loves Swifty King. He has no enemies. You would think this guy walks on water. I get sick of even hearing my own sister gush over the bastard. No, nobody has it in for him that I know of," Jake squeaked.

"Somebody has it in for one of you . . . somebody and Adam Breck."

Joe opened a stick of gum and popped it into his mouth.

Adam Breck convened the grand jury at the federal courthouse in Phoenix two days later. He explained to the press that "this is not a witch hunt, this is a serious look into illegal and organized activity involving citizens of Arizona. Witnesses have been called from other states, California, Georgia, and New York, but our primary objective is right here in your community."

Two young prosecutors sat in the conference room when Swifty entered. His Beverly Hills attorney, Craig Bosson, had to wait outside. Breck did not come in until late in the afternoon. All morning long, the young people, a man and a woman, grilled Swifty about his business, his friendship with Artie Leonardo, his dealing with Jake Leonardo, his wife's job, his clients, and his years in prison. Most of the questions were history, some were inane.

"Who is Nelson Leigh?"

"A man I met in prison."

"Do you consider him a friend?"

"Yes."

"Do you still see him?"

"Sometimes."

"So you admit to making friends with criminals and carrying on a long-term relationship with them?"

"Hard to make friends with anybody but criminals when you are in prison. Nelson became a good friend. He is a television producer now, not a crook."

"What did he produce?"

"He is co-producer of *The Dark Side*, on Fox. It's about con men."

"A subject he knows well."

"I guess."

At four in the afternoon, six hours into testimony, Breck pushed the door open and stood gazing at Swifty. One of the youngsters stopped the reporter.

"Well, Mr. King, long time no see. You have aged well." Breck's huge frame moved into the light. Swifty had seen him on television. He too had aged well, though his hair had thinned.

Breck bent and extended his hand across the table. Swifty took it, applied as much pressure as he received, and stared blankly at Breck.

"Proceed," Breck directed the young attorneys. They were back on the record.

After fifteen minutes, Breck broke in. "When did you decide to get into the illegal drug trade? Were you recruited by Artie Leonardo or his son? Did you meet Jake at college . . . is that it

. . . then he pulled you in with a promise of easy money?"

"You tell me, Counselor. I am all yours."

"So, after Jake Leonardo recruited you and introduced you to his father, the three of you formed a partnership to sell drugs to college students. Then you became a drug courier for Artie Leonardo, occasionally carrying laundered money around for him as well?"

"Whatever you say. I'll sign it."

"So you admit, that after you were released from prison, you continued your relationship with the Leonardos, expanding your operations into Mexico, where the three of you, joined by a man named Louis Peltz, ran a medical scam . . . bilking hundreds of rich sick people out of millions on a promise of restoration of health?"

"As you say, sir."

"My colleagues have a list of times and dates when illegal activity took place. Please listen and affirm or deny their questions . . . elucidating as you will." With this, Breck stood, stretched, and strode from the room.

That was it. Breck's people would tell him what to admit to, how to incriminate himself and the Leonardos. In exchange, he would release Kim's passport. He wouldn't touch Peltz until Kim received treatment. He would not intercede with the Thai government to have Peltz's Asian clinic closed, at least until Kim had been treated.

One can only guess what really goes on in a grand jury room, since it is closed. Witnesses don't even have an attorney present. But, if an enterprising reporter gets to a couple of jurors, listens carefully to the boasting of the prosecutors and pulls a few facts from the witnesses once they are identified, he can develop a scenario.

It didn't take a week until Swifty and Jake were arraigned on open charges. It only took a little longer until a complete transcript of the grand jury proceedings had been reconstructed.

Some further highlights of the proceedings after Swifty's testimony:
"Your name, sir?"
"Walter Allen Cope."
"Are you aquatinted with Mr. Colin King?"
"Yes, sir."
"How is it that you know Mr. King."
"My wife and I have worked with his wife for twenty years. We have seen him at company events."
"Do you know of Mr. King's criminal activity?"
"No, not specifically. I mean, we have all heard stories about Swifty and his thing with Artie Leonardo . . . but nothing specific."
"Mr. Cope, did you overhear Mrs. King telling your wife that she had been threatened by Mr. Jacob Leonardo . . . told not to testify against his criminal activity?"
"Well, that was over twenty years ago. Kim . . . Mrs. King, told Pam, my wife, that Jake Leonardo and another man had once come to her home and threatened her. She was supposed to tell Swifty not to testify against the Leonardos in the case that sent Swifty to prison. She told Pam that years after Swifty was in jail. She said that another man had given her cash to keep them quiet too."
"Cash."
"Yes, some man . . . I think his name was Augie Bash . . . he gave her cash from the Leonardos."
"She told your wife this?"
"Yes, sir."
"State your name please."
"Millicent Audrey Ussery. I am called Audrey."
"Ms. Ussery, did your father once have illegal business dealings with Mr. Leonardo senior and Mr. King?"
"Yes."
"Tell the grand jury the nature of this illegal business, please."

"My late father, Malcolm Ussery, was involved in organized crime in Baltimore, Maryland, mostly gambling. He suffered from bone cancer. He had traveled to Europe in an effort to find a cure. He was not successful, but he did obtain a formula from some men who owed him money. This formula was very complex, but it basically outlined how to grow human organs in animals without killing the animals or having them later be rejected by the humans into whom they were replanted. The formula wouldn't help him, but he used it as a bargaining chip to get Mr. Leonardo's associates to give him a supply of a rare drug that could cure cancer. This drug, K148 it was called back in the sixties, had been stolen from the European companies that had developed it. It was ordered destroyed by several European governments. But, this man, Mr. Peltz, saved a supply and smuggled it into this country. He was and is Mr. Leonardo . . . both Mr. Leonardos's partner."

"Well, if this rare drug could cure cancer, why was it ordered destroyed?"

"Because in the trial, which were closely controlled, several people died. Testing was stopped and the drug was ordered destroyed. It was a big thing in Europe in the late sixties and early seventies."

"Why did your father want a drug that was so dangerous?"

"Because, Mr. Peltz and his people had found the problem and corrected it. My father learned that many people had been saved using K148. He wanted it. But, he wanted his own physicians to administer it. He didn't trust Peltz or his people on that part of it."

"Did this illegal drug help your father?"

"Well, for a few months, but Mr. Peltz, Professor Peltz, said that my father's people did not have the skill to administer the drug. He, my father died in nineteen seventy-one."

"But he gave up this other formula in exchange?"

"Yes, he did. He was desperate and he said there really wasn't any other market for it. It was called . . . is called chimerics . . . this procedure."

"And what is your understanding of Mr. King's role in all of this?"

"He was the courier . . . both for the formula transfer and the money to pay the men who smuggled the chimerics' processes into the country. He was arrested, I understood, when he delivered the money to the smugglers."

"Please state your full name, for the record."

"Gladys Ann Ames York. York is my married name. I am divorced now."

"Thank you, Mrs. York. Do you know Mr. Colin King?"

"Yes, but when I first met him, in high school, thirty years ago, his name was Colin Koenig."

"Are you related to Mr. Koenig, or King, by marriage?"

"Yes, he has been married to my sister for over twenty-five years."

"Have you ever heard your brother-in-law speak of criminal activity?"

"I have."

"Please elaborate."

"Well, Swifty... that's his nickname, or professional name... Swifty talked all the time about his years in prison, the inmates and how they engaged in crimes. He told my sister in my presence that Mr. Leonardo... Arthur Leonardo... arranged to have one man broken out of jail, then returned... just to show his power."

"Who was that man?"

"Connor Grove."

"You were told that Mr. Leonardo had Mr. Grove taken from prison and returned, just to show he could do it?"

"Actually, I was supposed to be asleep in the bedroom, but I heard them talking. Swifty told Kim he thought Leonardo had broken Grove from jail and had him put back in to scare Grove and to prove he could have it done."

"Please state your name."

"Lou Ann Bryce."

"Miss Bryce, what is your occupation, please."

"Ski instructor."

"Oh, and where do you ply this trade?"

"Mostly Gstaad, Switzerland."

"Do you know a man named Connor Grove?"

"Yes."

"How do you know him?"

"First, I helped him improve his skiing. Later, we became lovers. I lived with Connor for two years in Gstaad."

"Isn't Mr. Grove somewhat older than you, Miss Bryce?"

"Yes, so? He's in his seventies now. Then he was fifty-five and I was twenty-six."

"I see, and this was over fifteen years ago?"

"Yes, I am now in my forties... still skiing and still instructing."

"Do you see Mr. Grove these days?"

"Yes, but, we had a falling out sometime back. He likes younger women, it seems."

The jury remained silent, but the lawyers chuckled quietly.

"Ms. Bryce... please tell the court what you shared with our investigators about Mr. Grove's source of income."

"Connor has money. He has invested wisely. The source of his original stake, I believe, was Mr. Arthur Leonardo and some other people he was associated with. Connor said Artie broke him out of jail and flew him to Switzerland just to prove the money was there. He said he was paid off for facilitating some transactions back in the early seventies. He never said how much or what transactions. He later said that Artie and Louis needed his 'blood' and that was the real reason they took him from the prison."

"Well, if this were true, why would they send him back once they had him in Europe?"

"He said he learned from another man in jail that they wanted to know where they could find him in case they needed more 'blood.'"

"Now, Ms. Bryce, you mentioned a man named Louis. Was this not Dr. Louis Peltz?"

"Yes."

"Oh, and Miss Bryce, why on earth would Mr. Leonardo and Dr. Peltz need Mr. Grove's blood?"

"Connor has a rare blood type. They needed to duplicate it in a laboratory in order to make some 'antigens' for experiments with animals. Connor said they found a way to use his blood type to uh, uh, act as a catalyst between human and animal blood. Something like that . . . it worked with certain types of dogs, I think."

"Interesting. Why would Mr. Grove share all of this with you? It would seem it could put him in some jeopardy."

"Well, Connor used to drink a lot. He would talk on the phone. He would talk loud. I maybe overheard him on some of this. Sometimes he would answer my questions when I asked about these things . . . but only when he had a lot to drink."

"Ms. Bryce, were you . . . are you in love with Mr. Grove?"

"Once I was . . . no more . . . not after the way I was treated. But this is no retribution . . . I really don't want to hurt Connor. The subpoena made up my mind for me. I would like to go back to Switzerland. My passport has been withdrawn until some things are cleared up. Hopefully, after this I can go back."

"Yes, hopefully. Thank you, Ms. Bryce."

You get the gist of it. Naturally, Jake took the Fifth Amendment.

Swifty, in accordance with his deal, gave Breck everything he asked.

The U.S. Attorney said and Breck had to agree that Swifty's testimony about Jake and Artie meant nothing. It was all old and unusable news. The phony story about illegal drug sales on college campuses was thrown out. There was no evidence, no proof, no witnesses. Swifty incriminated only himself. It was clear to Breck and the U.S. Attorney that no matter what Swifty confessed to, it didn't get them anywhere. Swifty had shared nothing usable about Jake or Artie. So Breck decided to squeeze Swifty even more, but he did okay the release of Kim's passport.

CHAPTER 44

IN RETURN

KYLE ACCOMPANIED KIM to Bangkok where Peltz greeted them. Swifty called every day, or Kim called him. Neither of them had any inkling that Gladdie had testified before the grand jury.

None of the lawyers believed that Swifty would be prosecuted. Craig Bosson was a little concerned that Swifty might be charged with withholding evidence back in the seventies, but even that would be a stretch since the statute of limitations had already run out.

Artie called three days after his grand jury appearance.

"I guess they didn't even want to bother with me. Too bad, I could have taken the fall for all of you. No way they would jail an old guy like me. Did you get a feel for what they're after?" Artie asked hoarsely.

"Yes, Arthur, it's clear they want headlines and a piece of my ass . . . and Jake's."

"What do they have?"

"Nothing I know of. Look, I confessed to everything they brought up, but they didn't seem to want it. Frankly, Arthur, if I had anything incriminating against you or Jake, I would have given it to them if that is what it took to get Kim's passport back."

"I guess I can see your point, Swifty. But, it's good neither you or Jake can get hurt."

"Yeah, it is."

"How is Kim doing over there?"

"So far it's going good . . . we'll know more later this week."
"Teresa and I will pray for her."
"Thank you, Arthur."
"Good-bye, Swifty."
"Arthur, wait. How are you doing?"
"Swifty, you worry about you and Kim. I'm fine. No more talk of me. Got that?"
"Got it. Good-bye, Arthur."

After considerable discussion amongst prosecutors, the indictment against Jake was dismissed. Swifty was left as Breck's sole target. Joe Seeley and Jeff Domres told Craig Bosson that they believed the indictment against him would be dismissed as well. There appeared to be no plausible evidence that any crime was committed.

Breck had another plan. The indictment against Swifty was expanded: conspiracy to traffic in illegal substances, transportation of illegal substances across national borders, and conspiracy to launder currency. Of course, Swifty had already been tried, convicted, and pardoned for his alleged part in the 1970s transfer of money for drugs and drugs for drugs. No, this was a new charge, based upon Swifty's transport of and payment for rehabilitation drugs used as follow-up treatment for Kim in the eighties. He figured he'd have to plead guilty. He had never paid Peltz for the drugs, and someone else brought them back from Mexico and had them delivered to his home, but Breck would never believe that. He fully intended to do whatever it took this time to get Kim the medicine she needed from Thailand. His wife's life was at stake.

Bosson thought it a ridiculous charge. No jury would convict on it. He was shocked that the grand jury would bring the charges. The other experts in his firm figured that it was a ploy to push Swifty to give them something else that he might not have disclosed on Jake or Artie. It was quite puzzling.

The *Arizona Republic* began to switch allegiances when the story of Kim's illness came out. Letters poured in, supporting Swifty and Kim. Breck fought back. He fired off releases to the press blasting the "torture of animals" and the "bizarre use of animals as living farms for the purpose of growing human organs . . . it sounds like something out of H. G. Wells or, worse, *Frankenstein!*"

Kim had been in Thailand for four weeks. Kyle had come home twice on business and returned to Bangkok as soon as practical. He reported to Swifty that she was having a rougher time than she was letting on. Dr. Steiger was having trouble stabilizing the doses of her medication.

Swifty was at wit's end. He couldn't be with her, he couldn't work, he didn't know what to expect from Breck. He began to drink again; just a little at first, "to calm his nerves," soon it was every night. No one seemed to notice, but he spent his days wondering if his hangovers were obvious. Kim called early in the morning, evening there, and filled him in on her day of therapy. She always asked how Spirit was doing. Swifty would say, "Fine, just a little slow." He lied. Spirit was barely hanging on to life. The vet recommended putting her to sleep, but Swifty said no. Pain medication and hand-feeding and Swifty's determination were all that separated her from a convulsive expiration.

Then, Swifty got word of his trial date. It was three months away, October 5. That same day Kyle called and told him he was bringing Kim home.

"She has to go back in a few months for monitoring. They're giving her a special diet. The medication she will have to take can now be prescribed in the States. It's the supplemental stuff that they have to give her here . . . so we'll just come back over when it's time."

"Kyle, I can never repay you for this." Swifty started to sob. Kyle could tell he was drinking.

"You shithead! Get your ass sober before we get back or I'll kick it. And don't ever talk to me about repayment of anything. I love you and Kimmie . . . you helped me have a real life . . . you asshole! Why are you back on the booze? Damn you!" Kyle felt like crying too.

"Fuck you . . . I'll stop today, tonight! I promise. This is it!" Swifty knew he would finish the rest of the bottle before he stopped. Kyle knew it too. Drunks know.

Swifty cleaned it up. It took three days, but he filled himself with diet Coke and coffee, fruit and vegetables, and got through it. When he met Kim and Kyle at the plane in Los Angeles, he was clean.

Kim looked gaunt and walked unsteadily, leaning on Kyle for support. She smiled weakly when she saw him. He rushed to her, taking her arm from Kyle. He kissed her on the nose.

"You look good, baby, I missed you so much."

"Me too . . . did you bring Spirit?"

"She was too tired, honey. She's at home waiting for you."

"Oh. I want to see her now. Do you mean home here, or home in Scottsdale?"

"Scottsdale, honey."

"Oh."

"Hey," Kyle said as they walked slowly toward the exit, "I'll help the porter get the baggage to the car. Is it waiting at the curb, Swifty?"

"Yeah. How did you come through customs? Did you have to stand in lines and all?"

"Kyle put me in a wheelchair and the porter helped with the bags. It wasn't bad. Honey, I want to get home to Spirit." Kim's eyes were full of tears.

Swifty thought for a moment. "Well, I got us rooms for today at the Hyatt, but we could go right on. I'm really not supposed to be out of Arizona, but screw it. Whatever you want, honey. We can go back now. Kyle's plane is just over on the other side of LAX."

Swifty had broken the rules by leaving Arizona, using Kyle's Cessna Citation X to meet them. It was a ten-minute ride in the limo to Jim's Air on El Segundo where it was parked. Swifty called the pilot on his cell phone and instructed him to have the plane readied for the return to Scottsdale. Fortunately, both men had anticipated the possibility of a quick return and waited over coffee until they heard from Swifty.

They arrived home two hours later. Air traffic control wouldn't release them for twenty-five minutes due to all the airline traffic. It was only twenty minutes to their house from the airport in Scottsdale once they got in.

Kim walked slowly up the two steps to the front door, braced by Swifty on one side and Kyle on the other. The door opened. Kim's housekeeper, Juanita, stood smiling tentatively, and just behind her, chin nearly touching the floor, tail wagging tentatively, stood Spirit.

Kim collapsed on the threshold and embraced the little dog that licked the tears from her face. The two of them went directly to bed. Swifty could hear Kim singing softly as if to a child. At six that evening, he awoke with a start. He had fallen asleep in a chair, in the small sitting room off their bedroom after Kyle had left. The door to the bedroom was ajar. He could hear her gentle breathing. Tiptoeing quietly into the room, he could see her clearly, though the drapes were closed to the summer sun, sleeping on her back, with Spirit curled under one arm. He crept nearer and instinctively let his hand pass over the slumbering ball of fur.

Something wasn't quite right. He looked more closely at Kim. Her eyes slowly opened. "She's gone. She waited for me and now she's gone."

It took a moment for the words to register. Then he understood. Spirit had passed on. He lifted the little dog from the covers and Kim's reluctant grasp.

"It's okay . . . we said good-bye. She isn't hurting anymore." Kim smiled softly and closed her eyes.

Swifty patted her arm with his free hand and, hugging the dog to him, left the bedroom.

They had a full funeral for Spirit with twenty-five mourners. Kyle said some words over the little gray casket, and everyone cried but Kim.

"She will always be with me. I will never lose her."

"I know, honey, I know" was all Swifty could say.

October 5, 1995. Judgment day. Like most trials and unlike TV, nothing started on time. The judge was late . . . something about a federal subpoena in another case. Four hours elapsed before Swifty was even allowed in the courtroom. The judge and the lawyers were going over pre-trial motions. The rest of the day was devoted to jury selection. Three days it would take before a jury was seated.

Kim and Kyle left the day before the trial for Bangkok. Kim looked good and had gained some weight. Kyle said not to worry; he would take care of her. Swifty never wanted a drink more than he did that day.

The government's case was direct and straightforward: Colin L. King, formerly Colin L. Koenig, had knowingly and willingly transported illegal substances into the United States from Mexico. He had paid for said substances with U.S. currency and had received a refund, also in U.S. currency, that he later delivered to Mr. Jacob Leonardo of Paradise Valley. Mr. Leonardo was "an unindicted co-conspirator." Shades of Watergate! Bosson and the Leonardo lawyers, Seeley and Domres, assumed that Breck was trying to "break" Swifty by letting him see Jake go unscathed . . . once again, while Swifty took the rap . . . once again.

After the direct presentation of the case by the prosecution, they called a litany of mundane witnesses, followed by Audrey Bryce, whose testimony was "immaterial," according to Bosson.

Then came the surprise: Gladdie! Swifty could not believe his first girlfriend and sister-in-law would testify against him, though her words were not particularly incriminating. Evidently, the prosecution wanted to establish, with her testimony, that Swifty talked liberally about his involvement with organized crime. At first, Gladdie wouldn't make eye contact with him, but when she finally did, she smiled sweetly. Swifty almost threw up. He wouldn't respond to her advances – she would nail his ass for it. "Good girl, Glad."

Next, another surprise: Louis Peltz. Peltz looked appealingly to Swifty who, until Louis appeared in court, had no idea Louis wasn't with Kim in Bangkok. The prosecutor pressed Louis – who kept looking nervously at Swifty – on his relationship with the Leonardos and with Swifty.

Breck was a skilled inquisitor, and while he relied mainly on his right-hand man and woman to ask the questions, stepped forward to pressure Louis Peltz.

"Dr. Peltz, if your scientific studies and their applications are so beneficial to mankind, why aren't you making them available to your fellow Americans? Why are you running off to Mexico and to Thailand to conduct experiments and administer the results? Please tell the court . . . the relevance will be clear in a moment, Your Honor."

The judge nodded.

"Our theories have been somewhat controversial and at first we had some problems – some failures among the successes. The FDA would not even consider our applications in the old days . . . though several are currently pending. Mexico, for fifteen years, embraced our activities . . . then they changed their minds. We were forced to go to Thailand to continue our therapies."

"Okay. When you decided to operate in Mexico, were people still dying from the results of your work?"

"No. No. You see, we ran into some trouble . . . due to our lack of experience . . . in dosages . . . back in the sixties. Some people died. But they would have died anyway. Later, we moved our operations to Chile . . . then the government there became uncooperative and we moved to Mexico. By that time, we had the procedures down pat. We have saved many, many lives."

"But, the therapies and the substances you administer were and are illegal in the United States?"

"Yes, but it is a political thing . . . I – "

"But, illegal, right?"

"Yes."

"Did a certain formula come into your hands, along with a small sample of the substances that you came to use in your experiments?"

"Yes?"

"When?"

"Nineteen seventy-one."

"Who placed it in your hands?"

"Mr. King, but – "

"No buts, thank you on that, Dr. Peltz."

"Now, Dr. Peltz, fast-forward to the eighties."

"Did you sell Mr. King a similar substance to be administered to his wife that he transported from Ciudad Obregón in Mexico to Scottsdale, Arizona? And, did you receive cash money from Mr. King for these substances?"

"I recall providing the substances for Mrs. King and being paid for them. I cannot be certain if it happened the way you say."

"In due course it will be obvious that it happened that way and that Mr. King was refunded the money . . . in a laundering effort." Breck smiled.

The next witness was Jake Leonardo.

"Good morning, Mr. Leonardo."

"Good morning, sir, Mr. Breck."

"Mr. Leonardo, how long have you known Mr. King?"

"Over twenty-five years . . . I can't remember the exact date when we met."

"Mr. Leonardo, let me help you. You met Mr. King, July 30, 1971, at an office your father had leased in Phoenix, Arizona, not one mile from where we sit today. You conspired with Mr. King on that date to transport an illegal drug to Tucson, Arizona, in exchange for yet another illegal drug, then to exchange that illegal drug for a certain amount of cash. The cash was to pay the smugglers of the original drug for their work. Is that not correct?"

"There is accuracy in your comments, but they aren't entirely true."

"Fine, we will get to the clarifications in a minute. But fast-forward to the nineteen eighties. Is it not correct, sir, that you gave Mr. King a certain amount of money that he transported to Clinique de Obregón in Mexico and paid to Dr. Peltz for an illegal drug? That drug was then transported to the United States, Scottsdale, Arizona, by Mr. King, and miraculously, a similar amount of money to that which was paid Dr. Peltz appeared in his luggage and he exchanged it with you for a check in the amount of three hundred twenty-five thousand dollars. Is this not correct, sir?"

Silence.

"Mr. Leonardo, I believe you have received immunity from prosecution in exchange for your free, frank, and truthful testimony, correct?'

Silence.

"Mr. Leonardo, are you ill? Do you need a break? Your Honor, it is nearing day's end . . . is it possible that we could consider recess now and resumption in the morning?"

"Court is adjourned until tomorrow morning at nine a.m."

Jake sat near his father's bed. He bent his head and listened very carefully. He nodded. He stood partially and kissed his father's cheek. His head dropped on his father's chest. The bed shook with the tremors of one or both of them releasing the emotion of fifty years.

"I love you, Jakie . . ."

"I love you, Papa . . . I'll do us honor."

Artie patted his hand lightly and was gone.

"I figure Breck got to Peltz because his wife is here in Palm Springs. As far as Jake is concerned, Seeley and Domres disappeared two days ago. I couldn't find them . . . didn't see 'em until today in court, so I can't ask them their position," Craig Bosson explained.

"We have to go on the basis that Jake has made a deal to protect himself, and since you didn't give them enough to nail Jake, Breck will settle for using Jake and Peltz to nail you. So far, I mean with Peltz, there is nothing. It all rides on Jake confirming what Breck laid in his lap today. By the way, how is Mrs. King doing?"

"Well shit, Craig, how do you think? She doesn't know if she is living or dying and she figures her husband is about to go away to jail for the second time."

"Oh, oh, sorry. I didn't mean to be insensitive."

"I know, and I am sorry . . . but this is so much bullshit!"

"Yeah. Well, we better get plenty of sleep and prepare for Jake's testimony tomorrow. It ain't likely to be good."

"Yeah, okay. See you in the morning."

The evening went slowly. They called each other twice and talked of the future.

"When you get ready . . . we'll get a new puppy."

"I know. But, I'm not ready yet. I have to get well first."

"Yes . . . get well."

"Honey . . ."

"Don't worry, I'm not scared. I can take it, whatever it is." Swifty thought the minute he said it what a dumb comment it was. Here his wife – her life in the brink, suffering great pain without complaint – was ten thousand miles away, existing in uncertainty, and he said he wasn't scared. Shoot!

"I know you aren't scared. You're my big guy. No, I mean don't worry. It is all going to be okay. You'll see."

"Good, honey. Good."

He was such a fool! He did not deserve this woman.

The morning came and Swifty dressed in his finest suit: a dark blue from Armani, with thin pinstripes. He made certain his shoes sparkled and found his most elegant tie. He donned all of his jewelry, contrary to legal advice. Rings, gold watch, bracelet, and diamond collar pin. "Supposed to look humble and conservative in court . . . bullshit," he mumbled to himself.

"If I'm going out, it's going to be in style."

He drove the Mercedes 600SL to the courthouse.

On the way, his phone rang. He answered it by voice: "King!"

"You sound chipper for a guy about to be hung."

"Who is it?"

"Joe, Joe Seeley."

"I thought you weren't supposed to talk to me, Counselor?"

"Screw it. You're my friend. Look, Swifty . . . I want you to know that as soon as this thing with Jake is over . . . I will gladly . . . Jeff too . . . uh, handle any appeal necessary . . . pro bono."

"Jake's got a wife and kids. He has to protect himself . . . but, since I am the designated 'go-down EE' I at least deserve free counsel . . . again. You tell Jake *and* Artie – "

"Artie's dead."

"What?"

"Artie died last night."

"Shit. I'm sorry . . . Jesus."

"Swifty . . . good luck today."

"Thanks, Joe."

Swifty pulled over and checked his book for Artie's number. He dialed. A strange voice answered.

"Hello, this is Mr. King . . . I know about Mr. Leonardo's passing . . . I was wondering if Mrs. Leonardo is able to speak."

"Swifty, it's Toni. I have a cold. Mom is up there with him. She won't believe he's gone. I came in during the night. I'll tell her you called."

"Thanks, Toni. Hey, sorry. Are you okay?"

"Yes, fine. He was ready. So much pain. Swifty, Daddy was seventy-seven and he had a really interesting life. God, he was shot four times!"

"Tell your mom . . . well tell her I loved him too, in my way."

"I will. Good luck today, Swifty."

"Thanks."

Jake had looked strained the day before. Today, he looked as good as Swifty: black double-breasted suit, white shirt, and paisley tie; cuff links that matched his gold watch, two gold rings, and a jade tie clasp. His shoes glistened. He stood straight, and Swifty noticed the small pouch that usually protruded below Jake's belt was almost nonexistent. Amber and her sons were in the courtroom. They were a fine-looking family. Why were they here?

Joe Seeley, looking dapper too, hugged Jake as he stood to take the stand. Domres looked off into the courtroom.

Breck suddenly looked shabby next to his witness and the defendant. He seemed uneasy as he approached.

"Good morning, Mr. Leonardo."

"Good morning, sir!" Jake boomed out, his voice not squeaky, not even high.

"Mr. Leonardo, we talked yesterday of the exchanges of illegal drugs and moneys between you and Mr. King. Do you recall that?"

"I do indeed, sir."

"Do you wish me to have the clerk reread the question we asked as we closed yesterday?"

"For the record, yes I do."

"Fine, if the clerk will please read back from line 23, page 267."

The clerk droned out the several paragraphs of testimony.

"Mr. Leonardo."

"There is accuracy in your comments, but they aren't entirely true."

"Fine, we will get to the clarifications in a minute. But, fast-forward to the nineteen eighties. Is it not correct, sir, that you gave Mr. King a certain amount of money that he transported to Cliniquè de Obregón in Mexico and paid to Dr. Peltz for an illegal drug? That drug was then transported to the United States, Scottsdale, Arizona, by Mr. King, and miraculously, a similar amount of money to that which was paid Dr. Peltz appeared in his luggage, and he exchanged it with you for a check in the amount of three hundred twenty-five thousand dollars. Is this not correct, sir?"

"That, sir, is a complete and total fabrication by your office!"

Jake began talking loud and fast over the objections of Breck and his associates. He spoke directly to the judge so that the recorder could hear him clearly over the prosecutorial objections.

"I deny that what you allege is true and I submit that Mr. King not only did not pay for the alleged drug transfer, a lifesaving substance to be administered to his wife. I paid for it! And I brought it to this country and I had it delivered to Mr. King's home!"

Jake looked first at the dumbstruck Breck, he then turned and smiled at Swifty.

"If there was anything illegal here or in 1971, I am the guilty party! Mr. King is and was guiltless in these matters! I apologize to him, to his wife, Kim, and to this court for not coming forward earlier, when I should have!"

Breck stood looking eye to eye with Jake, who was sitting in the raised witness box. Deep in his eyes, he saw something that had not been there before . . . a color . . . a deep gray color. He had thought Jake's eyes were brown. But the color wasn't it . . . there was a power. Breck felt fear, physical fear. He coughed and turned away. His hand went up as if to ask for a break. He stumbled to the prosecution table, leaning heavily upon it, gasping, as if to catch his breath.

The young female prosecutor rose and signaled the bench, "Your honor, a brief recess?"

"Ten minutes . . . get Mr. Breck a drink of water." The judge marched out as the courtroom stood, dumbfounded.

Looking one to another, the front row began to quietly applaud. Jake's two boys and Amber, wiping tears from her cheek, took up the effort. Swifty turned to Jake and saluted, as the applause grew louder before subsiding into a buzz of excited banter.

Breck did not return. The young prosecutor asked to approach the bench. She and Craig Bosson approached. They argued heatedly for ten minutes. The attorneys returned to their tables.

The judge looked at Swifty, then at Jake, and then again at Swifty.

"This case is dismissed!" The gavel sounded. "Mr. King, you are free to go. Mr. Leonardo, you had better stand by. I believe the U.S. Attorney has a forthwith subpoena for you. Ladies and gentlemen of the jury, thank you for your service. Court adjourned!"

EPILOGUE

THAT WAS OVER a decade ago. Jake did the only thing his father ever wanted him to do: behave with honor. And Jake had heard the words he always longed to hear: that his father loved him.

Jake was prosecuted, but not for drugs, not for money laundering, not for mayhem, or murder or anything like that. Investigators found that he had not claimed income for the profit he made in selling his "silent" interest in Wild Jack's Bar, an interest he had won from Gordon Macaw's brother, Paul, in a wager. Paul had been an employee of Jake's for years. He had accompanied Jake to Kim's early in the seventies when they both intimidated her. Paul had not told his brother that he lost his half of the bar in a wager with Jake. Gordon, when he learned of it, hated Jake and never got over it. In a drug-crazed rage he had attacked Jake's party, shooting Artie, Swifty, and Augie Bash. Jake beat him to death after Swifty shot him. He sold his interest back to Paul after the incident, but neglected to declare the gain.

He served sixteen months in prison and paid two million dollars in penalties. Jake Leonardo is again a successful businessman in Scottsdale, Arizona, and a national figure in health promotion and fitness. He has learned to play golf and can often be found with one of his sons on the Karsten links at Arizona State University or at Paradise Valley Country Club.

Louis Peltz lives in Rancho Mirage, California. His companies in Australia and South Africa have received approval to proceed with clinical trials in chimeric transplantation. He has eleven patents and four applications pending with the FDA.

Nelson Leigh is retired and often escorts Teresa Leonardo to social events in Los Angeles. They make a striking octogenarian couple.

Connor Grove lives in the nation of Andorra and only occasionally risks leaving its borders.

Toni Marie and Stu Rosenfeld divorced, and Toni finished medical school. She practices neonatal plastic surgery in Beverly Hills. Stu is still Dr. Look Good.

Gladdie Ames is president of Alderson College in Ohio. She and Swifty have not spoken since the trial. She has not remarried.

Norm Cellestine succumbed to Alzheimer's disease in 1996, leaving the bulk of his estate to the universities in Arizona.

Augie Bash died of emphysema in 1997.

Chet Levine died of AIDS complications in 1998.

Becky Strahman continues to run a worldwide investment business and manages the finances of the wealthy, including the Faust, Phenet, and King families.

Joe Seeley and Jeff Domres, though they have moved gracefully into their eighties, continue to practice law in the Phoenix area. Former Safford guard and law student Glen "Bo" Slattery is now the managing partner of Domres, Seeley, and Slattery and a confidant of both Swifty and me.

Adam Breck is a federal judge in the mid-Atlantic region.

Naomi Kulokowski Faust, my mom, passed away of diabetes in 1998 at age eighty.

Peter Phenet continues as chairman of Cellestine General Alliance, a Fortune 100 company.

What about me, Kyle, or K. K. Faust? I am president and CEO of the Cellestine General Alliance Group and owner of the Faust Company, a family-owned conglomerate. That is, when I am not being called upon to help Swifty King out with some interesting challenge.

My two youngest kids work for me. My oldest son, Ken, is an anesthesiologist in Scottsdale; his twin sister, Emile, is an OB-GYN in Philadelphia; and my son Philip is the youngest brigadier general in the air force. More on my kids at a later time.

And Kim . . . well, she recovered her health in Thailand, returned to the States after the trial, and thrived as president of Cellestine Enterprises, a division of Cellestine General Alliance until last year when we lost her to renal failure. We miss her. Spirit II still sleeps on her pillow.

Swifty King is, as always, the best man around, even in his grief. He remains in Scottsdale and in the world as SWIFTY KING, ADVICE.

He is my best friend.

Sincerely,
K. K. Faust

Any and all similarities to persons living or dead, business enterprises, or medical procedures, other than known public figures and established locales and processes, are purely coincidental. This entire story is a product of the author's imagination.

WATCH FOR THE NEXT SWIFTY NOVEL,
SWIFTY AND THE COUNT
COMING IN THE FALL OF 2010

Made in the USA
Coppell, TX
27 August 2020